"THE THOUGHT OF RIDING A PARADE WAGON DOES SOUND LIKE A GLORIOUS WAY TO HAVE SOME FUN!"

Mose stepped toward her, his heart hammering. When the rays of the setting sun glimmered on the gauzy back of her heart-shaped *kapp*, Sylvia glowed like an angel wearing a halo. Was that a sign that Mose should be paying her special respect? Or was it perhaps a subtle heavenly warning about the limited number of days this little woman had left?

Mose inhaled deeply to fortify his nerves. "You—you want to ride with me when I p-put them through their—p-paces t-tomorrow morning?" he stammered. "I'll b-be t-taking them out around eight."

The joy on Sylvia's face made Mose want to grab her up and hug her—which would be as wildly inappropriate as his invitation to ride the parade wagon. He seemed to have lost all control over his thoughts, because he'd gotten the sense that Sylvia was somewhat older than he, and far too fragile for a man his size to handle. And he'd face a stern talking-to when Bishop Monroe found out that he'd offered Sylvia a ride with a client's team.

And yet, the fact that he'd made her so happy made him happy, too.

Hidden Away at PROMISE LODGE

Charlotte Hubbard

ZEBRA BOOKS
Kensington Publishing Corp.
www.kensingtonbooks.com

ZEBRA BOOKS are published by

Kensington Publishing Corp.
119 West 40th Street
New York, NY 10018

All Kensington titles, imprints, and distributed lines are available at special quantity discounts for bulk purchases for sales promotion, premiums, fund-raising, and educational or institutional use.

Special book excerpts or customized printings can also be created to fit specific needs. For details, write or phone the office of the Kensington Sales Manager: Kensington Publishing Corp., 119 West 40th Street, New York, NY 10018. Attn. Sales Department. Phone: 1-800-221-2647.

First Printing: August 2023
ISBN-13: 978-1-4201-5441-2
ISBN-13: 978-1-4201-5442-9 (eBook)

10 9 8 7 6 5 4 3 2 1

Printed in the United States of America

Ask, and it shall be given you; seek, and ye shall find; knock, and it shall be opened unto you:

For every one that asketh receiveth; and he that seeketh findeth; and to him that knocketh it shall be opened.

—*Matthew 7:7–8*

Acknowledgments

Highest praise and thanks to God for this book—and this entire series!

Thank you, thank you to my agent, Evan Marshall, for so many years and so many books! Special thanks, as well, to my editor, Alicia Condon, for making the writing and publishing process so enjoyable over the course of all these Amish stories! And a note of thanks to Vicki Harding for providing research assistance from the Old Order Amish of Jamesport, Missouri.

A special nod to contest winner Karen Mercer, who agreed to share her name with a character in this story.

For Neal and Vera. You are my sunshine!

Chapter 1

Karen Mercer set her suitcase on the ground and shut the hatchback of her brother's car. "Thanks for the ride, Mike," she called out. "See you next Sunday!"

As he drove away, she smiled at her best friend, Andi Swann, who was tucking a stray lock of blond hair back into her heart-shaped *kapp*. "Well, here we are, following our dream of living Amish—not just reading the books, but walking the walk and talking the talk! For nearly a week!"

"Look at how this place has changed since we went to church camp here," Andi remarked as they stood at the entry to Promise Lodge. "This must be a new metal entry-way sign, because I don't remember it having sunflowers and wheat sheaves, do you? And this plot to the left was a mowed pasture for horseback riding. Now it's planted in green beans and tomatoes—"

"Probably to be sold at this produce stand," Karen said, nodding toward the wooden structure at the roadside. "And look at all the houses! And there's a tiny home with a dock on the far side of Rainbow Lake. How cool is that?"

"The old timbered lodge and the cabins look just the same as I remember them," Andi said wistfully. "Except the Amish here have obviously done a lot of painting—and that looks like a new roof. The summers we spent here as campers and counselors were some of the best times of my life."

"Yeah, they were." Karen pointed toward a large white barn. "And look at those adorable black-and-white cows! Everything looks too neat and perfect to be real—"

"But what about *us*?" Andi interrupted, her smile falling a notch. "Do *we* look authentic? We're wearing these calf-length dresses we made and the *kapps* we ordered from a store in Lancaster County—and we've read hundreds of Amish novels—but what if they call us out as fakes? What if they make us confess in front of everybody at church and then—"

"They can't do that, silly!" Karen reminded her with a chuckle. "We're only taking a little trip down memory lane while we live the Amish life instead of just reading about it. If we stick to our script and imitate the way these folks do things, we'll be fine, right?"

Andi sighed as though she wasn't too sure about that. "But we made our phone reservation request and sent our money as though we were Plain, and the Amish think it's a sin to lie. Maybe we should've—"

"But we didn't," Karen pointed out quickly. Her pulse was pounding with anticipation as she picked up the old-fashioned suitcase she'd bought at a thrift store. "If we follow our plan, we won't have any problems. We're just a couple of Amish *maidels* who've come to Promise Lodge for a week to check it out because we read about it in *The Budget* newspaper—which we did. Let's walk to the lodge before you get cold feet and back out on me."

Side by side the two of them strolled along the main dirt road, gazing at other changes that had been made since their days as teenage campers. "It must be quite a draw for these folks to have a bulk store now—and look at how many cars are in the parking lot there," Andi remarked.

Karen, however, was inhaling too deeply to reply. "I smell pie!" she whispered giddily. "And look way up on the hill—at that pasture where the sheep are grazing. What a picture that makes!"

Andi nodded, focused on the rustic, timbered lodge building they were approaching. "That porch hasn't changed a bit," she murmured. "I still remember the night Denny Willoughby kissed me on that swing."

"*Jah*," Karen said with her best Pennsylvania Dutch accent, "but we can't be talking about past stuff like that. According to our story, we've never been to Promise Lodge, remember? Now get your act together, because once we walk inside, we become Annie Stoltzfus and Karen Yoder for the next seven days."

Andi—now Annie—smoothed the front of her deep green cape dress, nodding nervously as Karen reached for the doorknob. When they stepped into the lobby, they gazed upward with wistful smiles, taking in the grand old space that was two stories high with an elaborate chandelier made of deer antlers. Ahead of them, the double curved staircase took their memories up to the level where they'd bunked so many summers as kids.

But it was the tantalizing aromas of sweet fruit, pastry, and spices that made them close their eyes in anticipation.

"Camp food never smelled this good," Andi whispered.

Karen giggled. "And you can bet they don't get their pie fillings from those big gallon cans, either. Shall we let them know we're here?"

As they passed through the huge dining room at the right, between the long wooden tables Karen remembered very well—because she'd secretly carved her initials on one of them—a wave of nostalgia washed over her. Everything seemed smaller than she remembered, yet it did her soul good to see the way these Amish had saved an abandoned church camp from rotting away and being overgrown by weeds. Voices coming from the kitchen made her pause to draw a fortifying breath.

"*Jah*, hall-o!" she said as she and Andi peered into the kitchen from the doorway. "It's Annie Stoltzfus and Karen Yoder, come to claim our rooms."

Two gray-haired ladies in flowery dresses and white aprons looked up from the pies they were making at the big counter in the center of the kitchen. Recalling that some of the folks living here were Mennonites, Karen gave them a little wave.

"And here you are, bright and early," the taller of the two said as she bustled toward them. "Welcome to Promise Lodge! I'm Beulah Kuhn—"

"And I'm her sister, Ruby, who talked to you on the phone," the other one said with a nod. "We're glad you're here, ladies. As you can see, we're hip-deep in pie preparation, getting ready for a wedding on Thursday—and our assistant, who just came here to live at Promise Lodge about a month ago, is Sylvia Keim."

The woman seated on a high stool at the counter nodded shyly at them. Dressed in black, with eyes that seemed to fill her entire pale face, Sylvia seemed more like a fragile doll than a flesh-and-blood woman.

Karen smiled at her, relieved that Ruby and Beulah were already striding through the dining room. She wasn't sure how to converse with a woman who resembled an invalid—or perhaps a grieving widow—in her somber black clothing.

"We'll show you upstairs so you can choose your rooms and freshen up," Beulah called over her shoulder as she clomped steadily up the stairs in her sturdy shoes.

"You must've gotten an early start this morning," Ruby put in, gesturing for Karen and Annie to precede her. "How far did you have to come? I don't recall where you live—not a town I'd ever heard of when you told me over the phone."

Andi's panicked expression prompted Karen to reply. "Cherrydale is south of here, along the Missouri River. It's about a three-hour trip, but we didn't want to miss a minute, so we had our driver come early!"

Luckily, as they reached the second level a few steps behind Beulah, they didn't have to fabricate any more fibs. It occurred to Karen that maybe Andi was right: maybe they'd made a big mistake, pretending to be Amish. But it was too late to back out.

"Ruby and I have apartments in the back corner of the building," Beulah was saying as she pointed down the open hallway to their left. "Our Sylvia lives right here in front of us, and beside her is Irene Wickey, who's baking pies in that little white bakery you passed on your way up the private road." She turned to point across the open hallway. "Our bride-to-be, Marlene Fisher, is in the front corner—at least until she gets hitched on Thursday—so you've got your pick of the other unoccupied rooms."

"If you want rooms next to each other, you might choose the ones directly across from us," Ruby remarked. "You'll have a nice view of the front lawn and Mattie Troyer's garden plots, as well as the Helmuth family's nursery over by the state highway."

As Karen nodded, pleasant memories nearly overwhelmed her again. This upper level had a railing all the way around the hallway, like a mezzanine, and she was gazing out over the lofty lobby area . . . where she and Andi had once been known to drop water balloons as other counselors passed beneath them.

"That sounds very *gut*," Andi managed, gesturing toward

the neighboring rooms that overlooked the front porch. "It's so nice and homey here."

Their hostesses nodded pleasantly. "We came to Promise Lodge because it's one of the few places where unmarried Plain ladies are allowed to run businesses and live without answering to a man in their family," Ruby remarked.

"We hope you'll want to join us," Beulah said with a warm smile. "And now, if you'll excuse us, we've got pies ready to come out of the oven."

"Come on down to the kitchen whenever you're ready," Ruby added as she followed her sister down the stairs. "If you missed out on breakfast, we can scare something up for you. Lunch will be pretty simple today, and we'll eat around noonish."

Grasping the handle of her suitcase, Karen nodded at the sisters and started around the square-shaped hallway. Because she recalled how voices carried in the open area above the lobby, she kept quiet until they reached the center front rooms, where the doors stood open. She ducked into the first one, hauling Andi in behind her before quickly shutting the door.

"I thought I was going to say something that would give us away at any second," Andi whispered. Then she giggled. "But isn't it fun to be back up here? And look out this window—"

"Where I sneaked out after hours one night to crawl along the porch roof and shimmy down the corner support pillar to meet Ronnie Larson," Karen recalled with a chuckle.

"And when you slipped, you took half of that big trumpet vine with you," Andi continued.

"Yeah, and I landed in a big rose bush, too," Karen said. "By the time the camp manager got done treating my scratches and reading me the riot act, I'd paid for my wicked ways. But here we are, back again. Wow. Just *wow*."

"Look at the wonderful quilt on this bed. And the furniture matches, like it was a set from somebody's house. Much homier than in our camping days."

"We'll each have a little bathroom, too. *That's* an improvement over sharing one with the other girls in this hall." Karen felt the tension in her shoulders relaxing as she gazed around the simple yet cozy room. "I'll go next door and unpack, and then we can gather our thoughts again before we go downstairs. I'm hoping Beulah or Ruby will offer us a piece of that fresh pie!"

As Beulah placed the last of the hot fruit pies on cooling racks, her mind was abuzz with conflicting emotions. She waited until her sister had slid five more pies into the oven, however, before she voiced her concerns.

"Are you gals ticking off the little discrepancies about our guests the way I am?" she asked quietly. She glanced up the back stairway to be sure their visitors weren't coming down. "If you ask me, something's fishy—"

"Oh, those two are so fishy, we could whip up tuna salad to last us for weeks!" Ruby put in with a mirthless laugh.

Sylvia nodded as she carefully cut slits in the top crusts of two more pies. "Every settlement sounds a bit different, far as how they say some of their words," she said, "but even as far away as I was sitting, I didn't think they sounded *Deutch*."

"*Jah*, my first clue was while Karen was on the phone a couple weeks ago, she called herself a may-del instead of a *my*-del," Ruby put in. "And she pronounced Annie's last name, Stoltzfus, ending with *fuss* instead of *foos*. Not to mention the zippers I saw in the backs of their dresses as we went upstairs just now."

"It was their *kapps* that first struck me," Beulah said as she rolled out dough for three more pies. "I'm not Amish, but I've been under the impression that those heart-shaped, filmy *kapps* were mostly found in Pennsylvania, and these gals have told us they live in Cherrydale, Missouri."

"*Jah*, we wear those heart-shaped *kapps* out East," Sylvia put in. She looked up with the hint of a smile lighting her emaciated face. "Nothing like a little mystery to keep us on our toes, eh? That's what I like about Promise Lodge. You never know what each new day will bring."

"*Jah*, well, we'll keep our eyes and ears open," Beulah said emphatically. "A fellow who came here under false pretenses last summer could've made off with a bundle of our residents' money if our apartment manager, Gloria, hadn't gotten snoopy."

Sylvia's eyes widened. "What happened? I had no idea people could be so malicious as to pass themselves off as Amish for profit."

Ruby shook her head as she recalled the details. "He was quite the smooth talker. Said he came here from the Council of Bishops in Lancaster County to inform Bishop Monroe that Promise Lodge had gotten way too progressive. He intended to take over as the bishop here and insisted that a donation to the Council's fund might make up for our wayward inclinations."

"*Jah*, he had folks worried sick because he was saying our married women shouldn't be running businesses, too," Beulah recounted. She poured sweet pink rhubarb filling into two empty crusts. "Luckily, Gloria found an English suit and tie hanging in the closet of the room he was staying in at Lester's place—along with a laptop computer. Turns out he was a fellow who'd gambled away most of the accumulated savings in the Willow Ridge district before running off to leave those folks in the lurch."

When Sylvia's jaw dropped, her sunken face reminded Beulah how frail their newest resident was. After coming to live out her final days following a terminal diagnosis involving a brain tumor, Sylvia Keim was emerging from her reclusive shell—and it was Beulah's intention to make every one of this sweet woman's remaining days fulfilling and worthwhile.

"It's a real joy to have you helping us with these wedding pies, Sylvia," she said, reaching across the counter to pat the little woman's wrist.

"*Jah*, just look at how pretty these pies have turned out with your slits that form a heart shape on the top crust," Ruby chimed in. "Marlene will think it's mighty special that you've contributed your talent to make her wedding day even nicer."

"And you'll tell us if we can be doing anything for you, to keep you going, *jah*?" Beulah asked gently. "And you'll rest when you need to, I hope?"

When Sylvia slumped on her stool, Beulah could've kicked herself for spreading it on so thick—for reminding the pixielike woman that she was ill, when Sylvia had been so happily engrossed in helping them.

"It's been nice to have a tall stool, and to have something enjoyable to do," Sylvia murmured.

"And I'm sorry I brought it up and burst your bubble, dearie," Beulah said with a sigh.

"You realize, of course, that around here we all tend to call it the way we see it," Ruby teased lightly. "You can put us in our places anytime, Sylvia. Believe me, I've spent my life telling Beulah when she's being a pain in the patoot—"

"And I've considered it my personal mission to inform Ruby that she's too much talk and not enough action,"

Beulah put in with a chuckle. "You'll notice, after you've been here awhile, that the three sisters who bought the Promise Lodge property—Mattie, Christine, and Rosetta—don't let anybody rain on their parade, either. So we'll go back to speculating about Karen and Annie—"

"At least until they come downstairs again," Ruby finished with a chuckle.

Chapter 2

As Mose Fisher strolled toward the lodge alongside his future brother-in-law, Lester Lehman, he was ready to relax after working all day with a team of six Clydesdales who'd kept him on his toes. Aromas of pie wafted from the lodge kitchen's open windows, making him aware of how desperately hungry he was. Lester, too, inhaled deeply.

"As much as I'm looking forward to marrying Marlene, I'll miss these suppers in the lodge dining room with the Kuhns and you and Dale," Lester admitted. "We get a lot more for our money than fabulous food."

Mose nodded, allowing Lester to precede him up the steps to the lodge's large front porch. "Can't beat the friends we've made here," he agreed. "And even if Beulah and Ruby fixed nothing but peanut butter sandwiches, it would be better than eating alone in my apartment."

"We'll have to find you a girlfriend, Mose," Lester teased as he held open the door. "You—and this bachelor store-keeper coming to join us. Hey there, Dale! How was business today?"

"Brisk!" the middle-aged owner of the bulk store replied. "If Marlene hadn't been there helping me keep the shelves stocked, I couldn't have kept up with all the picnic and camping supplies folks were buying. Sure hope she'll work for a while after you two get hitched, until I can find some more help."

Lester chuckled. "I don't think Marlene wants to give up her job until the first little Lehman shows up. She loves seeing all those customers and being busy in your store, Dale."

As the three of them entered the lodge's lobby, Mose noticed more ladies than usual bustling around the dining room table nearest the kitchen door. He quickly picked out his sister, Marlene, who stood head and shoulders taller than the others. Beulah and Ruby were easy to spot from across the big room because of their colorful floral dresses. The presence of two newcomers sent his antennae up— but only until he noticed the small figure clad in black, carrying a big bowl of something to the table.

Sylvia Keim. Because she was so shy and quiet at their evening meals, all he knew about her was that she had an inoperable brain tumor. He had no idea where she'd come from or how many family members she'd left behind so she could spend her final days at Promise Lodge.

"All right, fellows, we're ready for you!" Ruby called out. "We spent our day making wedding food, so supper will only be barbeque ham sandwiches and a few other things we threw together."

"It'll be wonderful!" Dale said as he led the men between the long wooden tables in the large dining room. "And come Thursday, when we're celebrating with Marlene and Lester, your wedding feast will be the finest food we've ever tasted."

"Hear, hear!" Lester chimed in. He flashed a special smile at Marlene before pulling out a chair to seat her. "If it wouldn't get me into trouble with the church, I'd get married again and again just to eat the fabulous spread these gals put on!"

As everyone around them laughed and found seats at the table, Mose sat down between his sister and Dale, who had pulled out the seat at the end of their side for Irene Wickey, another lodge resident and a partner in the Promise Lodge Pies business. He suspected Dale and Irene had feelings for one another, but they seemed determined not to show them.

"Our guests have arrived, fellows, so make Karen Yoder and Annie Stoltzfus welcome," Ruby put in as she sat down across the table, alongside Sylvia.

Mose nodded to the two young women on Sylvia's right, who were taking in everything around them with bright smiles. Beulah took her seat beside them, on the end nearest the kitchen door, and everyone bowed their heads to give silent thanks.

"Welcome," Dale said when they'd finished praying. "I'm Dale Kraybill, and I own the bulk store across the way. Where are you ladies from?"

The two guests glanced at each other before Karen, the one with the dark hair, replied. "We live on the outskirts of Cherrydale, south of here about three and a half hours—by car, that is."

"*Jah*, we hired a driver!" her blond friend chimed in eagerly.

Mose reached for the basket of warm sandwich rolls and took three. As always, he clammed up around strangers, so he focused on passing food after he'd filled his plate with thin sliced ham smothered in sauce, baked beans, and fruit salad. Seconds later he'd forked a large helping of meat between the halves of a bun and was hungrily jamming it into his mouth—

Until Sylvia glanced at him.

Mose closed his eyes, wishing he'd shown more control. His days of physical labor, working with Bishop Monroe's Clydesdales, left him famished, however, and no one else seemed to mind that he ate several mouthfuls before he attempted polite conversation.

Not that he had a clue what to say to Sylvia. She mystified him, with her huge hazel eyes and gaunt body. Mose forced himself to slow down and chew, so he wouldn't embarrass himself further by choking.

"Not sure I've ever heard of Cherrydale," Irene remarked pleasantly. "But then, there are plenty of places in Missouri I have no idea about. Other than living here in Promise all my life and going to church in Cloverdale and shopping in Forest Grove, I rarely leave town."

"From all the pies we've seen today, the wedding here on Thursday is going to be quite a grand affair," Annie remarked.

Mose noticed that Annie didn't take any bread, and because she also passed on the beans, the only things on her plate were a few thin slices of ham and a spoonful of fruit. He'd never met anyone who took such scanty helpings. Even tiny Sylvia was biting into her ham sandwich with relish and had spooned a little of everything onto her plate.

He made himself look away before Sylvia caught him watching her. Fortunately, the other folks kept the table talk going.

"You ladies are invited to come to our wedding, of course," Marlene put in before she tucked into her own plateful of food. "What with our friends and family coming from Coldstream, and Lester's kinfolk bussing in from Ohio, you'll have plenty of folks to visit with."

Karen and Annie looked as though they'd just won a million dollars. "Oh, that's so kind of you—"

"We'd be delighted to come!"

Mose blinked. Why did these women act as though they'd never attended a wedding? Something about the way they spoke and reacted seemed odd to him—but as he stuffed more slices of sauced meat into another bun, he didn't let their guests' behavior bother him. He did notice, however, that Sylvia's slender eyebrows had risen very subtly, as though she, too, was considering the ladies' idiosyncrasies.

"And speaking of all those pies," Ruby said, focusing on Marlene and Lester, "if you two have any further requests for your meal, speak now."

"We'll be baking the hams and chicken you've asked for," Beulah said, "and we'll stir up the macaroni salad with pineapple that Lester requested, along with green beans and mixed fruit—"

"And your chocolate wedding cake layers are baked, ready to frost with that mocha buttercream you like so much," Ruby continued with a big smile.

"Chocolate wedding cake? Not plain white?" Annie asked. "I've always read that—"

"Well, most brides have traditional white cake," Karen interrupted very quickly. "But I can see you folks here do things a lot differently!"

Marlene chuckled. "From the first time Ruby baked one of her chocolate cakes, most of us here have requested it for weddings and birthdays and any other excuse we can come up with," she explained. "But you're right, Karen. We Promise Lodge folks have a rather independent spirit, compared to other districts. And what about you, Mose? How was your day with the Clydesdales?"

His sister's questions caught him off guard. "I uh, well, they—they're about ready to g-go," he stammered. "I'll b-be taking them out for one m-more run with—with the parade wagon t-tomorrow before their owner c-comes to get them."

Luckily, Lester picked up the conversational trail Mose had botched so badly.

"Mose works with the Clydesdales our bishop, Monroe Burkholder, trains to perform at special horse shows and in parades," he explained to the two guests. "Those horses are a sight to see when they're pulling a wagon and going through their maneuvers. Mose is also a top-notch farrier and he's got some veterinary skills that've been a real boon to the community."

As his cheeks flushed, Mose focused on getting a spoonful of fruit salad into his mouth without embarrassing himself further. He'd had a stuttering problem ever since he'd been kidnapped as a kid, and being thrust into the spotlight made him even more tongue-tied around folks he didn't know.

"That is so cool," Karen murmured.

"Like watching the Budweiser Clydesdales on—well, we've seen them in TV commercials at Christmastime when we've walked past the furniture store," Annie added quickly.

Somehow Mose got through the rest of the tasty meal without having to say anything more. As he was at the sideboard helping himself to bars that were loaded with peanuts, chocolate, coconut, and other wonderful ingredients, Beulah spoke up.

"Can I convince you gentlemen to carry our steam tables up from the basement?" she asked. "There might be some pie in it for you, in addition to those seven-layer bars Mose has just discovered."

Lester laughed when he saw that Mose had taken an entire handful of the bars and was coming back to his seat. "Save your pie for the wedding, ladies. We'll be happy to help, as long as our big buddy here shares those fabulous-looking cookies with us!"

"Count me in as a carry-upper," Dale put in as he, too, headed for the cookie tray. "You ladies always feed us way too well, even after you've been preparing for a wedding all day. With all the *stuff* these bars are bulging with, they're practically a meal by themselves."

Ruby laughed. "That cookie recipe's as old as the hills, but easy-peasy."

"And you can't go wrong if it's chockful of chocolate and butterscotch chips as well as M&M's and peanuts—and then has sweetened condensed milk poured all over it," Beulah added with a chuckle. "Take your time, fellows, and enjoy the rest of your meal. Just thought I'd put in our request for some of your muscle."

Mose closed his eyes over the combination of sweet, salty, and crunchy ingredients that pushed all the right dessert buttons. When Marlene rose to start scraping plates, he and the other men followed Beulah through the kitchen and down the basement stairs to where the stainless-steel steam tables and pans were stored. After she pointed out all the other equipment they would need to serve the wedding meal, Lester cleared his throat.

"So, Beulah, what's the story behind those two guests?" he murmured. "I've missed out on what brought them here and—"

"Is it me, or is something a little off-kilter about them?" Dale chimed in softly.

Beulah chuckled. "They called a couple weeks ago, requesting rooms—for a *may*-del getaway, they called it," she explained. "Believe me, we women have pinpointed the details you've probably noticed, and we're keeping our mouths shut until something jumps out and exposes the real story. I don't think this will be as serious as when that fake bishop came here under false pretenses, but we're keeping watch."

Lester groaned softly. "*That* man was a piece of work. I'm still ashamed I didn't spot him as a phony while he was bunking at my place," he remarked as he approached the steam table. "Mose, can you grab the other end of this? You want to go up the stairs backward or be on the lower end?"

"You start up with it so I'll bear most of the weight," Mose replied.

About fifteen minutes later, the three of them had carried up the steam table, pans, and everything else Beulah had asked for. Mose quickly slipped past the ladies who were washing dishes to snag one last cookie before striding through the dining room to start back to his apartment. He paused on the lodge's wide front porch, steeping himself in the beauty of the May sunset and the well-tended produce plots and lawns around him.

He and his sister had done the right thing by coming here from Coldstream this past spring. Even if Marlene hadn't fallen in love with Lester and so quickly turned her life around, he and his twin had often remarked that they'd found such a sense of peace and happiness here—such a feeling that they *belonged* among the friendly, hard-working folks at Promise Lodge. Mose believed he'd found his true calling at last, caring for Bishop Monroe's magnificent Clydesdales and putting his experience as a veterinary assistant to good use in ways he hadn't been allowed in Coldstream. The bishop there had flat-out told him he had no business getting his high school diploma, let alone attending some entry-level college classes for veterinary assistants.

As he ambled along the private road that wound its way between the various families' properties, he smiled at each of the places he passed. Two little white buildings near Christine Burkholder's dairy barn housed the Kuhns' cheese factory and Promise Lodge Pies, operated by Irene and her partner, Phoebe Troyer. He waved at Preacher Amos Troyer and Mattie, who were weeding a flower bed—and Mattie's sons, Roman and Noah, who had built homes nearby when they'd married. Farther up the road he passed the home of Preacher Marlin Kurtz and his wife, Frances. At the curve sat Lester Lehman's old home, which he'd sold to Phineas and Annabelle Beachey last winter before he'd moved into Allen Troyer's tiny home on the shore of Rainbow Lake.

Mose gazed at the new house standing on the highest point of the rise, overlooking the pasture where Bishop Monroe's Clydesdales grazed. Lester had just completed this place, where he and Marlene would be living after they tied the knot on Thursday. It was yet another story of a new beginning and a fresh chance at love—a story that had been repeating itself ever since sisters Mattie, Christine, and Rosetta had started Promise Lodge. God was obviously at work here, and Mose felt grateful to be living in his new apartment in the loft of one of the Clydesdale barns.

He headed toward the gate of the white plank fence that surrounded Bishop Monroe's pasture, eager to see the horses as he fed and watered them for the night. When he spotted a childlike figure gazing between the fence slats, however, Mose stopped in his tracks. In the fading daylight, he wondered if it could be Preacher Marlin's daughter, Fannie, or her friend Lily Peterscheim, Preacher Eli's girl. But the black dress—and the wistfulness surrounding the visitor like a pale cloud—could only belong to one woman.

He'd assumed Sylvia had been in the kitchen washing dishes. Why had she ventured all the way up the road? As though she sensed his presence, she turned, appearing as startled as Mose felt.

"Oh! I—I just wanted to see the Clydesdales you were talking about at dinner, Mose," Sylvia explained hastily. "They're absolutely magnificent. They must make quite a sight when they're hitched to a wagon as a team."

The way she finished her statement with such prayerlike

reverence touched Mose's heart—but it also sent him into an emotional tailspin. He had the sudden urge to lift this tiny woman to his shoulder like a child, so she could see over the top of the fence, even as his ability to put one rational word after another abandoned him.

"Would—would you like to s-see the barns and the C-Clydesdales? You c-could come in with m-me while I put out their f-feed," he said in a rush.

What had possessed him to say that? He'd just broken one of Bishop Monroe's cardinal rules about not allowing strangers in with the horses.

Sylvia's wide eyes expressed something akin to terror. "Oh, I wouldn't have the nerve to get so close to such massive animals!" she blurted out. She laughed nervously, peering through the fence slats again. "But the thought of riding a parade wagon does sound like a glorious way to have some fun!"

Mose stepped toward her, his heart hammering. When the rays of the setting sun glimmered on the gauzy back of her heart-shaped *kapp*, Sylvia glowed like an angel wearing a halo. Was that a sign that Mose should be paying her special respect? Or was it perhaps a subtle heavenly warning about the limited number of days this little woman had left?

Mose inhaled deeply to fortify his nerves. "You—you want to ride with me when I p-put them through their—p-paces t-tomorrow morning?" he stammered. "I'll b-be t-taking them out around eight."

The joy on Sylvia's face made Mose want to grab her up and hug her—which would be as wildly inappropriate as his invitation to ride the parade wagon. He seemed to have lost all control over his thoughts, because he'd gotten the sense that Sylvia was somewhat older than he, and far too fragile for a man his size to handle. And he'd face a stern talking-to when Bishop Monroe found out that he'd offered Sylvia a ride with a client's team.

And yet, the fact that he'd made her so happy made him happy, too. Mose felt like a dog that couldn't wag his tail fast enough.

"When will I ever get another opportunity for *that*?" Sylvia marveled softly. "I'll see you bright and early tomorrow, Mose!"

Off she went, down the hill, as though she thought he might retract his invitation if she stuck around.

Mose gazed after her, wondering how he'd explain his blatant breaking of the bishop's rules—rules that both men agreed were for the safety of the Clydesdales and the "sightseers" who unwittingly got too close to such massive horses. With a sigh he entered the pasture, secured the gate behind him, and made his way toward the two barns that glowed a deep shade of maroon in the sun's last light. As the horses nickered at him, he called each one by name and chatted with them as they began their nightly walk to the barn.

He'd just stepped inside the nearest barn when he came face to face with the bishop. Monroe Burkholder stood only an inch shorter than Mose. Before he uttered a word, he exuded a sense of power few other men possessed. Fortunately for the folks at Promise Lodge, Bishop Monroe wasn't one to use his position—or his size—to his own advantage, as some bishops did. Even so, Mose knew he shouldn't keep quiet about the mistake he'd made while talking to Sylvia.

"I—I know it's not a *gut* idea," Mose began hesitantly, "but when Sylvia Keim wanted to ride on the parade wagon sometime, I um—I just now invited her to come along t-tomorrow morning. If you—if you want me to t-tell her she can't do that because of our rules, I'll go right this minute. I'm sorry I spoke before I thought, Bishop Monroe."

A few stalls away, the bishop set his bucket of water on the floor and straightened to his full height. The steady thunder of hooves on concrete echoed around them as the Clydesdales entered the barn and went to their stalls. Bishop Monroe considered his response with an unreadable expression on his face while Mose stood silently, awaiting a well-deserved lecture.

"*Jah*, you and I both know why I don't allow other folks around the horses," he stated beneath the sounds of his Clydesdales nudging their feed bins in anticipation. Then a smile softened his handsome face. "I don't see Sylvia as a guest who's likely to stir up trouble, however—and soon enough that team of six will be performing amongst hundreds of strangers and spectators, after all. I'll trust you to be responsible for her, Mose. *Denki* for letting me know. And have a *gut* time making the horses strut their stuff tomorrow."

Mose blinked. He felt like a scholar who'd just been excused from detention because he'd admitted his guilt to his teacher. "You—you're very kind," he said as relief rushed through him. "The best boss ever!"

The bishop laughed. "The best bosses have *gut* reason to be kind to their employees. It makes for smoother working relationships—and it's what God wants of us all, to love justice and show kindness and walk humbly with Him."

"Micah six, verse eight," Mose whispered. "Words to live by."

"And you're the best fellow I could ever have hired, Mose," Monroe put in, squeezing his shoulder. "Keep up the *gut* work—and now let's get the oats dished out before these horses get impatient with us."

With a light heart, Mose went to work alongside Monroe,

e b-barns until we've left—s-so let's g-get started,
"

sensed that for all his height and muscle, Mose
ght be the gentlest man she'd ever met. "Don't
ast across the pasture," she said as he opened the
k gate. "I've got short little legs, you know."

started off across the expanse of lush green grass
n, Sylvia was startlingly aware of just how large
cally powerful her companion was. Mose strolled
ong a few careful feet away from her, his hands
d uncurling at his sides, but even so, Sylvia was
o steps to every one of his. By the time they got
hill and near one of the barns, she was struggling
f and puff—

she saw the two massive lead horses watching
n the open doorway. All fatigue left her as Sylvia
o gawk at them. Their glossy brown coats shone
lth and their shaggy cream-colored stockings
own to huge hooves. They wore black leather tack
vith silver trim that sparkled in the sunlight. And
e standing absolutely still, intently focused on

ack here with me, Sylvia," Mose murmured as he
everal feet away from the door.
dn't dare do anything else.
ght, boys, forward. Easy now," Mose said in a low

snort of anticipation, the six Clydesdales started
barn, pulling a shiny black parade wagon behind
e moment Mose said *whoa*, they halted.
," Sylvia whispered. "*Wow!* I've never seen such
ses and—and even though you don't have a hold
ns, they're doing exactly what you tell them!"
ooked away, embarrassed by her praise. "It's my

putting out feed and filling the water troughs in both barns. When at last he went upstairs to his apartment and slipped into bed, he felt more convinced than ever that God had indeed intended for him to live a fulfilling life at Promise Lodge.

One of the bishop's remarks about Sylvia kept ringing in his mind, however, repeating with a sense of inescapable finality.

I'll trust you to be responsible for her, Mose.

Mose hardly slept a wink all night.

Chapter 3

As the sun's rays streamed through Sylvia's bedroom window Tuesday morning, second thoughts made her frantic. Why on earth had she invited herself to ride on the parade wagon? She'd put both Mose and herself in a ticklish situation because Bishop Monroe might object to her riding along—and because there was no way around it: Mose would have to put his hands on her to help her up.

The thought of such a heart-stoppingly handsome man lifting her onto the driver's seat gave her all manner of goose bumps such as she hadn't felt in years. But Sylvia was quite sure Mose had no interest in a dying, overly cautious woman who was way too old to be of interest to him. She'd made a schoolgirlish mistake by hoping she could ride along, and he'd been too polite to refuse her.

As she put on a clean black dress, Sylvia considered staying in her apartment, letting Mose figure out that she wasn't going to show up.

And why would I be so rude to the poor man? Why not go along with this once-in-a-lifetime chance . . . because everything of interest that I do now will be for the last time.

A welling up of sadness made her blink rapidly. She'd vowed not to become maudlin about her diagnosis—wanted to live every day to its fullest now that she was here among

such wonderful, accepting new
however, to maintain a positive a
idea how much time she had lef
wanted was to become a burden to
she'd left her former church distri
started fussing over her. Better to
not become an object of pity.

*So I'll ride on that wagon—bec
to sit up so high and watch such m
don't have a headache this morn
make advances, and he's strong e
Clydesdales, so I'll be perfectly saf*

A few minutes later Sylvia slipp
door to walk up the road, her heart
tion. She was so lost in her thought
to the homes she passed or their nea
a beautiful May morning, and she
adventure!

The sight of two tall, burly men
gate made Sylvia feel extremely sn
their smiles welcomed her.

"*Gut* morning, Sylvia!" Bishop
approached. "Mose tells me you're
puts our team through its final pac
to keep these horses moving along
cised when their owner comes to
noon. Mose is so used to handling
any demands of them, so you nee
them off."

"Me?" Sylvia blurted. "What
dales or handling a team or—"

"D-don't let the bishop p-pull y
a smile that looked as nervous as
all hitched up, ready to g-go—

s-stay in
shall we
    Sylvi
Fisher
walk to
white p
    As s
beside
and phy
slowly
curling
taking
down t
not to h
    Unt
them f
stoppe
with h
reached
adorne
they w
Mose.
    "Stay
stopped
    She
    "All
voice.
    With
out of th
them. T
    "Wow
huge ho
on the re
    Mose

j-job," he said with a modest shrug. "Now all that's left is t-training their owner this afternoon, so he fully understands all the c-commands his t-team has been t-taught to follow. You ready to ride, Sylvia?"

She swallowed hard, nodding as she gazed up at him. For a long, lovely moment Mose's deep brown eyes held hers, and she sensed that he, too, would have to get his nerves under control.

"I—I'll try not to hurt you," he murmured as his broad hands spanned her waist.

"Oh, I'm not as fragile as I look," Sylvia murmured, fibbing to make him feel more confident.

As though she weighed no more than a feather, Mose lifted her high above his shoulders until she was standing in front of the driver's seat. He gave her a moment to steady herself and sit down before he stepped up onto the wagon and took his place beside her on the wide wooden bench. He inhaled deeply, as though to collect his thoughts before he took up the leather lines that were connected to each of the six Clydesdales' ornate black harnesses.

"You okay?" he whispered.

"Never better," Sylvia replied—because suddenly she felt like the queen of the world, perched high above the team as she gazed across the expanse of Bishop Monroe's pasture. "Mose, this is the most fun I've had in forever, so let's not spoil it by talking about *me*, all right? Let's go!"

"Yes, ma'am!" he said with a chuckle. "My boss says you're in charge, so I'll do whatever you say, Sylvia."

Before she could think of a comeback, Mose gave a soft command. The horses took off at a trot that made a merry jingling sound.

"They've got bells on!" Sylvia exclaimed. "I have to say that this wagon and the team's tack don't look very Plain."

"You're right," the man beside her agreed. "Most of the

bishop's clients are English fellows who spend thousands of dollars on fancy parade and performance wagons, because they enter their horses in nationwide competitions. We train the teams with bells and flashy trim to simulate the conditions and equipment they'll experience at big-time competitive shows. Our gear is at least black, though, instead of a bright color."

She shook her head in disbelief. "Sounds like a pricey hobby."

"You've got that right, too," Mose said. "Bishop Monroe has suggested that he and I need to attend one of those big competitions someday, to be sure our training is up to snuff. I really hope we'll get to go!"

Sylvia couldn't imagine what a spectacle such an event would be, if all the teams were as elaborately equipped as this one. As they approached the white plank gate, the bishop swung it open so Mose could drive the wagon through. The shine in Monroe Burkholder's eyes told her what a thrill he got from working with these extraordinary horses.

"You kids have fun now," he called up to them. "Don't be surprised if everyone at Promise Lodge stops what they're doing to watch you!"

Sylvia sucked in her breath. She hadn't considered how *visible* she would be during this ride—hadn't thought about how her new neighbors might react when they saw her seated beside Mose, either. But it was too late to worry about that. And she would *not* hunker down between the seat and the wagon panel just because people would be watching her.

When the horses reached the private road, it was clear that the thunder of their twenty-four massive hooves—along with their harness bells—would announce their arrival. Sylvia sat up straighter, her heart hammering with excitement.

"Sure enough, there's Preacher Marlin and his son, Harley, watching from the sheep pasture," Mose murmured as he returned their waves.

"And Christine's looking at us from her garden. My *gut*-ness, the view from up here is amazing, considering what a shortie like me usually sees," Sylvia remarked with a laugh. "Folks are coming onto their front porches as though we're a *parade* passing their houses. There's Annabelle and Phineas!"

"We *are* a parade," Mose put in as he waved at the Beacheys. "Most days I work the teams in the pasture, or with a plainer wagon, so seeing the Clydesdales in full regalia is a treat these folks don't often get."

And this ride is a treat like I've never had in my life!

As this realization struck her, Sylvia hugged herself to keep from exploding with the wonder of the moment. Her life had been one of quiet wifely duty before Ivan had passed, and before debilitating headaches, fainting spells, and seizures had forced her to seek medical help. Coming to Promise Lodge on a last-resort whim was turning out to be much more rewarding and invigorating than she'd anticipated—

And the smile on Mose's handsome face made her heart turn handsprings.

"It's *gut* to see you looking so happy," he murmured.

Sylvia gaped, wondering if she was going to pass out from sheer exhilaration. "I—I can't recall ever having so much fun," she admitted in a rush. "*Denki* for letting me come along, Mose."

He turned away, maybe as embarrassed by her admission as she was—but not before she caught the flash of his delighted smile. Mose resumed waving at the folks they were passing, calling out to Frances Kurtz on her porch, and to Preacher Amos and Mattie, and then to Mattie's sons, Noah and Roman, who were returning from the dairy barn where they'd done the morning's milking.

Sylvia knew what she'd seen, however. And, if she was recalling Mose's sentiment correctly, he'd spoken to her without stammering.

Maybe—just maybe—Mose saw her as more than an almost-invalid who'd be turning the fateful age of fifty on her next birthday, if the Lord let her live so long. She wasn't sure how she felt about that, but she allowed herself to enjoy brushing against Mose's muscular arm when the wagon swayed with the curve in the road.

As the lodge came into view, the Kuhn sisters and Rosetta Wickey stepped out onto the porch to wave, smiling brightly. Across the road, Irene and Phoebe emerged from their little white pie shop near the dairy barn. Sylvia's heart sang as she waved at them all, forgetting to be self-conscious about whom she was sitting beside. She inhaled the aromas of sugar and pastry that drifted on the breeze as the Clydesdales headed for the arched metal sign at the entry to Promise Lodge. Mose waved at dark-haired Preacher Eli Peterscheim, standing outside his forge, before focusing again on the team in front of him.

Once Mose had guided the Clydesdales onto the road with a single command, they soon came to the stop sign at the state highway. When a couple of cars had gone past and no other traffic was in sight, they turned onto the blacktop. Mose clucked to the team to pick up the pace. On her right, Sylvia spotted the redheaded Helmuth twins, Sam and Simon, helping customers among the trees and bushes at their nursery. Their wives, Bernice and Barbara, straightened to their full height in their huge garden, waving merrily.

putting out feed and filling the water troughs in both barns. When at last he went upstairs to his apartment and slipped into bed, he felt more convinced than ever that God had indeed intended for him to live a fulfilling life at Promise Lodge.

One of the bishop's remarks about Sylvia kept ringing in his mind, however, repeating with a sense of inescapable finality.

I'll trust you to be responsible for her, Mose.

Mose hardly slept a wink all night.

Chapter 3

As the sun's rays streamed through Sylvia's bedroom window Tuesday morning, second thoughts made her frantic. Why on earth had she invited herself to ride on the parade wagon? She'd put both Mose and herself in a ticklish situation because Bishop Monroe might object to her riding along—and because there was no way around it: Mose would have to put his hands on her to help her up.

The thought of such a heart-stoppingly handsome man lifting her onto the driver's seat gave her all manner of goose bumps such as she hadn't felt in years. But Sylvia was quite sure Mose had no interest in a dying, overly cautious woman who was way too old to be of interest to him. She'd made a schoolgirlish mistake by hoping she could ride along, and he'd been too polite to refuse her.

As she put on a clean black dress, Sylvia considered staying in her apartment, letting Mose figure out that she wasn't going to show up.

And why would I be so rude to the poor man? Why not go along with this once-in-a-lifetime chance . . . because everything of interest that I do now will be for the last time.

A welling up of sadness made her blink rapidly. She'd vowed not to become maudlin about her diagnosis—wanted to live every day to its fullest now that she was here among such wonderful, accepting new friends. It was difficult, however, to maintain a positive attitude when she had no idea how much time she had left. The last thing Sylvia wanted was to become a burden to anyone, which was why she'd left her former church district before the folks there started fussing over her. Better to make a clean break and not become an object of pity.

So I'll ride on that wagon—because how often do I get to sit up so high and watch such magnificent horses? And I don't have a headache this morning! Mose is too shy to make advances, and he's strong enough to handle those Clydesdales, so I'll be perfectly safe.

A few minutes later Sylvia slipped out the lodge's back door to walk up the road, her heart skipping with anticipation. She was so lost in her thoughts, she paid no attention to the homes she passed or their neatly tended yards. It was a beautiful May morning, and she was about to have an *adventure*!

The sight of two tall, burly men standing at the pasture gate made Sylvia feel extremely small and vulnerable, but their smiles welcomed her.

"*Gut* morning, Sylvia!" Bishop Monroe called out as she approached. "Mose tells me you're riding shotgun while he puts our team through its final paces. I'm counting on you to keep these horses moving along so they'll be well exercised when their owner comes to pick them up this afternoon. Mose is so used to handling them, he might not make any demands of them, so you need to insist that he shows them off."

"Me?" Sylvia blurted. "What do *I* know about Clydesdales or handling a team or—"

"D-don't let the bishop p-pull your leg," Mose put in with a smile that looked as nervous as Sylvia felt. "The t-team's all hitched up, ready to g-go—and the other horses will s-stay in the b-barns until we've left—s-so let's g-get started, shall we?"

Sylvia sensed that for all his height and muscle, Mose Fisher might be the gentlest man she'd ever met. "Don't walk too fast across the pasture," she said as he opened the white plank gate. "I've got short little legs, you know."

As she started off across the expanse of lush green grass beside him, Sylvia was startlingly aware of just how large and physically powerful her companion was. Mose strolled slowly along a few careful feet away from her, his hands curling and uncurling at his sides, but even so, Sylvia was taking two steps to every one of his. By the time they got down the hill and near one of the barns, she was struggling not to huff and puff—

Until she saw the two massive lead horses watching them from the open doorway. All fatigue left her as Sylvia stopped to gawk at them. Their glossy brown coats shone with health and their shaggy cream-colored stockings reached down to huge hooves. They wore black leather tack adorned with silver trim that sparkled in the sunlight. And they were standing absolutely still, intently focused on Mose.

"Stay back here with me, Sylvia," Mose murmured as he stopped several feet away from the door.

She didn't dare do anything else.

"All right, boys, forward. Easy now," Mose said in a low voice.

With a snort of anticipation, the six Clydesdales started out of the barn, pulling a shiny black parade wagon behind them. The moment Mose said *whoa*, they halted.

"Wow," Sylvia whispered. "*Wow!* I've never seen such *huge* horses and—and even though you don't have a hold on the reins, they're doing exactly what you tell them!"

Mose looked away, embarrassed by her praise. "It's my

j-job," he said with a modest shrug. "Now all that's left is t-training their owner this afternoon, so he fully understands all the c-commands his t-team has been t-taught to follow. You ready to ride, Sylvia?"

She swallowed hard, nodding as she gazed up at him. For a long, lovely moment Mose's deep brown eyes held hers, and she sensed that he, too, would have to get his nerves under control.

"I—I'll try not to hurt you," he murmured as his broad hands spanned her waist.

"Oh, I'm not as fragile as I look," Sylvia murmured, fibbing to make him feel more confident.

As though she weighed no more than a feather, Mose lifted her high above his shoulders until she was standing in front of the driver's seat. He gave her a moment to steady herself and sit down before he stepped up onto the wagon and took his place beside her on the wide wooden bench. He inhaled deeply, as though to collect his thoughts before he took up the leather lines that were connected to each of the six Clydesdales' ornate black harnesses.

"You okay?" he whispered.

"Never better," Sylvia replied—because suddenly she felt like the queen of the world, perched high above the team as she gazed across the expanse of Bishop Monroe's pasture. "Mose, this is the most fun I've had in forever, so let's not spoil it by talking about *me*, all right? Let's go!"

"Yes, ma'am!" he said with a chuckle. "My boss says you're in charge, so I'll do whatever you say, Sylvia."

Before she could think of a comeback, Mose gave a soft command. The horses took off at a trot that made a merry jingling sound.

"They've got bells on!" Sylvia exclaimed. "I have to say that this wagon and the team's tack don't look very Plain."

"You're right," the man beside her agreed. "Most of the

bishop's clients are English fellows who spend thousands of dollars on fancy parade and performance wagons, because they enter their horses in nationwide competitions. We train the teams with bells and flashy trim to simulate the conditions and equipment they'll experience at big-time competitive shows. Our gear is at least black, though, instead of a bright color."

She shook her head in disbelief. "Sounds like a pricey hobby."

"You've got that right, too," Mose said. "Bishop Monroe has suggested that he and I need to attend one of those big competitions someday, to be sure our training is up to snuff. I really hope we'll get to go!"

Sylvia couldn't imagine what a spectacle such an event would be, if all the teams were as elaborately equipped as this one. As they approached the white plank gate, the bishop swung it open so Mose could drive the wagon through. The shine in Monroe Burkholder's eyes told her what a thrill he got from working with these extraordinary horses.

"You kids have fun now," he called up to them. "Don't be surprised if everyone at Promise Lodge stops what they're doing to watch you!"

Sylvia sucked in her breath. She hadn't considered how *visible* she would be during this ride—hadn't thought about how her new neighbors might react when they saw her seated beside Mose, either. But it was too late to worry about that. And she would *not* hunker down between the seat and the wagon panel just because people would be watching her.

When the horses reached the private road, it was clear that the thunder of their twenty-four massive hooves—along with their harness bells—would announce their arrival. Sylvia sat up straighter, her heart hammering with excitement.

"Sure enough, there's Preacher Marlin and his son, Harley, watching from the sheep pasture," Mose murmured as he returned their waves.

"And Christine's looking at us from her garden. My *gut-ness*, the view from up here is amazing, considering what a shortie like me usually sees," Sylvia remarked with a laugh. "Folks are coming onto their front porches as though we're a *parade* passing their houses. There's Annabelle and Phineas!"

"We *are* a parade," Mose put in as he waved at the Beacheys. "Most days I work the teams in the pasture, or with a plainer wagon, so seeing the Clydesdales in full regalia is a treat these folks don't often get."

And this ride is a treat like I've never had in my life!

As this realization struck her, Sylvia hugged herself to keep from exploding with the wonder of the moment. Her life had been one of quiet wifely duty before Ivan had passed, and before debilitating headaches, fainting spells, and seizures had forced her to seek medical help. Coming to Promise Lodge on a last-resort whim was turning out to be much more rewarding and invigorating than she'd anticipated—

And the smile on Mose's handsome face made her heart turn handsprings.

"It's *gut* to see you looking so happy," he murmured.

Sylvia gaped, wondering if she was going to pass out from sheer exhilaration. "I—I can't recall ever having so much fun," she admitted in a rush. "*Denki* for letting me come along, Mose."

He turned away, maybe as embarrassed by her admission as she was—but not before she caught the flash of his delighted smile. Mose resumed waving at the folks they were passing, calling out to Frances Kurtz on her porch, and to Preacher Amos and Mattie, and then to Mattie's sons, Noah and Roman, who were returning from the dairy barn where they'd done the morning's milking.

Sylvia knew what she'd seen, however. And, if she was recalling Mose's sentiment correctly, he'd spoken to her without stammering.

Maybe—just maybe—Mose saw her as more than an almost-invalid who'd be turning the fateful age of fifty on her next birthday, if the Lord let her live so long. She wasn't sure how she felt about that, but she allowed herself to enjoy brushing against Mose's muscular arm when the wagon swayed with the curve in the road.

As the lodge came into view, the Kuhn sisters and Rosetta Wickey stepped out onto the porch to wave, smiling brightly. Across the road, Irene and Phoebe emerged from their little white pie shop near the dairy barn. Sylvia's heart sang as she waved at them all, forgetting to be self-conscious about whom she was sitting beside. She inhaled the aromas of sugar and pastry that drifted on the breeze as the Clydesdales headed for the arched metal sign at the entry to Promise Lodge. Mose waved at dark-haired Preacher Eli Peterscheim, standing outside his forge, before focusing again on the team in front of him.

Once Mose had guided the Clydesdales onto the road with a single command, they soon came to the stop sign at the state highway. When a couple of cars had gone past and no other traffic was in sight, they turned onto the blacktop. Mose clucked to the team to pick up the pace. On her right, Sylvia spotted the redheaded Helmuth twins, Sam and Simon, helping customers among the trees and bushes at their nursery. Their wives, Bernice and Barbara, straightened to their full height in their huge garden, waving merrily.

After they'd passed Dale Kraybill's bulk store parking lot, which was filled with cars and buggies, Mose urged the horses to go even faster.

"Hang on to your *kapp*!" he teased as Sylvia clutched her lightweight prayer covering. "We have to push the team as fast as it can go out here on the highway, because the shoulder of this road is too narrow to accommodate the wagon."

With the wind blowing in her face as the countryside passed rapidly by on either side of them, Sylvia began to laugh out loud. The heavy, rhythmic clatter of the horses' hooves thundered so loudly, accentuated by their jingling bells, she didn't even try to talk. Riding high on an open vehicle meant that she felt more vulnerable to every sway of the wagon, however, so she grasped her *kapp* strings in one hand and scooted closer to Mose so she could hang on to his arm for dear life.

Jah, it is a dear life. And I wouldn't trade this moment for anything!

For several exhilarating minutes they traveled full tilt down the state highway, until Mose spoke to prepare the horses for turning off at the next intersection. Sylvia realized that, because the team of six stretched ahead of the wagon for more than twenty-five feet, it took forethought and expert driving on Mose's part and the cooperation of three pairs of huge horses to make the turn without tipping the wagon. Once they were on a narrow dirt road, he slowed the horses to a gradual stop.

"How did you *do* that?" Sylvia exclaimed. "You just sat here as though—as though it took no effort at all to maneuver those huge horses onto this side road, and—and—"

She suddenly realized that she was the one stammering while Mose smiled modestly.

"It all happens in my hands," he said with a shrug. "Each of the horses has a pair of lines that are woven between my fingers, and I'm sort of like a puppeteer controlling them. I moved my arms and body while we were making that turn, but I guess you were too entranced to notice."

Entranced. Sylvia blinked at his word choice, because he'd described her state of mind perfectly. Suddenly realizing that her body was snugly situated against his—and aware of how large and powerful and male Mose was—she scooted away so there was space between them.

"Sorry. I didn't intend to hamper your driving or—"

"I think we were both having too much fun to think about it. And it was fabulous, wasn't it?"

Sylvia caught herself gazing into his eyes, allowing the low, soothing timbre of his voice to wash over her. "*Jah*, it was," she murmured.

For a brief and slightly scary moment, she thought Mose was going to kiss her. He sat several inches taller than she, and if he took the notion, he only had to lower his face a bit to be touching her lips with his.

Sylvia swallowed hard, not daring to break their gaze until, with a sigh, Mose focused on the horses again. "Back," he murmured, positioning his hands slightly higher as he tightened the lines.

Without a moment's hesitation, the Clydesdales moved in one fluid motion. The wagon rolled backward for several feet, until Mose said, "Whoa, now. At ease."

Exhaling and shaking their massive heads, the horses stood in place as though they had no intention of moving for the rest of the day.

Sylvia realized she was holding her breath, awaiting each new maneuver. Such a level of perfection reflected well on Mose's training, and she'd gained a new respect for the younger man who sat through evening meals at the lodge as though he was tongue-tied.

"Let's go. Walk it now."

Again each pair in the team reacted in synchronized timing, so the wagon moved forward without a hitch. Mose let them amble slowly along—although, even at their reduced speed, the six massive horses were taking each step together. The man obviously shared a deep kinship with these Clydesdales: their ears were tilted back slightly, anticipating his next quiet command.

"That's amazing," Sylvia whispered.

"They're incredible animals," he remarked in his low voice. "I'll miss this team, but we have a couple of mares about ready to foal, so they'll keep me busy until another owner brings us a pair of Clydesdales he's bought separately. It'll take some time before they cooperate with one another, but I'm looking forward to the challenge. Now— if you peek between these trees up ahead, on your right, you can see parts of Promise Lodge."

Sylvia leaned forward and looked earnestly where Mose was pointing. "That's Bishop Monroe's house! And—is that the backside of Lester's new place?"

"*Jah*. Those homes sit high enough to spot them from here. When the leaves drop this fall, we'll probably be able to see more."

Sylvia blinked. Was Mose hinting that he might bring her back here someday? When she'd moved into her lodge apartment, she'd figured on being long gone by fall—yet she suddenly wanted to stick around, to see the various wonders Mose and her other new friends might show her, and to share the winter holidays with them—

Lord, if it's Your will, I hope to live beyond the time frame my doctor gave me. I've got things to do and places to see here!

For the rest of the ride Sylvia remained pensive, nodding whenever Mose pointed something out—although he, too, became less talkative as he guided the team into a very tight ninety-degree turn at another intersection. The Clydesdales showed amazing judgment and skill as they took their time moving to the far side of the road and pulling steadily until the wagon had cleared the intersection and they were going in a straight line again. About fifteen minutes later, Mose was driving them under the arched white sign at the Promise Lodge entry, and the team stepped along briskly, happy to be returning to familiar territory.

The bishop was nowhere to be seen, so Mose halted the horses at the gate and hopped nimbly down to open it. For a tall, burly fellow, he possessed amazing agility—

And why am I paying attention to the way Mose moves? He's obviously got a talent for training horses, but it's silly to think of him as anything but a patient, considerate younger man who helps little old ladies across the street— or up onto a parade wagon. I'm setting myself up for disappointment if I allow my thoughts to take the slightest romantic turn.

After he'd vaulted back up onto the driver's bench, he looked at her. "You all right, Sylvia? You got kind of quiet."

She found a smile, even though her emotions were in turmoil. "I'm fine, Mose. Better than fine. I stand in awe of your skills, and I'm grateful for the time you've spent with me today," she replied. When she considered the distance she'd have to walk uphill from the red Clydesdale barns to return to the road, she added, "I'd really like to get down here, please. I'm feeling too tired to hike back to the lodge from the barn—and that way, you can pay full attention to the horses before their owner shows up."

Mose nodded, watching her as she spoke, as though he wondered if she was giving him the full story. "I can circle back and drop you off at the lodge—"

"No, no, I don't want to be any trouble," Sylvia insisted. "*Denki* again for a wonderful ride, Mose."

With a lingering smile, he clambered down to the ground and reached up for her. "If you crouch and let yourself fall forward, I'll catch you. I don't think you can reach the first step on the side of the wagon."

For a fleeting moment Sylvia balked, picturing a catastrophic fall if Mose's arms did *not* close around her and she hit the ground from this height. It was a ridiculous fear, of course—the kind of idea that had limited her life even before she'd received her terminal diagnosis. She'd always lived so carefully, following the rules and taking every precaution.

Sylvia focused on Mose's deep brown eyes, bent her knees, and went over the side. For a fleeting moment she was airborne, and then a pair of strong hands were holding her firmly. Was it her imagination, or did Mose embrace her for longer than he needed to? She was aware of his muscled chest moving against her as they breathed together, and of the warmth of his skin beneath his shirt, and of the dark, masculine shadow covering his cheeks and neck where he shaved each day.

When he set her carefully on the ground to release her, Sylvia sighed. For a blissful few moments, she'd felt as sheltered and protected as a beloved child. As her emotions began to whirl, she waved quickly rather than risking words, striding away before Mose could catch the shine of the tears filling her eyes.

I don't want to die! This tumor business is so unfair.

She blinked rapidly, in case the Kuhns or anyone else was around when she entered the lodge. By the time she'd opened the mudroom door and started up the back stairway from the kitchen, her legs were so wobbly she hoped she'd make it without collapsing and causing a scene. Her temples were pounding as she opened her apartment door, and as she tumbled onto her bed, she knew she'd be there all afternoon, recovering from more exertion and excitement than she'd had in a long while—not to mention an oncoming headache that promised to be a doozy.

But if I die tonight, I'll die happy.

Chapter 4

Thursday morning started early in the lodge, with all the regular residents in the kitchen before dawn, preparing for Marlene Fisher's wedding. At seven, however, Karen and Andi were scrambling back and forth between their rooms, deciding which of their Amish-style dresses would be the most appropriate.

"I wish we'd known about the wedding," Karen said as she shook her head over her choice of new cape dresses. "I loved all these springtime colors when I was buying my fabric, but I'll stick out like a—a parrot in a roomful of crows if I wear coral or sea green."

"I've decided on this gray one," Andi said as she took it off the hanger. "But I was so fascinated by the photos I've seen of Plain women wearing sneakers and flip-flops, I didn't bring any dark shoes!"

"Well, I packed my black church shoes, but from what I've seen Rosetta, Marlene, and Irene wearing, they'll look totally out of place with the bows on the toes." Karen shook her head. "Can't waste any more time choosing our outfits, though, or we'll be late on top of looking inappropriate. Church starts at eight!"

"And look at all those buggies parked along the pasture fence by the dairy barn," Andi said, pointing out the window.

"Last night a *busload* of Lester's friends and family arrived from Ohio, too. Maybe we'll be crammed in among so many people that nobody will even notice our shoes. That's my story, and I'm stickin' to it!"

"At least our makeup won't take up any time," Karen put in with a chuckle.

Ten minutes later the two of them started down the main stairway, following the aromas of the pastries and breakfast offerings Ruby and Beulah had invited them to share—but they stopped halfway down. Amish men in black suits, white shirts, and various styles of beards, as well as women dressed mostly in black with their hair pulled tightly beneath their *kapps*, chatted noisily in the crowded lobby. Karen almost retreated upstairs to use the back stairway into the kitchen, but folks below them had already spotted her and Andi. Their smiling faces didn't disguise their curiosity—but luckily, Marlene spotted them.

"Come into the dining room and grab a bite to eat, ladies!" she called up to them. "Everyone, this is Karen Yoder and Annie Stoltzfus, come to visit us from Cherrydale."

As the folks nodded and called up greetings, Karen lost no time reaching the bottom of the stairs where Marlene was waiting for them.

"It's your big day!" Andi remarked as the three of them eased through the crowd toward the sideboard near the kitchen. "Are you nervous, Marlene?"

"You look so pretty in your royal blue dress—with such a beautiful white apron," Karen put in.

The bride flashed them a quick smile. "I'll relax once the ceremony's behind us," she admitted. "It'll be a wonderful day, and I'm so blessed to have Lester in my life. Most *maidels* who reach the ripe old age of thirty-five never marry, after all."

By the time they got to the array of muffins, rolls, and

coffee cakes, Karen's stomach was clenching with hunger. She quickly filled a plate with a square of lemon coffee cake, a muffin that appeared to be mostly oatmeal, and a big spoonful of fresh fruit salad before ducking into the kitchen to eat. Andi was right behind her, also hoping to eat without being observed by so many strangers.

At the nearby worktable, Ruby saluted them with her metal tongs. "Glad you ladies are joining us! We're getting the ham and chicken into the ovens before church, setting the temperature low so the meat will be juicy and tender come time to eat it," she explained as she positioned two long boneless hams in a roasting pan.

"A lot of the other food is sitting ready in the fridge— and the wedding cakes and pies were finished yesterday— so we're in great shape!" Irene remarked from the counter where she was seasoning a panful of chicken pieces.

"I cannot imagine preparing so much food," Andi murmured before sticking a forkful of eggs into her mouth.

Karen groaned inwardly at this admission, because real Amish women would be old hands at making wedding meals. "How many folks will be here today?" she asked as she broke off a bite of the oatmeal muffin.

"Lester and Marlene are guessing we'll have nearly two hundred guests—in addition to the folks who live at Promise Lodge," Ruby clarified. "It's such a blessing that so many people they love can share their big day!"

Karen's eyes widened at that number. When she'd swallowed her first bite of the muffin, she said, "Wow, what's in this? It's really soft and moist—and chewy, with so much oatmeal in it."

Beulah glanced over from the sink, smiling. "Those old-fashioned rolled oats are mixed with smashed bananas, brown sugar, and milk," she replied. "It's almost like eating a bowl of oatmeal, except you can hold it in your hand."

"And this egg thingy!" Andi blurted out, holding up a forkful. "Like a little omelet baked in a muffin tin! It's to die for!"

Ruby laughed out loud. "Well, don't go dying on us while we're cooking," she teased. "You probably like that so much because it's got a sinful amount of cheese in it, to disguise all the spinach and other veggies."

"It's another one of the go-to breakfast goodies we make ahead, for big crowds," Beulah remarked. "Even though Lester's kith and kin were staying with several of our locals and could've eaten in their homes this morning, folks prefer to congregate so they can visit."

"*Jah*, eating and visiting—they make the world go around!" Ruby chimed in.

How could these middle-aged, gray-haired ladies have the energy to work on so much food—and without a recipe card in sight? Karen knew better than to ask that question, however, and she was thankful that none of these gals had asked for her help in the kitchen. She had no doubt they'd be appalled to hear how often she and her family ordered pizza delivery or picked up suppers from the drive-through at fast-food restaurants.

"Oh—we'd better get a move on," Andi said as she glanced out into the dining room. "Looks like people are getting seated for church."

When Andi set her empty plate down, Karen grabbed her arm. "We have to go in with women close to our own age, remember?" she whispered. "Let's head out to the porch and see where we fit into the line."

Nodding as they passed several older ladies—trying to look as though she knew what she was doing—Karen followed other women outside. It was such a relief when a pair

of friendly twins holding wiggly babies motioned for them
to step into the line ahead of them.

"You two can sit with us! We're the Helmuth twins—"

"She's Barbara and I'm Bernice," the look-alike sister
put in.

"Our husbands—who are also twins—run the nursery out
on the state highway by the bulk store," Barbara whispered.
"We're glad you two can join us for today's festivities."

"And now we've got to be quiet, because the line's
moving inside for church."

Smiling gratefully, Karen allowed Andi into the line
ahead of her. Soon they were sitting very close together in
a large meeting room, with their new friends beside them
on the wooden pew bench. The young mothers were settling their redheaded babies—who also looked enough alike
to be twins—into their carrier baskets, inserting pacifiers
into their mouths. After a few more minutes, the younger
women and girls were all seated on one side of the large
room and the remaining young men had taken their seats
across the room from them.

Karen was surprised when she realized that this age-old
seating arrangement—the men separated from the women—
meant that families didn't sit together in church. Younger
boys sat with their *dats*, and toddlers and babies were with
their *mamms*, but school-aged kids and teenagers sat with
others of their age group. Who was going to keep these
children quiet and occupied if they got wiggly and started
talking during the service?

When the Helmuths picked up a worn book Karen
assumed was the hymnal, she glanced at their page number
and did the same, holding the heavy old book so Andi could
share it. She blinked. There was no musical notation on the

page—only paragraphs that resembled stanzas of poetry. And the lyrics were in German!

As one of the men sang out a phrase across the room, the three preachers on the bench up front removed their broad-brimmed hats in one impressive motion. Karen looked at Andi in sheer panic: the tune was totally unfamiliar—there was no organ accompaniment to help them, of course—and the congregation was singing in a language neither of them spoke! She moved her mouth, hoping no one around them would realize they weren't really singing. As the preachers left the big room, a glance at the page revealed that this hymn had seventeen verses.

The rhythmic singsong of the unfamiliar language, along with the warmth from so many packed-in bodies, lulled Karen into a dangerously drowsy state. Furtively, she glanced around at the walls. It was probably intentional that there wasn't a clock in the room. After what seemed like forever—well into a second lengthy hymn—the preachers returned and hung their hats on wall pegs before taking their places on their bench to begin the worship service.

As the preaching and prayers commenced, all in German, Karen came to a startling realization: because she and Andi had read so many Amish novels—which were written in English with the occasional word or phrase of *Deutch* dialect tossed in—they had assumed the folks at Promise Lodge spoke English on a daily basis.

Did this mean that the Kuhns and the other ladies were speaking English to her and Andi because they already knew the two of them weren't Amish? Were Beulah, Ruby, and their other hostesses laughing among themselves, just waiting for Karen and "Annie" to blunder badly before having to admit they were here under false pretenses?

Karen got so lost in these worrisome thoughts she didn't

realize when the sermon ended—until everyone else in the room was getting down on their knees. It was an eye-opening experience when she and Andi struggled awkwardly to kneel between the closely set benches for a silent prayer that lasted several agonizing minutes. When they finally got up off the hard floor, Karen's knees were so sore and stiff she almost toppled over trying to resume her spot on the crowded pew. After that, another church leader read from a huge Bible.

Bishop Monroe, whom they'd met the previous afternoon, stood up to preach. He was a tall, handsome fellow with a resounding, enthusiastic voice, but of course Karen couldn't understand a word he was saying even if his kindliness and goodwill filled the entire room as he smiled at the huge group gathered around him. How on earth did he preach so eloquently without any notes? And how did he speak, on and on and *on*, without running out of something to say?

Stifling a sigh, Karen sat up straighter to ease the fatigue in her back. She'd read in Amish novels, of course, that church services lasted about three hours, but as the morning dragged on and the room became unbearably warm, she wondered how Amish people sat for such a long stretch after breakfast without having to use the bathroom—or just get up and revive the circulation in their butts. As she glanced around, she also noticed that although toddlers might be standing on the floor near their mothers, the other children were still sitting quietly without any adult supervision.

"I can't take another minute of this," Andi whined under her breath.

Karen was ready to commiserate softly—until the woman seated in front of them turned around.

It was Sylvia, whom they'd met the day they'd arrived.

As the delicate, birdlike woman's gaze held hers, Karen's insides clenched.

Sylvia *knew*. The slightest rise of her brow confirmed her awareness that they were impostors. And she didn't approve.

As Sylvia turned to face forward again, Karen's heart was hammering so hard she could barely breathe. Thank goodness these devout Amish souls wouldn't interrupt their worship service to call her and Andi out for lying!

But how long would it be before that happened? And how would the Kuhn sisters and the other folks treat the two of them when Karen and Andi had to admit who they really were and why they'd come to Promise Lodge?

Chapter 5

Seated among the other men as the wedding ceremony wound down, Dale Kraybill smiled at a radiant Marlene and a boyishly joyful Lester as they finished exchanging their vows. Had two people ever looked so happy? At thirty-five, Marlene was a first-time bride who'd spent her previous years looking after aging parents with her twin brother, Mose, while Lester Lehman was ten years older than she and had been widowed for a while.

Even with the span of years between them, there's no doubt they're meant for each other.

The thought gave Dale pause. Ever since Lester and Marlene had become engaged, he'd felt more aware of his life's clock ticking. He'd declared himself a happy bachelor years ago, yet lately he'd felt a few twinges.

He'd turned fifty-six last winter. Would he find deeper fulfillment running his new bulk store—or would he become even more unsettled as he lived out his life alone in its upstairs apartment? Was that the life God had really intended for him?

Across the crowded room, he spotted Irene Wickey wedged between the Kuhn sisters and Mattie Troyer. Irene appeared as delighted as he was to watch Marlene and Lester become a couple—and she'd happily baked dozens of dinner rolls and pies for this afternoon's wedding meal. She'd been widowed for several years and had lived in a house up the road with her son, Truman, until he'd married Rosetta Bender about a year ago.

And there were no two ways about it: Irene baked the finest pie he'd ever put in his mouth. She was also an attractive woman who'd kept her figure, and her enthusiasm spilled over into everything she did. Dale looked forward to the four mornings each week when she brought fresh, boxed pies to restock the Promise Lodge Pies display in the bulk store. He really enjoyed spending time with her—there, and when they attended their Mennonite church services in Cloverdale, a few miles up the road.

Did Irene ever get the urge to live with a husband again, someplace other than her Promise Lodge apartment?

Bishop Monroe, standing between the bride and the groom, smiled broadly at the huge congregation. "Let me be the first to congratulate Marlene and Lester," he said in his resonant voice. "It's my privilege to introduce you to Mr. and Mrs. Lehman with wishes for all the happiness their hearts can hold, and all the blessings the Lord our God can bestow upon them!"

In a rush of enthusiasm, folks around the room rose to their feet, applauding loudly. Dale, too, stood up—eager to stretch his legs after a long morning of Amish worship and the wedding ceremony. As a Mennonite, he was accustomed to a shorter church service, but now that he lived at Promise Lodge, he was pleased to be included in this community's special occasions.

As he watched Irene make her way toward the kitchen with the other local women, Dale felt compelled to catch up to her. In this roomful of people who hailed from other places—and some church districts that were much more conservative—Irene stood out. Even in a gray pinstripe dress, she glowed with contentment—a sense of purpose and accomplishment that he suddenly wanted in his daily life.

By slipping between the clusters of conversing friends in the aisles, Dale made it into the large dining room quickly. Not surprisingly, Irene took up a station behind the table where desserts were to be served and began taking pies from the rolling metal shelves behind it. She lined them up with an efficiency Dale admired, so focused that she didn't notice him standing a few feet away.

With a circular metal cutter that divided a pie into eight even slices, Irene cut the rhubarb pies as though she could do it in her sleep. Even though she baked several days a week in her pie shop and then cleaned up all the equipment afterward, her hands were smooth and supple. Dale waited until she'd finished the five pies before he spoke, searching for words that would sound positive but not pushy.

"Wasn't that a wonderful ceremony?" he asked. "As I watched Marlene repeating her vows with such joy on her face, it occurred to me that you must've looked just as radiant on your wedding day."

Irene blinked, her spatula stopping above the slice of pie she was about to remove from a pan. She almost always came back at him immediately with a response, but his remark had apparently taken her back in time.

"It was a once-in-a-lifetime day," she murmured fondly. "There'll never be another one."

Dale exhaled quickly. He didn't believe Irene had intentionally popped his bubble of optimism, yet her message was loud and clear, wasn't it? She hadn't refused his potential proposal—hadn't said she would never marry *him*, specifically—yet it sounded as if her mind was made up.

And he knew, from spending time among these Promise Lodge ladies, he wasn't going to change Irene's belief anytime soon. Especially not while she was helping with a wedding dinner.

"How about if I set these dishes in front of you so you can plate your pies faster?" he asked on sudden inspiration. He quickly counted eight small white plates from the cart beside the table and placed them in a row in front of her. "No reason for me to stand around like—like a clueless *man* or something."

Irene's burst of laughter relieved the unintentional tension between them. "Oh, I could never think of you as clueless, Dale," she said, deftly lifting perfect slices of pie from the pan. "You have one of the most organized minds I know, and you're really *gut* at anticipating what your customers will want. I've seen some bulk stores with inventory that dates back several months just because the owners keep ordering what they always have, instead of changing to meet people's needs."

"It's a tricky business," he remarked as he counted out more plates. "I appreciate your compliment, Irene. I'd rather order smaller lots of merchandise more often, because I can't return opened bulk packages—and I certainly don't want to store seasonal baking ingredients or holiday items until the following year."

As they worked, Dale was happy to be conversing with Irene, even if the talk remained breezy and impersonal. By the time Ruby and Beulah were wheeling out carts loaded with sliced ham, pieces of baked chicken, and macaroni salad, Irene had plated all the pie slices and together they'd arranged the plates on the dessert table and the racks behind it. They'd worked as a couple, talking and moving efficiently, as only longtime friends could do.

And that's how it'll remain between us—unless I say or do something that will prove to Irene she'll be happier with me than without me.

"Dale, I appreciate your help!" she said as she beamed at him. "And now I'll head into the kitchen to get the rest of our big dinner ready to serve."

Dale stifled a sigh. Irene would always have the company of her women friends, and the satisfaction of working on whatever meal or project they were cooking up, wouldn't she? And as a side sitter, Mose would be eating at the raised *eck* table in the corner with the wedding party. His best bet for dinner conversation would be Preachers Amos and Marlin, Truman Wickey, or Bishop Monroe, whose wives would be bustling about refilling water glasses and replenishing the steam table.

Any of those fellows would welcome his company without a second thought, of course. But it was one more reminder to Dale that in a world where most folks were married with families, he was the odd man out.

As Karen cut through the kitchen with Andi to escape the noisy, crowded dining room, she waved at Beulah and Ruby. They were slicing another huge boneless ham for the steam table so the second seating of guests—and the servers—could proceed through the serving line with fresh food.

"That meal was fabulous!" Karen called out as she strode toward the back stairway. "I'm so full I might pop!"

"That zingy macaroni salad was my favorite," Andi put in. "We'll be back later for our pie and wedding cake!"

The two of them quickly ascended the narrow wooden stairs to their rooms. When Karen entered hers, Andi was following close behind her. "The Kuhns probably think it's odd that we're not helping in the kitchen," Karen murmured. "But the noise down there was driving me nuts!"

"Yeah, it never got that loud when we were campers," Andi recalled. "And the longer I talked to those redheaded twins—and the ladies from Ohio—the more I felt like I'd stumble over my story."

Karen nodded, slipping her cell phone out from under her mattress. "Uh-huh. The more details we made up about Cherrydale on the spur of the moment, the more chances they had to catch our—oh! I've got a call," she said, quickly silencing her ring tone. "I hope nobody else can hear me."

As she spoke quietly into her phone, Andi sat down on the bed and kicked off her tennis shoes. By the time Karen had told her friend back home what a wonderful time they were having at Promise Lodge—and how much wedding food they'd eaten—Andi looked like she might fall asleep.

After Karen hung up, she hid the phone under her mattress again. "I need to charge this soon," she said. "I sure hope the Kuhns don't stop by and see it plugged in."

"We're lucky the outlets are still intact," Andi remarked. "I'm surprised these Amish folks haven't removed the wiring—and the phone in the kitchen."

"Maybe it's because Mennonites live here, too," Karen said with a shrug. "And have you noticed that Ruby and Beulah are cooking on those same old gas stoves—"

"The black beasts, we called them."

"—and using the same fridges, deep freezes, and cooking utensils that were here when we were kids?" Karen continued as she headed for the overstuffed recliner in the corner. "That's amazing!"

"They've cleaned everything up and painted the walls. And those old metal cabinets look like new again," Andi put in, although her voice was fading as she relaxed. "I even saw those same old metal scrollwork crosses hanging on the wall above the back worktables."

Karen heaved a tired sigh as she dropped into the recliner. "I just want to chill for a while," she remarked. "Don't you wonder how these women got up before dawn to do meal prep before that *endless* church service and wedding, and they still have enough energy to deal with a second sitting of guests? And they're all older than we are. Sheesh! I'm totally shot."

"And they still have all those dishes to wash, and leftovers to deal with tonight—"

"Oh, I suspect they'll be serving another meal this evening," Karen put in. "I haven't done a count, but I think Lester and Marlene have more guests than they anticipated."

"And nobody seems to mind!" Andi blurted out. "I'd be rattled about running out of food, or wondering where all the out-of-town company would be sleeping, or—"

"These women work *way* harder than I'd figured on," Karen said with a tired sigh. "Maybe we should keep reading Amish stories instead of wishing we could live their lifestyle."

For the next forty-five minutes the two of them savored some quiet time, although they could hear the buzz of conversation below them. It was such a relief not to answer people's questions or make small talk with folks they didn't know. No matter where these Amish folks had come from, *visiting* was obviously their favorite pastime—right along with eating, of course. It amazed Karen that in a crowd of more than two hundred people, she'd only spotted one or two who could be considered plump, and she'd seen no one who was obese.

It's another testament to the Amish work ethic. When they

aren't at a special occasion like today's, they're doing manual labor from dawn to dark. No chance to get lazy or fat.

Fighting a yawn, Karen got out of her chair and smoothed her *kapp* and dress. "Even though we're paying guests, we should offer to help in the kitchen," she said to her drowsy friend. "Do you suppose they still have that ancient portable dishwasher?"

"The one where we used the hose for water fights while we were supposed to be cleaning up?" Andi teased as she sat up on the bed. "You're probably right. The fact that we're not helping is one more detail that'll make us stick out from the crowd."

When they went down the back stairway a few minutes later, Karen glanced toward the corner but saw a large painted cabinet where the camp's dishwasher had been. She turned quickly, before any of the women had seen her.

"No dishwasher—so don't ask about it!" she whispered.

Andi nodded in comprehension.

Karen composed her thoughts before stepping into the busy room, where several ladies were washing and drying dishes over at the two sinks. Others were placing the left-over ham, chicken, and macaroni salad into pans for the steam table. Among them, she recognized Mattie Troyer, Christine Burkholder, and their sister, Rosetta Wickey—the three original Bender sisters who'd purchased the camp-ground property and led the restoration of Promise Lodge as a new Plain community. Everyone was conversing cheerfully as Beulah and Ruby wheeled cartloads of dirty dishes in from the dining room.

"How can we help?" Karen asked Mattie and Christine above the chatter.

The sisters, who bore a distinct resemblance to one another, nodded toward the sink. "You could dry those pans

Frances and Rosetta are washing," Mattie replied. "Clean towels are in that big drawer across from the sinks."

Karen raised her eyebrows at Andi. *Same place they were back in the day.*

As they plucked folded towels from the drawer, Rosetta flashed them a grin. "Fresh recruits! Awfully nice of you ladies to help us."

"*Jah*," Frances chimed in, "we can be thankful that if we're washing and drying these steam table pans and big pots, the end of the cleanup is in sight."

Karen wondered if these women were always grateful for every little thing—and *happy*—as they worked. She began drying the familiar stainless-steel pans.

"I'm going to give you the last of these pots, Frances," Rosetta said as she carried them from the adjoining counter. "I'll run fresh dishwater and start on the plates the Kuhns have brought in."

At that moment, Andi grabbed the handle of a large round lid, laughing as she dried it. As the women around them worked and chatted, she swung around to face Karen, brandishing the lid in front of her.

"*En garde!*" she said in a stage whisper meant for only Karen to hear. "Remember when these lids were our shields, and we'd have sword fights with those metal crosses on the wall?"

The kitchen rang with sudden silence. The only sound Karen heard—besides her hammering heartbeat—was the gurgling of dishwater going down the drain . . . right along with their carefully concocted story. She swallowed hard as the Bender sisters, the Kuhns, Frances, and Sylvia Keim held her and Andi captive with their knowing gazes.

Rosetta cleared her throat. "So, when were you ladies here before?" she asked calmly.

Andi looked ready to pass out, mortified by the way she'd revealed their secret.

Karen let out the breath she'd sucked in. There was no escape. It was time to come clean.

"We, um—we came here for several summers as teenagers when this place was a church camp," she confessed in a quavering voice. "We thought it would be fun to—to sew some cape dresses and visit this place again, now that you Amish folks have taken it over—"

"We didn't mean any harm!" Andi bleated. "We've read practically every Amish novel ever published, and we just wanted to spend a week here because we admire your lifestyle and your work ethic and—"

"But we lied about who we were, and it was wrong to mislead you about why we came and—and we're really *sorry*," Karen continued in the firmest voice she could muster. "We'll understand if you want us to pack up and leave immediately."

She and Andi held their breath, waiting for the proverbial ax to fall.

Beulah began to chuckle. "Now that you gals have fessed up," she said, glancing at her friends, "we'll admit that we've kept a running list of little *clues* that you're not Amish."

"The latest clue was when I checked a road atlas and discovered that there's no such town as Cherrydale, Missouri," Ruby put in quietly. "Not to mention the zippers in your dresses, and the way you've pronounced some of our *Deutch* words."

"And you didn't sing any of the hymns or read the prayer from the book during church this morning," Sylvia added quietly.

Karen blinked back tears. How embarrassing that these ladies had seen right through their charade from the moment they'd arrived—or maybe since she'd called to reserve their rooms—and yet they'd allowed their two English guests to continue making fools of themselves. "Maybe we should just go upstairs and—I'll call my brother to come pick us up—"

"I don't sense any malicious intentions behind your stories," Rosetta interrupted, glancing at her sisters for their reactions, "so it's fine by me if you want to stay for the rest of the days you've paid for. Will that be all right with you, Beulah and Ruby?"

The Mennonite sisters chuckled as Beulah replied first. "Now that the cat's out of the bag and we know you were just having fun—"

"You're welcome to keep your rooms," Ruby chimed in. "I suppose we should feel honored that you wanted to live at Promise Lodge so you could be like us. It shows that you have the right mindset even if you had a devious way of making your dream come true."

Andi let out a grateful sigh. "You're very kind," she murmured. "And if we're coming clean, we should tell you that my real name is Andi Swann—"

"And I'm Karen Mercer. And—and I just thought of a way we might make amends for coming here under fake names and false pretenses!" she said with renewed enthusiasm. "Andi and I design websites and online businesses. What if we made Promise Lodge's products visible to a wider audience by creating a website for *you*?"

Andi sucked in her breath. "Yeah! You Kuhn sisters could market your cheeses, and Rosetta could sell her goat milk soap," she said in a rush. "Even if you didn't want to sell Irene's pies or Mattie's fresh produce online, you could advertise your items with color photos. I think potential customers would drive a long way to buy what you bake and raise here."

"And we could create order forms, so people all over the country could buy your products with just the click of a mouse!" Karen continued excitedly. "Some of you ladies with businesses would most likely double your sales! What do you think?"

Beulah set a stack of dirty dinner plates on the counter beside the sink before glancing at Ruby. "Give us some time to ponder it," she replied cautiously.

"*Jah*, and we'll also need to ask Bishop Monroe and the three preachers for their input and permission," Mattie pointed out. Her sisters nodded in agreement as they all resumed what they'd been doing before Andi had brandished the aluminum pot lid.

"We run our businesses without consulting our husbands about every little detail," Christine remarked. "But offering products online—and maintaining a website— would mean that someone at Promise Lodge would have to own a computer. And allowing us Old Order Amish to do that would involve a *major* turnaround of religious policy, as well."

Rosetta glanced up from the plate she was washing. "As a Mennonite, I could deal with the computer—and my husband, Truman, could help me with running the online store," she said in a thoughtful tone. "But *jah*, that would represent a major step toward allowing technology to become a part of our Plain lives. Not everyone will see advantages to that!"

"We'd also have to purchase boxes and mailers to ship our products—not that we could send our cheese that way," Ruby put in. "And then we'd have to drive the packages into town to send them to customers."

"We'll see what the men and the other residents say. We'll have an answer before you leave on Sunday," Christine said with a nod. "Meanwhile, it's very nice of you to offer your services—and I'm glad we can get to know you two ladies for who you really are!"

"*Jah*, I'm glad we've cleared the air," Beulah said with a decisive nod. "No matter how smart we are, or how much we think we can hide from other folks, God always knows exactly what we're up to."

"And it's never a *gut* idea to lie to God," Ruby put in. "I feel a whole lot better about you gals now that we're friends with the real-life Andi and Karen."

"Amen to that!" said Mattie.

Chapter 6

As Sylvia pushed an empty cart into the crowded dining room to fetch more dirty dishes, she passed the *eck* table where Marlene and Lester sat with the wedding party on either side of them. The table was situated on a dais that was high enough so most guests in the large dining room would have a view of the newlyweds and the huge chocolate cake that would be cut later in the day.

But it was Mose that Sylvia noticed. Mose, and the attractive young woman sitting beside him, laughing and talking as though she'd known him well for many years.

Yet he didn't say a word about having a sweetheart the other day while we rode that fancy parade wagon. Was it only my lonely imagination—my wishful thinking—that led me to believe Mose Fisher might feel a tingle of attraction for me?

Quickly, before he caught her gawking at him, Sylvia wheeled her cart toward the center aisle that ran between the long dining room tables. Because guests were getting up to choose slices of pie, or chatting with friends, it took several minutes for her to reach the tables farthest from the kitchen. As folks began passing her their soiled dishes, she was glad to have something to occupy her time—and to have a reason for standing with her back toward the *eck* table.

It was better than gazing at a handsome younger man who had his eyes on someone much more suitable.

As she filled her plastic bins with plates and silverware, Sylvia reminded herself that when she'd come to Promise Lodge, she'd had no plans whatsoever to welcome another man into her life. She'd been hoping to spend her remaining days in peace and relative comfort among like-minded, kindhearted souls until her brain tumor grew so large that it interfered with her bodily functions and she could simply fade away.

Puh! Maybe that scenario was just a fantasy—because who can predict how my condition will progress? I have no way of knowing how long I might last . . . just as I couldn't have foreseen meeting a fellow who makes me feel younger and more vibrant than I thought possible.

Sylvia focused on her task, occasionally chatting with the out-of-towners who filled the dining room. It took two trips to collect tableware as folks finished their meals—and she welcomed Christine's offer to take over as the dining room began to empty out.

"It's a beautiful afternoon, and you could probably use some fresh air after working in the kitchen all day, Sylvia," the bishop's wife said with a kind smile. "Or if you feel a nap coming on, that's fine, too!"

"*Denki*, Christine. After being amongst all these talkative guests, I think I'll enjoy a little quiet time outdoors," Sylvia remarked. "I'm not used to being around so many people anymore."

As she made her way to the mudroom door, she glanced at the kitchen clock. No wonder her stomach was growling! It was nearly three o'clock and she hadn't taken time to eat. On an impulse, Sylvia picked up a plate from the worktable.

She found a fork and a piece of paper towel before she plucked a couple of chicken legs from a roaster. She added a dinner roll, some green beans from a nearly empty steam table pan, and a spoonful of macaroni salad before heading outside.

"Enjoy your picnic, Sylvia!" Mattie called after her.

She turned to smile at Preacher Amos's wife, who was stacking clean plates in a lower cabinet. "I intend to!" she said. "Time to get off my feet for a while."

The moment she stepped outside, where the old maple trees created some welcome shade, Sylvia felt refreshed. Several trees between the lodge and the Kurtzes' sheep pasture formed a long canopy, so she followed that path across the grass. As she sat down against a tree trunk, the view of Harley Kurtz's ewes and new lambs soothed her. Across the lush green pasture, Queenie, a black-and-white border collie, spotted her and sat up taller.

Chuckling, Sylvia bit into a chicken leg as she watched the vigilant dog approach her. She'd heard that Queenie belonged to Mattie's son, Noah Schwartz, but guarding Harley's sheep had given her a mission that kept her at the Kurtz place most of the day—unless other activities on the Promise Lodge property prompted her to check them out. The dog gradually made her way along the back of Preacher Marlin's barrel factory, stopping now and then to glance at the sheep before continuing toward Sylvia.

By the time Queenie sat down several feet away, her ears raised in anticipation, Sylvia was chuckling. "You think you're going to share my picnic, *jah*?" she asked. "But dogs aren't supposed to have chicken bones."

The border collie woofed softly, gazing steadily at Sylvia's plate.

She finished her macaroni salad, considering how she should handle Queenie's request for a handout. "If you come closer and lie down, like a *gut* dog, I might have a couple bites of dinner roll for you," Sylvia said softly.

As though she'd understood every word, Queenie stopped about six feet away. The border collie sat down in the thick grass before lowering her upper body, never taking her eyes off Sylvia's hands and plate.

"Such a *gut* girl you are, Queenie," Sylvia said with a nod of approval. She took her time catching the last of her green beans with the tines of her fork, pleased with how polite her black-and-white companion was. She wrapped the chicken bones in her paper towel and slipped them into her apron pocket. After taking one last bite of her roll, she broke it into small pieces and left it on her plate, which she placed in the grass beside her.

Obediently the dog waited, her face alight with focus.

"All right, girl, come over and eat."

Queenie quickly lapped up the scraps of bread before licking the plate clean. After a moment, she leaned against Sylvia as though she expected a nice scratching.

Sylvia closed her eyes as she stroked the dog's soft coat and massaged between her ears. "I kept a dog around the home place all the time—until my Ivan died a couple years ago. Cocoa passed on shortly after that," she murmured. "I didn't realize how much I miss her."

"Hmmm. Whom do you miss more, Sylvia? The dog or Ivan?" a low, familiar voice teased.

Sylvia jumped, her heartbeat racing. "Mose! I wasn't expecting—I mean, when I saw you had a girlfriend at the table—"

"You mean Ruth Ellen?" He crouched beside her before settling against the same large tree. "She's our cousin from Coldstream. Marlene invited her to be a side sitter, and Lester wanted me to stand up with him, so we ended up together. But only for today."

Even as Sylvia felt a tingle of attraction rushing up her spine, she warned herself not to expect too much from this chance meeting.

Who says Mose came out here by chance? He must have looked in a lot of places before he found me behind this tree . . .

"Ah. It's nice you two could catch up with one another today," Sylvia murmured. "I could tell you had a special relationship with her, and—"

When Mose's large brown eyes focused on her, Sylvia forgot the rest of what she'd intended to say. He appeared pleased that she'd noticed Ruth Ellen—and maybe he sensed she'd been a teeny bit jealous.

"Ruth Ellen didn't have brothers or sisters, so she spent a lot of time with Marlene and me when we were kids," he explained. He glanced at the dog that was lolling in the grass with her head on Sylvia's lap. "Seems you've made a new friend. Queenie's so comfortable, she doesn't look as though she's going anywhere soon."

"Queenie wanted some of my lunch," Sylvia pointed out with a chuckle. When a yawn escaped her, she added, "I hope you won't take it wrong if I drift off for a nap, Mose. Now that I'm off my feet and my stomach's full—"

"You worked hard today, Sylvia, helping with that huge wedding meal. We've both been up since before dawn, so I might just doze off myself." Mose let out a contented sigh. "*Gut* meal, *gut* company, a cool place in the shade—what's not to love about that?"

Sylvia wondered if she was crazy, wanting to nap when the handsome man who'd haunted her thoughts had shown up from out of nowhere. He'd never looked more attractive, wearing his black trousers and vest with a crisp white shirt—and she'd never expected his muscular arm to gently enfold her, coaxing her to rest against him. Her pulse pounded with the unexpected joy of this simple moment.

As Mose's large body relaxed, he began to snore softly.

Sylvia chuckled. Should she feel disappointed that Mose had fallen asleep? Or should she be delighted that he seemed every bit as comfortable as Queenie, who was also breathing deeply?

When Sylvia closed her eyes, the steady rhythm of Mose's heartbeat sang a soothing lullaby that soon had her drifting away on a soft cloud of sleep.

Mose awoke to realize that the bark of the tree was digging into his back, yet he didn't dare move. Queenie had returned to the pasture, but Sylvia was still snoozing. Something about the way she'd drifted off with her head on his chest and her tiny arm slung over his midsection touched him deeply.

When he'd left the crowded, noisy dining room to look for her, napping had been the farthest thing from his mind. Waking up to find Sylvia in his arms, however, filled him with a contented sense of awareness.

She was so small, so delicate. Through the pale skin of her neck, he saw veins and the gentle flutter of her pulse—and it suddenly saddened him that she'd come to Promise Lodge to *die*. The unfairness of her condition struck him like a coiled snake, and Mose had to blink back sudden, hot tears.

As though she'd felt the shift in his mood, Sylvia stirred. She reminded him of a little kitten when she yawned, blinking sleepily. At that moment, Mose wanted nothing more than to shelter this woman and protect her forever—even if her version of *forever* didn't sound nearly long enough to suit him.

It occurred to him that he was falling in love with Sylvia. And he didn't have the slightest idea what to do about it.

"Oh my," she murmured as she looked around to get her bearings. "I must've done some serious dozing off."

"That makes two of us," Mose remarked gently. "But it was nice, wasn't it, to get away from the crowd and give in to what we really needed? I mean—"

Sylvia's startled expression told him he needed to back-track. She sat up to put a few inches of distance between their bodies.

He chuckled, already missing her warm weight. "We didn't give in to anything improper, you know," Mose assured her. "We were both so tired we fell asleep together—"

"You'd better not tell the others that we've *slept* together!"

He laughed out loud and was then struck by a revelation. "Listen to me, Sylvia. I'm not stuttering and stammering anymore," he whispered. "That means I've gotten so comfortable with you—"

"What caused you to stumble over your words in the first place, Mose? Is that something you care to share with me?"

He swallowed hard. Everyone he'd grown up with—as well as his newfound friends at Promise Lodge—had heard about his childhood trauma, yet he hesitated to tell Sylvia about his darkest hours. Would she reject him? Would she believe he should've gotten over that long-ago event rather than allowing it to affect his speech every time he was around unfamiliar people?

Mose sighed. "I—I guess I was about five when our *mamm* and *dat* took Marlene and me to the county fair," he began timidly. "Something caught my eye and—from what they've told me—I wandered off in a different direction and got lost in the crowd along the midway."

"Boys will be boys," Sylvia remarked gently.

She didn't appear ready to poke fun at him, so Mose continued. "Next thing I knew, somebody snatched me up from behind. I—I have no idea why they took me, but I vaguely recall that they were a couple, and the man put his hand over my mouth while they hurried to their car with me," he said. His voice had grown husky with emotion, and he looked away. "I must've put up such a fuss that they locked me in the trunk. At that point the details get pretty fuzzy—"

"Well, no wonder!" Sylvia whispered, gazing anxiously at him. "I suspect you were such a cute little Amish boy that they might've had bad intentions about—well, who knows what evil they might've had in mind?"

Mose shrugged, relieved that she'd taken his side. "I don't recall how long I was in that trunk, and we don't know how the police found me," he recounted in a low voice. "But once I got home again, it was a long time before I wanted to leave, even to go to school."

He sighed, his pulse revving even now as he recalled his trauma of thirty years ago. "No matter how hard I tried, I couldn't get three words out without tripping over two of them," he recalled softly. "My schoolteacher helped me some, but there was only so much she could do. She suggested that my folks take me to a speech therapist, but the idea of working with an English stranger only upset me more."

Sylvia placed her small, warm hand on his. She was blinking away tears, shaking her head in sympathy and disbelief. "I can only imagine how frantic your family became when they couldn't find you on the fairgrounds," she murmured. "Not to mention how the other children probably teased you about your speech pattern. Kids can be so cruel."

Mose gazed gratefully at her, covering her hand with his. "*Denki* for understanding, Sylvia. It—it means a lot."

She glanced away, as though his gratitude felt too intense to bear.

Mose inhaled to settle his nerves, and then let his breath out again. "One thing I do recall is that Teacher Carolyn encouraged me to *sing*," he said softly. "We discovered that if I focused on a song or made my words fit a melody, I could express myself more clearly."

Sylvia's face glowed. "Maybe that's why, when I distinguish your bass voice from the other men's during church, it sounds so special. I could listen to your singing all day, Mose."

His face went hot, and he looked away. "You don't have to say that just to be—"

"I said it because I wanted to," she murmured. "Because it's true."

Mose swallowed hard. Was it his imagination, or did Sylvia seem sincerely interested in him—as a *man*, and not just as another person who'd known affliction? Her hazel eyes held his gaze long enough that he suddenly felt nervous. Rather than do or say something stupidly adolescent, he slowly stood up.

"I see how the party's progressing," he said. But rather than hurry away from her, he watched his hand reach for hers of its own accord. "Care to come with me?"

Sylvia accepted his help up before retrieving her dishes. "I imagine Ruth Ellen's wondering where her date disappeared to," she remarked. "It'll soon be time for Marlene and Lester to cut the wedding cake. And from what I've heard about Ruby's chocolate cake with the mocha frosting, we don't want to miss out on *that*!"

Mose thoroughly enjoyed the slow walk back to the

lodge with Sylvia. As she strolled beside him, her head barely came as high as his chest. She still reminded him of a tiny, fragile doll, yet he'd gained a new appreciation for her depth of understanding.

Would it be so wrong to explore the possibility that he and Sylvia might make a compatible pair?

Will I be able to handle it if she passes on—and takes my heart to the grave with her?

Chapter 7

As Karen and Andi returned to the lodge Friday morning after a shopping spree at the bulk store, they were laughing and talking. With so many purchases, Dale had allowed them to borrow two of his shopping carts.

"Can you believe how much cool stuff was in that store?" Andi exclaimed as they approached the big front porch. "There were so many little plastic bags and cartons of spices and baking decorations—not to mention varieties of dried beans and muffin mixes and candies! I could go back this afternoon and find stuff I didn't see this morning!"

Andi gave her cart a final shove as they reached the wooden steps. "Maybe we should go back and get one of those little Styrofoam coolers," she mused aloud. "I'd like to take some of the Kuhns' cheese home."

"And what if we got a fresh pie from Irene's bakery, as my brother's payment for driving us here and picking us up?" Karen suggested. She looked at their numerous plastic shopping bags and laughed. "But right now, we'll get our weight-bearing exercise toting all this stuff to our rooms! We'll be ready for lunch by the time we've carried it all upstairs."

Andi sagged, probably considering all the exertion of going up and down the porch and lodge stairways. "Why don't we ask Beulah and Ruby if we can stash our bags somewhere on the main level? On Sunday when we leave, it'll all have to come down again."

"Great idea!" Karen brightened, inhaling deeply. "I don't know what those ladies have been cooking, but it really smells good. After all the food they handled yesterday— and all the prep that went into that wedding meal—do you suppose they're *tired* of cooking?"

As they passed down the center aisle of tables in the dining room, Karen smelled sausage. When she peered through the kitchen door, she had to chuckle: the Mennonite Kuhn sisters seemed to be competing to see who could wear the wildest dress. Ruby sported a flashy tropical print in reds, oranges, and yellows while Beulah's dress was made from a tie-dye print in purple, neon green, and magenta. When Karen and Andi stepped into the kitchen, the sisters looked up.

"What'd you think of Dale's store?" Ruby asked. "I always find way more items than I wrote on my shopping list—"

"And I can't get out of there in less than an hour," Beulah chimed in as she took her skillet of sizzling sausage off the burner. "Decided to leave off the *kapps* today, eh? I bet it was a challenge to keep your collar-length hair under a prayer covering."

Karen nodded, appreciating the way these sisters had accepted them for the English tourists they were—without any sign of judgment. "I caught myself fiddling with the strings all the time, too."

"We *loved* Dale's store," Andi replied to Ruby. "We loved it so much, we're wondering if you have a place where we can stash our shopping bags until we go home on Sunday— rather than hauling them upstairs, you know."

The sisters looked at each other as they considered their

answer. "I don't see any problem with storing them in those big front closets just off the meeting room. That way, your bags won't be in the way when there's church on Sunday," Beulah said.

"Just don't forget your stuff's in there, come time to go home!" Ruby put in. "We'd hate to—"

"Hello, ladies!" a woman called out from the lobby. "By the looks of those two carts outside, a couple of shoppers have cleaned out Dale's shelves!"

Karen and Andi chuckled, poking their heads into the dining room as Rosetta approached. "You've got that right," Karen teased. "He told us not to come back until he'd had a chance to restock."

Rosetta's laughter rang out in the large, empty room. "I bet he misses Marlene today, now that she's taking a few days off to be a newlywed. A lot of our guests from Coldstream and Sugarcreek said they planned to stop by the store before they headed home, so I suspect business has been *gut* this morning."

"Those buses to Ohio were pulling out of the parking lot just as we arrived," Andi remarked. "It was nice that so many of the Lehmans' friends and family members came out for Lester's wedding."

Nodding, Rosetta entered the kitchen and greeted the Kuhns. She cleared her throat as though she had something important to say.

"Ladies, I've spoken with Bishop Monroe, as well as with most of the other folks who run businesses here at Promise Lodge," she began pleasantly. "Everyone appreciates your offer to put us on the Internet, but we all agree that offering our products for sale online will force us to increase our production—not to mention spend a lot of time shipping what customers buy."

"*Jah*, Ruby and I are already making more cheese than

we ever anticipated, just to maintain our display at Dale's store," Beulah remarked.

"It would be the same story for my goat milk soap, and for Preacher Marlin's barrel products," Rosetta added kindly. "So, in the interest of living our Plain lives to the fullest, we Promise Lodge folks prefer to be more like the tortoise than the hare in that old fable. I hope you understand where we're coming from."

"Oh, we do," Karen put in quickly.

"It's your slower, family-and-faith focused lifestyle that we English envy, after all," Andi remarked. "It's been so relaxing these past few days, not being constantly connected to my phone or my laptop."

Rosetta nodded. "Glad to hear it. Even if you don't convert to the Plain life, you can take some of our habits home with you. That alone would probably be worth your week's rent."

Karen nodded, hoping the idea that had just occurred to her wouldn't seem like an insult to these wonderful new friends. "Don't take this wrong," she began hesitantly, "but maybe it would be best if we left on Saturday rather than staying through Sunday's church service."

Andi's face lit up with comprehension. "To be honest, the rest of the congregation could probably focus better on worship if Karen and I weren't sighing and whispering about how hard those pew benches feel after a looong service conducted in a language we don't understand."

Rosetta glanced at the Kuhns and the three of them burst out laughing. "We're Mennonites, remember," she pointed out.

"And truth be told, we find the Amish services a bit lengthy, too!" Ruby admitted.

"But we often attend—especially on wedding days— because we love our Amish friends here," Beulah said. "I can see why one dose of church on Thursday would be enough!"

"And don't even think about refunding any of our money," Karen insisted. "The food and friendliness here have been worth *way* more than what we've paid you."

"That said, we should probably empty our carts so they're not blocking the porch steps," Andi said. "Thank you so much for letting us store our stuff in those front closets."

As Karen led the way toward the lobby, she recalled how different the dining room had looked for the wedding, with all the tables draped in nice white tablecloths. "This place has come a long way since we were campers here," she murmured.

"It has," Andi agreed. She chuckled as they opened the front door and stepped out onto the porch. "And you were a genius, suggesting that we leave tomorrow instead of on Sunday. My backside will be forever in your debt!"

Late Friday afternoons had become one of Dale's favorite times, because that's when Irene delivered the pies she and Phoebe Troyer had baked that morning. She was perfectly capable of handling her portable wooden pie carriers and stocking the endcap reserved for Promise Lodge pies, but he made a point of assisting her.

"As always, these smell absolutely divine," Dale remarked as he stacked the neat white boxes on the shelves. He also caught an enticing whiff of the rose-scented soap she'd showered with after spending her morning in the hot bakery.

"That's because you're hungry," Irene pointed out in her no-nonsense way. "I suspect you didn't take time for lunch, so you're ready to sit down to the Kuhns' cooking after a busy day."

Will there ever come a day when I sit down to your *cooking, Irene?*

Dale smiled fondly at her. After the way she'd shut him down at the Lehman wedding, he knew better than to ask that question aloud.

"You've got me pegged, dear. Nothing ends a busy day—a busy week—better than *gut* food eaten amongst friends. And for many of our regular customers, nothing starts a weekend like a Promise Lodge Pie fresh off the rack," he added. "Do you have any idea how many folks get here before the store opens on Saturday mornings? They rush in as soon as I unbolt the door to choose a pie before they do the rest of their shopping—and some folks come only for the pie!"

Irene blinked, apparently startled by his revelation. "You're just saying that to get my attention so I'll—"

"It's the absolute truth," he insisted as he stacked the final four pies on the shelves, label side out. Irene and Phoebe always wrote the flavor on the box to make it easier for customers to spot the different varieties. "Your pies have become such a staple item, I'd be hard-pressed if I had to explain why we didn't have fresh ones four times each week. There are folks who wish you and Phoebe would bake six days a week—but I can certainly understand why you don't want to!"

"That would be too much of a *gut* thing," she remarked as she straightened to her full height and smoothed her apron. "I need my time off a lot more than those folks need more pies!"

As their laughter drifted up toward the store's ceiling, Dale savored the happy sound of it. After they'd exchanged a few more pleasantries, Irene went back to the lodge, and he returned to helping the final customers of the day. His feet and back were telling him he needed to look for another employee or two, because someday Marlene would stop storekeeping to become a mother.

Dale sighed as he locked the door and removed the money drawer from the cash register. Recalling the joy on Marlene's and Lester's faces during their wedding was one more reminder of what seemed to be missing from his life.

After counting the money and locking it into his safe, Dale spent a few moments gazing into the main room of his store. Moving to Promise Lodge had been his best business decision in years, because his store on a gravel road in Cloverdale had never seen the volume of traffic he'd known here, located on a state highway.

But what is a man profited if he gains the whole world and loses his soul?

The words Jesus had spoken to his disciples struck Dale as a warning. Six days a week he was focused on running his store—not unusual, in the Plain way of things. Yet hadn't Irene made a point about working less so she could live more?

Maybe her priorities, especially at their time of life, were in better order than his. Maybe the way to win such a woman's heart was to spend more time with her—because time was a gift that became more precious with each passing year.

Dale pondered these ideas as he crossed the lot behind the store and started toward the lodge. Halfway there, however, he stopped.

What was it about the stillness of the air, the odd yellowish cast to the sky, that raised the hairs on the back of his neck? Such conditions were rare, and they usually signaled a disturbance in the atmosphere—a sudden change in the weather.

Or a tornado. We haven't seen one of those in years.

As Dale reached the lodge's front porch, he waited when he saw that Mose was heading down the hill to come in for dinner.

"Looks like we're in for a storm," the big man called out. "The horses have been skittish all afternoon, and I suspect they're an accurate indicator of nasty weather."

Nodding, Dale climbed the steps and held the door open for his friend. As they entered the lobby, aromas of meat and cheese made his stomach rumble, but the little red flags in his mind seemed more important than his hunger.

"Do you ladies have some candles and matches?" he asked as the Kuhns set bowls and a large flat pan on the table. "Looks like we have some bad weather brewing. We should be ready to head to the basement—just in case."

Ruby and Beulah went to look out the nearest window.

"We've been so busy in the kitchen, I hadn't noticed anything unusual," the shorter woman remarked. "But it can't hurt to be prepared."

"I'll round up a few battery lamps and those emergency candles," Beulah said as she turned toward the kitchen again. "We Plain folks can be thankful that when the power goes out, we know how to handle it better than most English do."

"What's this about the power going out?" one of the *maidel* guests asked as she and her friend carried plates of dessert to the sideboard.

Dale noticed they were no longer wearing *kapps* with their calf-length dresses—and it occurred to him that they hadn't worn them during their shopping spree, either. He suspected the discrepancies in their mannerisms had caught up to them—something he could ask Irene or the Kuhns about later.

"Do I spy pizza?" Mose asked excitedly. "I can't recall you ladies ever making that for us. I *love* pizza!"

Irene and Sylvia emerged from the kitchen carrying two more flat, steaming pans. "I suspected you did, so we convinced Beulah that two wouldn't be enough," Sylvia remarked.

"Not if the rest of us want anything to eat," Irene teased. "Let's sit down and enjoy it, in case Dale's weather predictions come true."

After the eight of them had found places around the table, they shared a few moments of silent thanks. Because Irene, Beulah, and Sylvia sat closest to the pizzas, they served everyone rather than passing the hot pans. Dale helped himself to the green salad and watched hungrily as the ladies placed generous slices of cheeseburger, sausage, and pepperoni pizza on his plate.

Mose groaned with satisfaction as he crammed the first wedge into his mouth.

"Somebody sounds pretty happy," Dale teased as he decided which of the hot, cheesy, slices to cut into first. "But then, who wouldn't be delighted with all this meat and cheese?"

"Really *gut*," Mose put in as he chewed. He stopped eating, however, when he noticed Sylvia shyly eyeing him from across the table.

Hmm, are the sparks flying between those two? Mose didn't seem self-conscious until he realized Sylvia was paying attention to him.

For Dale, it was yet another reminder that all around him—even between a tiny woman who was dying and a tall, muscular man who stammered—springtime romance was in the air. He tried to make eye contact with Irene, but when she turned toward the window, her eyes widened.

"My word, look how dark it's gotten! And the wind is making those old trees dip and sway as though they're possessed by demons."

At the end of the table nearest the kitchen, Beulah stood up. "Let's grab our plates and the food and head downstairs," she said urgently. "The battery lamps and candles are in a box, ready to carry down there, as well."

Nobody had to be told twice. As everyone picked up what was in front of them, the wind began whistling loudly through the windows in the dining room and above the kitchen sinks.

"Better leave those windows open to help equalize the pressure," Dale suggested as he grabbed his plate and the pizza in front of it.

"At camp, we went to the center room downstairs during storm drills," Karen recounted as she started for the basement door. "No windows there, because it's below ground level."

"At least we still have the electric lights so we can see to get down those creaky old stairs," the girl called Annie remarked as she followed her friend.

Dale smiled. Apparently the two guests were quite familiar with the lodge from its earlier days as a church camp. He was guessing they'd told the ladies about their true identities and that more of their story might be revealed while everyone waited out the storm. He'd only been in the storage area of the basement nearest the stairs, where the Kuhns kept their steam table and other large equipment, so he was pleased to see that the room their guests led them to contained old chairs, sofas, and tables that probably dated back to the camping era.

As Mose helped arrange the old furniture, Dale returned to the dining room. The ladies carried down the remainder of their meal, so he followed them with the large box that contained the battery lamps, candles, and matches. The basement light fixtures were bare bulbs screwed into ceiling sockets—and some of them didn't work—but he was grateful for their weak illumination as he made a final trip down the stairs.

He was also pleased that after the others had taken seats and placed their plates on nearby tables, the space next to Irene remained unoccupied. Dale smiled at her and sat down on the other half of an old love seat that had seen better days.

"This room smells musty, but at least it's cool and safe," Ruby remarked as she resumed eating her meal.

"And we have something besides the floor to sit on," Beulah put in cheerfully. "As always, things could be a lot worse. But thanks to the *gut* Lord, we have—"

Everyone gasped when the lights blinked out.

Chapter 8

Mose reminded himself to inhale slowly and deeply to quell the sudden shock of being plunged into darkness. Most of the folks seated around him knew he'd been kidnapped when he was a kid, but he hadn't shared the fact that the incident had left him desperately afraid of the dark—probably because he'd endured an untold amount of time locked in the trunk of a car.

It was such a childish fear, he felt ashamed of it. Only his twin sister, Marlene, knew that each night when he went to bed, a small battery lamp burned on his dresser. Mose also kept two flashlights under his bed in case the batteries in one of them died.

As he swallowed hard, struggling to keep his panic at bay, Mose was grateful that no one else in the room could see the stricken expression on his face. Rain began pelting the lodge above them.

"Hang on," Dale said from across the room. "We'll have these lamps going in a moment."

"*Gut* thing you suggested we have them ready, Dale," Irene said. "I certainly wouldn't want to find my way up those stairs in the dark to locate them."

"*Gut*ness, listen to that downpour," Ruby remarked with

a nervous laugh. "And it's coming right in through the kitchen and dining room windows—"

"But if this is the worst weather we see, a little extra water is an easy mess to mop up," Beulah pointed out in a hopeful tone.

The familiar voices helped Mose settle his jangled nerves. Within moments, a lamp came on in the center of the table where Dale and Irene sat. Ruby lit another lamp from the box and placed it on the table next to her old, over-stuffed chair.

"You fellows might not be aware," Beulah said as she took a votive candle and some matches from the box, "but there's a toilet in that first room we passed through. It's enclosed in a wooden stall, so I'll put this candle in there in case anyone feels the *need*."

"Let's hope we won't be down here very long," Sylvia said in a tiny voice.

"In case we are, however," Beulah said as her match sparked into a flame, "I suggest we save the rest of the candles to use if our lamps go out. It's been a while since they had new batteries."

Now that the faces around the room had appeared in the lamplight, Mose inhaled again to tamp down his fear. When he glanced at Sylvia, who sat on an old wooden chair next to his ancient recliner, he realized that her hesi-tant remark had come from another poor, frightened soul who didn't like darkness. Her eyes looked huge. Her too-slender face was whittled down even more by the shadows that framed it.

Instinctively, Mose placed a hand on her arm. "It'll be okay," he whispered. "I'm right here beside you, Sylvia."

His bravado, come from out of nowhere, apparently sounded real to the petite woman seated beside him. Sylvia gazed at him gratefully, nodding slightly.

"I—I don't know about the rest of you, but I'm going to finish my supper now," Sylvia announced. "It's been a blue moon since I had pizza. We made these with the Kuhns' fresh cheese, so they're too *gut* to leave on the pans."

"Amen to that!" Karen piped up from across the room. "This old lodge has weathered storms before, and no place is safer than this shelter we're in. We'll be fine, no matter what's happening outside."

Mose suspected Sylvia had been faking bravery, just as he had, but he went along with it. If they could be strong for one another—if he and the childlike woman beside him could focus forward instead of dwelling on their past traumas—perhaps it was another sign that God had meant for them to be together.

Above them, the wind suddenly roared at fever pitch. It sounded as if a locomotive was barreling full speed over the tops of their heads, so loudly that no one attempted conversation. For once, food was the farthest thing from his mind, yet when Sylvia resolutely picked up a slice of her pizza, Mose followed her example. She'd made a good point: all three varieties tasted delicious, so why let them get cold and greasy?

And who knows when we'll see our next meal? The weather we're having sounds mighty serious.

Despite the deafening roar of the storm, Mose managed to eat a few bites of pizza. Some of his companions were also eating, and some sat absolutely still, as though focused on what might be going on above them. Gradually, it sounded as though that high-speed train was roaring off into the distance.

After a few moments of eerie silence had settled in, Dale cleared his throat. "I wonder if we've just had a tornado? They say a funnel cloud sounds a lot like a train as it's passing through."

"I'm in no hurry to go upstairs and find out," Beulah remarked.

Irene opened her mouth to say something, but an ominous moan and a loud *crash!* interrupted her.

Everyone sat still, looking upward. A few moments later they heard an intense pounding, as though the lodge might be surrounded by an angry mob throwing rocks.

"Hailstorm," Mose murmured.

The racket continued, keeping everyone suspended in an edgy state of silence—until the lamp on the table near Dale winked out. A collective sucking-in of breath rang around them as Mose realized Sylvia was clambering into his lap.

She didn't say a word, and she didn't need to. Mose wrapped his arms around her, praying Sylvia would feel safe in his embrace—and that she wouldn't suspect the jagged, ravenous fear that made him want to light every one of those candles in Beulah's box.

Once again, he was reminded how fragile she was. He might have been holding a life-sized doll, except that Sylvia was shifting against him, burrowing against his chest. When her arms went around his body, Mose's heart swelled—and a sense of awareness blazed to life inside him. She was clearly seeking protection and comfort while he, on the other hand, began thinking of a more physical side to their relationship—even as he warned himself not to let his thoughts go down that path.

He was still single at thirty-five because his speech impediment had convinced him that no girl would want to court him, much less consider him as a mate. The torment he'd endured from other kids had also taught him just how small and worthless other people could make him feel, so he hadn't dared to kiss a girl or invite one home from a Singing. Surely a widow like Sylvia wouldn't entertain any notions about a clueless, inexperienced fellow like himself.

And if Sylvia was dying, the last thing she needed was a bull moose of a man who craved intimate relations that might cause her harm.

Or does she want me, too? And if she does, what will I do about it?

Irene watched with envy as Sylvia climbed into Mose's lap. She was trying hard to remain peaceful and positive as the storm raged above them, hinting at massive destruction, yet she would've given anything to have her husband, Ernest's, arms around her again. She worried about Truman and Rosetta, up at the house on the hill. Had they been struck by that possible tornado, as well? Was the old roof keeping the rain out?

In the chair to her right, Ruby began to sing "Amazing Grace." As the rest of them joined in, a welcome hush settled over the room and into Irene's soul. The hymn's last word had barely left their lips when Beulah started reciting the Twenty-third Psalm. As Irene chimed in, the images of sheep and green pastures soothed her even as she wondered how Harley Kurtz's flock was faring. She prayed that the ewes and lambs were safely in the barn, out of harm's way.

Following the Psalm, Mose sang the first line of "What a Friend We Have in Jesus." His voice was rich and low, and as they all joined in the singing, Irene felt Dale's hand gently closing around hers. He smiled at her from the other side of the love seat yet seemed to realize that she wanted him to stay on his side rather than scoot closer to her.

And why is that? Why do you repel Dale's hints at affection?

Before she had time to ponder such questions, however, the other battery lamp went out.

"Well, now," Beulah said quietly. "We should remember that before God gave His light to the world back in the days of the creation, the earth had no form, and everything was in darkness. But He cared enough to create the sun and the moon and us mere mortals, and He's looked after us ever since—"

"And He's loved us no matter how badly and how often we've disappointed Him," Dale pointed out. "I don't know about you folks, but I want to wait a while before we go upstairs, to be sure the storm has left the area."

"I'm fine with that," Mose chimed in. "But I'd feel better if we lit some of those candles so we can see the folks around us. Friendly faces mean a lot when we're not sure what we'll find when we leave this shelter, ain't so?"

"You've got that right, Mose," Beulah replied. "Let there be light!"

Moments later, after the Kuhns had fumbled in the box between them, a match flared to life. Soon there were candles on each table in the room and a warm sense of peace returned.

Irene's shoulders relaxed. She smiled at Dale, content to let her hand remain in his. "Maybe we should pray for our family and friends in the homes around us," she suggested. "We have no idea whether anyone else was in the direct path of the storm. For all we know, some of them might've been out in their buggies or—"

A loud, thundering *crash* made them all jump.

Dale squeezed Irene's hand. "Sounds like we lost another one of those big trees behind the lodge," he murmured. "As we pray, we should also ask God for guidance about how we can safely proceed, and how we can rebuild whatever's been damaged."

Along with the others, Irene bowed her head. During their silent prayer, she became aware that some folks breathed faster than others, or deeper—because the sounds of their breathing seemed to be magnified by the dim

stillness. She was glad everyone had remained calm, and
that nobody insisted that the men go upstairs and report
back on the damage. Those huge trees had fallen on the
backside of the lodge—the side where her apartment was.
Sylvia's and the Kuhns' were there, too.

Irene was in no hurry to learn what she might've lost
during the storm.

In the flickering light of the candles Beulah had placed
on their tables, Irene saw some of the others picking at their
food again. Andi and Karen appeared completely calm as
they lifted fresh wedges of pizza from the metal pans on the
center table.

Irene watched Mose hold a slice of pizza in front of
Sylvia, softly encouraging her to eat. After the tiny woman
had taken a mouthful, Mose devoured the rest of the slice
in a couple of large bites. It seemed so personal, so intimate,
that they were sharing their meal—

She blinked. Dale was holding a slice of sausage pizza
in front of her.

Tentatively, Irene took a bite. She closed her eyes over
the chewy hint of Italian spices—not to mention the layer
of gooey cheese that was firming up as it cooled. Even after
all this time had passed, the Kuhns' pizza seemed like the
most delicious food Irene had eaten for days. And that said
something, considering the fabulous spread they'd served
for Marlene and Lester's wedding yesterday.

As Dale bit into the wedge of pizza and held her gaze,
Irene felt funny little bubbles in her stomach. Even if he'd
gotten the idea from Mose, it was still a novelty to be sharing food as though—

As though we're family. Husband and wife.

Tentatively, Irene opened her mouth in anticipation.
When Dale held the pizza slice for her again, his delighted
smile spoke volumes about the relationship she'd been

trying to deny. Who would believe that fastidious, nitpicky Dale Kraybill would eat from the same plate as she, much less from the same slice of pizza?

And what possessed him to do it in front of all these other people? Even if they're our close friends?

Before Irene could consider that subject, Ruby rose from her chair. "I've got to use the bathroom, and then I'm going to try the upstairs door," she said in a low voice. "It's been quiet for a *gut* long while now."

"Once you get it open, I'll be right there to help you," her sister put in.

"You'll not be going into the kitchen without me," Mose insisted. "There's no telling what sort of damage the storm did to the structure of the building."

"Don't wander around," Dale chimed in. "It's after dark by now, and no doubt the power won't be back on for—"

"Not to worry!" Ruby interrupted with a nervous edge in her voice. "I—I'm just curious, not stupid!"

Irene and the others sat in heightened silence until a few minutes later, they heard the flush of the toilet. Soon they saw the flickering light from her candle move toward the other room. Her footfalls echoed eerily on the old wooden steps like the collective beating of their hearts. When Ruby reached the top, she stopped—and each of them held their breath.

"Oh. *Ohhh.*"

Irene's eyes widened as she glanced at the friends around her. Everyone listened intently as Ruby came back down the stairs with the same slow, careful tread she'd used going up. She stopped in the doorway to their concrete room, shaking her head.

"I couldn't open the door," she said, sounding deeply shaken. "Then I noticed that the top of the door frame was three or four inches farther to the right than the bottom. Our world has seriously shifted, my friends."

Chapter 9

Dale felt Irene stiffen with fear and shock—and why wouldn't she? He gently squeezed her hand before he set down the crust of the pizza they'd shared.

"That means we've got some serious structural damage, probably from those trees falling," he said as he rose from the love seat. "And it's highly possible that storm debris is blocking the door, too."

"Storm debris?" Irene echoed. "You mean, maybe part of the building has broken loose?"

"What'll happen if we're *trapped* down here, and the candles all go out?" Sylvia blurted in a tiny, tight voice. "And—and how do we know that other folks aren't trapped in their houses, as well? What if *days* go by and nobody comes to look for us?"

"It won't come to that, honey," Mose insisted gently. He eased her out of his lap so he could stand up. "What about other doors? Do you ladies know of another way out of this basement?"

Beulah's wide, frightened eyes spoke volumes—as did her sister's. Dale had never seen his steely-haired lodge hostesses beset by panic or vulnerability, and the Kuhns' fears would become contagious if they multiplied before he—or someone else—took control of the situation.

"Or what about windows?" Dale asked, hoping he sounded calm. "We'll figure this out, ladies, if we all remain rational about—"

"Windows?" Ruby shot back. "We're underground, remember? I think there are some very small windows in the storage area—"

"But none of us could wiggle our wide behinds through them, if that's what you're thinking," Beulah chimed in. "This building doesn't belong to us, so the only time we've come down here is to get the steam table and other equipment in that room closest to the stairs. I haven't done any exploring, so maybe we should each take a candle and search the walls for a doorway in these other rooms—"

"Wait! That's it!" Karen cried out. "Andi, don't you remember? Back when we were counselors, the camp managers brought us down here for storm drills. They said something about a door leading out of the root cellar, where they used to keep those mountains of potatoes and onions. Didn't they?"

"A root cellar?" Ruby asked incredulously. "I never thought to look for such a place when we moved here. Maybe Rosetta knows about that because she owns the lodge—"

"But Rosetta's up at the house with Truman," Irene pointed out.

Karen's face fell. "Phooey. I can't call her, either, because in my attempt to be more like the Amish, I left my cell phone up in my room."

"Me too," Andi murmured.

Irene smiled kindly. "But if you're saying there's a door down here, that implies that it opens to a way outside, right?" she asked the two young women. "Where should we be looking for it—and for the root cellar you've mentioned?"

The darker-haired young woman reached into Beulah's

box and took out a white utility candle, lighting its wick from the flame of Ruby's. "I only recall peeking in there once," she murmured, gazing at the concrete walls of their shelter.

"I think it's over this way," Andi put in as she, too, lit a candle. "There used to be a lot of camp gear and boxes of craft materials stacked along the walls down here, so if you folks have stored some of your own boxes in addition to that old stuff—"

"We might need to move things away from the walls to see that doorway," Karen finished with a nod.

Dale lit a candle, and so did everyone else. "I can't imagine Rosetta and her sisters left a lot of camp materials down here after they purchased the place," he remarked.

"I can recall those ladies carrying boxload after boxload of old books and papers out into the yard after they moved here," Irene said. "Back then, I was so curious about the new owners of this place that I'll confess to spying on them with my binoculars from my house on the hill. I suspect Rosetta can tell you exactly what's in these various nooks and—"

"In here! Bring more candles," Andi called out from a different room.

Karen followed her friend's voice, walking past stacked trunks and other items to push aside an old gray curtain. "Yeah, this was where they used to store all those potatoes and onions and apples!"

"That's because it's deeper under the ground and naturally cooler in here," Ruby put in as she entered the room behind Beulah. "We'll have to keep this room in mind if . . . if we ever have the occasion to store food and—and to cook meals in the lodge again."

Dale ducked his head slightly to enter the cavelike room,

which was had been dug out beyond the lodge's concrete foundation.

"We *will* resume our normal lives, Ruby," he said emphatically. "It's no wonder you gals didn't realize this unfinished root cellar was back here. The entry's narrow—around the corner and out of sight from the main basement. And the curtain's the same color as the concrete."

Mose had also entered the dark, musky space and was studying the walls. "If there's a way out of here, you'd have to pass through some sort of tunnel to come out above the ground outside," he reasoned aloud. "And if the camp folks had designed it as a passageway from a storm cellar, they would've made it substantial enough for the counselors and campers to get through it safely—right?"

Karen frowned, thinking. "You know, those old trunks out there look familiar, but I don't know why. Let's shift some of that stuff around. I'm not seeing anything that resembles a doorway in here."

Nodding, Dale let their guests lead the way. He could understand why Rosetta and her sisters might've left some of the original items from the camp stashed in this forgotten corner of the lodge's basement: when they'd come here, they were establishing a whole new community, so more important matters had required their immediate attention.

Karen and Andi had handed their candles to Sylvia and were struggling to move a thick, flat pole away from the stack of items in the shadowy corner. Dale gave his candle to Irene so he could help them.

"Look at this—an old iron cross!" he said when he realized it had been stored upside down. "And some old-fashioned metal snow shovels and rakes."

"That cross used to hang on the stone fireplace up in the lobby," Andi remarked. "But one year when we painted and redecorated, we didn't put it back up."

Once the cross was out of the way, Mose also handed off his candle to move a trunk that was stacked on top of two others.

"This feels empty," he remarked. "Could be Rosetta and her sisters got rid of the stuff inside it and kept it for storing their own belongings."

"I don't think there's anything in this one, either," Ruby remarked as she and Beulah lifted the next trunk off the stack. "But as much grit and grime as we're knocking loose, I doubt our landlady ever got around to clearing out this corner."

With everyone eager to help, the remaining trunks and boxes were soon out of the way—as well as a few old canvas cots that had been stacked upright against the wall. As Mose shifted the last cot, his laughter echoed in the concrete room.

"Well, how do you like that?" the big man asked. "Here's a doorway, all right—but why would anyone with a lick of sense pile all that other paraphernalia over the top of it?"

Andi laughed as she glanced at Karen. "Remember how, one summer, some of the guys loved to sneak in through the outside cellar entrance to make scary noises at night—"

"So the adults made a point of showing them that the way was blocked!" Karen crowed. "It's all coming back to me now!"

"But I don't remember actually going *through* this door to whatever's beyond it," Andi recounted. "Thank goodness we never had any serious storms the summers we were here."

Dale took hold of the knob, relieved to feel it turning in his hand. "Well, ladies—and Mose—we're about to find out where it leads."

Chapter 10

Sylvia's pulse pounded painfully in her temples, so loudly that she had to concentrate to hear what the other folks were saying. She thanked God that the storm had passed, however, and that they had found another way out of the basement before she'd spiraled downward into panic mode. It was another blessing that Mose hadn't questioned her need to crawl into his lap; when Ruby had discovered that they couldn't go upstairs because of structural damage, Sylvia's emotional control had nearly reached the breaking point.

Reminding herself not to delve backward into the terrifying incident that had made her so afraid of being alone in the dark, Sylvia focused on the door Dale was opening very cautiously.

"Here's that passageway we've been speculating about," the storekeeper said in a hopeful tone. "Mose, let's take our candles and check to see that it's safe—"

"And we'll hope the door at the other end hasn't been blocked by other storm damage," Mose put in matter-of-factly.

"Oh, this is exciting!" Ruby whispered as she handed

back their candles. "A secret passageway in the lodge, just like in a murder mystery!"

Beulah let out a short laugh. "I'll feel a whole lot more excited when I'm out of this basement, so I can see exactly what's happened to our home."

Sylvia nodded in agreement. When Mose smiled at her, she tried to return his confident gaze before he entered the passageway behind Dale.

"Yikes! Duck down, Mose, or you'll hit your head like I did," Dale cautioned.

"*Jah*, because look at this! We're in a cave—and it runs underneath the cabins, most likely."

Sylvia and the rest of the ladies exchanged surprised glances. They remained quiet, hovering near the doorway to catch whatever the two men might say. After a few moments, however, the dim light from their candles was swallowed up by the cave's darkness—which did nothing to reassure Sylvia about how she'd make her way to the exit. What if she froze in fear and had to be carried out? What if she began crying and couldn't stop? What if—

Sounds of the men's exertion reached them from a distance, along with their muted conversation. Before long, Sylvia could hear them returning.

Mose's expression was impossible to read as he reentered the basement. "Well, there's a door down that way, all right—"

"But when we tried to open it," Dale continued, pausing to catch his breath, "it only budged about a foot. I suspect it's covered over with years of dirt or debris from not being used, so we'll need to dig our way out—or push the obstruction beyond the opening."

Mose nodded, exhaling loudly as he gazed around. "Why don't you ladies find something to scoop with—maybe small metal cooking pots. And Dale, do you suppose we could use that iron cross like a battering ram?"

Dale looked doubtfully at the large cross, which rested against the wall. "As heavy as that thing is, I won't be much help battering anything—"

"But one of us needs to keep the door open and hold a candle, right?" Mose asked with a kind smile. "You ladies can join us when you're ready—but be careful not to bang your heads against the cave's low ceiling."

"I'll take one of these snow shovels," Dale remarked. "I can handle that much, anyway."

As burly Mose hefted the cross to carry it into the cave, Sylvia felt a thrill of pride. It seemed he was going to be the one who got them out of captivity because he was so strong.

Strong enough to care for me. Strong enough that he's able to move beyond his childhood trauma and get us both out of the dark and into the light again.

Feeling reassured, Sylvia followed the other ladies back into the room where the Kuhns stored their cooking equipment. She suspected she'd be holding candles while the other folks did the digging, but hadn't Mose just pointed out that even the smallest and weakest among them could play a vital part in their evacuation? She hoped the dimness would disguise her trembling arms and legs. The last thing she wanted was folks feeling sorry for her—or asking questions about why she felt so fearful.

Armed with a few small, sturdy pots, the women returned to the doorway that had been so mysteriously hidden. Beulah smiled at them.

"It's getting late and we're all feeling the stress of the storm, but we'll get through this crisis together," she said. "No matter what, God's got plans for our future and He's walking with us every step of the way. Sylvia, maybe you should lead us with a couple of candles so we can see when we need to duck."

Sylvia's eyes widened but she nodded. If Beulah, the bedrock resident of the lodge, believed she could be the leader, then she'd have to prove her new friend right, wouldn't she? This wasn't the moment to cower or to protest that she wasn't up to the task.

As she stepped into the cave, dankness enveloped her—which was common for the air in underground caverns, as she understood it. Sylvia wasn't going to admit that she'd never been inside a cave . . . or that this one reminded her of a tomb from back in Bible times. She took a deep breath, held her candles high, and stepped forward into the dim, low-ceilinged room that stretched in front of her. The walls appeared craggy and irregular—downright spooky in the flickering light of her candles.

"Here we go," she said as confidently as she could. "I can't see the men, but I can hear them at the far end."

Sounds of Mose ramming the iron cross against an obstruction kept Sylvia focused as she walked. Behind her, the other ladies followed in silence.

Are there bats in this cave? Are other creepy-crawly creatures watching us from the shadows? Who knows what might've died down here—

Sylvia sucked in her breath, forcing such frightening thoughts from her mind. She concentrated on walking where the ceiling appeared to be the highest, hoping the taller women like Beulah, Karen, and Andi wouldn't have to hunker down too much. After several long, cautious moments, Sylvia spotted the welcome glow of Dale's candles.

"Almost there—but be careful not to bump your heads!" Sylvia warned over her shoulder. "I see Dale and Mose a little way ahead of us."

At the sound of her voice, Dale turned toward their little

parade. Mose took a moment to set the heavy cross against the wall.

"Just in time!" the storekeeper called out. "If a few of you ladies can hold the candles for us, I'll shovel this loose rubble out of Mose's way so he can make more progress."

"It's mostly dirt and dead leaves," Mose put in, his breathing ragged from exertion. "Looks like it's been several years since anybody has used this exit. It must've been completely covered over from the outside."

"Time goes by faster than we think," Irene remarked, "but I suspect the camp was unoccupied for at least five or six years before Rosetta and her sisters bought it. That's time enough for a lot of soil or mud to accumulate in a doorway that was probably built very close to the ground."

"*Jah*, as you can see, the door we've found is nearly level with the top of the cave, with a few large, flat rocks to serve as a stairway up out of here," Dale remarked. "Reminds me of the storm cellars that were built years ago, adjoining basements that had no other way out of them. We had one like this at our family's old farm."

Sylvia nodded, taking in what Dale said—but she was mostly aware that Mose's purple shirt had become soaked with sweat and was clinging to his torso . . . his very muscular torso, and shoulders that bulged beneath his dark suspenders.

Why am I so fascinated by a man's body at a time like this? Gut grief, I just want out of this creepy, claustrophobic hole!

And yet she couldn't deny that her attraction to Mose involved more than the traumas they had in common—more than the shared fear that had already bonded them. Sylvia reminded herself to hold her candles high near the doorway so that Dale and the ladies with pans could move a small mountain of old leaves, soil, and paper trash out of Mose's way.

Her heart skipped lightly when Mose caught her gaze and held it. Then he, too, seemed to realize he had more important priorities.

"I've caught my breath, and you gals have cleared the stairs. I can knock away more blockage now," Mose said as he lifted the large iron cross again.

Sylvia stepped out of his way, amazed at his stamina. By grasping the cross's horizontal arms, he could ram the end of the longer vertical piece against the packed debris that still blocked their way to freedom. It was gut-wrenching work, but after a few more moments another large pile of debris had landed on the stone stairs and the cave floor.

"Surely there can't be too much more," he said as he took another break. "I'm starting to wonder if we're blazing our own trail out of here rather than following a way that was clear at one time."

"Oh, we can recall guys who came in from the outside this way," Andi assured him.

Karen laughed as she scooped more dirt and leaves out of the way. "Yeah, and if you look closely, you might even find their old cigarette butts—because smoking was forbidden at camp," she added with a wry chuckle.

Mose pulled a bandanna from his pants pocket and mopped his shiny forehead. "All right, here we go again."

Sylvia hoped, for Mose's sake, that the way outside would soon be open. The candles in her hands and Irene's were burning dangerously low, so they'd soon be in the dark again unless somebody fetched more candles from Beulah's box. She tried desperately not to let her fear of entrapment flood her mind again.

"Let this be a lesson to us to keep more emergency

candles around," Ruby murmured. "We've run through our supply—"

"Open air!" Mose cried out from the doorway. "We're almost out of here."

As everyone around her sucked in hopeful breaths, Sylvia said a quick prayer of thanks. No matter what sort of damage the lodge had sustained during the storm, the residents had survived a monumental crisis. And no one had been hurt.

Mose redoubled his efforts with the cross and then stepped back inside, his chest heaving with exertion. "If you ladies can clear off the stairs and floor one more time, I'll climb through the opening and help everyone outside," he said as he leaned the cross against the wall.

Eagerly, the Kuhns and the two guests scooped more debris out of the way. Sylvia shifted the sputtering candles in her fingers, letting melted wax drip down onto the dirt floor. A few minutes later Mose hoisted himself up and disappeared into the darkness outside.

"Come on up here, Dale, so the two of us can assist the ladies."

The storekeeper gazed up through the opening. He set aside his snow shovel and reached up so Mose could grasp his hands.

"All right, Buffalo Gals," Dale teased, "time to come out and dance by the light of the moon. One by one. Easy does it now."

"Go on ahead," Sylvia urged her friends. "My candles are too low to hand over to anyone else."

"*Jah*, mine, too," Irene said.

When the other women realized how close they were to being in the dark again, they moved quickly. With a few grunts and some scrambling, which knocked more loose dirt onto the stone stairs, Sylvia's friends clambered up to freedom. Irene dropped her candles and snuffed them out with her foot before stepping into the opening.

Sylvia had no choice but to do the same so she wouldn't get burned. The momentary darkness threatened to overwhelm her as she stepped carefully up the stone stairway—until she saw two familiar arms reaching down through the opening.

As she stood on tiptoe to grasp Mose's huge hands, Sylvia heard words that would remain etched on her heart forever.

"I've got you, sweetheart. You're out of the dark now, Sylvia."

She felt herself rising from the cave and past ground level. Rather than setting her on the ground, Mose lifted her effortlessly against his chest and wrapped his arms around her, as though she was a treasure he wanted to hold close forever. Sylvia laid her head against his damp neck and hung on gratefully, trying not to cry. Being out in the open air again sent a whirlwind of thoughts and feelings through her system as she realized her ordeal was finally over.

Mose seemed to sense that her emotions had momentarily gotten the best of her. He simply held her, allowing her to regather her strength. Sylvia realized then that night had fallen and the temperature had dropped, as well. Except for an occasional set of headlights out on the state highway, the property around them was steeped in total, silent darkness.

"Where are we?" Irene asked in a thin voice.

Dale, standing close enough to be holding her hand, cleared his throat. "Can you see the outlines of the cabins and the lodge?" he asked as he pointed in that direction. "And not very far away on this side, you'll see the Helmuths' nursery and the silhouette of the bulk store."

When the clouds shifted, the moonlight illuminated a

part of the Promise Lodge property that Sylvia wasn't very familiar with. She felt so contented resting against Mose—and so emotionally drained—that she let her eyes drift shut again, until Beulah let out a ragged cry of desperation.

"Oh my *gut*ness—oh my stars, the back half of the lodge has been crushed by—by those two old maple trees."

"*Jah,* ladies," Ruby murmured with a hitch in her voice. "We're not going to be living in our apartments anytime soon. Maybe never again."

It was all Sylvia could do not to cry, because her apartment—her final earthly dwelling place—was on the same side of the lodge as the Kuhns' and Irene's. Where would she live now? Would she ever reclaim her personal items? Squeezing her eyes shut against tears, she pressed her face into the collar of Mose's shirt. She was trembling all over, so he surely knew she was upset—

"Don't worry about a thing, Sylvia," he murmured, shifting her weight so he could hold her more easily. "Folks here take care of their own, and that includes you. Don't think for a minute that I'll let anything bad happen to you."

She was trying to wrap her mind around what Mose had just said when a man behind them cried out, "Irene and Sylvia? Ruby and Beulah? Can any of you ladies hear us? Are you all right in there?"

Chapter 11

At the sound of her son's voice, Irene came out of her anxious woolgathering about where she would live and what would come next. "Truman! Truman, we're over here," she called out, waving her arms above her head.

"Oh, but it's *gut* to hear your voice, Irene—and see all you folks over there in the darkness!" Rosetta cried as she hurried toward them with a lantern. "Did everyone make it out unharmed?"

When Irene reached Truman and her daughter-in-law, she threw her arms around them with a love so fierce it made her cry. "*Jah*, thanks to Karen and—and Andi—we came out through a secret passageway. Then Mose dug us out—"

"Secret passageway?" Rosetta's eyebrows rose in a pale face highlighted by her lantern. "What on earth are you talking about?"

Irene hugged the couple again for good measure. Now that she was saying those words aloud, the concept of their escape route *did* sound rather hard to believe.

"Our two guests recalled a cave with a doorway that opens at ground level over there, just past the cabins," she explained as the rest of the evacuees joined her. "The door in the basement had been completely covered with old trunks and items left from when this place was a camp, so it's no wonder you didn't know it was there."

"But thank the *gut* Lord it was," Truman put in as he glanced at the backside of the lodge. "When I saw what those two fallen trees had done to your apartments, I was afraid—well, let's just say we're grateful to God to see all of you out here, safe and sound."

Irene nodded. "It's also a *gut* thing that Dale warned us about the approaching storm, and that he and Mose kept us women from getting upset, and—well, all of us together made a strong team," she added gratefully. "Did you two have any damage up at the house?"

"Nope, just a lot of wind and noise," Rosetta replied. "It was scary, watching from our basement window as that dark funnel cloud wound its way through the Promise Lodge property. It hit Christine's dairy barn, and . . ."

Truman sighed along with his wife. "Sad to say, there's not much left of your Promise Lodge Pies shop, Mamm," he murmured. He looked over at the other folks standing nearby, who were hanging on his every word. "And Ruby and Beulah, I'm sorry your cheese factory took a hit, as well."

Beulah sighed dejectedly. "It's not what we wanted to hear, but we're grateful to be standing here talking about it rather than still trapped inside the lodge."

"And the way we've seen things work around here," Ruby put in, forcing herself to sound cheerful, "our neighbors will soon construct a new building for us, and we can order new cheesemaking equipment—"

"I'll be happy to help you ladies replace your supplies and machinery," Dale said as he gently put his arms around the two sisters' shoulders. "From what I can see, the bulk store is still intact, so helping anyone who lost a business is the least I can do. I'm going over to see if the power's on," he added. "If not, I'll need to crank up the generator to keep my refrigerator and freezer units going."

Before Dale turned to go, he held Irene's gaze for a few moments. She felt self-conscious, knowing he could see the tear streaks on her face, yet she sensed the evening's ordeal had strengthened their bond of friendship. She hadn't thought much about their relationship before the storm—but she realized the storekeeper had indeed taken care of her comfort and her needs.

"If you need to speak to Mamm about those supply orders, she'll be living up at the house with us for a while," Truman called out to Dale's retreating figure. "And *denki* for your help this evening!"

Irene suddenly felt exhausted. "Before we go, we need to be sure these other folks also have places to stay—"

"Hey there, you folks behind the lodge!" Bishop Monroe called out as he came around the corner of the cabin nearest the lodge. "I can hear your voices, but I can't see you in the—ah, you've got a lantern! Is everyone accounted for? Anybody injured?"

"We're all vertical and ventilating, Bishop!" Ruby replied. "Did you folks up the way get hit, too?"

The bishop, along with Preachers Marlin and Amos, held their lanterns high as they walked quickly toward the little group. Their lamplit faces were etched with concern as they made their way around the huge, uprooted trees—and then focused on the damaged lodge building.

"We were very fortunate at our end," Bishop Monroe replied. "The only damage I've seen so far has been a few missing fence planks around my pasture and the Kurtzes'—"

"What a blessing that none of you gals were in your apartments when that twister went through!" Preacher Amos blurted out as he stared at the caved-in roof. "We went to the front of the lodge first and had no idea the backside had sustained so much damage."

"I'm sure you're all upset and exhausted, too," Preacher Marlin said gently. "Rest assured that some of you can stay with Frances and me—"

"And Christine and I have two guest rooms," the bishop added.

"Mattie and I have a spare room, as well," Preacher Amos insisted. "Whenever you ladies feel ready, we'll walk you up the hill so you can get settled in."

Irene had been listening closely, tallying the number of guest rooms the men had mentioned. "Someone's welcome to the other spare room at our place, as well," she put in.

"It's a little cluttered," Rosetta added with a rueful laugh. "But we can fix that."

The group grew silent, contemplating the options.

"Bishop, if you have two rooms—and you and Christine can put up with a couple of old busybodies—Ruby and I would be grateful for a place to lay our weary heads," Beulah said.

"*Jah*, and if Christine needs any help getting her cows back after the storm—or help with anything at all, we're on it," Ruby put in.

Bishop Monroe's handsome face lit up. "Christine, along with Mattie and her two boys, are already working on that dairy cow roundup, ladies. You can head on up to our place anytime you're ready."

"And I'll stay with you, Preacher Amos—if you're sure Mattie won't mind," Sylvia said meekly.

"Mattie will look forward to having someone besides me for company," Amos assured her kindly. "Shall we walk on over to the house? I bet you're worn to a frazzle, dear."

Irene didn't miss Sylvia's quick glance at Mose before she joined Preacher Amos and the two Kuhns. When she noticed the uncertain expressions on Karen's and Andi's faces, however, she didn't linger over the potential romance between Mose and Sylvia.

"That spare room I was talking about has twin beds in it," Irene said, walking over to place her hands on their English guests' shoulders. "If that would work for you two, we can find nightgowns and everything you'll need until you go home."

Andi blinked, shaking her head in disbelief as she took in the view of the two uprooted trees that had crushed the backside of the lodge. "Do you suppose we'll be able to get our stuff out of our rooms?" she asked. "They're on the front side of the building—"

"And I really feel bad about leaving tomorrow morning, considering all the cleanup that needs to be done," Karen put in, "but I've already called my brother to come and get us."

"Let's see how things look in the daylight," Truman said. "We don't want you to risk tripping over uneven floor-boards—or having some of that collapsed roof fall through while you're inside."

"We'll do what we can," the bishop assured them. He smiled at Mose, who'd remained quiet as he'd listened to the plans for the ladies' lodging. "How about if you and Marlin and I look at the damage on this end? We'd better turn off the lodge's gas valve, too."

"*Jah*, you're right about that," Mose said. "We don't need gas leaks—or the stoves exploding—on top of every-thing else that's happened."

Nodding, Irene smiled at Andi and Karen. "Let's head up the hill, shall we?" she suggested. "I don't know about you, but I've had all of this long, eventful evening I can handle."

* * *

Karen had a hard time sleeping even after Andi had drifted off in the twin bed across the room from her. Considering all the things folks at Promise Lodge had lost in the storm, it seemed petty to be worried about retrieving her cell phone from the room she'd rented—yet she couldn't stop thinking about how much personal information she wouldn't be able to access if the men declared it was too dangerous for her and Andi to pack their belongings. And when she wasn't obsessing about her phone, she couldn't stop hearing the tornado roar through her thoughts, just as she couldn't quit reliving the adrenaline surge of locating the cave and the door that had been hidden away beneath Promise Lodge for so many years.

It was almost dawn when she fell asleep—and then she awoke much later than she'd intended.

"Andi!" she said, grasping her sleeping friend's shoulder. "I told Mike to be here by nine o'clock, and it's already after seven."

Andi yawned and swung her feet over the side of the bed. They made quick use of the bathroom and went down to speak with the Wickeys about fetching their belongings.

Rosetta offered them mugs of fresh coffee and pointed to a pan of warm breakfast casserole on the table, where Irene was eating. "I doubt any of us got much rest last night," their hostess remarked sympathetically. "I still can't believe the lodge has been so badly damaged on the backside. I almost don't want to go and look at it," she added as her eyes suddenly filled with tears. "But it's what we need to do."

"What about church tomorrow morning?" Karen asked as she placed some casserole on a plate. "Will you call off your service, or—"

"Oh no!" Rosetta wiped her eyes with her sleeve, quickly composing her emotions. "Christine has already announced that everyone's to bring lawn chairs to the Burkholder home for church in their backyard."

"No time's too tough or inconvenient to worship the God who spared every one of us from that awful storm," Irene pointed out. "We're all meeting at the bishop's place this morning, so everyone can be informed about safety procedures and start planning our cleanup."

Truman entered the kitchen, appearing as weary as Karen felt. "When you've eaten a bite, ladies, let's fetch your stuff," he suggested. "I was just at the lodge for a quick look-around. If we go straight upstairs to your rooms—"

"We have a bunch of shopping bags stashed in the front storage closets, too," Andi put in with wide eyes. "But your decision is the one that counts, Truman. If it's too big a risk to get our things, so be it."

"We appreciate your willingness to accept whatever Truman decides," Rosetta said before she took a long sip of her coffee. "As for me, I'm *so* curious about that cave you folks passed through, but we need to be extremely cautious about exploring it. We'll wait for our carpenters to assess the safety of entering other parts of the lodge."

Karen nodded, chewing a mouthful of the delicious, cheesy breakfast casserole. "Remember—you can't get into the kitchen from the basement, because the doorway's blocked," she said. "When Ruby told us the top of the door frame had shifted a few inches from the bottom, we realized just how badly those old trees had damaged the building."

Rosetta, whose brown hair was pulled neatly up into a small, round Mennonite *kapp*, smiled gently at her and Andi. "Who knows? Maybe God led you ladies here for a visit because He knew you'd be able to guide our dear friends away from danger," she murmured with a hitch in her voice. "I'm upset about the condition of my poor, beautiful lodge, for sure and for certain. But if we'd lost any of you folks who were in the basement, we'd all be inconsolable."

"*Jah*, that's the way I see it, too," Truman said with a nod. "A building we can replace. Our friends and my mother? Not so much."

Ten minutes later, the five of them climbed into Truman's big pickup truck. Karen's pulse thrummed with anxiety and hope during the short ride as she looked through the side window. In the shimmering light of early Saturday morning, the lodge appeared the same as it had back when she and Andi had been camp counselors—except for the absence of the trees behind the building.

"Well, it's a comfort that the timbered peaks and the front porch weren't damaged," Andi murmured as she, too, peered eagerly at the lodge.

"Do we dare believe we can rebuild the back section of the building and keep the front intact?" Rosetta asked in an emotional whisper. "Oh, Truman—"

Truman reached over to grasp his wife's hand, his handsome face alight with love for her. "That's what I'm hoping, honey-girl," he replied. "We'll know more after Preacher Amos and Lester and the other men skilled at carpentry assess the damage."

He pulled the truck up near the building and shut off the engine. "Mamm, you can go upstairs with me and our guests, but after looking toward your apartment when I was here earlier, I'm insisting that you can't go anywhere near it to retrieve your clothes or belongings right now," he said softly. "I'm just taking Karen and Andi up to pack—and we'll have to ease very carefully past the damage at the top of the main staircase."

Irene stifled a soft sob. "I—I understand," she murmured after she regained some control over her emotions. "I've been telling myself that it's only *stuff*, after all."

"Same thing goes for you, Rosetta," Truman continued. "If you want to go inside, don't even *think* about entering the dining room or the kitchen or the big meeting room, all right? The lobby is as far as you should go."

Rosetta slumped in the passenger seat, swallowing hard. "I probably shouldn't go inside yet," she said sadly. "Is there any chance of recovering what our residents left behind in their apartments, Truman? Or anything from that kitchen we all love so much?"

"Maybe." Her husband smiled gently. "If Bishop Monroe and the other men agree to it, I could rent a cherry picker that would lift us into the apartments from the back, so we wouldn't have to stand on the floors. But don't get your hearts set on that until we hear what Amos and the other fellows have to say."

"I'll just stay outside," Irene remarked as she opened her door. "On my way up the hill to the Burkholder place, I'll look at the tree damage at the back of the building and keep my distance from it. Too much temptation to poke around if I go in."

"*Jah*, that's probably best for me, too," Rosetta agreed with a sigh. When she turned in her seat to smile at Karen and Andi, the hollows beneath her eyes made her look tired and wrung-out. "Meanwhile, we wish you two Godspeed as you return home, and we thank you again and again for leading everyone outside through that cave and covered-over doorway. Without your help, I'm not sure how we would've gotten them out of the basement."

"And what a nightmare *that* would've been, even though we were perfectly safe in the shelter room," Irene put in with a nod. "I'll say my *gut*bye, as well. Have a safe trip home, ladies. God bless you both."

Karen felt special, being blessed and thanked by two of the women she and Andi had deceived when they'd arrived for their visit. "You ladies have all been so gracious and welcoming," she said.

"We've had such a fine time," Andi agreed. "Please give our best to Beulah and Ruby, too. We probably gained five pounds while we were here, but it was worth every delicious bite!"

Rosetta and Irene chuckled before sliding out of the truck and closing their doors. Karen's heart was pounding as she and Andi also stepped down onto the lawn in front of the lodge. She was glad Truman was going inside with them—and as she climbed the steps to the porch and followed him into the lobby, she made a point of not looking around too much.

"We'll be quick about gathering up our stuff," she said. "It's awfully nice of you to let us do that—"

"We know you've got a lot on your mind, and a lot of reconstruction ahead of you," Andi added as they started toward the double stairway that curved around both sides of the lobby.

"Happy to help," Truman replied. "I'd be pretty upset if I had to leave my clothes and my cell phone—and my shopping bags—behind. Let's take the stairs on the left and turn left toward the Kuhns' apartments, staying close to the railing as we go. Their end of the building isn't damaged as badly as the other side."

Nodding, Karen followed him up the stairs. It had been such a treat to revisit the lodge where she'd spent so many happy summers in her youth—even if their plan to pretend to be Amish had backfired. The big chandelier made of antlers was still intact in the lobby, as was the glossy wooden railing that went around the open upstairs hallway. Once they reached the top of the stairway, however, she couldn't miss the skewed, cracked front wall of Sylvia's apartment and the way its door hung open at an odd angle.

Down the hall to their right, the door to Irene's apartment also hung ajar, nearly broken from its hinges. Daylight and large leafy tree branches came through the crushed walls, and the wind had broken her windows. Large shards of glass glistened on the overturned furniture and the rugs.

"What a mess," Andi murmured as she quickly followed Karen and Truman to their rooms. "I'm so sorry your *mamm*'s home has been destroyed."

Truman stopped between the doorways of their two rooms, shaking his head sadly. "Now you know why I didn't want her to come up here. She'll see the place soon enough—and we'll have to take comfort in whatever we might be able to reclaim if we go in with a cherry picker."

Nodding, Karen entered her room and quickly folded her clothing into her thrift-store suitcase. Being on this upper floor so close to the damage gave her the willies—and she gasped when her cell phone began to ring on her night table.

"Hello?" she breathed, glancing at the caller ID. "Is that you, Mike?"

"Yup, I'm five minutes away," her brother said. "Just making sure you're about ready."

"Oh, you have no idea. The tornado that passed through last night has left everything in a mess," Karen said sadly. "We'll see you soon. Bye."

After she snapped the old suitcase shut, she went out into the hall. Andi wasn't far behind her. Truman led them back the way they'd come in, and as they descended the wonderful old staircase, Karen felt a pang of sadness.

"Sure hope you folks can put this lodge back together again," she remarked as they stepped outside onto the big porch. "If you have to rebuild the whole place because the structure's been compromised, it just won't be the same."

"You're right about that—but it's about more than appearances, isn't it? It's all in God's hands, and He'll help us make the right decisions." Truman smiled at them, glancing up when they heard the rumble of an approaching car. "Again, we can't thank you enough for helping my mother and our friends last night. Let's get those shopping bags, shall we?"

Waving at her brother, Karen hurried inside again, grateful that the Kuhns had allowed them to store their purchases on the front side of the building. She and Andi grabbed the handles of several plastic bags apiece before heading out to the car, where Mike waited beside the open hatchback.

Karen's brother let out a laugh. "Did you leave anything in the store for the other customers?" he teased as he helped them arrange the bags.

"Let's call it retail therapy," Karen replied. "When we tell you about everything that's happened in the past twenty-four hours, you'll understand why we need all the fun stuff we bought."

Truman helped load the suitcases into the car. As Karen hopped into the back seat beside Andi, a surge of nostalgia and relief washed over her. She waved to the man standing on the front lawn, and then focused on the road as Mike turned the car around to drive away.

It was sad to think that they would probably never return to Promise Lodge. But the residents—their newfound friends—were right: God had seen them through a horrifying storm, and whatever happened next was in His hands.

Chapter 12

As Sylvia stood at a safe distance from the backside of the lodge, she tried not to cry. All during a sleepless night she'd reminded herself how blessed they were that everyone had gotten out of the lodge safely after weathering the storm in a secure place. It was still very difficult, however, to look at the two massive maple trees that had destroyed the back apartments. She felt so tired and dragged out, she wanted to sleep and sleep, yet she was too keyed up to rest.

Beside Sylvia, Beulah shook her head sadly. "I've been thanking the *gut* Lord for sparing us all," she murmured, "but I'm not sure I can look at the wreckage of my apartment and our little cheese factory much longer. That tornado took the starch right out of me."

"It's the end of an era," Ruby chimed in with a sigh. "And it's not just my cozy little rooms I'll miss. It's that kitchen where we've cooked so many wedding meals and Saturday night suppers and—"

"Pizza," Sylvia put in softly. "That pizza you made last night was simply divine."

"Our last supper, so to speak," Beulah said with a hitch in her voice.

Mose, who stood head and shoulders above the other

men congregating near the mudroom door, gave Sylvia something much more uplifting to look at than her crushed apartment wall. As he conferred with Lester, Preachers Amos and Eli, Bishop Monroe, and Truman, his haggard face showed signs that he, too, had lost sleep. It gave her a spark of hope, however, that he was nodding as he talked—as the men focused forward on the day's work rather than dwelling on the previous evening's destruction.

Bishop Monroe gave his companions a final nod before he turned to address the women, who waited several yards away.

"Here's how we'll proceed—and here's how you ladies can help us," he announced with a patient smile. "First, it's *gut* news that the power is back on, so the food in the refrigerators and freezers should be fine. We've turned off the gas to avoid any explosions, of course."

"That's a blessing. No wasted food," Rosetta murmured as she grasped Beulah's hand.

"Our first order of business will be to remove these two fallen trees, so you'll hear a lot of chain saws whining today," the bishop continued. "Truman, bless him, will be coming over with his crew and some heavy equipment later this morning to move those two huge trees. We'd really appreciate it if you ladies could rustle up meals for us—and for Preacher Marlin and the other folks who're hunting Christine's last few dairy cows and fixing her pasture fences."

"Count on us, Bishop!" Ruby piped up. "And *denki* for the *gut* news about the food in the lodge's freezers and refrigerators. We'll put it to *gut* use once you tell us we can fetch it."

"*Jah*, I'll be a lot better off when I'm cooking in somebody's kitchen," Beulah admitted. "Where shall we work today, ladies? The sooner I get away from this depressing mess, the better off I'll be."

"Let's go to my place," Frances Kurtz volunteered. "We'll all get our turn to provide food, considering how long it'll take us to rebuild the lodge, Christine's barn, the Kuhns' cheese factory, and the Promise Lodge Pies bakery—not to mention Mattie's produce stand."

"*Jah*, plenty of work to keep us all out of trouble for a while," Preacher Amos agreed amiably. "Meanwhile, our motto has to be *safety first*. I know you ladies are itching to see if you can salvage any of your personal belongings—or the kitchen equipment. But please be patient! We have a lot of structural damage to inspect before we can let *anyone* inside these damaged buildings."

Ruby smiled as the women started up the hill to Preacher Marlin's place. "He's making it sound as if we might try to sneak inside on our own," she murmured to Sylvia. "Surely we're in no hurry to have our own clothes and underthings to wear!" she added ironically.

In a surprising burst of merriment, Sylvia laughed out loud. "That's the way it is when you escape with only the clothes on your back. Any dresses my friends loan me will drag on the ground—"

"And probably wrap around you twice," Beulah observed. "Here again, we're thankful we're not in the hospital—or headed to the funeral home. If that tornado had ripped through Promise Lodge while we were in bed, we'd be singing a much sadder tune today. Or playing our harps up in heaven."

As the conversations around her continued, Sylvia allowed herself to drift along on their rhythms. It was a pleasure to enter the home Frances shared with her second husband, Preacher Marlin, and his two younger children, Fannie and Lowell. The boy was with his *dat*, helping round up Christine's Holsteins, but Fannie had stayed home to start casseroles and other food for the noon meal. Sylvia inhaled the yeasty aroma of rising bread dough mixed with the salty smell of the ham slices that were sizzling in the skillet. Frances offered everyone coffee and suggested various ways the ladies could help.

"We've got dough about ready to shape into rolls," she said, "and that ham can be chopped for the mac-and-cheese casserole as well as a big green bean casserole."

"I couldn't sleep, so I baked a couple pans of bars and brownies," Mattie put in. "They should be cool enough to cut now, so I'll go get them."

"How about if I fetch a few jars of canned peaches from my shelves?" Annabelle Beachey asked. She and her husband, Phineas, were among the newer members of the Promise Lodge community; they'd bought Lester Lehman's home next door to Frances.

"Oh, canned peaches are my favorite!" Ruby exclaimed. Then her face fell. "I was about to suggest that we stir in a bag of frozen dark cherries and a jar of sliced pears, but I guess I won't be getting those from the lodge . . . although, if we came *out* through that cave exit last night, why couldn't I go back inside that way and—"

"Preacher Amos just told us *not* to do that very thing, sister!" Beulah teased, shaking her finger. "But the way around that is to sweet-talk some of the men into fetching what we want from the basement. And why couldn't they go in through the front door and bring some of our tables and chairs outside, for serving lunch? After all, Truman took Karen and Andi upstairs, and nothing dangerous happened to them."

Beulah's suggestions inspired a volley of chatter as the women began stirring up casseroles. Sylvia took a seat at the end of the kitchen table to roll the soft, fragrant dough into

balls. It was a job that didn't require much concentration—
or conversation—and that suited her fine. She was forming
the second row of dough balls in the metal pan when young
Fannie sat down beside her.

"Sylvia, I'm really sorry that big tree crashed into your
apartment," she said softly. Her slender fingers pinched and
rolled the dough with an agility Sylvia envied. "It must be
horrible, not knowing when you'll be able to check on your
furniture and the favorite things you brought here."

Sylvia blinked. Fannie was a coltish, slender adolescent
who resembled her handsome dark-haired *dat*—and who'd
lost her mother a few years ago, before they'd moved to
Promise Lodge. Her soft brown eyes were filled with compassion, and her sentiments touched Sylvia deeply.

"Truth be told," Sylvia admitted, "I arrived at Promise
Lodge with only a suitcase. My apartment was already furnished, and I didn't figure I'd be staying long, so—"

"But what about clothes?" Fannie assessed Sylvia, her
expression thoughtful. "You're close to my size, I think, but
shorter. When we've finished making these rolls, let's check
the trunk upstairs. I've had a growth spurt, so my previous
dresses come nearly to my knees—and I'd only worn them
a few months!"

Sylvia's eyes widened. When she'd come to the Kurtz
home to cook, she'd never expected such a timely solution
to the problem she and the Kuhns had been discussing.

"That's very kind of you, Fannie," she murmured. "As
you can see, growth spurts weren't something I experienced
very often. I recall being about this same height when I was
in fourth or fifth grade."

Fannie's face lit up with her smile. "My stashed-away
dresses might as well be doing you some *gut*, ain't so? If
they can save you the effort of making all new ones—or

get you by until you see if your own clothes survived the storm—I'd be pleased for you to have them."

About ten minutes later, after they'd left the rolls to rise beneath a towel, Sylvia followed her teenaged benefactor up the stairs. In her room, Fannie lifted the lid of a wooden chest and took out a stack of folded dresses. As the pungent aroma of cedar wafted around her, Sylvia told herself not to express her knee-jerk objections: of *course* a young girl would have more colorful dresses than she'd worn since she'd lost her husband. Her thoughts spun into a whirlwind.

What if I'm not ready to wear anything other than black? What if folks think I'm forgetting Ivan or disrespecting his memory? What if I put one of these pretty dresses on, and everyone thinks I'm trying to attract a man? What if—

When Fannie shook out a dress and cape the color of gingerbread, Sylvia quickly composed her facial expression. The teenager turning toward her would have no idea how much inner turmoil she'd just stirred up with her thoughtful—and practical—gift.

"Oh, look at the way this color brings out your pretty eyes," the girl said as she held the dress in front of Sylvia. "It was one of my favorites, and I was sorry I outgrew it so quickly."

Pretty eyes. How long had it been since anyone commented on her hazel eyes?

Will Mose think this color looks nice on me? Will he notice my eyes, too?

Where had *that* thought come from? Sylvia quickly shifted her focus, hoping her words sounded coherent—and grateful. "It doesn't look too awfully long for me, either," she remarked, fingering the knit fabric. "And if it is, putting in a hem will give me something to do while I'm bunking at the Troyers' place."

"You can try it on in the bathroom if you want. If this one fits you, they all will."

Sylvia shook her head. She didn't want to take time away from helping the other women fix lunch—or to change clothes while Fannie waited to see how the dress looked on her.

"How about if I take two or three, and I'll try them on tonight when I'm getting ready for bed?" she suggested. "You're very generous and thoughtful, Fannie. *Denki* for thinking of me."

Fannie quickly picked out another dress of mauve and one the color of grass before adding two ivory aprons to the stack. "You're welcome, Sylvia. Maybe these colors will make you feel so much better, you won't remember that you're at Promise Lodge because you're ill. When I'm feeling slow—or low—wearing a bright color perks me right up!"

After they put the remaining dresses back in the cedar chest, Fannie found a bag for Sylvia's new wardrobe. As she anticipated, the women in the kitchen thought Fannie's dresses would be just right for her—and no one remarked that the colors were inappropriate, either.

On the way down the hill to set tables for lunch at the lodge, Sylvia took the dresses to her room at Preacher Amos's house. After he and Mattie went to bed, she'd try them on—she did *not* want anyone else to see her in them until she'd gotten used to the idea of wearing bright colors again. It would be another adjustment altogether to show up for church the next morning in such flashy attire rather than a black dress.

Flashy? Beulah and Ruby will think those dresses are drab, compared to the wild, flowery designs they usually wear!

Chapter 13

Mose watched in awe as Truman maneuvered a dozer blade behind one of the big maple trees and rolled it away from the lodge. It was an effortless mechanical move that would've taken several men—with draft horses—a long time to perform safely. Not long after that, the second tree hit the ground with a resounding *thud* that sent vibrations up Mose's legs. Along with the tree, dozens of branches, broken boards, shingles, and some window glass showered the area around the lodge's foundation.

"All right, Mose," Bishop Monroe called from beside two of his harnessed Clydesdales. "Let's hook up this first tree and let these big boys haul it out of the way."

Mose moved quickly, slipping a log chain around the maple tree that had landed on Sylvia's apartment. As he worked, he once again gave thanks that the tiny woman hadn't been asleep in her bed when the tornado had blown through.

"Heave ho!" he said loudly.

As the bishop urged his horses forward, the tree followed them, leaving a deep trail through the debris behind the lodge. About fifteen minutes later, Mose wrapped the heavy chain around the second tree, which had landed on

Irene's place, so the huge horses could pull it off in the opposite direction. He felt a surge of pride and adrenaline as he watched the Clydesdales work. Soon some of the men would cut the two trees into more manageable sections with their chain saws, well away from the half-destroyed building.

A pang went through Mose as he gazed into the three exposed apartments with their contents in such disarray. Dirt and debris covered everything, and he wondered if the residents would reclaim any of their belongings. At ground level, the mudroom was all but demolished. It would take several days to clear away enough of the clutter to determine how many of the large kitchen appliances they could salvage.

"It's a depressing picture, ain't so?" Preacher Amos remarked as he stopped alongside Mose. "When the ladies come back down here with our supper, I expect we'll see more tears."

"*Jah*, they're sure to be upset—even more than when they first saw the damage in the daylight," Bishop Monroe said with a sigh. "After we finish working today, we should spread tarps over this whole backside to protect everything from the rain and the wind."

"I'll go to Dale's store and see if he has enough in stock to get us through," Mose offered. "This job's going a lot faster than I expected, thanks to Truman's equipment. Once we whiz off the smaller tree branches and section the tree trunks with our chain saws, he'll haul them off for us."

"We owe him yet another debt of gratitude," Amos said with a nod. "We'd still be clearing away dead trees and underbrush—and we'd have been digging our house foundations by hand—if Truman and his crew hadn't helped us when we first bought this property."

Mose sauntered across the lawn behind the line of

cabins, which had sustained considerable storm damage they hadn't seen clearly until this morning. He and his neighbors faced a daunting task, restoring property and buildings—most of which belonged to the three sisters who'd founded Promise Lodge. Mattie had merely lost her roadside produce stand, but Rosetta's lodge and cabins and Christine's dairy barn would take a lot longer to repair or replace.

It would be a long while before he could get the images of dead or maimed Holsteins out of his mind, too—not to mention the sound of their pitiful bawling. Very early that morning he'd gone to Christine's barn with the folks who were going to hunt the missing cows, to check the condition of the herd they'd already rounded up. He'd done the merciful thing by euthanizing the badly injured cows, but it had still upset him. Christine had lost about half her herd, and the cows that were left were probably so traumatized that they wouldn't produce much milk for a while.

It lifted Mose's spirits to step inside the bulk store, where English and Plain folks were doing their Saturday morning shopping as though nothing disastrous had happened in the night. He looked for Dale and found him assisting a woman in the frozen-food section.

As he moseyed down the aisles toward the lawn and garden department in the back, he noticed a large display of colorful silk flowers in the craft section. When he passed alongside the bins bursting with spring blooms and colors, something caught his eye.

It was such a simple thing, and rather small: a white basket that held a handful of bright pink roses.

Mose immediately thought of Sylvia. Would she enjoy having a cheerful silk flower arrangement in her room at the Troyer place? Or would she prefer fresh flowers?

*Or would she get the wrong idea altogether and think
I'm getting serious about her?*

He picked up the basket and then put it back, caught in
a quandary. Although Amish women sometimes made floral
wreaths to sell, it would be unusual to give someone a silk
bouquet. With a sigh, Mose continued toward the area where
the tarps would be. What was so complicated about giving
Sylvia a gift to cheer her up after she'd lost her belongings?
Why was he suddenly overthinking everything when it
came to his feelings for her?

"Hey there, Mose! How's it going at the lodge?" Dale said
as he came up beside him. "If you're buying items to help
with the cleanup, why don't I start a tab? I'm sure Rosetta
won't expect you to pay for the things you'll need—and
indeed, Monroe might suggest that such items could be
covered by the congregation's emergency fund."

Mose nodded. "*Gut* point. Right now, I'll need several
sturdy tarps and bungee cords so we can cover the backside of the lodge," he said. "Truman has dozed away the
two trees, and I suspect they'll have them cut up and hauled
away by the end of the day."

"I've got just the thing," the storekeeper said, motioning
for Mose to follow him. "You have a lot of area to cover, so
I'll get you some unopened cases of tarps and bungees. You
can return whatever you don't use, of course."

"You won't have to restock your shelves that way, either."
Mose glanced at the display of silk flowers they were passing and found himself making a quick detour. As he followed Dale through the swinging warehouse doors, he
considered how he'd explain his personal purchase.

Dale, however, had it all figured out.

"A little something for Sylvia?" he asked kindly as they
passed stout wooden shelves loaded with boxes and crates.

"She'll love that, Mose. A cheerful little reminder that you're thinking about her as she deals with the loss of her apartment. It'll be a while before she and Irene and the Kuhns can live in the lodge again—and who knows what will stay the same and what will have to be totally rebuilt?"

"Don't put this basket on the tab for the lodge supplies." Mose reached into his pocket for his wallet, but Dale held up his hand.

"It's a gift, friend. I'm pleased you've found somebody to care about—somebody who obviously feels better when she's in your presence, too."

The storekeeper flashed Mose a smile before he pulled a large box from a nearby shelf. "It did my heart *gut* to watch her crawl into your lap when we were hunkered down in the basement. Sylvia hasn't said much about her late husband—or about her family or anything else in her past—but it's clear she's getting ready to bloom again, just like these pretty pink roses."

Blinking, Mose couldn't think of a thing to say. Were his feelings for Sylvia so obvious to other folks even though he wasn't at all sure about their relationship?

Dale put the little basket in a shopping bag for him. The storekeeper then started a record of supplies for the lodge and loaded the two large boxes of tarps and bungee cords into a low wagon that Mose could pull to the work site.

"Give everyone my best," Dale said as he held the back warehouse door open. "If you're still working after I close the store this evening, I'll be there to help."

"Could be you'll arrive in time to share our picnic supper," Mose teased. "After we carried some tables and chairs from the dining room onto the lawn, Bishop Monroe insisted that nobody else should spend any time inside the building until they've determined how sturdy the beams and interior walls are."

"That's wise. We don't want anyone getting hurt because their curiosity got the best of them."

Mose nodded. "Truman's going to bring in a cherry picker so we can go inside the upstairs apartments without having to walk on the floors. They're also taking the apartment residents up so they can bring out whatever belongings they can save."

Mose chuckled, even if the subject wasn't terribly humorous. "Apparently the ladies are eager to get their underthings and clothing out. Can't imagine why they'd feel that way, can you?"

The storekeeper laughed, waving him off. "Careful there, Mose," he teased. "Thinking about women's underwear can get you in big trouble. But seriously—I hope the work at the lodge goes well," Dale added. "The sooner you men know how much is damaged, the sooner you can plan your rebuilding."

As Mose started back to the lodge, pulling the wagon behind him, he wasn't sure what to think. Did Dale believe he had women's underthings on his mind—Sylvia's in particular? Until the moment he'd mentioned *unmentionables*, Mose hadn't given a thought to anything Sylvia wore, except that everything was black. Images of what might be underneath her dark widow's dresses fluttered through his mind—

And that's a subject best left alone! When I saw Mamm's and Marlene's underwear hanging on the clothesline back home, I didn't give two hoots about what it looked like on their bodies. It's not as though I ever plan to see Sylvia undressed.

By the time he'd reached the grassy space behind the cabins, however, his curiosity was unfurling like wisps of smoke from a forbidden fire.

To keep the other men from asking questions, Mose

slipped his shopping bag into the farthest cabin from the lodge. He could already picture Sylvia's delighted smile when he gave her the simple bouquet. And who knew where his gift might lead?

The constant whine of chain saws and the time-consuming task of helping Amos, Eli, and Marlin secure the tarps across the lodge's gaping backside kept Mose focused on safer topics. Lord forbid that the three preachers should guess he'd been speculating about Sylvia's underwear.

Chapter 14

As Dale strode behind the row of ten cabins that evening, carefully carrying his tray of sliced sausage and cheese, he slowed down. The cabins looked the worse for wear after the tornado's winds had buffeted them. Some of them appeared to need only a few new shingles, but the windows had been blown out of most of them—and a few had a definite *lean* to them, as though it wouldn't take much to knock them over.

As he approached the lodge, he shook his head sadly at the patchwork of tarps covering the open, gaping wound that disfigured the magnificent old building. Sawdust and twigs littered the ground where the men had cut up the two maple trees—another loss that couldn't be replaced anytime soon. He fully expected his friends would be gathering for this evening's meal with glum expressions and heavy hearts. He was thankful that Irene had gone back to her longtime home to stay with Truman and Rosetta. He couldn't imagine the sadness the Kuhns and Sylvia were also suffering after losing their cozy apartments as well as the kitchen they loved so much.

And yet, as he rounded the corner of the building, the familiar voices sounded pleased and positive. Several tables and chairs had been set up on the side lawn, and it required two long tables set end to end to hold all the casseroles, bowls, and trays of food the women had prepared. Everyone from Promise Lodge had shown up to share this meal and lend their emotional support to the folks who'd lost their homes and businesses.

"Dale! *Gut* to see you!" Preacher Marlin called out.

"Just in time for supper!" Bishop Monroe chimed in as he waved Dale over to join the crowd. "It wouldn't be the same without you here, Kraybill—and you brought food!"

Dale chuckled, deeply pleased to feel so welcomed, as though he belonged here among these people. "As you can see, I slaved over a hot stove all day to make this tray of sausage and cheeses. And it took a real effort to open a couple jars of olives."

Irene came up to relieve him of his tray, smiling brightly. "Who doesn't love finger food? We're glad you could be here, Dale. You survived the storm with us, and helped get us out of the basement," she added. "And having your store nearby saved us the trip into Forest Grove to get those tarps and supplies so we could protect what's left of our apartments."

As she held his gaze for a few extra seconds, Dale dared to hope that Irene was pleased to see him for her own personal reasons, as well. When she carried his tray to the serving table, he suspected she was wearing one of Rosetta's dresses because it was somewhat shorter than her own—and it revealed several more inches of her shapely legs.

"Folks, let's take our seats to pray before we fill our plates with all this fine food," Bishop Monroe said over the crowd's chatter.

Dale hung back for a moment as families and friends found places to sit. He waved to Lester and Marlene, who'd just returned from their traditional visit to relatives' homes to collect wedding gifts. He noticed an empty spot beside

Mose—and he saw that Sylvia was seated at a different table, near the Kuhns—but Irene saved him from his habit of sitting with his bachelor buddy.

"Let's take these seats," she suggested as she slipped her hand into his. "They're closer to the serving table, in case I need to get up and help."

Dale didn't argue. Any reason Irene devised for sitting with him suited him just fine. By the time the two of them were wedged between Preacher Eli's family and the red-headed Helmuth twins with their wives and babies, a respectful hush had settled over the crowd.

"Shall we bow our heads?" the bishop asked.

Dale closed his eyes, aware of the sense of great peace that had enveloped the crowd. No matter what Monroe Burkholder would say, nothing compared to the power of group prayer, where every soul present focused on a single purpose: honoring God.

"Most holy Father God, we gather here for this meal with hearts filled with gratitude to You for sparing every one of our lives," Bishop Monroe intoned reverently. "We ask Your continued presence with us as we discern Your will and move forward with repairs to our property. We thank You for the skills and materials You've provided us to undertake the work that lies ahead. Each time we come to the table together, Lord, we're aware of Your bountiful providence and the love You've shown us. Bless this food and the hands that prepared it, that we may have the strength and energy to serve You and our friends in the coming weeks. Amen."

Before anyone could stand up or speak, a distant ringing drifted toward them.

"That's the phone in the lodge kitchen," Irene murmured as it rang again.

"What if somebody's calling to order some cheese?" Beulah asked at the next table.

"Could be it's our brother, trying to find out if we're all right after that storm passed through," Ruby speculated aloud.

As the ringing continued, folks glanced at each other, uncertain what to do.

"We'll just let it ring," Bishop Monroe stated—probably to quell any thoughts about slipping inside to settle the questions that were buzzing like Ruby's bees.

"Sylvia, maybe you and the Kuhns should call your kinfolk, in case they're wondering about you," Mattie suggested. "Feel free to use our phone shack—"

Dale glanced over in time to see Sylvia shake her head. "Nobody to call, *denki*," she remarked quietly.

"*Jah*, we should probably give Delbert a ring," Beulah said with a nod. "For all we know, *his* house might've been damaged by the storm."

"Guess we've been so busy, I hadn't even thought about that." Ruby stood up with the rest of the folks around her to go to the serving table. "But it'll have to wait until after our supper. I'm bone-tired and I need to eat something."

When the phone finally stopped ringing, the folks around Dale relaxed.

"We had a message on our phone late this morning from Coldstream," Christine remarked above the rising chatter. "I called back and told that neighbor we were all doing fine. When I mentioned the tornado hitting us, he promised he'd get up a work crew to help us with the rebuilding, whenever we're ready for them."

"It's yet another blessing, having friends and family who will travel three hours to come when we need them. But we're not quite ready for their help," Preacher Amos said as he, too, got into the line that was forming near the serving tables. "As we were spreading those tarps today, we decided that our lodge residents can go up in Truman's cherry picker first thing Monday morning to see what they can save from their apartments. After that, we men can move all the ruined furniture and broken glass out of the way so the carpenters can get started."

As Dale stood up to pull Irene's chair back from the table, she was frowning. "Is there any reason volunteers can't come early next week to rebuild Christine's barn and Mattie's produce stand, as well as the cheese factory and our little bakery?" she asked. "Those workers wouldn't interfere with our crew at the lodge, after all."

"*Gut* idea!" Dale put in with a nod. "I had some mighty disappointed customers this morning because they couldn't buy fresh pies, and my supply of the Kuhns' cheese won't last much longer. I think we owe it to our business owners to get them up and running again, don't you?"

As soon as the words left his mouth, Dale realized he'd overstepped. He wasn't on the reconstruction crew, after all—and he wasn't even a resident of Promise Lodge. The immediate responses around him eased his concerns, however.

"*Jah*, that's the ticket! Christine's cows need a permanent place to live!" Amos's daughter, Bernice Helmuth, cried out.

"After all the Kuhns have done for us, let's repay the favor sooner rather than later!" newlywed Marlene joined in.

"What *gut* are Mattie's nice vegetables if they're still in her plots? Won't take a *gut* crew but a few hours to build her a new roadside stand!" Frances Kurtz pointed out.

Preacher Amos's expression was priceless as his mouth dropped open. Then a smile eased over his face. "Once again, our women have spoken—and they make a *gut* point," he remarked with a chuckle. "If helpers are willing to come as soon as Monday, I see no reason to wait."

Bishop Monroe was also chuckling as he slipped his arm around Christine's shoulders. "We meant no disrespect, ladies," he said in his strong, resonant voice. "We men were focused on our own plan of action today at the lodge, but we should've included you in our decision-making. Will you forgive us—especially if I call that fellow from Coldstream back, and urge him to bring helpers as soon as possible?"

As laughter rippled through the crowd, Irene slipped her hand under Dale's elbow and squeezed it. "We all appreciate the way you support us, Dale," she said as she gazed at him. "You're a fine man."

For a few moments, the crowd around him disappeared and it felt as though he and Irene shared their own private bubble.

We all appreciate the way you support us . . . you're a fine man.

Did he dare believe that Irene's feelings toward him—and a second marriage—were shifting in his favor? "I—I'd be happy to support you, Irene," he murmured. "Maybe we can talk about that sometime, *jah*?"

When her eyes widened, Dale feared he'd said too much too soon. Sure, she'd warmed up to him last night while they were sharing pizza—but that was a far cry from committing to a marriage for the rest of their lives.

Irene stepped ahead of him to pick up her plate. She moved slowly behind the folks ahead of her, spooning up macaroni casserole and other hot entrées. When she reached the tray he'd brought, she snatched up a slice of the summer sausage and took a bite of it.

"Maybe we can," she replied.

Or at least Dale *thought* that's what she'd said. Her

mouth was full and her voice was so low, he wasn't sure he'd heard her correctly—and he wouldn't ask her to repeat what she'd said. He followed her along the serving table and returned to their seats, totally unaware of how *so much food* had ended up on his plate.

Dale didn't know whether to feel ecstatic or terrified. Was he pursuing the right path? Had he thought about what it would *mean* to marry Irene—a woman who, until recently, had been accustomed to living in a large house, and who was running a very successful business?

Dale didn't know much about Irene's first husband, either, and he was suddenly worried that he wouldn't measure up. Folks who'd been widowed tended to elevate their deceased mates to a pedestal of sainthood, didn't they? Why did he think Irene would let go of her pleasant memories—not to mention the independent lifestyle to which she'd become accustomed—to hitch up with *him*?

When Rosetta went back for seconds, Sylvia rose from her chair, as well—except she put her plate and utensils in the plastic bin full of soapy water on the clean-up table. She slipped away, hoping not to attract attention.

"Are you all right, Sylvia? It's been a tough and tiring day."

Turning, Sylvia put a smile on her face. "It has," she replied to Rosetta. "I just need to use the bathroom."

It wasn't a complete lie. But Sylvia's main concern, as the sun was setting on the horizon, was which dress she would wear to church in the morning. She needed to slip into her room at the Troyer place and try on the three colorful dresses Fannie had given her, because if she couldn't face herself in the mirror, she'd have to launder her black dress and underthings—which she'd worn for two days—

and pray everything would be dry in time to go downstairs for Sunday breakfast.

As she hurried up the main road, she prayed she could make up her mind—and wash her dress, if necessary—now, before Mattie and Preacher Amos returned home, rather than waiting until later. They were wonderful, compassionate hosts, but she hated to impose or ask for their help with this wardrobe matter.

It would be wasteful to run a load of laundry for only one set of clothes, so she'd have to wash them out in the bathtub. She didn't have a bathrobe, so how could she do that unless she wore one of Fannie's dresses while she worked? She didn't want to tie up the bathroom—especially after Amos returned to the house. And she hated to cause a fuss by borrowing something of Mattie's.

Mattie would understand. Even if her clothes are too large, she'd let me borrow whatever I need. And God won't care what I'm wearing to church—

But even if one of Fannie's dresses will work, I need to rinse out my underwear. I can't stand to wear it a third day in a row. And I can't launder any of these things tomorrow, on the Sabbath.

With her thoughts circling frantically, Sylvia stepped onto the Troyers' porch and entered their single-story home. By Amish standards, it was smaller than most places because widowed Preacher Amos had built it before he'd married Mattie—figuring he'd have no more children to raise. Sylvia was staying in the guest bedroom off the back of the house, which was small but almost as cozy as her lodge apartment.

Almost. Sylvia tried not to think about her wrecked apartment, because it upset her.

She entered her room and shut the door. Spreading Fannie's three dresses on the bed, she shook her head again over the array of bright colors. In the fading daylight, the dress that reminded her of cinnamon or gingerbread seemed the most conservative.

In the bathroom, Sylvia stepped out of her black dress and removed her underthings, as well. She ran hot water in the bathroom sink, added some liquid hand soap, and put her skivvies in to soak. The sooner she hung them up beside her open window, the better chance she'd have of wearing dry underwear to church tomorrow.

Gathering her nerve, Sylvia dashed back to the guest room to put on the cinnamon-colored dress and matching cape. It felt odd to have the polyester fabric against her bare skin, but the hemline fell to the middle of her calf—right where it was supposed to. With a couple of pins, she adjusted the fit, and tying an apron around her waist made it feel very much the same size as the dresses she'd sewn for herself.

But how did it look?

When she turned to face the small dresser mirror, Sylvia's mouth dropped open. It was like seeing a version of herself from twenty years ago—so unsettling that she was ready to wash her black dress in the bathtub—

But someone knocked on the back door.

"Sylvia, are you okay? It's me, Mose."

The blood rushed from her head, and she grabbed the dresser to steady herself. Why, this evening of all times, had he followed her to Preacher Amos's place? And how had he known she'd be on this side of the house?

More to the point, how can you possibly open the door without any underwear on?

Stepping over to the wall near the open window, where Mose wouldn't be able to see her, Sylvia inhaled deeply to settle herself. "I—I'm fine, Mose. Just tired after a long day. *Denki* for checking on me."

His pause made her dare to hope he'd be satisfied and leave her be.

"I, um, b-brought you a little s-something, Sylvia," he said from right outside the window. "C-could you c-come out and talk to me?"

He was stammering again, a sign that he was nervous. Sylvia closed her eyes, praying frantically for an answer to her dilemma. She knew, in her mind, that she was decently covered, and that Mose would have no idea about what was missing under the dress, but her long-ingrained modesty cried out against seeing him.

"It's not much," he admitted plaintively. "B-but I s-saw it today and thought it might cheer you up while you c-can't live in your own apartment."

Sylvia's heart swelled painfully. What a sweet man, to realize how bereft and displaced she felt, and to bring her a gift. She also sensed that he'd followed her here to prevent prying eyes from watching him give her something—to protect their privacy and her feelings. And hadn't Mose comforted her during the storm and kept her from caving in to her fears in that dark, claustrophobic basement?

"Um, give me a minute," she murmured. "I'm trying on some clothes Fannie loaned me, and—"

"She's a mighty nice girl, ain't so? Take your time, Sylvia," Mose added. "But then, I have no idea when the picnic might break up and folks will be headed home."

"*Jah*, you're right about that." She let out a long sigh, weighing pros and cons. "Okay, here I come."

Somehow Sylvia fought back her misgivings as she quickly slipped into her shoes. And somehow she went to the back door, gripping the knob to steady her nerves before she opened it.

Please don't let him notice I'm not wearing any underwear—and please, please, Lord, don't let shock or disapproval or disbelief show on his face when he sees me in a teenager's dress.

Mose stood outside gripping a white plastic sack, gazing earnestly at her as though he might bolt if she looked at him the wrong way. The smile that immediately transformed his anxious expression, however, shone as bright as the sun on a perfect May morning.

"Well, look at *you*," he whispered.

It was all he said, but his words embraced her frightened, lonely heart. Sylvia hadn't heard a man's compliment since Ivan had courted her, as her husband hadn't been one to slather on the flattery even though he'd loved her dearly.

Sylvia released the breath she'd been holding. "Do—do you think it'll be all right for church tomorrow? Appropriate?" she asked shyly. "Fannie was nice enough to share, and beggars can't be choosers, but she's a lot younger than—"

"I hope you'll consider wearing it for more than church," Mose replied matter-of-factly. "You've had a long, tough day and yet you look—well, you seem refreshed and renewed, Sylvia. As though you're not sick anymore."

Her eyes widened—but she swallowed the protest that rushed into her mind. Mose was a kind, simple man who had no reason to lie to her. And he wasn't the sort to make such a complimentary remark if he didn't mean it.

"Oh," she murmured. "*Oh*."

"That was out of line and—well, I didn't intend to mention the part about you being sick, or—*here*." Mose opened the plastic sack and brought out a little white basket, thrusting it at her. "I better just keep my mouth shut. I—I hope you like this, Sylvia. It's not much, really—and if you think it's a stupid little—"

"What a sweet bouquet of roses," Sylvia said as she held it up to study the bright pink blooms. "I'll put it on the dresser and think of you every time I see it, Mose. It'll be a real mood lifter."

Her guest focused on the ground in front of him, as though he were a bashful little boy caught in a man's body, unsure of what to do or how to respond.

Sylvia saw beyond his shyness, however. Mose was a man in love.

His tormented expression told her he'd had no experience with courting or expressing his affection, probably because the girls he'd liked had been put off by his stuttering— or he'd assumed they would be, so he hadn't asked them out. And yet here he was, baring his soul to *her*.

What should she do? Whatever she said and did next would change Mose Fisher's life for better or worse. And if Sylvia hinted that she welcomed his affection, there could be no changing her mind later—unless she wanted Mose to feel totally worthless and rejected. Her rejection might even cause him to spend the rest of his life alone.

Sylvia sighed. She knew more than she wanted to about living alone, and she didn't wish that fate on anyone. But, knowing she had only a short time before she died, would it be fair to indulge in a last romance that would leave Mose alone again—probably by summer's end?

Torn, yet deeply touched by the risk he'd taken and the tug-of-war of emotions that played over his handsome face, she stepped outside and slipped her tiny hand inside his larger, trembling one. If it didn't matter to Mose that she was several years older than he, and not long for this earth, maybe she shouldn't let those details stand in her way, either.

"Mose," she murmured. "*Denki* for thinking of me—and for being such a sweet, special man."

His eyes widened. Gripping her hand, Mose searched her face for signs that she was about to say *but* and let the other shoe drop on his hopes and dreams.

"Would tomorrow afternoon, following church and the common meal, be a *gut* time to go for a walk?" Sylvia suggested. Her heart was pounding. She'd never asked a man for his company before, and it felt foreign to her—yet exhilarating. "After last night's storm and all the hubbub about the lodge today, I could use a little quiet time. And there's no one I'd rather spend it with than *you*, Mose."

"Me too, Sylvia!" he blurted out before laughing at himself. "I mean, I want to spend my time with *you*, as well. And we'll start tomorrow! I hope it's all right if we don't dawdle over lunch."

The joy in his deep brown eyes suddenly made Sylvia feel taller—younger and more alive—than she had in years.

I hope we made the right choice, Lord. Come what may, for however long I have left, Mose and I will be together.

Chapter 15

Sunday morning as Mose sat in a chair on the Burk-holders' large lawn, he didn't hear a word of the main sermon Bishop Monroe was preaching. Even though the bishop was speaking in his usual uplifting, positive tone, his encouraging words couldn't dispel the fears swirling in Mose's mind.

Sylvia changed her mind about our walk. Rather than tell me about it head-on, she's stayed home from church to avoid me.

As he searched the women's side of the congregation, trying not to appear obvious about it, he caught himself sighing loudly. Because the church leaders hadn't wanted to risk carrying the wooden pew benches out of the meeting room in the back of the lodge, everyone had brought a chair—which made it more difficult for him to see who was present.

"We should never stop believing in the Lord's love and mercy, friends," Bishop Monroe exhorted as he gazed around the spread-out crowd. "And we should never fail to give Him thanks for His abundant blessings, because we, as a community, are a prime example of His power to save us from a raging storm—"

Mose swallowed hard, feeling the effects of his own inner storm. Why had he ever believed Sylvia would accept his silly little gift? He'd been trying to win her heart—her love—and he'd botched it so badly, it was no wonder she wanted nothing to do with him. He'd been so excited he'd barely slept last night, thinking of all the things he hoped to say during their walk. Now it appeared that he'd wasted his time. His dreams.

"We should also express our gratitude to Him for the friends who're coming tomorrow from Coldstream to start our rebuilding," Bishop Monroe continued, "as well as for the crew from the Mennonite Fellowship in Cloverdale that will be here later in the week. And we ask His presence and blessings upon us tomorrow when Truman takes the lodge residents up in a cherry picker to assess the possessions in their apartments."

Mose was aware that folks around him were nodding, but in his angst, he felt far removed from the present moment.

"It'll be the first step of many to come as we rebuild the homes those ladies have lost—not to mention the kitchen where so many of us have enjoyed their fine meals on special occasions and our wedding days," the bishop said.

Wedding day.

Mose blinked, hoping none of the fellows near him could see how upset he was. In the brief time since he'd visited with Sylvia the previous evening, he'd built them a home and a whole new life in his dreams—but maybe it was only a house made of imagination. Maybe Sylvia had only felt sorry for him yesterday. Maybe she didn't love him at all, but she hadn't known how to break it to him gently.

When the men around him rose from their chairs, he realized that the service had ended. As the women across the lawn also began to move around, Mose looked again, but his fears were confirmed. Sylvia was a no-show.

The last thing he wanted to do was sit through the common meal, even though his stomach had been growling for hours because he'd been too excited to eat breakfast. He didn't want to leave, however, because then folks would know something was seriously wrong: he wasn't the type to miss dinner. As he stood amid the friends who were shifting tables into place, lost in his doubtful thoughts, someone placed a hand on his arm.

"Mose, I'm supposed to tell you that Sylvia has one of her serious headaches this morning, so she's not leaving her room."

He blinked. Mattie's sympathetic smile hinted at her suspicions about why Sylvia wanted him to know that.

"I—*Denki* for letting me know," he exclaimed. "I was wondering why—so is she all right? Will she be coming over to eat, do you think?"

Mattie shrugged. "She looked pretty weak and washed out. After she ate a few bites of a biscuit so she could take her pain medication, she went right back to bed," the preacher's wife replied. She raised one eyebrow slightly. "But it wouldn't hurt if somebody checked on her and took her a plate, ain't so? Maybe some food and friendship would help her recover."

Mose knew he looked like a lovesick puppy that couldn't quit wagging its tail—but he didn't care. "*Gut* idea. I'm on it."

A short while later he was loading a doubled paper plate with all manner of ham slices, sandwiches, and salads. After he stuck some silverware into his shirt pocket, he covered the food with another plate, put several cookies and two slices of pie on a third plate, and carefully balanced it on top of the main meal.

"Eating for two, Mose?" Lester teased good-naturedly.

Mose paused, considering his answer. If Sylvia had

asked Mattie to tell him she was ill, what harm would it do to tell his good friend what he was doing?

"Sylvia's feeling poorly," he explained in a low voice. "Mattie suggested I take her some lunch."

"Ah." A knowing smile eased over Lester's face. "Give her my best. I hope she's feeling stronger by tomorrow so she can go up in the cherry picker."

Nodding, Mose slipped away from the serving line. He felt very obvious, carrying two loaded plates between his hands, but he was too hopeful to care. Who knew? Maybe months from now, he and his friends would recall this day as the beginning of his happy ending with Sylvia.

He walked carefully down the road toward the Troyer place and cut across the grass to reach the back of the house. It took a lot of finesse to set the plates of food on the back stoop without dumping them over. He noticed that the window in Sylvia's room was open about an inch, and he hoped she would be awake—and receptive to his presence.

"Sylvia? It's me—Mose," he said near the window. "I—I brought you some lunch, honey-girl. Do you feel like eating with me?"

Mose held his breath, hoping he would hear her response if she was still in bed. He wished with all his might that Sylvia didn't have a brain tumor—and that she didn't dwell in the shadow of a constant cloud, anticipating her demise.

Not that wishing was an acceptable way to spend his time. He'd spent his younger years wishing his stutter would disappear, too, but to no avail.

When a pale face appeared at the window, Mose stepped back. As his mother would've put it, Sylvia looked like death warmed over.

"Hey there," she murmured weakly. "Sorry I couldn't come to church—"

"It's okay," Mose hastened to reassure her.

"—and it'll take me a few minutes to get dressed," Sylvia continued in a voice he could barely hear. "But I should eat something. You're a saint, Mose. Hang on."

You're a saint, Mose.

After a remark like that, he could hang on for however long it took her. He sat down on the side edge of the concrete stoop and decided Sylvia wouldn't care if he snarfed half a sandwich while he waited. And then another one. It hardly made a dent in all the food he'd brought.

When the back door opened slowly, Mose stood up, wiping his mouth. He was disappointed—but not surprised—that she was wearing her black dress rather than one of Fannie's more colorful ones. "I—hope you don't mind that I sampled a couple of things," he said nervously. "I didn't eat breakfast, so—"

Sylvia focused on the two loaded plates. She chuckled gingerly, as though it hurt to laugh. "A man your size requires a lot more fuel than I do. I'll just sit myself down and—ohh!"

When her knees buckled, Mose caught her in the nick of time. It seemed only natural to sweep her up into his arms and sit down on the stoop with her. Sylvia was trembling like a newborn foal who hadn't gotten her legs under her yet.

Her eyes widened in alarm. "I didn't mean to—you must be thinking I did that on purpose, so you'd have to pull me close and—"

"And what if you did?" Mose teased. "It doesn't seem all that different from when you crawled into my lap during the storm Friday night. And I wasn't complaining then either, was I?"

Sylvia's eyes resembled plates the color of hot, steaming tea. "Maybe before we get any more, um, *involved* you should know that I'm terrified of being in dark rooms that close in on me. It's a fear I can't seem to get over. I got into your lap because it was less traumatic—and embarrassing—than having a panic attack in front of our friends."

Mose decided not to be disappointed. Even if Sylvia hadn't sought his company out of affection, she had still wanted to be close to him, rather than seeking comfort from someone else in that dark, scary basement.

"All right, so maybe you should know that I'm afraid of the dark, too," he admitted in a low voice. "I never go to bed at night without a light burning—and that started when I was five, after I was kidnapped."

Sylvia gazed at him solemnly. "*Jah*, you've mentioned that incident. And I'm sorry it happened to you, Mose."

She looked off into the distance, as though deciding what else to admit about her condition. "For me, it involved being trapped in an elevator. I was at the little funeral home in town, paying for—for Ivan's embalming—when a storm blew up and knocked the power out. It was a creaky old elevator and it stopped between floors as I was leaving the building."

As though she was reliving her ordeal, Sylvia inhaled a ragged breath before she could continue. "By the time the funeral director and the firemen could open the doors to free me an hour later, I'd all but lost my mind—being trapped in that creepy old building on a dark and stormy night. I figured there'd be dead people around, you know. And of course, in my imagination, they were coming to get me."

Mose considered this, frowning. "You went to the funeral home by yourself to pay the bill? No one offered to take you?"

Sylvia shrugged. "My parents had passed, and I was an only child without any children," she explained. "Our little farm was a distance from Ivan's family, so I was taking care of business a couple weeks after we'd buried him. I was doing just fine by myself, too," she insisted in a stronger voice, "but sometimes the nightmares about being held captive in that funeral home still haunt me—especially during storms."

"I can't imagine," he murmured, shuddering at the ideas that must've run rampant through Sylvia's head during that horrible experience. And yet she'd sounded quite comfortable about living on a farm alone, apparently at a distance from friends and family.

"I also can't fathom living without any family close by— even though I'm a grown man who's supported himself for years," Mose remarked after a few moments. "If Marlene hadn't wanted to move to Promise Lodge, I wouldn't have come either, because now that our parents have passed, we only have each other."

Sylvia smiled wanly. "Except that now, Marlene has Lester. So you're the odd man out—even though you and Lester are *gut* friends, both of you having Marlene's welfare as your top priority."

Mose smiled at her insightful remark. "Actually, because Marlene and I are twins, Lester is often the odd man out. But we don't remind him."

When Sylvia's laughter tinkled like tiny wind chimes, Mose was a goner. Childlike and fragile though she might be, she'd corralled him with a sturdy grip on his heartstrings— and she'd found an inside track to his very soul with her story about fearing dark, enclosed spaces. He was ready to say something about their common fear of darkness, until she glanced at the nearby plate of food on the stoop.

When she chose the remaining half sandwich, Mose's gaze was riveted on her lips as she nibbled one corner. He'd seen toddlers take larger bites than Sylvia's—which was yet another reminder of how small and vulnerable she was.

"Does it bother you that I'm so much bigger—that I eat like a horse and move like a bull moose?" he blurted out. "I could crush you without realizing—"

"Does it bother you that I'm so much older?" Sylvia shot back. Her pale brown eyebrows rose like question marks above her expressive hazel eyes. "I'll turn fifty in October, Mose, if—if I live that long."

He shrugged. "Why are you so sure you won't, sweetie?" he whispered. "Folks can latch onto ideas that aren't true—until they become self-fulfilling prophecies. If you believe you'll die soon, you might. But if you believe you're going to lead a long, happy life with me, maybe you'll do that instead. Which plan do you prefer?"

Sylvia sucked in her breath. "But the doctors have told me my brain tumor will—"

"Which plan do you prefer, Sylvia?" Mose repeated emphatically.

His heart was pounding with the audacity of his challenge. He was skating on thin ice, speaking as though he knew more than her doctors—or more than God. But he had to give it a shot. "Seems to me that if you focus on living rather than dying, at least you'll be in a better frame of mind—and you'll feel more fulfilled—when check-out time arrives, *jah*?

"And please don't think I'm making light of your condition," he added quickly. "It's just that, at my age, I don't spend much time thinking about death. So I hate to see *you* bogged down by those thoughts. I'm thirty-five, by the way. Plenty old enough to know a *gut* woman when I've met her."

As Sylvia held his gaze, her sandwich forgotten, a tear trickled down each of her cheeks.

Mose kicked himself for being so insensitive. "I'm sorry

I spoke out of turn about—I had no business insinuating that—"

"No, no," she whispered, gently stroking his face. "You're the first person who's dared me to see my condition from a different angle instead of just accepting that my time is short. You've given me a reason to rethink my situation, Mose. And truth be told," she added softly, "you're giving me a whole new reason to recover, *jah*?"

Mose felt his shoulders relax as relief washed over him.

"It might take me a little time to adjust my attitude completely," Sylvia said in a stronger voice, "but—but I'll be doing us both wrong if I don't try."

He held her close, as he would cradle a precious child— because Sylvia had already become *very* precious to him.

"I have clothing older than you, by the way," she said with a perfectly straight face. "It's in a trunk at my farm. I didn't figure I'd be needing much when I came here—"

"You still own your farm? Where is it—and who's overseeing it while you're away?"

"It's outside of Lititz, Pennsylvania," she replied with a wistful smile. "A neighbor's newlywed son needed a home, so I was pleased to rent the place to him. I figured it would be a source of income to pay my medical bills and my . . . final expenses, so nobody else will be burdened with those." Sylvia met his gaze, as though trying to read his reactions. "I stashed my extra clothes in trunks and left the house furnished for the newlyweds. It worked out well for everyone."

Mose blinked. She'd come a long way—by herself—to live out her days at Promise Lodge. His opinion of Sylvia Keim had always been high, but his esteem for her self-reliance had just climbed a notch or two. When she set aside her sandwich, he was ready to tell her she needed to eat more—except the endearing way she curled up against him made his heart turn handsprings.

Bubbly tingles shot up his spine when she pressed her lips to his face, in the sensitive spot in front of his ear.

Mose's pulse went wild. He held his breath as she kissed him some more, little baby pecks on his cheek as she made her way toward his mouth. Thankfully, he was so agog with wonder that he didn't have a chance to worry about making a wrong move. When Sylvia's lips found his, it was a kiss so sweet, so instinctual, that he got lost in it. For countless moments he surrendered to the sheer pleasure of intimate contact he'd only dreamed of until now.

When Sylvia eased away, her sigh mingled with his. "Oh my. Oh, *Mose*," she murmured. "I've gone and done it now."

"High time. For *years* I've been wanting that kiss, Sylvia, and it was even better than I'd dared to imagine."

He thought he'd died and gone to heaven when Sylvia kissed him again, longer and more insistently. Mose hugged her close, reveling in his newfound exhilaration.

After he held her for a few more blissful moments, he shifted backward so he could sit against the door. Sylvia leaned out and grabbed the plate of food.

"Seems the least I can do is to hold this plate while you eat," she said with a winsome smile. "I've felt your poor empty stomach gurgling the whole time I've been on your lap."

Mose was almost too giddy to think about food, but he pulled the two forks from his shirt pocket. "You've got to eat with me," he said. "My whole point in coming over was to get you on the road to recovery."

"Really? That's *all* you were hoping to do?" Sylvia teased. She took the fork he offered her and obediently scooped up a small bite of slaw.

Laughter bubbled up inside him. Was this part of falling head over heels, that he could joke so easily with her moments after they'd shared a life-altering conversation and their first kiss?

"Well, maybe I *was* hoping for a little more," Mose admitted with a grin. "And I loved what you gave me, Sylvia. A *lot*."

Chapter 16

Irene stood a safe distance from the site of the Promise Lodge Pies bakery, watching in gratitude as a crew from Coldstream started up a large generator. The carpenters had arrived with a trailerload of lumber and tools in time for lunch, and they had already torn down the outer walls and other parts of the structure that had been damaged by the tornado. Not much remained on the foundation, because Phoebe's husband, Allen, had already removed the ovens and the big refrigerator so he could check their wiring and make some repairs. A smaller guest crew was reconstructing Mattie's produce stand out by the road.

Because most of Christine's milking equipment had been shattered in the storm, she and her herd manager, Roman Schwartz, had been milking the surviving cows by hand, in the various neighbors' barns where they were temporarily housed. Christine had agreed that the bakery and her sister's stand should be rebuilt first—and the Kuhns went along with that because they, too, had needed to order new equipment to process their cheeses, which were made from Christine's milk.

When movement up the hill caught her eye, Irene waved

at her baking partner, Phoebe Troyer, as she came down the unpaved road from her home.

"It's a big day!" the young blonde called out above the rumble of the generator.

After thanking the folks who'd come to help, Phoebe stood alongside Irene, out of the workmen's way. "When I heard that customers at the bulk store were disappointed not to find our pies there on Saturday morning, I bought a bunch of flour, frozen fruit, and aluminum pans to bake some at my house. Would you like to come up and make the filling for them? I've gotten so used to being in our bakery four mornings each week, I needed to fill some empty time."

Irene slipped her arm around Phoebe's slender shoulders. "It's different, not baking, that's for sure—just as it's not the same to wake up in a guest room at Truman and Rosetta's place instead of in my apartment," she remarked with a sigh. "But I'll pass on the baking, dear—at least for today. Truman says he'll be taking us lodge ladies up to see what we can save from our apartments, so—"

"And here he comes, pulling a metal basket contraption behind his truck," Phoebe said, waving as the white pickup approached them. "I can see why you'd rather do that than stir pie fillings this afternoon! Just thought I'd ask."

Nodding, Irene watched her son skillfully back the truck so the platform with the cherry picker ended up exactly where he wanted it, near the corner of the lodge. The Kuhns and Sylvia, as well as other curious folks, were making their way toward the badly damaged building. A satisfying pneumatic *whack-whack-whack* behind her announced that the carpenters from Coldstream were already nailing parts of an exterior bakery wall together.

Shading her eyes with her hand, Irene smiled at Truman as he approached. He'd filled out since he'd married Rosetta, and from her brief time living as their guest in the house she'd given them when she'd moved to the lodge, she knew they were delightfully happy together.

"I'm glad you and Phoebe could save your bakery appliances, so it won't be long before Promise Lodge Pies is back in business," Truman said with an encouraging smile.

"It helps that Phoebe's Allen got his electrician's license during his *rumspringa*, before they married," she pointed out. "He'll also be installing a bigger exhaust fan to circulate more air while we're baking. Come summertime, Phoebe and I will be happy to have that."

Nodding, Truman glanced over to where other folks had gathered behind the lodge. "Are you ready to go up into your apartment? I'll ride in the cherry picker with you, to steer it wherever we need to go."

Irene inhaled deeply. Although she desperately wanted to salvage everything possible, she was hesitant to see the tornado's damage to her home. "I get to be first, eh?"

Truman chuckled. "If you'd rather I take one of the Kuhns or Sylvia now, I can—"

"No. Let's get this over with."

He gently squeezed her hand. "It'll all work out, Mamm. We'll drop your clothing and other non-breakable things onto that tarp that's spread on the ground, so we'll have room for other items in the picker cage with us. Here's a pair of my heavy work gloves," he added, handing them to her. "We'll be handling a lot of broken glass."

Irene slipped her hands into the bulky leather gloves that were much too large for her. Many of the lodge windows had been blown out during the storm, which meant the construction crew would have to clear everything from the ladies' apartments so they could work safely.

"*Denki* for helping me do this, Truman," she murmured. "Let's go now, before I lose my nerve."

They walked quickly toward the cherry picker, exchanging greetings with Ruby, Beulah, Sylvia, and the others who'd gathered to see how this process would be carried out. Irene was grateful for the side rails on the basket as she stepped into it. Once Truman got in with her and grasped the steering mechanism, they rose through the air faster than she'd anticipated.

Grasping the rail, she let out a nervous laugh as the basket lurched before stopping on the level of her apartment. As her son unhooked the bungee cords holding the tarps over the gaping hole where the lodge's back wall had been, Irene tried not to let her emotions get the best of her.

Her bed—the one she'd shared with her husband, Ernest, all her married life—and her dresser and rocking chair had been blown into a heap in the corner of her bedroom. Shards of glass sparkled everywhere, and the once-beautiful wood was in splinters.

Bless him, Truman sensed her shock and slowly maneuvered the basket farther into the apartment. "Shall we get an overview and then decide where you want to start?" he suggested gently.

"I—I suppose."

Irene's heart thudded dully. It was all she could do not to cover her eyes and tell Truman to whisk her outside again. The interior walls were partly blown away, so he moved the cherry picker into her front room without any trouble. Her poor little home was lifeless and still, except for the mechanical whir of the basket she was riding.

Her favorite overstuffed chair . . . her end tables and the lamps she and Ernest had bought with wedding money . . . the rugs she'd so lovingly cleaned before arranging them on the apartment's hardwood floors. All ruined. The cedar chest where she'd stored blankets and linens gaped open, because its lid had been partially torn off and left hanging askew. Her *dat* had made it for her when she'd been a young girl, and her *mamm* had helped her fill it with embroidered pillowcases and dresser scarves.

Everything was waterlogged. Every piece of her furniture, every little memento on her whatnot shelf, had been tossed about or thrown against a wall. A heavy, wet smell permeated the air. And again in this room, shattered glass covered everything.

Tears streamed down Irene's cheeks, and she was too stunned to wipe them away.

"Oh my," Truman murmured, slipping his arm around her shaking shoulders. "I expected a mess, but I had no idea it would be so difficult to look at."

For a few moments they stood together in silence, deciding what to do next.

"Do you want to see if you can pick any of your clothes out of the dresser? Would you like to locate any specific items to take out with you?"

Irene curled forward and hugged herself. She was crying so hard she couldn't speak as her son kept his arm around her.

"Let's go," she finally managed. "My poor old underwear was worn thin anyway, and most of my dresses were several years old. It seems like a perfect excuse to sew an entire new wardrobe, ain't so?"

"You've got a point," he said with a wry smile.

"And while there's no way to replace the things your *dat* gave me, I still have my best memories of our life together," Irene added with a loud sniffle.

"You still have several pieces of furniture and other things up at the house, too," Truman pointed out. "Plenty to choose from, come time to set up your new apartment, *jah*?"

Nodding, she wiped her face on the sleeve of her dress. "And I still have you and Rosetta, son," she murmured. "Things feel a little bleak right now, but my life could be a whole lot worse."

After he kissed her temple, they shared a long hug. Truman steered the basket slowly toward the back wall of the building again, as though giving her one last look.

But Irene had seen enough destruction to last her a lifetime.

It was a relief to be outside again in the fresh air. As they slowly descended in the basket, Irene felt her friends' questioning gazes. She and the Kuhns had shared so many good times in the lodge that she couldn't recall ever feeling so devastated or sad. Even Sylvia's reason for being here had bonded her, Ruby, and Beulah with the purpose of helping their newest friend feel welcome and comfortable in her final days.

And yet Irene sensed this disaster was one more thing they would have in common. One more reason to sigh and forge ahead rather than dwell on their temporary misfortune.

"You, um, didn't bring anything out," Ruby said quietly.

Shaking her head, Irene carefully stepped out of the cage onto solid ground. "I suspect that my corner of the building bore the brunt of the tornado," she reasoned aloud, "so maybe you gals will find belongings worth saving. As for me, I see a trip to Dale's store—and maybe the big fabric shop in Forest Grove—in my immediate future. I—I'll probably be such a fashion plate in all my new dresses, you won't recognize me."

Although her attempt at humor fell flat, the Kuhns and Sylvia smiled sympathetically. If nothing else, Irene had prepared them for their own rides in the cherry picker, hadn't she?

Rosetta stepped away from the small crowd that had gathered. Although she appeared exhausted and pale from dealing with the stress of the tornado's damage, her smile was warm as she gazed into Irene's eyes.

"Would you like me to go to Dale's with you right now?" she asked as she grasped Irene's hands. "Maybe it would lift your spirits to look at that new fabric he got in last week, and we can cut out some dresses this evening after supper. Of course, you're welcome to keep wearing my clothes for as long as you need to, Irene."

Irene sighed gratefully, trying to keep a smile on her face. "*Denki* for your offer, dear, but right now I just want to go home and sit on the porch with a glass of iced tea. I have a lot to process. A lot to think about."

Sylvia couldn't help overhearing Irene's conversation with Rosetta—just as she hadn't missed the expression of utter devastation on her friend's face as she'd descended from her apartment in the cherry picker. And Irene had found nothing worth saving.

Nothing.

As Truman glanced her way, Sylvia's thoughts whirled like leaves caught in their own little tornado. Did she really want to put herself through the same emotional torment, only to emerge empty-handed?

She'd noticed that Mose wasn't in the crowd gathered behind the lodge, which meant he was working with Bishop Monroe's Clydesdales this afternoon. When Sylvia realized she'd be facing the destruction of her apartment with Truman—who was nice, but whom she barely knew—her decision became easy.

Sylvia saw that Truman was climbing into his pickup, probably to reposition the platform that supported the cherry picker. "Truman, wait!" she called out as she hurried toward him. "May I have a word?"

Rosetta's handsome husband turned the key, making his truck rumble to life, but he leaned out his window. "Ready for your ride upstairs, Sylvia?" he asked with an encouraging smile.

"I—I see no need for you to take me up there," she replied quickly. "After all, one of the trees fell directly onto my apartment, so I'm guessing the place is all but destroyed. The only things that belong to me are a worn-out old suitcase and a few clothes of the same vintage as the ones your *mamm* is ready to replace, so why should I waste your time? You might as well position the picker platform farther down and take the Kuhn sisters up instead."

Truman held her gaze for a moment. "You're sure? It's really no bother, Sylvia."

"Positive. Matter of fact, I'm going to head on over to Dale's store right now and buy fabric," she said resolutely. "Making a few new dresses seems like a useful way to occupy my time, instead of stewing over the mess I really don't want to see up there."

"Probably a wise choice," he murmured. "It'll take Mamm a while to get over the sight of her ruined furniture. And when Rosetta sees the condition her lodge is in up close, she'll be awfully upset, I guarantee you.

"*Denki* for telling me, Sylvia," he added with a nod. "Enjoy your shopping trip."

To avoid the questions folks were likely to ask, Sylvia headed straight for the road. Walking quickly toward the Troyer place to fetch her purse, she felt filled with a sense of exhilaration. She had the perfect reason to replace her black dresses, didn't she? What if this was a sign from God that He wanted her to move beyond mourning Ivan so she could get the most from whatever time remained for her— time she intended to spend with Mose?

She stopped in the middle of the road, frowning. It hadn't occurred to her that her purse was still in her apartment— as were Irene's and Beulah's and Ruby's. Several days often passed between times when they needed money, so none of them had even considered dashing upstairs Friday night to fetch their pocketbooks before they'd hunkered down in the basement.

Oh, but I hate to think about going inside that wrecked apartment! I'd do just about anything to avoid seeing such devastation because I won't be able to stop seeing it.

Sylvia turned, walking quickly, hoping Truman would understand the big favor she was going to ask of him. She reached the cherry picker as Ruby was bravely stepping into the basket.

"Truman, I still don't want to see my apartment," she began in a low voice, "but I just realized I left my purse up there. It was hanging on the back of my bedroom door, so who knows where it might've blown to? If—if you don't want to look for it, I could ask Mose to go in—"

"I'll be happy to give it a shot, Sylvia," Truman replied immediately. "And if I don't find it right off, I'll be sure our crew looks through everything so your purse doesn't end up in a dumpster."

Relief rushed through her as she smiled gratefully. "*Denki* so much for understanding," Sylvia said in a rush. "And I'm betting your *mamm*'s pocketbook is still in her apartment as well. She was too upset to think about that when she went up there with you."

"You're probably right. *Denki* for mentioning it," he said.

"I'm glad you said something about that, Sylvia," Ruby put in with a nod. "Beulah and I will be sure to find our purses—and look for yours—and we need to get our coffee can out of the pantry downstairs, too. We've accumulated quite a nice lodge emergency stash, and we don't want *that* going in a dumpster, either!"

Sylvia smiled, wishing she had a fraction of the Kuhn sisters' bravado. Rather than dwell on the way her fears tended to play upon her mind, however, she waved at Beulah and the others and started toward the bulk store. The lawn behind the ten cabins—or what was left of them—was littered with splintered boards, sawdust, and small branches, so she cut around in front of them and continued.

As she walked, she wondered what Rosetta would do about the cabins. They hadn't been luxurious by any means, but they'd provided temporary housing for many guests and for folks who were waiting for their new homes to be built after they'd moved to Promise Lodge. They'd also been a place for men to stay, because males weren't allowed upstairs near the ladies' apartments unless they had special permission and a reason to be there.

When she reached Dale's store, however, Sylvia turned her thoughts in a different direction. She'd come to shop without a dollar in her pocket, so before she picked out a new dress pattern and fingered the fabrics—got up her nerve to sew a totally new wardrobe—she needed to consult with the proprietor. Dale knew who she was, of course, but she hadn't been talkative during the evening meals he'd eaten with the lodge ladies. And his attention had been focused on Irene, anyway.

Several cars were parked in the lot, and when Sylvia entered through the front door, she stopped to let her eyes adjust after walking in the bright sunshine.

"*Gut* afternoon, Sylvia! How's it going at the lodge with Truman and his cherry picker?" the storekeeper asked loudly.

It took her a few moments to find Dale, who was high on a ladder, changing a light bulb. Should she elaborate on Irene's sadness and desperation?

"It's—well, after I watched Irene ride in that contraption," Sylvia hedged, "I didn't need to survey the wreckage in my apartment, because none of the furnishings are mine—and because I'd already decided to, um, upgrade my wardrobe."

Aware that other customers were following their conversation, Sylvia smiled patiently at Dale. "When you've got a moment, I have something to ask you, please. I'll be back in the fabric department."

As she strolled along the aisles, she sensed other shoppers were looking at her. Was it curiosity about what she wanted to ask Dale? Did they think Fannie's gingerbread-colored dress looked too young for her? Or were they simply aware that she was too short to see over the tops of the store's shelves?

Sylvia finally reached the section of the store where fabric bolts were neatly stacked on end. She bypassed the quilting prints and the fancier fabrics English folks probably used for dressy occasions, heading for the solid-colored material Plain seamstresses would choose. On the other side of the sturdy Tri-Blend fabric for making men's pants, the wrinkle-resistant polyester blends were arranged in an array of colors that rivaled the flowers in a summer garden.

She held her breath, running her fingertips over the bolts. Lilac, fuchsia, goldenrod, and morning glory blue progressed into the purples, grays, and black. Sylvia wanted a new black dress for church and funerals, of course, but she was determined to liven up her clothing—and liven up her life—so Mose wouldn't think she was forever mired in her past.

But how many dresses should she sew? And which colors should she buy?

Temporarily overwhelmed, Sylvia walked over to the patterns for Amish and Mennonite dresses, which Dale displayed in an upright rack. The cape dress style that Promise Lodge women wore was prominently displayed, as well as the kind with slightly more elaborate sleeves and collars she'd seen the Kuhns and Irene wearing in colorful prints.

When she spotted an envelope containing patterns for shirts and broadfall trousers, Sylvia turned it over to look at the sizing chart. Her Ivan had been several inches taller than she, but thin as a rail—which made her wonder what size Mose would wear. When Marlene made his clothing, did she have to cut the shirts broader and the pants longer than the pattern to—

"Ah, here you are, Sylvia! Looking to make Mose some new shirts perhaps? Some of his have been around a while, I suspect," Dale remarked cordially.

"No! I—I'm replacing the poor old black dresses I lost in the storm!" Sylvia blurted out. Her face felt flaming hot and she sucked in air to settle herself.

"Sorry I startled you, dear," the storekeeper murmured. "And it's not my place to presume anything about who you want to sew for, either. Please forgive me, Sylvia."

She let out a nervous laugh, determined not to leave the store empty-handed because she'd lost her nerve. "Dale, I have a favor to ask," she said quickly. "Until we dig my purse out of my demolished apartment, I don't have any money—and I don't have any clothing, either, so—"

"So your credit is absolutely *gut* with me," the storekeeper assured her in a low voice. "I'll get you a cart, Sylvia.

Fill it with *kapps* and fabric and shoes—everything you need, all right? I was so fortunate that my store and apartment were spared by the tornado, providing for my friends is the least I can do."

As Dale hurried down the aisle, Sylvia was filled with a warm glow. All her life she'd lived within her means, and she and Ivan had only purchased what they could pay for at any given time. Yet Dale hadn't hesitated to extend credit to her. When she saw him wheeling a cart toward her, she flashed him a grateful smile.

"I really appreciate your understanding, Dale," she began. "I felt funny asking—"

The storekeeper held up his hand. "I'm delighted that you see this as a time to start fresh, Sylvia—to be reborn, like a butterfly emerging from its cocoon," he added. "And I'm happy to be part of your transformation."

Sylvia blinked. No one had ever spoken to her in such encouraging language. It made her think that Dale could be entrusted with a little more detail about Irene's situation.

"*Denki* for saying that. Truth be told, every one of us whose apartment was hit is going to need cheering up." She cleared her throat, focusing on him. "Let's just say that Irene was much braver than I, going into her apartment to see the damage firsthand. And she came out saying that *nothing* inside was worth saving. She'll be chewing on that for a long while, Dale."

His eyes widened as his face fell. "Oh my. That poor woman," he whispered. "Irene would never admit such a thing to me, Sylvia—she would put on her stiff-upper-lip act and soldier on. I'm grateful you've told me. I—I'll let you get on with your shopping now."

Nodding, Sylvia gripped the handle of her cart. First she selected some new underthings, a pair of shoes and some dark stockings, and a nightgown. Still feeling the uplifting effects of Dale's remarks, she even chose two new pleated *kapps* so she'd no longer appear to be a guest in her heart-shaped Pennsylvania prayer covering. Finally she returned to the fabrics.

Her energy was dwindling, so Sylvia put a pattern in her cart and picked up a bolt of black fabric. After she laid it on the cutting table, she rang the service bell and chose bolts of magenta, bittersweet, and—flinging inhibition to the winds—periwinkle blue.

She was delighted to see Marlene coming up the aisle to cut her fabric. Was it because Sylvia was feeling tired, or did Dale's assistant look especially young and vibrant and healthy? With her dark hair and distinctive brows, Marlene was the spitting image of her handsome twin brother—except that Mose was taller and brawnier.

"How's the new bride?" Sylvia asked cheerfully. "I hope you and Lester had some nice visits while you collected wedding presents. And I bet you're glad you moved your belongings into your new home before the tornado struck—even if your apartment wasn't directly affected."

"Our poor lodge is in a bad way, isn't it?" Marlene asked as she deftly unrolled the bolt of black fabric on the cutting table. "How many yards will you need, Sylvia?"

Sylvia smiled. "Short as I am, I can get a dress out of a couple of yards of that wide polyester," she replied. "Give me four yards of the black, and two of each color—"

"And *look* at these colors!" Marlene put in excitedly. "Sylvia, I'm so happy you feel like wearing brighter clothing now. These new dresses will be just the thing to keep you from getting depressed as you wait for your new apartment. I'm wondering if the entire lodge might have to come down—either because the structure's been compromised, or it's just more financially feasible to start fresh."

Sylvia blinked. She hadn't thought about the possibility that the lovely old lodge might not exist any longer. "You know, it's one thing that folks have built their nice new houses with off-white siding from Lester's company, but—well, Promise Lodge just won't have the same *character* without its weathered, timbered gables and our old-fashioned front porch and—"

Suddenly feeling drained after an emotionally taxing day, Sylvia sighed. "I guess we'll see what our carpenters decide about that, won't we?"

Chapter 17

That evening after he closed the store, Dale arrived at the lodge in time to see Rosetta and Truman descending in the cherry picker with a few large plastic bins. Rosetta, wearing leather work gloves and an old kerchief over her hair, appeared tired but purposeful as her husband steered the metal basket down onto its platform. Before folks noticed him, Dale left his large shopping sack at the end of the building, out of sight.

Beulah and Ruby stepped closer to the platform with a pull cart, as though anticipating some of the items the Wickeys had salvaged.

"We'll take these up to the bishop's place and get them washed right away!" Beulah was saying as Dale approached. "They'll make a wonderful-*gut* surprise for—"

"Oh, *hello,* Dale!" Ruby said loudly. "Once we got past the initial shock of seeing the wreckage in the apartments, we turned our cherry picker trips into a treasure hunt."

Rosetta's smile hinted at a secret they might be keeping, but Dale played along. The ladies weren't the only ones hiding things away, after all. It was such a relief to see them acting happier than Sylvia had hinted at, considering Irene's depressing discoveries earlier in the day.

"If anyone can turn disaster into a frolic, it's you gals,"

he said with a chuckle. "Were you able to bring some things down from your apartments, I hope?"

"*Jah*, our clothing's pretty nasty from being whipped around in the rain," Beulah replied, "but a few loads of laundry will remedy that."

"Our end of the building got off easy," Ruby pointed out. "And most of the furniture—which was already there when we moved in—can be fixed up and used again. Just a matter of time and carpentry work."

Dale nodded, watching Rosetta and Truman carry two large plastic bins over to the Kuhns' wagon. "And what's your take on the situation, Rosetta?" he asked kindly. "You've put so much time and attention into your lodge, it must be hard to see what the storm did to it."

Rosetta deposited her bin and came over to him. "It's heart-wrenching," she said with a sigh. "We're going to raze all the cabins, and I'll decide later whether to replace them. We've got a crew coming from our church in Cloverdale in a few days, and I want them to concentrate on Christine's barn and restoring the apartments first. If you'll excuse me, I want to retrieve the food from the freezers and fridges and get a better look at the kitchen," she added with a purposeful smile.

"Looks like everybody here's got a job, so I won't stand in your way," Dale said. "I'm on my way to visit Irene—unless she's napping, or—"

"I suspect she could use some company, whether she'll admit it or not," Truman put in. "She took it hard this morning, seeing her apartment in ruins. Ah—take this with you."

Truman went over to a small pile of belongings beneath a tree. When he picked out a brown leather handbag, Dale recognized it immediately. "Irene's purse! She'll be happy to see that—even if it's water-stained and not fit to take into town anymore."

"Give her our best!" the Kuhn sisters called out. Beulah grabbed the wagon handle and the two sisters started for the road that led up to Bishop Monroe's place.

Other folks had gone home for their dinner, most likely, so when Rosetta and Truman refocused on their task, Dale retrieved his shopping sack. As he strode around the lodge toward the road, his thoughts took several different directions. It surprised him that Rosetta had decided to raze all ten of the cabins—and he wondered what she'd do with that empty tract of land if she didn't rebuild them.

The sound of air-driven hammers made him glance toward Christine's barn—except it had been completely taken down during the day. The carpentry crew had made great progress on the Promise Lodge Pies shop, however, as well as getting a good start on the Kuhns' new cheese factory. Dale had always marveled at the meticulous efficiency of Amish builders. As he passed beneath the arched metal sign at the Promise Lodge entry, he saw that Mattie's new produce stand had been rebuilt and was ready to be painted.

A few minutes later he was approaching the Wickey home, walking up the long lane. He'd never been inside Irene's two-story house, but Dale suspected it had been built around the same time as the lodge—maybe seventy or eighty years ago. He sensed it might be a little too full of furniture even after Irene had taken some to her apartment—but that was often the case in a home where several generations had lived.

Through an open window at the front corner, he heard a *whirrrr . . . whirrrr . . . whirrr.*

Dale paused. Irene was the only one home, so what might she be doing? He didn't want to interrupt a project that was keeping her happily occupied—but he didn't intend to go back home without seeing her, either. It occurred to him that it had been *years* since he'd approached a house to visit the young woman within—

Because after Louisa turned me down flatter than a pancake, I decided women weren't worth my time.

Dale paused, swallowing hard. Despite a few encouraging hints, he'd already heard Irene's opinion of getting remarried, yet here he was like a man come courting, bringing her gifts. He reminded himself that he merely intended to cheer up a good friend, so if Irene acted less than interested in visiting with him, he could walk away with his pride intact. She had good reason to feel depressed after what she'd seen this morning, after all.

Gathering his courage, he walked closer to the open window. "Hey there, Irene, it's Dale! I—I brought you something I bet you'll be glad to have."

That had sounded lame. What sort of man talked up his gifts as though he knew what a woman really wanted?

Whirr . . . whirr . . . whirrrrr.

He sighed. What mechanical contraption made such a sound? Was Irene so engrossed she hadn't heard him—or was she ignoring him? He was starting to recall why he'd found women so frustrating when he'd been a young man.

"Irene?" he called out again. "You won't believe how delicious Phoebe's fried pies are! They flew off the shelf today, but I—I saved you a few."

A moment later Irene appeared at the window. She was smoothing the dark blue bandanna she'd tied over her hair—obviously not expecting company. But at least she'd responded.

"Phoebe made fried pies? Last I heard, she was bringing you full-sized—"

An exasperated sigh escaped her. Irene shook her head as she raised the window and screen high enough to lean out.

"Where are my manners, Dale?" she asked sheepishly.

"I've been tied into so many knots today that I got more excited about fried pies than the fact that you've taken the time to bring me some. Shame on me."

"It's all right. Very understandable," Dale said. He held up the big shopping bag, as well as the purse Truman had given him. "Shall I bring these in, or—"

"Come around back to the patio. I'll be right out with some milk and plates. I just realized I haven't eaten anything since breakfast, and I'm suddenly starved out of my mind."

It wasn't the affectionate welcome he'd hoped for, but Dale was pleased that a few fried pies had gotten his proverbial foot in the door. By the time he'd walked past the huge lilac bushes at the side of the house, as well as a large vegetable garden, Irene was setting a pitcher and two plates on the patio's picnic table. Large old shade trees provided relief from the setting sun's intense rays, and Dale smiled at the homey, comfortable feeling he got as he approached the Wickeys' backyard retreat.

He also realized that Irene's beloved husband, Ernest, had provided her with this wonderful home. Why would she settle for less—or for an efficiency apartment above a bulk store—from any other man who wanted to win her heart?

When she smiled at him, however, Dale set aside his troublesome thoughts. It was much too soon to be worrying about where he and Irene would live—*if* they both decided to give up their very comfortable, independent lifestyles.

"Here you go," he said. He set her purse on the table so he could reach into the shopping bag for the small white bakery box.

"Oh my word. I'd forgotten all about leaving my purse upstairs," Irene murmured as she looked it over. "Just goes to show you how deeply that storm disrupted life as I've known it. *Denki* for bringing it, Dale."

"Truman and Rosetta thought you might want it," he remarked gently. "When I was there a few minutes ago, the two of them were bringing things down from the apartments in big plastic bins. I couldn't see what was in them, but Beulah and Ruby seemed tickled to be taking them back to Bishop Monroe's place."

As he spoke, he took out two of the fried pies. "Would you like pineapple-lemon, dear? Or rhubarb?"

Irene looked up from gingerly rummaging around in her purse. "Phoebe made pineapple-lemon filling? That's a new one!"

"I confess that I tried one of those for lunch. I sure hope she bakes more of them—and more fried pies in any flavor," he added as he placed the golden brown pastry on Irene's plate. "I think you ladies would attract a whole new audience for your handheld goodies. Folks who live alone don't always want to deal with an entire pie."

Irene didn't respond. She was closing her eyes over her first bite of the pastry, and the expression on her face held Dale spellbound. As she chewed, the tension left her shoulders. The smile he'd come to love returned to her face, erasing an entire day's worth of despair.

"Oh, but that's tasty," she murmured. "I'm sure glad you've had one, so I don't have to share."

Dale laughed out loud, delighted that Irene's mood was improving—even if it wasn't his presence she was enjoying so much. As she took a second large bite and chewed it, he could only hope that someday she'd appear as genuinely ecstatic about *him*. He bit into the rhubarb pie and poured them both glasses of milk, allowing her to finish her treat without his chitchat intruding upon her enjoyment.

A few moments later, Irene let out a contented sigh. "Dale, you've rescued my day. I've been in such a funk since I saw my apartment, I've been buzzing from one task to another like a crazed bee seeking out the right flower— but not having any luck," she added with a shake of her head. "When you got here, I was at the sewing machine making a dress from different-colored fabric remnants Rosetta had stashed away. She offered to bring me over to your store, but I felt too bumfuzzled to choose fresh fabric."

Dale picked up the shopping bag, smiling. Never in his life had a woman offered him such a perfect opening—and he hoped he wouldn't blow it by saying something stupid.

"For you, Irene. And if you don't like what I picked out, bring it back and you can choose something you really want. No hard feelings."

Her eyes widened as she accepted the sack. "You didn't have to bring me a—it was gift enough to come over with a fried pie and my—oh! Here's a new dress pattern. And look at this pink and purple striped fabric!"

Dale tried not to let his excitement run away with him. *She likes it!*

"I got in a new shipment of polyester blends yesterday, so I brought you a few pieces before the Kuhn sisters could snatch up the prettiest colors," he said softly. "I can't imagine how devastated you must've felt when you found all your clothing had been ruined, Irene."

Irene blinked, probably to keep from crying. After she placed the striped fabric on the table, she reached into the sack again. "And here's a nice houndstooth in deep green and celery—and a pretty summer-weight tweed in French blue, white, and yellow."

She looked at him in something akin to amazement. "Dale, you have fabulous taste in fabric. I'm really looking forward to making these dresses!"

Something in her expression made Dale stand up. Next thing he knew, Irene was hugging him fiercely, holding him as though she couldn't let go.

To Irene's horror, she burst into tears. Not only had she startled poor Dale, but now she was weeping inconsolably, and she couldn't seem to stop.

It was very important to stop, too, because she knew firsthand how uncomfortable men became when women cried. She'd loved Ernest to his dying day, but early in their marriage he'd told her sternly, pointing his finger, to go to the bedroom until she could stop blubbering—to behave like a grown woman instead of a spoiled child trying to get her way.

Ernest's reaction had made an indelible impression on her. For the rest of her life with him, she'd repressed her need to cry until she could steal a few moments alone. Yet here she was in the arms of another man, releasing her pent-up fears and frustrations—the losses of home and property that had hit her so hard.

And this man chose to hold her close.

"I—I'm sorry I'm such a—a crybaby," she said with hitches in her voice.

"You have every reason to be upset, Irene," Dale murmured. He swayed gently with her, as though comforting a small child. "Cry it out, dear. You'll feel a lot better after you wash away some of your desperation."

Irene sniffled loudly. Dale was such a fastidious fellow, neat as a pin, so she hated soaking his striped shirt with her tears. She appreciated his point of view, however, and allowed herself to sob a little longer. It felt so good to express her deep sorrow without having to hide it.

"*D-denki* for your patience," she said after a few more

minutes. "I don't usually go on and on this way, bawling like a baby—"

"You don't usually see that your apartment's been totally ravaged, either."

"I should be thankful," Irene countered, wiping her eyes with the back of her hand. "It's not as though I don't have a perfectly nice home to live in—"

"But this is your son and daughter-in-law's home now," Dale pointed out. "You probably feel like a guest—or an intruder, even though that's not your intention."

Irene blinked. When had a man ever behaved so patiently with her? And he'd hit the nail on the head: she'd moved to her apartment so Truman and his new bride could have their privacy, without a nosy *mamm* insisting that the household routine continue the way *she* wanted it. Truman and Rosetta had welcomed her immediately after the storm Friday night, of course, and they'd done everything possible to make her comfortable.

But it wasn't the same, living in the guest room. Not after she'd spent so many years of her life here with Ernest raising Truman, and then managing the household so Truman could concentrate on his very successful landscaping business.

"Truth be told," she murmured, "I felt so comfortable in that apartment, doing exactly as I pleased without all the cooking and cleaning. The only thing that might've kept me from spending the rest of my life in the lodge was the stairway, if my hips or knees gave out."

Dale's chuckle rumbled in his chest. He was still holding her close, with no sign he wanted to let her go—which made Irene very aware of the intimate way their bodies were pressed together.

"From what I've seen of your hips and knees, and the

lively way you walk, Irene, physical disability is a long way off for you."

Her eyes widened. Dale had watched the way she moved? She'd known him for so many years while attending the Mennonite Fellowship services in Cloverdale—even while Ernest had been alive—that she'd come to think of him as a bachelor immune to feminine allure. A blank canvas of a man with no sexual inclinations.

But maybe her mental picture of Dale Kraybill lacked the dimensions, the nuances, belonging to this fellow who seemed in no hurry to release her. If he'd so astutely chosen fabric she liked—patterns and colors he felt would be flattering—maybe he'd been paying more attention to her than she'd assumed.

What might she discover about Dale if she thought of him as a man who wanted her as a woman, rather than as a friend she'd known for so long that she barely noticed him?

The hand that had been slowly following the curve of her body to her hip was telling her that *he* certainly noticed *her*. Meanwhile, she'd stopped crying. For the first time in years, her body was on high alert.

Irene didn't have a chance to protest that her hair needed combing or that she was exhausted, or that she looked a mess in a bandanna and one of Rosetta's old dresses. When she raised her head from Dale's shoulder to ask what he thought he was doing, he kissed her.

She sucked in her breath at his audacity—but she didn't back away. His lips felt gently urgent, eager to please her and not inclined to stop kissing her anytime soon. Irene hadn't even looked at another man since Ernest had died. She'd assumed that the intimacies and affection of a man-woman relationship were behind her—and she'd been fine with that.

But when Dale finally eased his lips from hers and held

her gaze with his soft brown eyes, Irene suspected she'd be rethinking her future.

"Where'd you learn to kiss like that?" she blurted out.

Although Dale's eyebrows rose, his dimples winked at her mischievously . . . dimples she'd never noticed before.

"Why do you ask?" he teased. "And why does it make a difference?"

Irene's mouth dropped open. Once again, her assumptions about his private life had to be set aside, didn't they? Just because she'd never seen Dale with a woman didn't mean he'd lived the same chaste sort of life she had, as a widow.

"I—I suppose I've always figured you for a man who was married to his store," she stammered. "Too busy for a social life. Or so fussy about the kind of woman you'd pair up with, you never found one who met your standards."

"Maybe you need to refigure, Irene. Or maybe you're right," he added, his smile edged with mystery, "but I'm planning to change my ways. Starting right this minute."

Irene sensed that the man standing in front of her was having way too much fun at her expense. "You're going to stop spending all your time in your store? You're going to quit being so fussy?" she challenged. "I'll believe that when I see it!"

Dale gently grasped her shoulders. "Believe *this*, Irene," he murmured as he lowered his lips to hers again.

She wasn't sure where his bravado had come from—and she was in no position to ask. Apparently Dale's first kiss had set something free deep inside her soul, because as Irene slipped her arms around his neck and began to kiss him back, she became totally caught up in the warm, exhilarating sensations he was stirring within her.

When at last Irene eased away enough to catch her breath, reality returned. She'd still lost her apartment and almost everything in it. She was still wearing Rosetta's dress and an old bandanna. But Dale had somehow convinced her that she could get past those setbacks. He'd even provided her fabric to start a whole new wardrobe.

And if she could sew some lovely new clothes, couldn't she also create a lovely new life?

Chapter 18

On Thursday morning Mose was working from the metal basket of the cherry picker, dragging the ruined contents of Sylvia's apartment out the open back end of the lodge building. It wasn't a challenge physically, but the sight of her mangled furnishings took a toll on his emotions.

What if she'd been up here in her bed during the storm, asleep after taking her pain medication? We'd be picking up the pieces of her tiny body—

He shook his head fiercely, forcing such depressing thoughts from his mind. He and the other residents had agreed that *what if?* was a question that could only lead to more anxiety than they were already facing. After he'd fastened a rope around what was left of Sylvia's bed and steered the basket to the edge of the room to let the splintered wood and sodden mattress fall to the ground below, it was time for a break. He could drag out everything else that remained in the center apartment with a large shop broom while Truman steered the cherry picker—as they'd already done in the two Kuhns' apartments.

Mose lowered the metal basket, careful not to hit the men who were picking through the debris that had landed on the tarps they'd spread on the ground. It would've been easier to position their dumpster so the broken, ruined objects landed in it—but everyone had agreed that, on the chance they'd find something the lodge residents could salvage, they would pick through the trash before scooping it into the dumpster. Fortunately, Beulah and Ruby had located their purses and Sylvia's earlier in the week, so those ladies weren't concerned about losing any cash or other personal items.

"Three down, one to go," Truman remarked as he shut down the cherry picker's motor. "We've made *gut* progress this morning."

Mose stepped out of the metal basket with a deep sigh. "I'm reminding myself that it's a blessing the rest of the building is stable enough so we can reconstruct the apartments, the kitchen, and the back exterior wall, rather than tearing down the entire lodge," he put in as he removed his heavy gloves. "But today's work is making the situation *personal*. You can't help thinking about how Sylvia and your *mamm* lost everything they came here with—except their lives and the clothes on their backs. That's hitting me hard right now."

Truman smiled gently. "I know where you're coming from, Mose. I'll be glad to get Mamm's apartment cleared out so we can put this part of the tornado's destruction behind us and move forward."

Nodding, Mose inhaled deeply. "From what my nose is telling me, she and Phoebe are baking their pies this morning," he remarked. "That has to make Irene feel a lot better. She's back to running her business, acting somewhat normal."

"It also helped that she left the house in a new dress this morning," Truman said with a chuckle. "Would you believe *Dale* chose the fabric for it and took it over to her Monday evening—along with fabric for two more dresses? I haven't seen her smile so much in years."

"Glad to hear it. I—"

From across the road, the *whack-whack-whack* of a nail gun interrupted him. While he'd been inside Sylvia's apartment, the crew from Coldstream had raised two completed exterior walls of the new dairy barn into place, and the carpenters were securing them to the old foundation. Not far away, Bishop Monroe waited with two of his Clydesdales. When the builders were ready, they would fasten strategically placed ropes on a third wall. After guiding the ropes through a simple system of pulleys, Monroe would attach them to the harnesses on his massive Clydesdales and lead the horses steadily forward to pull the wall into position.

It wasn't a high-tech method, but Mose still got a thrill from watching those fine horses accomplish such a feat.

"Well, *that*'s progress," he remarked, nodding toward Christine's new barn.

Truman untied his leather apron, nodding. "Truth be told, that old barn had been hanging together on a prayer," he said. "When the Bender sisters first came here, Mattie's two sons and Amos made some quick repairs to the structure so Christine could get her herd settled in. She was lucky that parts of her barn hadn't collapsed before Friday night's storm."

"No doubt she'll be glad when her new milking equipment arrives, so she can replace the cows she lost and get back to milking a full herd again," Mose remarked. "I won't soon forget the expression on her face when she found the ones that didn't survive—and the maimed ones I put down for her the next morning."

Mose turned, again hoping to redirect his thoughts in a more pleasant direction. While Preacher Marlin, his adult son, Harley, and Preacher Eli continued searching through the rubble from the lodge, he thought about going over to

speak with a couple of the fellows working on the barn—
longtime friends from Coldstream.

Then he saw Sylvia.

He nearly melted as he watched her coming down the
road alongside Mattie Troyer. Mattie was pulling a cart that
held a big metal coffee urn while Sylvia carried a basket in
each hand—a sure sign they thought it was time for some
refreshments. As the two women chatted amiably, Mose
couldn't help noticing the spring in Sylvia's step and the
easy smile on her face.

She was still too thin. But her new red-violet dress,
which she must've sewn in the past day or so, was a huge
improvement over the black ones she'd worn before the
storm. And as Sylvia got closer to the lodge, Mose noticed
something else.

"You're wearing a pleated *kapp*!" he blurted out before
he could think to greet the women properly. "And—and don't
you look pretty in that new dress!"

Was it his imagination, or had the air hammers and all
conversation stopped after his outburst? Sylvia was so
startled that she gaped at him—but only for a moment.

"I needed new *kapps*, after all," she reminded him with
a shy smile. "I don't intend to return back East, so it's time
I dressed like a Missouri girl, *jah*?"

Missouri girl. That has a nice ring to it!

Mose's heart danced in his chest. Did this mean that—
even on the slim, bold chance that she might outlive her
doctor's grim prognosis—she was leaving her farm in
Pennsylvania behind for good? Sylvia sounded like a
woman who intended to stay right where she was . . . where
he could be with her.

"When you two have a spare moment," Mattie teased,
"we can set up for a coffee break, with some of Sylvia's

frosted sugar cookies and her coffee cake with peaches and chunks of cream cheese—"

"Who'd like a fried pie, still warm from the fryer?" Irene called out from the bakery. "Looks like Phoebe and I finished them just in time to go with fresh coffee!"

The mention of so many fresh-baked goodies immediately attracted the Kurtzes, Truman, and the others working around the lodge. The carpentry crew at the barn also looked over to where the ladies were setting up at one of the long wooden tables in the yard.

"Hey, we'll be there in two shakes of a cow's tail!" Preacher Amos hollered from the barn.

"Soon as Burkholder's horses pull this wall into place," another man put in. "So don't eat everything before we get a chance at it! Okay, Bishop—let her rip!"

Bishop Monroe urged his team of Clydesdales forward, slowly and steadily. Everyone standing in the yard stopped what they were doing to watch in awe as the completed white wall of Christine's new barn rose from the ground, guided by a couple of carpenters on either side.

"Now *that's* progress," Preacher Marlin said in a low voice. "Christine's going to be delighted when she comes this way again and sees her walls up. The way this crew works so well together, I bet they'll have the roof on it by tomorrow at this time—and that's just one more thing we have to be grateful for."

Nodding, Mose slipped one of the frosted sugar cookies off the tray as Sylvia removed the cellophane covering. When she playfully swatted his hand, he popped the entire cookie into his mouth. They were small—but the combination of moist, chewy cookie and buttery frosting packed a flavorful punch.

"I've eaten my fair share of sugar cookies, but this one

takes the prize," he said after he'd chewed and swallowed. "What's in it, sweet Sylvia?"

Her cheeks turned a pretty shade of pink as she shrugged modestly. "We rescued several boxes of cream cheese from the lodge fridge, so it seemed like a *gut* time to share it with you folks who've been working to get us back to rights."

"Those were my thoughts, too," Irene remarked as she set a large tray of fragrant fried pies on the table. They were half circles of golden pastry with fork crimping, sprinkled with powdered sugar. "You men were nice enough to bring out several jars of canned fruit from the lodge basement, so we have peach and cherry fried pies today. Phoebe made some to sell in Dale's store earlier this week, and they were gone in a heartbeat."

"No wonder!" Harley Kurtz said as he grabbed one from the edge of the tray. "They're warm, and just the right size to fit in a man's hand—"

When he bit into the pastry, he closed his eyes in sheer ecstasy. "And my advice is to keep them coming, Irene," he said as he chewed. "You've got a winner here. A great new product for Promise Lodge Pies."

"That's what Dale said, too," Irene remarked as she filled coffee cups for the men gathering around the table. "Maybe that storm shook up some of our old ideas. Maybe God's trying to prove that new opportunities can come out of our misfortunes."

"Like the mythological phoenix rising from the ashes of its predecessor," Mose murmured as he helped himself to a generous square of the peach and cream cheese coffee cake. He moved away from the serving table so other folks could pick up their coffee and treats—and kept going toward the front side of the lodge, hoping Sylvia would follow him.

He sensed her presence as he ascended the stairs to the front porch. "I thought this would be a nice place to take a load off while I enjoy your coffee cake," he said. "I was in the cherry picker most of the morning, clearing out your apartment after we emptied the furnishings and other stuff from the Kuhns' places."

Sylvia perched on the edge of the porch swing beside him, a faraway expression on her face. "I'm glad I was baking. I didn't want to watch you men pull out all that rubble."

"Understandable." Mose savored a bite of the moist, peach-filled cake—unique because it had chunks of cream cheese in it. "It bothered me more than I anticipated, watching the contents of your home fall to the ground like trash. Soon as I sweep out the small pieces with a broom, we'll get Irene's apartment cleaned out, too."

Sylvia sat quietly for several moments. He fought the urge to pull her close, thinking the other folks might have the same idea about resting in comfortable porch chairs.

"What did you mean about a phoenix rising from ashes, Mose?" she asked softly. "I hated to appear clueless amongst our friends, but—but I've never heard anything about that."

After a moment of thinking about it, he said, "The phoenix was part of Greek mythology, centuries ago. It was always shown as a magnificent, colorful bird rising up from destruction to symbolize how new life—resurrection—happens after the old life passes away."

Sylvia's hazel eyes widened. "How do you know about such stories? When I was in school, I never studied anything about that."

"Me, neither, until I finished my high school diploma and took some college classes so I could become the local vet's assistant." Mose smiled, thinking back. "The bishop of Coldstream was dead-set against me continuing my education—as most bishops are. But my parents hoped I'd learn some new, useful skills to help me get started in life. You see, after my kidnapping incident, I was much more comfortable around animals than I was around people."

Sylvia's mouth dropped open. "Wow," she murmured. "You went to *college*, Mose?"

The last thing he wanted was for Sylvia to feel inferior. He'd worked hard to earn his veterinary tech license, however, so he didn't intend to downplay his accomplishments, either.

"I completed a two-year program," he clarified, gently stroking her cheek. "That certainly doesn't mean I'm a genius—"

"But you stuck by your guns and went on to *school*," she said proudly. "You didn't let anyone stand in the way of what you wanted to become, Mose. That's special. And it explains why you use words that most Amish men have probably never said in their lives."

Mose set his fork down, intrigued. "Like what?"

"Well, like *predecessor* a few moments ago. And *phoenix*," she shot back. "And that day we rode on the show wagon with those Clydesdales, you said I must've been too *entranced* to notice the effort you'd put into steering the team around the sharp turn onto that side road."

He blinked. "If you can recall exactly what I said during that ride, sweetie, it means there's nothing lacking about *your* memory or mentality—because *I* don't recall using such a word. So don't go thinking I'm such a hotshot—"

"You were so *entranced* by the company you were keeping, it's a wonder you remember anything at all about that ride," Sylvia teased.

Mose laughed out loud. As he reached for Sylvia, she leaned into his embrace and met his lips for the kiss he'd been yearning to give her.

Sylvia might have a few years on me, but she sure doesn't kiss like an old lady!

As he chuckled—because Sylvia seemed anything but *old*—he deepened the kiss, heedless of whomever might come around the corner of the lodge and catch them. It wasn't exactly a *sin* to kiss in public, but church leaders frowned on such displays of affection.

When Mose sighed contentedly and eased away, Sylvia's eyes shone like whiskey and her gaze packed a similar punch. "How dare you laugh at me while I'm kissing you, Mose," she teased.

He grinned. "I might be a little wet behind the ears, as far as winning a woman, but I know better than to laugh at you, Sylvia," he pointed out. "Especially if I expect to taste any more of your fabulous cookies—or *you*—ever again. I was laughing at *myself.*"

Sylvia's expression suggested she didn't believe him, but the sound of approaching voices made her scoot away as though nothing had happened between them.

"Those two recipes are among my favorites. I'm glad you like them," she said demurely. "I'll get back to the break table now, to see if I can be of any—oh, hello, Preacher Marlin! And Harley, you were enjoying your fried pie so much, I believe I'll go try one myself—if there are any left."

"They're going fast," the preacher's son informed her. "It's *gut* to feel fortified before we step inside the lodge to see where we need to install some temporary support poles."

"We're thinking it'll be easier to haul that heavy black stove and those industrial-sized freezers and refrigerators out this front way," Marlin put in. "When we asked Rosetta about replacing those old workhorse appliances, she agreed that this remodeling process would be a fine time for some major updates in that kitchen."

"That's exciting!" Sylvia said as she scooted off the swing. "I'll leave you fellows to your work."

Mose waited until the Kurtzes had gone inside to let out his sigh, knowing he sounded like a lovesick puppy. He *was* a lovesick puppy. He found it absolutely adorable, the way Sylvia's feet didn't touch the porch floor when she sat in the swing—or anywhere else. And he was still thrumming all over with the pleasure of their kiss.

And didn't she look vibrant in that colorful new dress? If I didn't know better, I'd think Sylvia was perfectly healthy. A little thin, but certainly not expecting death anytime soon.

The thought of her potential passing cast a dark shadow over him, so Mose got up from the swing and joined Harley and Preacher Marlin inside the lodge. He spent the rest of the day working on the renovation project, but his thoughts were never far from Sylvia . . . and how he might convince her to marry him sooner rather than later.

When Sylvia went to bed that evening in her room at the Troyer home, her mind was brimming over with joy and a sense of adventure and success. Mose had loved her treats, and he'd complimented her new dress—and *kapp*—and every time she'd glanced at him, he'd been gazing at her.

Tomorrow seemed like a good time to call her neighbor, Abe Stoll, in Lititz and tell him she wanted to sell her farm—wanted him to have the first chance at it for his newlywed son. It was also nearing the time when she was to check in with her doctor in Lancaster. Wouldn't it be wonderful to tell Dr. Sutherland she was feeling so much better?

As she said her nightly prayers, Sylvia thanked God again for the remarkable improvement in her health and well-being, and for leading her to Promise Lodge. She drifted off to sleep with happy thoughts of Mose and the wonderful future they surely had together.

Hours later, however, she awoke with a pain so startling and severe, it felt as though her brain had grown to the size of a watermelon inside her skull.

Sylvia lay absolutely still, trying to think. As the clock in the hall struck three, she began to breathe in short, shallow breaths to minimize the excruciating pressure. Her pain meds were on the nightstand, but her vision was playing tricks on her, and she wasn't sure she'd count the pills clearly—or get them out of the right bottle. She hated to waken Mattie and ask her to call an ambulance at this hour—and she wasn't even sure she could walk to the Troyers' bedroom without falling. She thought about yelling, but even at its best, her voice wasn't strong enough that Mattie would hear it above Amos's snoring.

So Sylvia stayed in bed, trying to remain rational as she planned out what she should do when she heard Mattie stirring in a couple of hours.

Mose . . . Mose . . .

I hope you know how much I love you.

Chapter 19

About an hour before the bulk store opened on Friday morning, Dale was in his office clicking through the online pages of an institutional appliances catalog. Rosetta sat beside him, wide-eyed with excitement.

"Look at these new stoves and ovens," she whispered. "Why, we couldn't find *anything* like these at stores around here. These pictures make me realize how old and tired our lodge kitchen looks. I had no idea how much appliances have changed!"

"That's because we Plain folks hang on to our furnishings and appliances by maintaining them carefully," Dale put in. He smiled wryly. "I'll warn you, though, that the Kuhn sisters won't be too enthusiastic about digital technology. And when I asked Irene if she and Phoebe wanted to replace their bakery's ovens, they steered completely clear of it."

"That's because Allen is qualified to repair the ovens they already had, at no charge," Rosetta pointed out. "Irene and Phoebe aren't making enough profit on their pies to justify investing in pricey new equipment, after all."

"True enough. But when Ruby and Beulah were choosing their new cheesemaking equipment, they felt overwhelmed by how everything has been updated with electronic controls." He clicked back to the institutional ranges Rosetta had seemed most interested in. "Have you decided? Or do you want to mull it over? I'll submit your order whenever you're ready."

Rosetta flashed him a smile. "I appreciate your help, Dale. I never thought I'd say this, but your store's computer has come in handy since the tornado overturned our lives."

"I dragged my feet about incorporating online inventory control and ordering," he admitted. "As you've pointed out, though, it gives us rural customers access to a lot more selection than we'll ever have in the little towns around here."

Rosetta nodded. "I'm going to think about my appliance choices for a day or so—but while I'm here, could you choose a couple more fabrics Irene would like for new dresses? Her birthday is next Tuesday—and by the way, you're invited to the surprise party we're—"

"I'd be delighted to do that!" Dale blurted out. He didn't intend to divulge the details of his visit with Irene on the Wickeys' patio, but he'd been basking in his success ever since. "Matter of fact, I have some bolts of polyester blend I haven't had a chance to display yet, and you're welcome to look at them first. Let's wheel them out into the fabric section, shall we?"

"Of course we can. I've been taking up the time you usually spend restocking your store, so the least I can do is help you," Rosetta insisted.

"Marlene will be here any minute now," he said as he turned off his computer. "Something must've detained her."

Dale's thoughts were spinning as he pushed his loaded cart through the swinging warehouse doors into the store. As he flipped the light switches, he hoped to illuminate some ideas about what to give Irene for her birthday— without getting nosy and asking Rosetta how old her mother-in-law was. At this stage of their lives, it didn't really matter anyway.

He had a building full of merchandise at his disposal . . . yet merely *buying* Irene something didn't feel right to him. Didn't she deserve a gift much more special than something any of his customers could purchase in his store?

As he began setting bolts of fabric on the cutting table, a wild idea struck him.

"Rosetta, did I hear correctly that you're going to raze all the cabins?" he asked. "What if—what if I bought a small parcel of that land, nearest my store, so I could build a house there?"

In her surprise, she fumbled the bolt of polka dot fabric she'd been admiring. "Seriously? I wasn't expecting *you* of all people to—"

The sudden wail of a siren made them rush to look out the nearest window at the front of the store.

Dale frowned as he peered through the glass. "That sounds really close! If it's a fire engine—"

"I didn't hear it coming from farther down the state highway, did you?" Rosetta asked. "It just started blaring moments ago and—oh no, it's an ambulance." Her hand fluttered to her heart as she watched the boxy vehicle rush past the store with its lights flashing. "Do—do you suppose it's someone from Promise Lodge?"

"Let's ask the Lord to be with whomever it is," he replied in a whisper. "And let's hope the back of the lodge didn't collapse on any of the folks who might be working there."

Rosetta's brows furrowed as the siren faded into the distance. "Whenever you get a moment in the next couple of days, cut three dress lengths from whichever bolts of fabric you think Irene will like," she murmured. "I'm going to see if anyone knows who's in that ambulance. And about your question concerning the land where the cabins are—"

Rosetta smiled knowingly at Dale. "If you're thinking what I *think* you're thinking, dear man, I wish you all the best at winning Irene's heart. She's like a fish out of water now that she's lost her apartment. Offering her a home would be a wonderful gift—"

"But this has to be our little secret!" he insisted. "Don't breathe a word of it to Irene, all right? And I'll be happy to come to her surprise party."

"We'll discuss your plot of ground soon," she assured him. "See you later, Dale—and *denki* for helping me with my appliance selections. I'll get back to you when I've made up my mind."

He nodded as Rosetta strode toward the warehouse to leave the back way. "That'll be fine, dear. Keep me posted about—"

An urgent pounding on the front door made Dale glance up at the clock above the checkout counter. The store didn't open for another twenty-five minutes, yet he sensed the person outside had come to get his attention rather than to shop.

"Dale! Open up—is Rosetta in there?" a familiar male voice cried out.

Rosetta turned quickly. "Truman! Oh no, what can this mean?"

"Just a moment!" Dale yelled as he reached the entrance. He twisted the dead bolts and threw open the door. "*Jah*, she's right here—"

"Rosetta, I thought you should know that Mattie found Sylvia in her bed—unconscious but still breathing," Truman said in a rush. His voice was calm, but undertones of concern and compassion were discernible just beneath the surface. "When Mose saw the ambulance pulling away from the Troyer place, he came unhinged. Insisted on following it. Mattie realized that Mose knows as much

about Sylvia's condition as any of us—so she gathered up
the prescription bottles on her nightstand to send along
with him—"

"And you're taking him to the little regional hospital
between here and Coldstream?" Rosetta asked, grasping his
hands. "Drive carefully, Truman."

"*Jah*, it's a *gut* forty-five minutes from here to Latham
Memorial," Dale put in. He sighed, sadly shaking his head.
"Give Mose our best and tell him our thoughts and prayers
are with him and Sylvia. Let's hope this isn't her final ride."

After quickly kissing his wife's cheek, Truman rushed
back out to the white pickup he'd left idling near the door.
Through the passenger-side window, Dale saw Mose sitting
with his head bowed.

As the big, burly man wiped his eyes with the back of his
hand, Dale sensed his friend was in for a long, painful day.

Mose gazed blankly out at the passing scenery, grateful
that Truman didn't fill every moment of their trip with
chitchat. The moment he'd spotted the ambulance parked
at the Troyer place, his pulse had shot into overdrive—
and his fears had taken over all rational thought. He and
Marlene knew from experience with their parents that
if an ambulance traveled without sounding its siren, the
patient involved had probably already passed on.

*But Sylvia was still breathing. Mattie was sure of that—
and the way the ambulance raced off with the siren
blaring and the lights flashing is proof that there's hope
for her. I can't let my fears and dramatic imagination get
me down. Yet.*

"You know," Truman mused aloud as he focused on the
road, "I thought Sylvia looked better yesterday than she
had since she moved into her apartment."

Mose sighed. He agreed. Remembering their kiss in the porch swing nearly made him cry again.

"And all things considered, after the tornado, she's sewn new clothes and seems to be moving forward with more energy than we've seen before," the man beside him continued softly.

Nodding, Mose still didn't answer. Didn't trust his voice.

"Just my opinion, but I'm thinking *you* are the main reason for Sylvia's improvement," Truman said in an encouraging tone. "So if you intend to be helpful to her now, Mose, you have to take care of *yourself* these next few days."

Mose frowned. "Wh-what do you mean? I'm perfectly fine—"

"But you're so worried about her, you're liable to sacrifice your sleep, your health, your well-being while you wait to see how this episode will end," Truman countered softly. "You're so far gone in love with Sylvia, you might just lose *yourself*, man.

"It's not a bad thing to be so attached to her," Truman added quickly. "I'd feel the same way if it had been Rosetta in that ambulance. But don't forget that if—*when*—Sylvia gets out of the hospital, she'll need a man who's focused and rested enough to truly help her."

"Duly noted," Mose said with another sigh. "I'm not sure why you're telling me this, Truman, but I appreciate your concern."

Truman's smile indicated that he didn't think Mose would follow his advice. He drove in silence until they arrived at Latham Memorial Hospital nearly forty minutes later. An ambulance was parked near a side doorway marked EMERGENCY in big red letters, but Mose reminded himself that several such vehicles came and went from this place every day. Sylvia was exactly where she needed to be—and God would be with her, no matter what happened next.

Mose thought he was holding his act together until they entered the main door and headed for the admittance desk. Latham Memorial brought back difficult memories of times his *mamm* and *dat* had needed treatment as they'd approached the ends of their lives. The décor still appeared as institutional and sterile as he remembered—and he vaguely recalled the same woman with dyed black hair and fake eyelashes who greeted him and Truman.

"Yes?" she asked abruptly. "How can I help you?"

Mose choked on his words, grateful when Truman responded for him.

"Within the last half an hour you've admitted our friend, Sylvia Keim, who came here in an ambulance," Wickey said as he took the white plastic bag Mose was holding. "We thought it might be helpful if her doctors had access to her prescription information—"

"Neither of you are her next of kin?"

Mose blinked. He knew where this line of questioning would lead. "N-no. Sylvia just moved to M-Missouri from P-Pennsylvania this p-past spring, and she has no f-family that we know of."

The woman stared as though she remembered Mose because of his stuttering. Her ridiculously long lashes made him think that several large, black spiders had given their lives—and legs—so she could adorn herself in such ghoulish style. The spider image made him want to laugh, but he knew better.

"I'll be sure the staff attending to Ms. Keim gets these medications." Her speech was clipped, and it left no room for argument. "But you won't be able to see her until after the doctors have run their tests—and even then, you won't be able to discuss Ms. Keim's condition with her care providers, unless she's able to sign the necessary documents to allow it."

When Mose showed no sign of accepting that answer, the clerk added, "If you'll leave a contact number, we'll notify you when the doctor has released her . . . or when we need to know which funeral home should come for her."

Mose nearly exploded in the woman's face. What a nervy, unnecessary—unprofessional—thing to say! Truman grasped his arm, reminding him to remain calm.

"I'm n-not leaving," he stated tersely. "N-nobody should be left all alone in s-such a s-scary, impersonal place."

The clerk shrugged and headed down the hallway behind her with the plastic sack. Mose almost wished he hadn't surrendered Sylvia's medications to her, but there was no way to grab them back.

Truman gently steered him toward a row of molded, modernistic chairs in the nearby lobby, leaning toward him after they'd both sat down.

"This is what I was talking about on the way here, Mose," he murmured. "Sylvia's going to be undergoing all sorts of tests, and there's no point in hanging around here in these hard plastic chairs—"

"You can go on back, Truman," Mose insisted. "But *nobody* should be left all alone here. Can you imagine how scared Sylvia will be when she wakes up with tubes attached to her and monitors all around her and—"

"But you won't be allowed into her room," his friend pointed out. "Why not get the phone number of the nursing station where she'll be and call from home—"

"Nope."

Truman let out an exasperated sigh. "But who knows how long you'll be here? What if they don't—"

"Doesn't matter. I can't abandon her." He held Wickey's

gaze. "You wouldn't walk away if Rosetta had been checked in—"

"That's different. I'm her husband, so I'm her next of kin," Truman pointed out. "That legality counts with medical issues."

"*Legality*," Mose muttered harshly. "That's the thing, Truman. *Nobody* will look after Sylvia the way I will. The law has nothing to do with love!"

"True enough. But the clerk was only telling you the way it's going to be, Mose. I'll bring you back tomorrow if you—"

"Nope. I'm staying right here." He reached into his pants pocket, frowning. "Next time somebody comes, though, I could use my wallet. When I left my apartment this morning, I wasn't figuring on leaving Promise Lodge."

After a few more moments, Truman stood up. "All right, I'll head on back and let folks know what's happened so far. But while you have hours to roam the halls or sit here, remember what I said about taking care of yourself. Sylvia will need your help when she checks out of here, you know."

Mose waved as Wickey turned to go. His friend was right: he was in for a long wait, and nothing was more exhausting than hanging around in a hospital. But as Sylvia's thin face and tiny, fragile body came to mind, he firmly believed he could make a difference in her stay.

He smiled to himself. This wasn't his first time at Latham Memorial, after all. God had provided inspiring ideas for getting what he'd needed when his parents had been patients here, and Mose was sure the Lord would work with him this time around, as well.

Chapter 20

As Irene entered the bulk store early Friday afternoon with two tall wooden carriers that each held six fresh pies, she saw Rosetta and Mattie chatting with Marlene at the cash register as she checked out their purchases. She didn't see Dale, but she'd restocked her Promise Lodge Pies display often enough that she didn't need his help.

"I'm not surprised Mose insisted on staying at the hospital for the duration—or at least until he's sure Sylvia's going to be all right," Marlene said with a shake of her head. "When each of our parents had to be hospitalized, he refused to leave them—probably because he despises hospitals, and he doesn't want anyone to feel isolated and alone there."

"But what if Sylvia's in a coma?" Mattie asked. "And—although we hate to think about it—what if her tumor has grown to the point that she's not going to come *out* of that coma?"

"*Jah*, I've heard that's the way it often goes with brain tumors," Rosetta put in ruefully. "And I'd been thinking lately that Sylvia was starting to live again—starting to feel some real purpose and excitement in her life."

Irene agreed with that as she neatly stacked her white bakery boxes on the shelf. Before she'd even unloaded her first carrier, two customers had selected pies and placed them in their shopping carts.

"My concern is also for Mose," Mattie continued. "I hate to think about him hanging around in the hospital for so long—especially because he's not likely to be admitted into Sylvia's room. And he won't be able to ask her doctors about her progress."

"If I could get off tomorrow, I'd go keep him company," Marlene confided. "But I can't leave Dale shorthanded on the busiest day of his—"

"Did someone say my name?" Dale teased as he pushed a loaded cart through the swinging warehouse doors.

Rosetta and Mattie quickly gathered their purchases so the next customers could check out. As Irene saw the concern on Marlene's face, it occurred to her that she might be able to help. The Fisher twins were very close, and she hated to think about poor Mose wandering around the hospital alone all night. She placed her last pie on the shelf and walked over to greet the storekeeper.

"Dale, *gut* afternoon!" she said. "I've been restocking my pie shelf—"

"And you should've come back to get me, Irene!" he insisted. As always, he looked exceptionally well groomed and tidy, even after working most of the day in his store. He smiled at her over the cardboard boxes on his cart.

She shook her head. "I've got one more carrier to bring in, and I'll be finished," she said. "Would you be willing to let me fill in for Marlene tomorrow while she keeps her brother company at Latham Memorial? I'd be happy to help."

Dale's eyes widened. "Mose looked mighty upset when Truman drove him away this morning," he recounted softly. For a few moments he seemed uncertain of his decision, until he caught the anxious expression on Marlene's face.

"Seems the least I can do, to allow her some time off, however. When can you start, Irene?"

Irene sucked in her breath. "I—we've done the day's baking, so I could be here in half an hour or so," she replied quickly. "I'll ask Phoebe to finish cleaning up so I can take Marlene's place."

Nodding, Dale turned toward his assistant, who was checking out a couple of English ladies. "Marlene, I'll be happy to let you keep your brother company if you can give Irene a crash course in restocking the shelves and where most of our items are located when she comes back in a little while. If someone can take you to Latham Memorial—"

"Truman and I will!" Rosetta volunteered. "And we'll gather a few things into a duffel for Mose. He left his apartment this morning not knowing he'd be staying with Sylvia."

The relieved expression on Marlene's face—and her eager nod—made Irene glad she'd offered to help. It seemed like such a minor effort, considering that Sylvia's life-and-death situation had everyone at Promise Lodge praying for a positive outcome . . . not only for their newest resident, but for Mose, as well.

Dale turned to Irene then, lowering his voice. "This will be a chance for you to experience life as the co-owner of a busy bulk store, ain't so?" he asked with a gentle smile. "It wouldn't be a bad idea for us to see how it goes, working together."

Irene's pulse shot up with a burst of nervous energy. What had she just let herself in for?

Maybe he's right. If we're to follow through on the feelings we share, I should spend some time in Dale's world. I can't assume my life will remain the same if we become a couple.

"I—I'll bring in the rest of those pies," she said in a rush.

"Then I'll tell Phoebe what I'm doing, and change into a fresh dress—"

"You look delightful in those pink and purple stripes," Dale put in. "Anything you wear will be fine with me, dear."

Flustered, Irene hurried back to the pie display to grab her carriers. Phoebe's Allen had built the portable wooden shelves when the two of them were falling in love, to make it easier to transport their pies in Irene's van. As she went out to the parking lot, it occurred to her that she and Dale were going through that same process at a later stage of their lives, but it still involved some trial and error—trying new ideas on for size, before they decided if they were meant to be together. Being married before hadn't prepared her for a new husband's expectations—or her own, now that she'd lived independently for several years.

I must give this my best shot. Dale has high standards—which is one reason I've always respected him—and I don't want to let him down.

Irene toted the last carrier inside and placed the boxed pies on the Promise Lodge Pies shelf. It was gratifying to see the smiles on customer's faces as they realized they were selecting fresh desserts from the woman who'd baked them only a few hours ago. Irene acknowledged their compliments, even as her emotions were spinning into high gear.

"I'll be back in about half an hour, Marlene," she said. After waving at Dale, she went out to get into her van.

As she sat for a moment in the driver's seat, Irene exhaled loudly. If she was going to pass this test—measure up to the challenge she'd just accepted—she needed to have her thoughts in order and her emotional ducks in a row. She turned the key in the ignition.

Here we go, Lord. I'm glad You'll be with me, because

I have a feeling the next day or so will be quite a ride. I know absolutely nothing about storekeeping.

Aware that admittance and testing procedures took a long time, Mose had spent most of the morning refreshing his memory of the hospital's layout and routines. Latham Memorial was a small rural hospital, not as complicated as big-city medical centers, and most of its staff were small-town folks, just as he was. He'd learned from taking college-level courses, however, that most English folks believed the Amish were clueless about things outside their own unsophisticated farming communities.

When professors had first seen his broadfall trousers, suspenders, and basic, solid-colored shirts, they'd assumed Mose couldn't comprehend their professional jargon or the concepts they were explaining. And they'd associated his nervous stuttering with mental and social deficiency, as well.

Mose had used this to his advantage. While getting his veterinary technician degree, he'd immediately gained his teachers' amazed respect by acing his exams and turning in thoroughly researched, carefully composed papers—and his lifelong experience with farm animals had given him an edge over urban students, too. He'd also figured out, during his parents' stays at Latham Memorial, that if he learned the hospital's systems, he could work around them. Living without electricity and other English conveniences had taught Mose how to *adapt* and achieve the results he wanted.

By noon he'd made himself inconspicuously comfortable in the waiting area nearest the intensive care unit. A partial wall provided a corner where he could watch the TV while keeping an eye on the information desk beside the double doors that opened into the wing where Sylvia would probably land. Driven by hunger pangs—but still without his wallet—Mose made his way toward the hospital's main kitchen on the lower level.

He was in luck! Two unattended carts stacked with meal trays from patients' rooms stood outside the doors, and—as he recalled from being here with his parents— many individual dishes still contained untouched, perfectly edible food. Mose reasoned that he wasn't stealing, because the two bananas, three pieces of bread, and jelly packets he snatched were headed for the trash anyway. And because the bread was still wrapped, patients hadn't handled it. It wasn't a filling meal, and he didn't enjoy wolfing it down after he'd ducked around another corner, but it would hold him until someone brought him some money.

Somewhat fortified, he arrived back in the ICU waiting area as the new desk attendant was starting her shift, focused on the computer. His timing was spot-on.

Rule number one: act like you're supposed to be here. And play along with whatever they tell you.

Mose took his hat from the shelf on the coat rack, put it on, and hurried to the desk wearing an urgent expression.

"I—I got here as quickly as I c-could," he said breathlessly. "They told me at the m-main desk I'd find my Sylvia here—Sylvia Keim."

As the attendant glanced at the computer monitor, her eyes told Mose when she'd found Sylvia's name.

"She's still in radiology having X-rays, Mr. Keim, so you'll have to wait here," the lady said. "No indication which room she'll be in, or whether you'll be able to see her anytime today. I'll let Dr. Mannering know you've arrived, and perhaps he'll be out to speak with you when he's gotten her test results. Please have a seat."

Mose nodded, spearing his hand through his hair. He

kept the smile off his face until he was seated in his corner
again. A little educated bluffing—and a sympathetic attendant who'd probably told him more than she was supposed
to—had confirmed his hunch that Sylvia would be in this
wing when they moved her to a room. It was a real plus that
the woman had assumed he was Sylvia's husband and had
also assumed that the folks at the main desk had gotten
enough information from him to verify who he was and
point him in this direction.

*In another hour or so, I'll meander into the wing and
find Sylvia's room number on the monitor above the nurses'
station. Timing is everything.*

As he flipped absently through an old magazine, Mose
shook his head at what passed for entertainment on the
big flat-screen TV. Three shows in a row dealt with couples
looking to buy homes for outlandishly exorbitant prices.
The hosts were either real estate agents who acted as
strangely as they dressed, or they were a couple of so-called
renovation experts who fast-forwarded through the various
stages of the remodeling they'd done. The buyers were behaving as though every home they viewed was exactly what
they'd been dreaming of, and their gushing remarks and
hyped-up reactions made Mose wish the shows were over.

When he couldn't handle any more, he used the restroom
and then waited for a nurse to come out of the intensive care
unit so he could slip in through the double doors before they
shut. From here, if someone questioned him, it was all
about charm.

Mose spotted a large digital monitor above the nurses'
station, noting that the technology—and the bland gray
décor—hadn't changed since Dat had been a patient here.
He stood back against a wall and focused intently on the
monitor, grateful that his eyesight was sharp for distances.

The name KEIM made him hold his breath. There was her room number, her pulse rate and blood pressure, her—

"Sir, you are *not* supposed to be here!" a sharp female voice informed him.

Mose turned, acting sheepish. "I—I thought I was heading for the cafeteria—"

The nurse's raised eyebrow cut him off, yet he sensed she was subtly checking him out, and liking what she saw.

Rule number two: if a woman finds you attractive, don't do anything to convince her otherwise.

He clasped his hands, holding her gaze with a wide-eyed, clueless smile. He'd been horribly awkward with girls when he was younger, but he'd always gotten along well with women. It didn't hurt that his stomach growled loudly to substantiate his story.

"You'll need to go back through the double doors and down the first hall to your left," she informed him in a gentler voice. "I can recommend today's hot roast beef sandwich. The mashed potatoes are out of a can, but they pour on enough gravy to disguise that pretty well."

"*Jah*, thanks, I'll keep that in mind," Mose murmured. He grimaced. "And I just realized that in my panic to get here, I left my wallet at home. I'll go figure something out."

He turned obediently and went back to his corner in the waiting area. Sylvia was in a room down the hall! Her vital signs were stable! Her situation was looking *so* much better than when he'd seen the EMTs wheeling her into the ambulance this morning. Most of his story had been factual, so Mose didn't think God would mind that he'd fibbed a little to get this information.

Mose glanced at the television and chose a chair facing a different direction so he wouldn't be distracted by the laugh track of a program that appeared totally pointless. It was only a matter of time before Truman or someone else from Promise Lodge showed up, so he relaxed and considered the next steps toward getting in to see Sylvia. With the sun warming him through the window, he lapsed into a light doze . . . dreaming about food that was so warm and delicious, he could practically taste it—

"Hey there, how about a little something to tide you over?"

Mose awoke suddenly to see a carryout container brimming with fragrant hot beef and gravy on the small table beside him. The nurse who'd shooed him out of the ICU wing was standing nearby, watching him with a smile that twitched on her lips.

"You didn't have to—I didn't mention m-my wallet was at home to m-make you f-feel sorry for me!" Mose blurted. "My friends'll be here any time now—"

"But meanwhile, a little lunch might make you feel better," she said with a shrug. "Who are you here for this time? I could swear I've seen you before—"

Familiar voices and soft laughter coming down the hall made them both turn. Mose raised his arm to hail Truman, Rosetta, and Marlene, who carried a duffel and a small cooler.

"Aha! *Now* I remember," the nurse added. "That's your sister, right? It's hard to forget a duo as tall and attractive as the two of you. And you were looking after your father."

Mose nodded. It was probably just as well that this nurse—her name tag said RENEE—had figured him out, so he wouldn't have to keep faking his way.

"This time Sylvia Keim's the patient. She has an inoperable brain tumor—a terminal condition—so when she didn't get out of bed this morning, unconscious, we called the ambulance."

As his visitors arrived, he rose from his chair. "This is Truman and Rosetta—and you remember my sister, Marlene," Mose said to Renee. "They've come with my wallet— among other things, it appears—so now I can pay you for this nice lunch you so graciously brought me."

The nurse greeted the trio and then held up her hand. "Nope, no need. My buddy in the kitchen was clearing out the steam table to start serving supper, so these leftovers are on the house," she said. "You folks have a nice visit. Let me know if I can do anything else to make you more comfortable."

As Renee returned to the ICU through the double doors, Marlene raised her eyebrows. "Mose, have you been flirting with the nurses again? You're incorrigible."

He shrugged, glancing at the covered carryout container. "What matters most is that Sylvia's resting in a room and her vital signs are stable," he remarked as he took the wallet his sister was handing him. "Hope you folks don't mind if I tuck into this meal of beef, potatoes, and gravy while it's still warm."

Chapter 21

Irene collapsed into an overstuffed chair and kicked off her shoes with a tired sigh. Although she was accustomed to spending long hours on her feet while she and Phoebe baked four days a week, she'd foolishly changed into a dressier pair of pumps to work alongside Dale until the bulk store closed. The hot throbbing on the backs of her heels suggested that she'd worked up some blisters.

Grateful to be home alone for a while, she lolled in the chair. She couldn't recall the last time she'd felt so exhausted. She'd taken so many pointers from Marlene and had then straightened displays, assisted customers, and bustled from one task to the next without a break until closing—because Dale hadn't stopped working, either.

My word, why does that man never appear drained? I had no idea storekeeping required so much mental and physical energy.

After resting about half an hour, Irene walked to the kitchen, limping part of the way because her feet hurt so badly. Too tired to cook, she poured a bowl of cold cereal and doused it with milk.

Why have I never seen Marlene acting as weary as I

feel right now? I'm not sure I can face an entire day of this tomorrow.

Rubbing the back of her neck, Irene reminded herself that Dale's assistant was more than twenty years younger than she was—and that she'd only agreed to cover a day and half. It wasn't as though she'd have to come back on Monday—

But what if I was Dale's wife? The "co-owner of a busy bulk store," as he put it? If that were the case, he wouldn't have to find another full-time helper when Marlene and Lester start their family—

Irene blinked. Was that the real reason Dale had encouraged her to fill in? And one of the reasons he was hinting at marriage?

She slurped the last of her milk straight from the bowl, too tired to delve into Dale's ulterior motives. A long, hot soak in the tub seemed like a fine idea—especially while Truman and Rosetta weren't home.

Steeped in the sudsy, scented water, Irene tried to organize her thoughts so she'd be ready to face an entire ten-hour day. Thankfully she'd sewn the blue-and-yellow tweed dress, and it would look acceptable with her high-support low-heeled blue shoes. If she arrived about twenty minutes early, she could receive her assignments from Dale—and request some sit-down time in the warehouse, perhaps filling and labeling bags at the worktable. He was a considerate fellow, so he'd surely understand her need to be off her feet for part of the day. And if she packed a sandwich, she could eat while she worked back there.

When she rose from the cooling bathwater, it was only eight o'clock but she put on her nightgown and robe. Rather than be caught snoozing on the sofa when the kids came home, Irene took the newspaper to the recliner in her room. To rest her eyes briefly, she shut them, just for a few moments . . . drifted off . . .

Her thoughts swirled into a downward spiral. She heard the impatient voices of Saturday customers who told her she hadn't shelved their favorite items in the correct spots . . . saw an irate Amish woman whacking off lengths of fabric from a bolt with uneven slashes of the scissors because Irene hadn't come to help her . . . spotted large boxes tumbling down from Dale's high storage shelves to land on her head—

Irene awoke with a loud gasp. She was so terrified she was panting, and her mouth felt like a desert from hanging open during her troublesome dreams. The dresser clock—a gift from Ernest, which she hadn't taken to her apartment—chimed midnight. As she rose from her recliner to crawl into bed, she chided herself for dozing off in the chair. She was sure to have a sore neck and achy muscles from falling asleep in such an uncomfortable position.

Worse yet, once she was in bed, sleep refused to come. The clock's delicate tinkle had been such a comfort years ago that she'd never noticed it at night, but now every hour it marked gave Irene more reason to believe she'd be cranky all day in the store. As her night of tossing and turning crept by, she also became more convinced that Dale wanted her for an assistant storekeeper more than he desired her as a wife.

She rose before dawn on Saturday in such a foul frame of mind, she picked up the phone to leave a voice mail telling Dale she couldn't come to work. But she hung up.

Irene wasn't a quitter. And she didn't make excuses. And she didn't wiggle out of her commitments.

She dressed in her pretty tweed dress and sensible shoes and arrived at the bulk store an hour before it opened. Of *course* Dale hadn't come downstairs from his apartment yet, so the doors were locked. Irene sat on a sturdy wooden porch chair out front, watching the traffic go by on the state highway—until, in her frustration, she began pounding on the door . By the time Dale finally responded, it was all she could do to greet him civilly.

"Irene!" he said with a surprised smile. "I wasn't expecting you quite so early—"

"Just show me what I have to do today," she muttered. "Some of it needs to be back in the warehouse, so I don't bite people's heads off. I was up half the night."

Dale's eyebrows rose and he gestured for her to enter the store. "I'm sorry you didn't rest well, dear—"

"You don't know the half of it. And you don't want to."

Irene was appalled at her brusque tone of voice, but maybe Dale needed to see her grouchy side. Maybe he would realize he didn't want to become permanently attached to a woman who became such a shrew when lack of sleep allowed her to conjure up negative ideas.

"Let's have you start by restocking the frozen vegetables," he suggested as they walked toward the warehouse. "I'll cut the tape on the boxes, so all you'll have to do is place the bags in the freezer units behind the older ones that're already there. Sound okay?"

"Sure."

Dale nodded, holding one of the double doors. "Marlene has a pair of work gloves you can use. They should be your size."

About fifteen minutes later, Irene was propping open the tall door of a freezer—and wishing she'd brought a jacket. But she refused to complain, because she'd already gotten off to a grumpy start. Dale was being extremely nice, sounding sympathetic, so she curbed her irritable notions about why he *really* wanted to marry her.

It was an easy job, stacking fresh bags of frozen vegetables and then placing the older stock in front, but by the time she'd emptied two cardboard boxes, she was chilled to the bone. Customers were coming in, so Irene reminded herself that she had to smile and step out of their way—or move her cart—as they shopped in the freezer section.

"*Gut* morning," she murmured, but what she really wanted to say was *I'd kill for a cup of coffee.* Why had she left home so early this morning instead of taking the time for a bigger breakfast and her usual second cup of strong, black mood-lifter?

After she'd emptied all her cardboard boxes, Irene steered her wheeled cart to the warehouse to fetch the other boxes Dale had opened for her. When she returned to the main store, however, she overheard an exasperated outburst from a woman as she spoke with the storekeeper.

"Why can't I find the green beans? Or the corn?" she demanded, gesturing into the open freezer door. "I've shopped here since you opened this store, and I know exactly where everything is—"

Irene's heart sank like a stone. She had just restocked green beans and corn, and she was sure she'd placed them in their previous spots.

If you know exactly where everything goes, lady, maybe you should take a job here!

Yet the puzzled expression on Dale's face as he valiantly looked through two different freezer units told her she'd made a mistake—

And it's just like that weird dream I had when I fell asleep in the recliner.

Finally the storekeeper found the vegetables, and the

woman moved on to another section of the store. Sheepishly Irene wheeled her cart toward the scene of her mistake.

"I—I guess I wasn't paying close enough attention," she murmured apologetically. "Did I mess up your freezer shelves?"

Dale rolled his eyes as he pulled several bags of corn out and set them on top of her boxes. "The customer is *not* always right, even if we're supposed to act as if they are," he confided under his breath. "I reserve the right to reposition my stock, after all. But *jah*, dear, this corn was behind the peas and carrots. No harm done. I'll just check the rest of these freezer units and—"

His expression told her he'd found another spot where she'd misplaced her bags. "Maybe it's a *gut* time for you to fill bags back in the warehouse, like you suggested," he said softly. "I'll be back to get you started, right after I ring up the folks at the checkout counter."

Irene felt as crushed as a little girl who'd failed a simple test in school. Had she been so inattentive that Dale would have to redo everything she thought she'd accomplished? She hadn't intended to double his workload—and she had no idea how to operate his cash register, so she couldn't help him with that, either.

As she slumped in the chair at the worktable, resting her head on her folded arms, Irene began to think that she might be even more unqualified to work in the store than she'd been in her disjointed dreams. Maybe she should stick to baking pies with Phoebe in their rebuilt bakery. And in a matter of weeks, she could move back into her cozy refurbished apartment to take up the comfortable, independent lodge life she loved . . .

The warmth of Dale's hand on her shoulder made her sit up with a start. "*Ach!* I must've drifted off—"

"Let's get you going on some sanding sugars and

jimmies," he said as he considered her options. "Marlene explained how to run the label maker yesterday, *jah*?"

"She did," Irene replied with a sigh. "Dale, I'm so sorry I messed up—"

"You're learning," he put in quickly. "If you can fill these little plastic tubs with the colored sugars, label them, and bring them out into the store, that'll be great. I've got a line at the cash register."

As he strode back into the store, Irene realized that Dale's lifelong occupation required much more effort and expertise than she'd ever imagined. How did he maintain his unruffled composure while staying on top of his customers' demands? Her respect for him rose several notches as she gathered a couple dozen empty oval-shaped containers and placed the big bin of colored sugars on the worktable.

Maybe this is another sign that I'm not cut out for the storekeeping life. Maybe I should break the news to Dale sooner rather than—

"Oh! Oh my—*phooey*!" Irene cried out as four bulk containers of sugar hit the floor. Their lids popped off, making a dramatic splash of red, blue, yellow, and green that rivaled a fireworks display—except this was no reason to celebrate. All the sugar that had spilled needed to be swept up—and what a wasteful mess she'd made.

"Irene, are you all right?" Dale asked as he hurried back into the warehouse. "I heard you holler, and—oh my."

"*Jah*, that's what I said, too," she whimpered as she gazed at the amount of inventory she'd ruined. "I didn't realize I'd put those sugar bins so close to the table's edge, and I was careless yet again, and—oh, Dale, I'm so sorry. I'm causing you more trouble than I'm worth!"

At that, she burst into tears. It was exactly the wrong thing to do, because it made Irene feel even more embarrassed and it put Dale in the difficult position of dealing with her when he should be minding his store.

Bless him, he paused for a moment before he said anything—although he could surely think of all manner of pertinent remarks.

"Some days we just get up on the wrong side of the bed," he said with a sigh, "and it happens to all of us. Maybe you'd be better off going home—"

Irene covered her face with her hands, although she was nodding her agreement. "Truth be told," she said with a hitch in her voice, "I'm obviously not cut out to be an assistant storekeeper—or a storekeeper's wife, either. Why don't you go back and tend your customers, Dale? After I sweep up this mess, I'll leave you to run your store—and your life—in your usual flawless, organized way. It—it's just better that way."

Dale's face fell. "We'll talk about this at a better time," he said softly.

When he'd returned to his cash register, Irene cleaned up the floor, sniffling and hiccuping. All told, she must've wasted three pounds of colored sanding sugar and she'd left Dale short of those four colors until he could order more. It was only right to compensate him for what she'd thrown away, so she took a twenty-dollar bill from her purse and left it on the worktable with a scribbled note.

Dale, please accept my apologies and my money to cover the sugars I wasted. And please believe me when I say I'm not the right person to be your wife and helpmate. I wish you all happiness as you find qualified help to work in your store—and a wife, if that's what you truly want.

> *Still friends, I hope,*
> *Irene*

Chapter 22

Mose swung his legs over the side of the twin-sized bed and stretched his arms languidly. The sound of running water told him Marlene was already up and taking her shower. They'd both slept quite a lot later than usual—but then, they'd had a long, worrisome day on Friday, and they'd stayed up talking late after Truman and Rosetta had gone home last night.

He smiled as he glanced out the window, which faced the hospital's back parking lot. He and his twin had stayed in this little guest room a time or two while tending their parents, so he'd been waiting to see if Nurse Renee or anyone else on the staff would offer it as an option. His sister, however, had simply asked Renee if the room was unoccupied, and if they could use it again.

"You absolutely may. That's why we have it," the nurse had replied. She'd been nice enough not to mention how Mose had fibbed to her and sneaked into the ICU. "When I checked on Sylvia about ten minutes ago," Renee had added, "she was still stable and under sedation. I don't see a reason for that to change, so get a good night's rest and we'll see what tomorrow brings."

"I like that smile on your face," Marlene said as she

came into the main room. "It's a big improvement over your expression yesterday."

Mose gazed at his twin, noting her fresh goldenrod dress. Because he knew her so well, he anticipated the direction this conversation was likely to go.

"It was *gut* news to hear that Sylvia's condition has stabilized," he hedged.

"And when she returns to Promise Lodge, what are your plans? I've never seen you so emotionally involved, Mose."

There was no dodging her question. Marlene wouldn't let him off the hook until he gave a satisfactory answer. "I intend to marry her," he replied, holding her gaze.

"And what if the doctors here tell you Sylvia's not long for this world, even though they've pulled her through this particular crisis?" she asked in a softer voice.

"That would give me even more reason to make our relationship permanent," he said emphatically. "I want the world—and Sylvia—to know that I love her enough to take care of her. You can't tell me you would've turned down Lester's proposal if he'd been diagnosed with a terminal condition."

Marlene's dark, distinctive eyebrows rose. "After caring for our parents for so long, I'd have thought very hard about marrying a man I knew was ill," she murmured. "Being a full-time caregiver was exhausting when Mamm and Dat neared the end—as you know. That's why I'm surprised you're signing on for more of that emotional wear and tear."

He sighed as he thought back over their parents' lingering illnesses. "It was tougher for you because you were home with them all the time," he pointed out. "When I wasn't out on veterinary calls, I was tending our farm, working outside."

"I felt blessed to devote myself to them. I just wouldn't do it again anytime soon."

His sister's honesty touched Mose deeply and made him think. "I can understand that sentiment," he said. "But if I don't marry Sylvia, I'll be missing out on a chance to love a woman who truly appreciates and understands me—a woman I believe God has brought into my life for a reason."

Marlene came over to him and took his hand in hers. "All right then, I won't pester you about it any further. I was just—"

"You were sounding me out, making sure I wasn't chasing a rainbow just because I've been alone all these years," he finished. "You're the best sister ever, Marlene. Let's go get some breakfast."

They shared a filling meal of eggs, sausage, and pancakes in the cafeteria, which was relatively quiet at this midmorning hour. Mose enjoyed spending time with his twin, the one person in the world who was so tuned in to his thoughts and feelings. He hadn't seen Marlene very often since she'd married Lester, because being a wife and working at the bulk store occupied all her time these days.

As they walked back toward the ICU waiting area, he considered ways to gain access to the nurses' station again—or better yet, ways to get into Sylvia's room, so he could see for himself that she was resting comfortably. He wasn't sure if Renee was on duty this morning, or if he'd have to charm a different nurse for the latest information. It would be helpful if a doctor or someone in the wing could give him an idea about how long he might need to be here, because he didn't want to leave Bishop Monroe shorthanded for much longer.

When Mose and Marlene entered the waiting area, Renee rose from the chair where she'd apparently been watching for them.

"I'm going off-duty now, but I wanted you to know—unofficially, of course—that Sylvia was supposed to be moved into a regular room later today, except her doctor received some information that's changed his mind." Renee was keeping a professional expression on her face, but the urgency of her tone told Mose she was concerned about this change of plans. "I'm sorry, but I don't know any more—"

"Don't know, or won't tell me?" Mose challenged. His pulse was galloping, and he reminded himself not to jump to any fearful assumptions. "I understand about doctor-patient confidentiality, but I hate to think you've been getting my hopes up only to let them drop now that you're going home. Sylvia has nobody else to help her, Renee, so someone needs to know what's going on."

Renee frowned, glancing away. "I've told you more than I should as it is, because you folks have been through so much," she murmured. "I honestly don't know what this turn of events means, except that the doctor appeared startled—"

"And who is this doctor?" Mose asked. "What's his name? Surely you can tell me that much."

Renee grabbed her purse as though she wanted to leave before anyone on the hospital staff overheard her. "Dr. Mannering has been ordering Sylvia's tests—and of course, he's been consulting with the technicians and other doctors who've been reading the results. He found it very helpful that you brought in her prescription bottles, by the way."

She smiled at him and Marlene. "I wish you all the best. I won't be back until the middle of next week," she said before she turned to hurry down the hallway.

Mose watched her for several moments, unsure what this conversation with Renee had meant. "At least we have a doctor's name," he said with a sigh. "But we can only speculate about why Dr. Mannering changed his mind about moving Sylvia into a regular room, and what he found out that supposedly *startled* him."

"*Jah*, that might mean she's taken a sudden turn for the worse," Marlene said.

"Or we can choose to believe he learned something so unexpected—so off-the-charts incredible," Mose said, his voice rising like a hot air balloon, "that he's rechecking Sylvia's test results. Maybe ordering new MRIs or other tests to reconfirm a huge improvement in her prognosis. Wouldn't *that* be something!"

"Mose, don't get your hopes up just because—"

"Why not?" he challenged, grasping his sister's sturdy hands. "Hope is all I've got, Marlene, so I intend to play it for all it's worth. One way or another, I intend to find out exactly what to expect when Sylvia's released. And right now, I feel compelled to pray about it. Will you join me?"

Together they returned to the guest room, where they wouldn't be interrupted. Marlene sat on the edge of her bed as Mose pulled a chair in front of her. As he sat holding her hands again, he felt an inexplicable power bubbling within him, a potent combination of optimism and unshakable faith. He closed his eyes and bowed his head.

"Lord, You work in mysterious ways, and You've led us to this place at this time for reasons only You know," he began in a reverent rush. "You've promised us that wherever two or three gather in Your name, You are present—and I'm asking You to include Sylvia in our circle as we pray for her healing and recovery. After all's been said and done for her medically, You alone have the power to grant her a healthy life . . . or a life with You eternally."

Mose paused, refusing to allow the possibility of Sylvia's death to dampen his spirits. "We ask that You work out Your will for her, and for us, and that You grant us Your presence and Your peace no matter what happens in the days to come. If it's my turn for a miracle, Lord, why don't You give it to Sylvia instead? Surround her with Your comfort and love. Remind her that she's not alone—and she never will be."

After a moment, a sense of serenity and fulfillment settled over him. He'd said all he could say. The rest was up to God.

"We ask these things in the holy name of Your Son, Jesus Christ, our Lord and Savior," he whispered. "Amen."

"Amen," Marlene echoed softly. She sighed as she held his gaze. "Mose, I stand in awe of the effortless way your words come out when you pray—the perfect words, spoken without a single hitch. You've always been such a blessing to me. Sylvia's a lucky woman."

His eyes widened at his twin's praise. Mose smiled wryly. "Maybe that's a sign that I should pray more and worry less, ain't so? Let's visit the gift shop, shall we? I've got an idea, and I may need to make a call or two to bring it off."

As Irene left the bulk store Saturday, feeling horribly humiliated, she wanted nothing more than to hide in her room at the house on the hill. She'd caused Dale endless trouble and extra work this morning—and she didn't feel good about leaving him a note to end their relationship, either. An afternoon to lick her wounds and take a long nap seemed the only cure for her funk—

Until she saw folks gathering at the outdoor tables near the lodge. Her women friends had prepared another hearty meal for the workmen, and they were sitting down to enjoy it, too. The last thing Irene needed was to be quizzed about her downcast mood and her pink-rimmed eyes, yet when she spotted an empty chair at the end of a table, she hurried toward it. Her nap would be so much more satisfying if she didn't keep waking up with hunger pangs.

As Bishop Monroe rose to bless the food, the conversations stopped. All eyes were on the church leader as he clasped his large hands in front of him, considering what he'd say.

"Friends, as our work progresses, we have much to be thankful for," he began, glancing around at his congregation and the carpenters who'd joined them from Coldstream and Cloverdale. "And because so many of us are here for this meal, it seems like a *gut* time to pray for Sylvia Keim, for we believe that the power of our prayers is magnified when we address God as His gathered people, with a unified request. Rosetta and Truman don't think Sylvia had regained consciousness when they were at the hospital yesterday, and as time goes by, that circumstance becomes more worrisome. Shall we pray?"

Irene felt some of the tension easing from her shoulders. She would never join the Amish church because shunning didn't feel right to her, but she believed Monroe Burkholder was one of God's chosen messengers. She bowed her head along with everyone around her and let the bishop's resonant voice and providential wisdom wash over her.

"Dear Lord and Father of us all, we're grateful once again for the friends who've come to help us rebuild, and for the food You've provided so we may sustain ourselves to do Your work and Your will," he began reverently. "Today we also lift up your daughter Sylvia. We ask Your presence with her doctors and caregivers. We pray that her body will heal and her health will be restored, even as we know that You might have other plans for her."

Irene swallowed hard. Her own troubles seemed so trivial compared to what tiny, birdlike Sylvia was going through.

"Give us the faith to believe that with You, all things are

possible," Bishop Monroe continued more emphatically. "And grant us the courage to answer Your call, to help Sylvia when she returns to us—or to serve as her final friends on this earth as You welcome her to Your kingdom. Either way, Lord, we can't lose because You are with us— in life, in death, and in our resurrection. And You're with Sylvia, even if she can't perceive Your presence. All thanks be to You for our Savior Jesus, in whose name we pray. Amen."

"Amen," the folks at the tables whispered.

For a moment, Irene sat quietly, aware that workmen were being encouraged to fill their plates first. The bishop's words—especially about God being present in life, death, and resurrection—stirred something deep inside her.

Resurrection. Weren't they all witnessing that as Mattie's produce stand, Christine's barn, the Kuhns' cheese factory, and the Promise Lodge Pies bakery came back to life after the storm? And they all lived in anticipation of the day when the lodge would stand fully restored, too—with a re-modeled kitchen and apartments they could call home once again.

As the folks at her table stood up to get into the buffet line, Irene walked behind the lodge instead. The entire back wall had been removed, so the building resembled a large dollhouse with all the rooms open. She was amazed to see that new beams and interior support walls were already in place, and that a new roof on the back half of the building was ready to be shingled. With the storm's damage com-pletely cleared away, the air was redolent with the scents of sturdy new lumber and fresh paint.

It smelled like *hope*. And the large stack of boards wait-ing nearby suggested that very soon, the workmen would be enclosing the lodge with a new back wall.

Irene muffled a little sob as she gazed up at the corner,

where her new apartment would soon be ready. It wasn't the end of the world if she and Dale didn't marry. Her morning's mistakes had shown her that she wasn't the woman he needed—in his store, or in his life—but wasn't it valuable to know that *now*? What if she'd gotten so caught up in the excitement of a midlife romance that she'd married him and had *then* discovered, too late, that storekeeping as Mrs. Dale Kraybill wasn't the life she was intended to lead?

Quickly wiping her eyes, Irene felt a smile easing over her face as she walked toward the serving line. A good meal would go a long way toward making her feel like herself again.

"Irene! What a pretty new dress!" Mattie called out.

"*Denki*," she said. "Losing all my clothes in the tornado gave me the perfect excuse to sew a whole new wardrobe, *jah*?"

And when she recalled the moment she'd pulled the blue, yellow, and white fabric from Dale's bag, Irene smiled fondly. He might not be the man she wanted to spend the rest of her life with, but she couldn't argue with his sense of style.

Chapter 23

Sylvia had the sensation of floating up from the bottom of a deep pool, toward light that seemed to be welcoming her . . . welcoming her home. As she slowly approached the surface, gentle waves supported her, rocking her as though she were a baby again.

Is this what it means to be born again?

The question startled her, but she wasn't yet ready to open her eyes. The air was cool and fresh. From a distance she heard faint voices, but she felt no connection to them. Every few moments, something beeped softly, yet she had no need to discover where the sound came from. When Sylvia drew in a deep breath—because she was no longer underwater—a sweet fragrance filled her being with a sense of beauty and euphoria.

She allowed her eyes to flutter open and was engulfed in *pink*. Everywhere she saw pink, even after she blinked repeatedly to clear the fog from her vision. Sylvia didn't know why, but she sensed her eyes had been closed for a long time. Did that mean that all the marvelous or strange or somewhat frightening images she'd experienced lately had been in her dreams?

When she turned her head to focus on the array of pink

closest to her, she realized it was a huge bouquet of roses. Blinking again, Sylvia spotted a spray of exotic lilies in various shades of pink, just beyond the roses. Moving her head slowly so nothing would hurt, she focused on more roses, more lilies, along with carnations, cyclamens, gladiolas, and varieties of flowers she couldn't identify—all of them pink, and more beautiful than any she'd ever seen.

I'm in a garden.

Sylvia wanted to get up, to walk around this paradise she'd awakened in, yet her body felt lethargic. And she was in no hurry to move around, because again she sensed that it had been a long time since she'd been on her feet walking. She didn't want to fall, to ruin this sensation of glorious peace and perfection all around her.

Is this the garden in that song, where He walks and talks with me and tells me I'm His own?

Sylvia sucked in her breath. She'd died and gone to heaven. Any minute now, Jesus might step into view! And while that idea filled her with awe and delight, it also made her strangely sad. She clearly recalled a life on earth that had taken a turn for the better, and she hadn't been nearly ready to leave it.

A movement in the distance made her turn her head, and there He was. It was Jesus, looking larger than life and darkly handsome—and He was here to visit with her! Jesus didn't resemble the Savior with the halo and the light brown hair, as He was depicted in religious paintings she'd seen. In fact, as the figure slowly approached her, He appeared distinctly Amish: dark trousers and a green shirt, rather than glowing white robes. But then, the Amish believed their faith was the one true way to salvation, so who was to say that Jesus—or even God—didn't wear suspenders?

"Sylvia?" he whispered. "Have you come back to me? I've been waiting—"

Her eyes widened. He knew her name, just as it promised in the Bible! He'd been watching her all through her life, and now He was welcoming her to her heavenly home—

"Oh, honey-girl, it's s-such a b-blessing—s-so exciting!—to s-see you looking at m-me again! I—"

Sylvia sucked in her breath. Was it a coincidence, or did Jesus stutter exactly the way—

"Mose?" she blurted. "What're *you* doing up in heaven?"

He stopped at her side, leaning over her with great caution, giving her the sweetest, gentlest smile she'd ever seen.

"That's exactly where I am when I'm with you, Sylvia," he replied gently. "I can't stay, sweetie—I'm not supposed to be in here, because visiting hours don't start for another couple of hours. But I'll be back!" he added happily. "We'll get you home to Promise Lodge as soon as they let you out of here. You rest easy, Sylvia. Everything's going to work out!"

As he slipped away, Sylvia longed to follow him, yet when she reached toward him, she realized something was attached to her arm. Tubes.

She blinked. Were there visiting hours in heaven? If she and Mose were both there . . .

The next little *beep* made her realize that those tubes taped to her arm were attached to machines and monitors that whirred softly.

She wasn't in heaven, it seemed. Somehow she'd ended up in a hospital bed—

I had such a headache I must've passed out. Someone—Mattie, probably—must've called the ambulance when I didn't wake up.

Sudden tears ran down her cheeks. She recalled staying in bed in her room at the Troyer place because she'd been in such excruciating, debilitating pain that she hadn't been able to get up to take her pain meds—or to tell anyone. She must've passed out . . . and she might well have passed on but for the help her compassionate friends had provided.

And now Mose, bless his heart, was here at the hospital with her—and he'd undoubtedly been the one to fill her room with more flowers—*pink* flowers—than she'd ever seen in one place.

Sylvia took in a deep breath and slowly let it out. She hadn't gone to heaven and seen Jesus, but that was quite all right. If Mose said everything would work out, she believed him with all her heart.

But the best part? She inhaled fully and deeply again, smiling with the wonder of it: for the first time in recent years, she didn't have a headache. Not even a dull one. No pain whatsoever.

On Sunday morning after the service at the Mennonite church in Cloverdale, Dale made his way between the folks chatting over coffee and cookies in the crowded hall to visit with Irene. His emotional antennae had shot up when she'd avoided him in the sanctuary and had barely met his gaze when he'd slid into the pew a few rows ahead of her.

Why? Had he upset her yesterday when he'd suggested she could go home from the store?

Putting on a smile, he approached her. Irene was surrounded by some of her longtime female friends, Doris and Gladys and Greta . . . almost as though their presence would protect her from him. Again, Dale sensed she was trying not to acknowledge him. Had they not kissed a few days ago—

had Irene not seemed so open to trying out a new life that would include him—the little alarms wouldn't be jangling in the back of his mind.

He positioned himself behind the woman in front of Irene, so she couldn't miss him. During a pause in the ladies' conversation, he spoke up.

"Irene, you look very nice this morning, in those shades of green," Dale said, keeping his tone light.

Thankfully Doris chimed in. "I was just asking where she found that pretty houndstooth fabric," she said. "Do you sell it in your new store, Dale?"

"*Jah*, we sure do miss having you here in Cloverdale," Gladys remarked with a nod. "The local bulk store's just not the same under its new management."

As Dale smiled at all four of the women, he couldn't miss the way Irene glanced toward the coffee urn.

"I have a nice selection of new summer-weight polyesters," he replied, "and I'd be delighted to help you select some. I miss seeing you ladies—but I have to say business is really booming now that I have a store on the state highway in Promise."

"And your new building is so nicely lit, and you have more space to carry a wider variety of items," Greta pointed out. "I've only been there once, but I plan to come again soon to get one of Irene's fresh pies and some of the cheeses the Kuhn sisters make—and some more of Rosetta's goat milk soap."

When Irene slipped away, apparently to refill her coffee cup, Dale refused to let her escape—because that's what her body language suggested she was doing. Indeed, she was setting her cup on the table and heading out to the parking lot, but why? She'd come to church with Truman and

Rosetta, so it wasn't as though she could drive herself back to Promise.

"Irene!" he called after her.

A few other folks were walking to their vehicles, glancing at him, but Dale didn't care. If something was coming between him and the woman he'd fallen in love with, he wasn't going to let it fester. And if other members of their church surmised that he and Irene were behaving as a couple after all these years, that was fine with him.

"Irene, please," he said as he caught up to her. "What's the matter, dear? Don't let a couple of mishaps at the store discourage you from—"

"*Mishaps?*" She'd reached Truman's white pickup, and she was opening the door behind the driver's seat. "I made a total mess of your freezer units—and I wasted so much of your sanding sugar—"

"It's my own fault." Dale grabbed the door before she could enter the truck and close him out. "I should've known Marlene's crash course wouldn't prepare you for working in her place. It was so generous and kind of you to fill in for her at the last minute, Irene. Please don't let a false start in the store affect our—our relationship."

Her hand fluttered to her mouth as though she might cry—which seemed to distress Irene even more.

Dale's eyes widened. Did she believe he would write her off for shedding a few tears, when he had been the cause of them?

Irene turned away to compose herself. Or was she looking for another escape route?

"Can we sit in the truck and talk this over?" he asked gently. "Or, if you don't want Truman and Rosetta to interrupt us, we could sit in my car—"

"Oh, I couldn't do that!" she blurted out.

He frowned, puzzled now. "Why not? I'm suggesting a

simple conversation, dear. We're beyond the stage of, um, *misbehaving* in the back seat, after all."

The idea of kissing Irene until passion wiped away their inhibitions suddenly seemed appealing—yet Dale could see that his choice of words had upset her even further.

He sighed, stepping away from Truman's pickup. "I'm sorry. I've bungled this whole situation," he murmured ruefully. "Please give me another chance, Irene. I—I *love* you. And if you never want to help in the store again, that's quite all right," he added emphatically. "I'm hoping you'll spend the rest of your life as my wife—not just as someone who can help me run my business."

"It won't work, Dale. We've been *gut* friends for years, and that's how it'll have to stay." Irene stepped up into the truck and sat down. "Please close the door. I—I don't know what else to say."

Stunned, he did as she asked. The last thing he wanted was for Irene to think he wouldn't respect her space, her need for privacy. What did he know about pleasing women, or dealing with their moods? Maybe if he gave Irene time to get over her current upset, she would reconsider the stand she'd taken about marrying him.

"Dale, you look like a man who's been turned away— or turned down," Truman observed as he and Rosetta approached the truck. "How can I help?"

"*Jah*, Irene's got a bee in her bonnet, and she won't tell us why," Rosetta said softly. "Did something happen at the store yesterday?"

Dale sighed, aware that Irene could hear what they were saying. He had to answer Rosetta's question, however, so she and her husband would at least know his side of the situation.

"Irene feels terrible because she bungled some restocking and spilled some sugar in the warehouse," he replied with a shrug. "And she seems to think that such minor mistakes—which anyone new to storekeeping could make—have spelled the end of our . . . our blossoming romance. I—I wish I knew how to change her mind."

Rosetta plucked the keys from Truman's hand and handed them to Dale. "Here—let's trade vehicles. What woman doesn't like a Sunday drive in the country?"

"*Gut* idea!" Truman said with a chuckle. "You've got a full gas tank and the rest of a pretty day—and our blessings," he added. "High time my mother went for a ride with someone besides her son."

Chapter 24

A short time after he'd left Sylvia's room, Mose's patience was rewarded: a doctor in dress slacks, with a white lab coat over his shirt and tie, went in to see her. Mose assumed this was Dr. Mannering, and the eager expression on the physician's face—the way he gripped the charts in his hand—suggested that he had some positive news for Sylvia.

"I'm impressed that he's come on a Sunday," Marlene murmured from the chair beside Mose's. "When our parents were here, it was impossible to get attention from their doctors or test results on weekends."

"I'm going to listen from the doorway," Mose said as he rose from his seat. "I know it's against the rules, but somebody besides Sylvia ought to hear what Doc Mannering's got to say. If you see a nurse headed this way, distract her, all right?"

Marlene's furrowed brows and dropped jaw made Mose chuckle—but his twin would do as he'd asked, because she understood just how deeply he cared for Sylvia. He stopped a few feet from Sylvia's doorway, nonchalantly leaning against the wall as though he was studying the artwork across the hallway.

". . . wonderful to see you looking so chipper this

morning, Sylvia," Dr. Mannering was saying. "Your vital signs are good. How do you feel?"

"It would be hard to feel sick with all these beautiful flowers around, ain't so?" she replied without missing a beat. "At first when I woke up, I thought I'd died and gone to heaven—"

The doctor chuckled, but Mose wondered if he'd remain so jovial if Sylvia told him about her earlier visitor.

"—but then," Sylvia continued, "I realized that, for the first time since I was diagnosed with an inoperable tumor, I have absolutely no pain! My headache's completely gone! And considering the excruciating way my head hurt before my friends had me admitted here, this is a *miracle*."

"I use that word *miracle* very sparingly," Dr. Mannering remarked after a moment. "But in your case, Sylvia, I have to concur. I've spent considerable time discussing your tumor with Dr. Sutherland in Pennsylvania—thanks to your friends' sending along your medication bottles, which gave me his name. He's just as amazed as I am by what we've seen in your most recent MRI."

Mose held his breath. He'd been agog at the dosage on those bottles, and at the type of pain prescriptions Sylvia had been taking just to function somewhat normally. The absence of her headache was a major improvement indeed.

"Dr. Sutherland didn't give me much hope for any sort of recovery," Sylvia remarked cautiously. "During my last appointment, he told me I probably wouldn't live to see my fiftieth birthday in October. He said my tumor would grow until it eventually interfered with my bodily functions—"

"Which is why he and I are both astounded. I ordered a second MRI to be sure the original images were correct— and that they didn't belong to another patient," Dr. Mannering said in a rush. "Your tumor is *gone*, Sylvia. We don't know why, or what happened to it, but your brain now looks as though you never had one."

Mose's mouth dropped open. How could a tumor simply disappear? In his experience as a vet tech, he'd never heard of that happening.

With God, all things are possible.

He blinked, believing that Bible verse with all his heart and soul and mind. He kept listening, because nothing could've stopped him at this point.

Sylvia sucked in her breath. "Disappeared?" she asked in a loud whisper. "Do you . . . do you suppose I had such excruciating pain in my head the night before I came here because the tumor had broken open or—or exploded? It hurt so bad, I couldn't get up out of bed. I was pretty sure my time had come."

Sudden tears stung Mose's eyes. When he saw his curious twin approaching, he waved her over. "Can you believe this, Marlene?" he whispered in her ear. "Sylvia's tumor is gone! Totally gone!"

"Oh my—thank the Lord!" his sister cried out.

Marlene clapped her hand over her mouth as her outburst reverberated in the hallway. Mose slumped against the wall, knowing he and his sister deserved whatever reprimand Dr. Mannering would surely deliver. He knew better than to eavesdrop on a confidential conversation.

Moments later, the physician peered around the doorway. He was a middle-aged fellow whose eyebrows had remained somewhat darker than his graying hair—and one of those brows was raised in displeasure.

"You folks have no business hovering outside a patient's door," Dr. Mannering began sharply. "If you don't leave immediately, I'll have to call security—"

"Mose, is that you out there, with Marlene?" Sylvia called

loudly. "Dr. Mannering, I give them my permission to come in and hear what you're saying to me!"

The doctor paused, turning so he could see Sylvia while he kept an eye on Mose and his sister.

"We'll leave if you want us to, Doctor," Mose said apologetically. "I love Sylvia with all my heart, but we're not married—"

"*Yet!*" Sylvia put in emphatically. "Dr. Mannering, Mose is the man who filled my room with all these beautiful flowers, not knowing if I'd live or die. Can you imagine how much money he paid to have this *garden* delivered to my room, so I'd know how much he loves me?"

Mose thought his heart was going to thump its way out of his rib cage. Sylvia had just stated her case for all the world to hear, removing the last shadow of any doubt from his mind. She wanted to marry him! *And* she no longer had a tumor! No matter how much the doctor disapproved of his eavesdropping, Mose wouldn't trade these past few moments for *anything*.

Dr. Mannering cleared his throat, as though assessing the two Amish folks who stood before him in their guilt.

"This is highly irregular," he pointed out, "but if Sylvia is giving her permission—"

"Mose, honey, come here!" Sylvia blurted out. "I need a kiss—right this minute—to celebrate my tumor being gone!"

Mose's cheeks flushed red-hot, but he smiled at the doctor. "What man in his right mind would argue with *that*?"

Dr. Mannering chuckled in spite of his earlier displeasure. "Sounds like you'd better get used to following orders, sir, because now that Sylvia's feeling better, she seems ready to have her say—and have her way."

Mose was aware that his sister was introducing herself and chatting with the doctor, but when he saw Sylvia carefully sitting up to swing her legs over the side of her bed, he lost track of everything else. The church leaders would be declaring that it was indecent for him to see so much of Sylvia's bare skin in a skimpy hospital gown before they were married—

But Bishop Monroe and the preachers weren't here, were they? When Mose spotted a spare blanket in the open closet, he grabbed it. Sylvia smiled gratefully as he draped the blanket around her without disturbing her IVs and tubes.

With his pulse pounding, Mose perched cautiously beside Sylvia. When she beamed at him, her joy erased at least ten years that had lined her face while she'd been facing death. As he slipped his arm around her, he was again aware of how tiny and fragile she was—and aware of the mind-boggling responsibility God had given him, along with the love he'd assumed he'd never find.

Sylvia kissed him exuberantly, then eased away.

"I'm so glad you were listening when the doctor told me my tumor was gone, Mose," she confessed in a whisper. "I'm not sure I could've found the words to tell you myself, because I'm still wondering if I might be caught up in a wonderful dream, and when I wake up—"

"Every bit of this is real, sweetie," he murmured as he carefully held her close. "God has blessed us with a miracle, for sure and for certain. Let's believe that, and promise each other we'll live up to such a marvelous gift every day of our lives, all right?"

Irene sat tight in the back seat of her son's truck, too flustered to protest the way Truman and Rosetta had conspired against her. Dale had stepped up into the driver's seat and started the engine. He was smiling at her in the rearview mirror, appearing awfully pleased about the turn their morning had taken.

"Will you sit up here with me so we can talk, dear?" he asked. "Your kids are right—it's a lovely day for a Sunday drive and dinner out somewhere. But I feel pretty lonely with my date in the back seat."

"I didn't intend to be your *date*," Irene sputtered. "We're too old for such—"

"On the contrary," Dale interrupted gently. "It's just occurred to me that some courting time is exactly what we need. I've seen you at church and in the store and in the lodge dining room countless times over the years, but if I'm to convince you to be more than my *friend*, we need to spend some time alone together."

Irene swiveled her head to stare out the truck's window. All she wanted was to go back to her room at the house—

But, like it or not, the only way I'll get there is to ride with Dale.

Exhaling impatiently, she grabbed the door handle.

Somehow, Dale, ever the gentleman, got down from the truck and opened her door in time to help her to the ground. He gently kept hold of her hand as they went around the vehicle, and then he gallantly opened the door and assisted her into the front seat—even though Irene had stepped up into Truman's truck dozens of times without help.

She held her tongue, however. She sensed that the quickest way to get through this ordeal was to go along with Dale's wishes—for now.

Dale steered the truck onto the county road that led to Promise before he spoke again. As always, his voice was low and cultivated, and he put some thought into what he was saying.

"What if . . . what if the store wasn't an issue? What if I never expected you to help there again—even though I know you'd be really *gut* at storekeeping if you had a chance to learn," he added quickly.

Irene frowned. "But if I were your wife, everyone would expect me to—"

"But what if *I* don't expect you to work in my business?" Dale's expression brightened, as though he had a completely new idea. "What if I *sold* the store, so it wouldn't even be a concern?"

Irene's mouth fell open. "Sell your store? Why would you want to do that, Dale? You're such a successful businessman—and how would you make your living?"

He shrugged as he stopped at an intersection. "What if I went to work for *you*? What if we expanded Promise Lodge Pies and sold our products to more stores and restaurants? After all, once Phoebe and Allen start their family—"

"Have you lost your mind?" Irene blurted out. "We wouldn't make enough money selling pies to—"

"Ah. But I got you to join the conversation, didn't I?" he asked with a smile. "And truth be told, we're both thinking outside the box now. After more than thirty years of store-keeping, maybe I'm ready to take up something new."

Irene could only gape at him as he remained at the stop sign with the engine idling. Dale speared his long, elegant fingers through his steely-gray hair with a smile that was boyish yet wise.

"I wouldn't suggest such a venture if I couldn't afford it, dear. I could sell the store tomorrow and retire, and still keep you in the manner to which you've become accustomed," he stated softly. "But I would have to have something to *do* with myself—"

Behind them, a car horn blared.

Chuckling, Dale continued down the road. "I like to think I'm still trainable, so why not consider it, Irene?" he said. "I've been cooking for myself for years, and you could show me how you like to have things done in your pie shop. Or, I could become your business manager and line up more places to sell your products—leave the baking to you and whomever you'd hire to help you."

"Absolutely not." Irene's thoughts were spinning so fast and furious, she thought her head would explode. What on earth had possessed Dale to suggest selling his store? It was a big point in his favor that he could afford to retire, but—

"You don't want me to partner with you? Why not?"

"I don't want to expand Promise Lodge Pies," she stated. "Phoebe and I discovered long ago that working four mornings a week is about all the time we can handle standing on hard floors. The pie shop was originally Phoebe's idea, and I felt honored that she wanted me to partner with her."

Shaking her head, Irene wondered how Dale had lured her into this conversation unawares. But if he was willing to sell his store—and could afford to—maybe she had nothing to lose by discussing her own circumstances.

"Like you, I need something useful to do more than I need an income," she explained softly. "When I moved from the house to my apartment, I suddenly had so little housework and so much time, baking pies sounded like *fun*."

Dale stopped at the next sign before turning onto the road that led to Promise Lodge. "But it's not fun anymore? Your pies—and now your fried pies—are such a quick sellout, I just assumed you enjoyed baking them."

Sighing, Irene took a moment to consider the direction their conversation had taken. Until this moment, she hadn't thought much about the business venture she and Phoebe had begun several months ago: she'd been committed to it, and she wasn't one to quit on a whim. Now, however, if Dale was suggesting that he could sell his store and walk away—apparently without regret—maybe she could do that, too.

"I do enjoy baking," she murmured. "But truth be told, the tornado—and losing my apartment and the bakery— have overturned my apple cart. Maybe I should consider a business that doesn't require so much time on my feet. But I'd talk it over with Phoebe before I made such a move."

"Of course you would," he put in softly. "You've never been a quitter, Irene. It's one of the qualities I've always admired about you. I've always admired your pies, too, but I can understand why all those hours of baking could wear on you after a while. I confess that I have days when managing my store is the last thing I want to do," he added with a sigh. "But I can't just close up on a whim. I have a commitment to my customers to keep regular hours."

"And it's not as though you could leave thousands of dollars of inventory sitting on your shelves," Irene put in. "If you ever walk away from your store, you'd have to have a buyer lined up. You're the kind of man who would have his ducks in a row and his exit plan in place."

"See there? We know each other pretty well, Irene—but that's all I'm going to say on that subject." Dale drove past the entryway to Promise Lodge, stopping at the intersection of the state highway where the Helmuths' nursery sat. "Are you in the mood for the Skyline Inn out past Forest Grove? I haven't eaten there in years, but it was always a great place—especially at a table by the back windows that over-look the wildlife preserve."

Irene's eyes widened. Ernest had always considered the Skyline Inn too pricey, even for special occasions. "I've never been there, but—well, are we dressed up enough? I've heard they have white linen tablecloths and waiters in tuxedos and—"

Dale's smile, and the warmth of his hand as he clasped hers, made Irene realize again what an attractive man he was.

"You're wearing a very nice church dress, and I'm in a

shirt and tie," he pointed out. "If the maître d' doesn't think we're properly attired—"

"I would *never* accuse you of being improper, Dale Kraybill!"

His low chuckle reverberated in the cab of the truck as his expression took a mischievous turn. "Maybe it's time I changed that. Maybe I should channel my inner scoundrel— give you something to *think* about, Mrs. Wickey."

Irene's cheeks went hot as Dale refused to drop his gaze. It had been years since a man had looked at her with such *intentions* shining in his eyes—intimate intentions that were written all over his clean-shaven face.

"You've given me quite a lot to think about," she admitted in a whisper.

"Glad to hear it."

Chapter 25

As Truman's truck pulled into Promise Lodge late Tuesday morning, Sylvia looked eagerly through the back seat window. It was wonderful to see Christine's new barn with some of her black-and-white Holsteins grazing nearby, as well as the Kuhns' new cheese factory, and the Promise Lodge Pies bakery building—all of them up and running, thanks to the carpentry crews from Coldstream and Cloverdale. Even better, as Truman drove her and Mose up the hill, Sylvia turned to see that their local carpenters had begun constructing the new back wall that would enclose the lodge.

"You fellows made a lot of progress while I was away!" she said to Truman. "I'm sorry you had to leave your work to drive me home from the hospital."

"Not a problem," Truman assured her. "We've been very concerned about you, Sylvia. Seeing you at Mamm's Rainbow Lake birthday picnic this evening will be the frosting on everyone's cake, believe me."

"So I got home for Irene's party?" she asked with a chuckle. "It's the perfect time for a *lot* of celebrating, ain't so?"

"Sure is," Mose chimed in beside her. He'd been holding her hand the entire way home from the hospital, and his happiness accentuated his boyish good looks. "We all have so much to be thankful for these days—and I'm especially grateful to God. It's so *gut* to have you back home, honey-girl."

Honey-girl. Ivan hadn't used endearments very often during their marriage, but Sylvia was becoming accustomed to Mose's romantic vocabulary. When they pulled up in front of the Troyer home, he slid down from the back seat and immediately turned to help her—because for a short person, the ground was quite a distance from the seat. Mose had just released her when the front door flew open.

"Sylvia! Look at you!" Mattie cried out. "Oh my! When I watched them rolling you into the ambulance Friday morning, I—I wasn't sure you'd make it."

Truman laughed as he opened the topper on the bed of his truck. "Sylvia's not all I came back with, Mattie," he said. "You ladies can open your own florist shop with all these flowers."

When Mattie peered into the back end of the truck, she sucked in her breath. "Where'd you get all these *pink*—oh, silly me," she added quickly. "I don't have to look very far to see who sent them, do I?"

"Truth be told, when I woke up from being sedated, I thought I was in heaven—or in that garden in the song, where Jesus was walking and talking with me," Sylvia said. As she grasped Mose's large hand again, she beamed at him. "It was so generous of the Fisher twins to leave their jobs so they could look after me."

"When I saw Marlene at the store this morning, she—and Dale—were back to their normal routine," Mattie remarked, still gazing at the packed-in planters and pink blooms. "But they agreed that your care took top priority,

Sylvia. Especially because you had no next of kin to help you navigate your hospital stay."

"Where would I be without my friends?" Sylvia murmured, still holding Mose's hand and his gaze. She sighed, knowing how blessed she was, before focusing on the matter at hand. "And where shall we put all these flowers, Mattie? Most of them are bouquets, but a few are potted plants—"

"What if we decorate the tables for Irene's birthday party this evening?" Mattie suggested. "I think we've managed to keep it a surprise. The birthday girl will be even more thrilled when she sees all these beautiful blooms, don't you think?"

Sylvia had known the Troyers didn't have enough room for so many flowers in their small home, so Mattie's suggestion seemed like a practical solution. She walked a short distance from the truck to gaze toward Rainbow Lake, where a few tables had already been put up near the water. Mose had come with her, to be sure she didn't stumble in the thick grass.

"Is it all right if I share my beautiful flowers with Irene?" she asked softly. "You must've spent hundreds of dollars on me—"

"Because I wanted to," Mose insisted. "I didn't think about what you'd do with them when you were released. Sharing them with Irene seems like a fine solution, Sylvia."

Her heartbeat raced. Was there any reason not to express the other idea she'd been considering, now that he'd given her the perfect opening? Sylvia inhaled deeply, telling herself the time was right—and no one else was close enough to hear their conversation.

"Is it all right if I share the rest of your life, Mose?" she asked demurely. "I wasn't teasing when I told Dr. Mannering I wasn't your wife *yet*. But I want to be."

Mose's jaw dropped. He knelt before her to look into her eyes. "You—you'll marry me?" he asked breathlessly. "I don't have to think up some flowery, perfect way to propose to—"

Sylvia cupped his jaw, marveling. On his knees, the man she loved was a few inches shorter than she was.

"Why beat around the bush?" she murmured. "God's given me a whole new life and I want to share it with *you*, Mose. Why put you through all the agony of a proposal— unless you *want* to propose? You know I love you, *jah*?"

Mose appeared dumbstruck—overwhelmed yet overjoyed. "Well, we *have* said that a lot this past day or so."

Sylvia smiled at him, the dearest man in the world. "Take your time if you need to think about it, or—"

"No! I've loved you practically since I met you. Let's announce our engagement tonight when everybody's at the picnic," Mose suggested.

As he hugged her close, Sylvia felt a hitch in his shoulders, as though her big, burly man might be fighting back tears. Her eyes misted over, as well, but they were tears of joy because she was at Promise Lodge rather than in a heavenly garden.

You'll just have to wait, Jesus. God—and Mose—aren't finished with me yet.

"I'll let you take care of our announcement," Sylvia replied, wrapping her arms around his broad, muscular shoulders. "Let's help Truman get all those flowers out of his truck, and we can talk more later, *jah*? He and Mattie are, um, *watching* us, I suspect."

"They won't see a happier man on the face of God's *gut* earth," he said as he rose to his feet.

* * *

When Rosetta went into the kitchen to answer the phone Tuesday afternoon, Irene peered out the back window of the Wickey house. It was just as she suspected: Mattie, Christine, Frances, and some of the other women were setting up tables near Rainbow Lake for the birthday party she wasn't supposed to know about. Irene gaped at the huge bouquets of pink flowers—

Oh dear, did Dale have those delivered as his way of convincing me to say yes?

Irene sighed. The two of them had shared a magnificent dinner at the Skyline Inn on Sunday, and in light of her qualms about becoming his life partner—or having him as a partner for Promise Lodge Pies—Dale had kept the conversation light. She'd asked his forgiveness for taking out her storekeeping frustrations on him, and he'd once again assured her that anyone could've made those mistakes.

Dale's such a lovely, agreeable person. Why can't I go along with his ideas about getting married? Any woman would be lucky and blessed to have him for a husband.

Now, however, it seemed Irene would have to attend a party for a birthday she'd rather gloss over. Sixty-three wasn't one of those landmark ages, so why were her friends going to such lengths to celebrate? To prove it was just another day, Irene had gone to the bakery before daybreak as usual and made pies with Phoebe. Then she'd delivered them to the café in Forest Green as well as to Dale's bulk store, restocking her shelf while Dale had assisted a customer. Truth be told, after such a busy day, she'd be happy to relax and eat leftovers at home—

The sound of gagging followed by the splatter of liquid hitting the kitchen sink made Irene turn. All thoughts of

Dale and her birthday vanished when she heard Rosetta vomit again.

Ordinarily Rosetta recovers quickly from adversity. What if her recent exhaustion and pale complexion have been caused by something other than stress from the tornado damage? Have I been so caught up in my own turmoil that I haven't connected Rosetta's frequent tears and the circles under her eyes to something entirely different?

Irene hugged herself, grinning, yet she knew better than to rush into the kitchen. A wise mother-in-law tiptoed into this situation rather than stomping on a delicate, potentially life-altering moment.

A few minutes later Rosetta returned to the front room as though nothing had happened. "Irene, I'm going to the lodge to speak with Dale about—oh!" she said as she joined Irene at the window. "I guess you've noticed we're having a picnic for your birthday, *jah*? Planning for happiness every chance we get!"

Her daughter-in-law squeezed her shoulder. "You might want to change into a fresh dress and join us for supper and Ruby's chocolate cake with the mocha frosting—because *nobody* wants to miss that!"

Irene smiled, taking Rosetta's hand. "Well, for Ruby's chocolate cake, I suppose I can make an appearance. But is there a possibility we're also celebrating something else, dear?"

Her daughter-in-law frowned, genuinely confused. "Well, we're all happy that the renovation is going so well—"

"And might you and Truman be turning one of the guest rooms into a nursery soon?"

Rosetta's blank expression told Irene that the idea hadn't even occurred to them.

Irene hoped she hadn't already rushed in where angels

feared to tread. "Think about it," she suggested gently. "You're pale and unusually emotional, and not sleeping well, and—and *maybe* throwing up—"

"But that's because I've been so upset about the lodge and all the repairs we've had to make and—"

"Maybe it wouldn't hurt to pay Minerva a visit."

"Teacher Minerva?" Rosetta gazed at Irene as though *she* might be the one who was behaving strangely. "Irene, I have no desire to take over the schoolroom—"

"Midwife Minerva."

Rosetta's eyes widened as her mouth dropped open. "Oh my word. You don't think . . ."

"Better to be sure than to second-guess such a possibility, right?"

Her daughter-in-law stifled a laugh that sounded a bit like a sob. She turned to look out the window again, to settle herself by watching her sisters and the other women who were arranging food on the long, decorated tables by the lake.

Rosetta inhaled deeply. "Don't breathe a word of this to anyone, *please*?" she pleaded. "We need to be certain—at my age, we can't take any chances—"

"My lips are sealed, dear," Irene whispered. "This is your announcement to make, not mine."

For a long, gratifying moment Rosetta hugged Irene as though she wouldn't let go. Then she eased away, resuming her plans for the evening—trying to act as though she wasn't connecting the dots of her symptoms, drawing a picture of her possible pregnancy.

"Supper's at six!" she said with a nervous chuckle. "See you there if I don't happen to make it back beforehand."

After a few minutes passed, Irene saw Rosetta striding

down the hill toward the lodge, which the local men had been hard at work renovating.

Irene stood straighter, spotting Dale as he walked methodically around the area where the cabins farthest from the lodge had once sat. He was placing one foot directly in front of the other, heel to toe, as though—

Why would he be pacing off a piece of ground? If he were going to expand his store, he'd be walking off the dimensions near the back of the warehouse.

Her curiosity got the best of her. Irene changed into her pink and purple striped dress, smoothed her hair, and headed to the lodge. If Rosetta or Dale asked why she was there, she'd say she was interested in how the new back wall was coming along—checking it out before the picnic. Secretly Irene was also hoping to find out where all those pink flowers had come from.

By the time she was passing Mattie's produce plots, Rosetta and Dale were engrossed in a serious conversation near the spot the storekeeper had been pacing off. Then, of all things, they shook hands.

"This will be a fine spot for your new house, Dale!" Irene heard Rosetta exclaim. "I'll just replace a few cabins near the lodge and call it good."

Irene's heart thudded faster—and it wasn't because she'd walked too quickly from the house. There could only be one reason Dale would build a new home.

I need to save him from such an unnecessary investment. As a longtime friend, I owe him that much.

"I'll speak with Amos and the other men about floor plans!" Dale put in exuberantly. "That way, they can start my house right after they've completed your lodge. This is exciting, Rosetta! I've never owned a freestanding home—"

"And why would you *want* to, Dale?" Irene called out as

she approached the two of them. "I know we've patched things up, but—but I haven't changed my mind. I don't plan to remarry. Ever."

Dale's eyes widened slightly. "You've made that quite clear, Irene. I don't plan to propose to anyone, either— especially if she's not going to accept," he added with a nonchalant shrug. "As I mentioned on Sunday, I might retire and sell the store someday—so I won't be able to live in the apartment upstairs anymore, will I?"

Irene's breath left her in a rush. Her cheeks flared with heat. She'd made a total fool of herself, assuming Dale intended to build a house for *her*.

Before he or Rosetta could say something that made her feel even more stupid, Irene turned and made a beeline for Rainbow Lake. She didn't know whether to laugh or cry. Now she *really* wanted to go home and eat leftovers, because she'd jumped to a conclusion that her daughter-in-law and the storekeeper were probably already laughing about behind her back.

Well, at least I know all those pink flowers didn't come from Dale, so I won't make the mistake of thanking him for them.

As Irene crossed the road, Rainbow Lake shimmered in the late-afternoon light. A large fish leapt out of the water near the dock. As it splashed down, she wondered if Dale wouldn't be just as comfortable in the blue tiny home sitting on the far side of the lake. Lester Lehman had lived in it for several months, before he'd met Marlene, and he'd seemed quite happy there. Allen Troyer had designed and built the compact little unit—and had lived in it himself, as a bachelor. Maybe Dale should ask Allen to build him a tiny home—or move the blue one to the plot of ground he was buying from Rosetta.

*And maybe I should stay out of it. I'll have a nice new
apartment soon—and maybe a grandchild—so where Dale
lives and how he spends his time are none of my concern.*

For some reason, that thought pinched a little.

"Irene! Welcome, Birthday Girl!" Beulah called out.

The other women greeted her as well, exclaiming over
her pretty striped dress and asking if the party had remained
a surprise until the last minute. Several casseroles and
bowls of food were already on the serving tables, and the
dining tables were draped in colorful pastel tablecloths—
each of them with a pink floral arrangement that looked
especially festive.

Irene smiled at her friends. "You shouldn't have gone to
so much trouble—"

"Nonsense!" Ruby said with a laugh. "After what we've
all been through, why wouldn't we spend this lovely springtime evening at Rainbow Lake having a picnic? And why
wouldn't we share food and fun with one of our favorite
friends on her special day?"

"*Jah*, happy birthday, Irene!" Frances chimed in. "We're
all so thankful you and the rest of the lodge ladies survived
the storm, we'll *never* run out of reasons to celebrate!"

"You said that exactly right, Frances! And I've got another surprise to start Mamm's party!"

Irene turned to see her son approaching, hand in hand
with Rosetta, along with other folks coming down the road
with dishes of food and big smiles on their faces. The Kuhn
sisters were nodding, as though they knew about the surprise and had possibly been in on it.

Truman kissed Irene's cheek, slipping his arm around
her. "Why don't you have a look at what's inside this trunk,
Mamm?"

When he nodded toward a large wooden chest sitting a
short distance from the tables, Irene let out a little cry and

broke away from him. "But this is—my *dat* built this for me, and it was ruined in the tornado—"

"Well, it was actually just the lid that was torn off," Truman explained. With his handkerchief, he gently blotted the tears streaming down Irene's face. "I sanded it down and refinished it and reattached the top with new hinges—"

"But it looks like new!" Irene exclaimed. "Oh, Truman, what a wonderful surprise—"

"Look inside," Rosetta prompted.

Irene took a deep breath to compose herself, because nearly everyone from Promise Lodge had gathered around to watch her. What could possibly be in the hope chest Dat had given her so long ago? And why were all her friends watching as though they knew she'd be even more over-joyed when she saw its contents?

Slowly she lifted the trunk's lid.

Irene's hand fluttered to her mouth as she began to cry in earnest. With a loud sniffle, she carefully lifted a quilt her mother had made her for a wedding present, in a double wedding ring design. The worn spots had been lovingly repaired, and the blues, greens, and purples looked fresh and bright again—better than they had in years.

After handing the quilt to Rosetta, Irene reached into the trunk again. The crazy quilt she'd made with her older sister—who'd passed on years ago—had also been totally restored. Even the feather stitching around each irregular piece had been re-embroidered where it had come loose. Holding the treasured piece was almost like hugging her sister again.

Irene gazed at the women standing closest to the trunk, unable to speak for a moment. "These—these were *ruined* in the storm, covered with tiny pieces of broken glass and saturated with rainwater that had come through the roof," she finally rasped. "But after I wrote them off as a total loss, you saved them for me. I see it on your faces. And—and I can't thank you enough."

Ruby, Beulah, Frances, Mattie, Christine, and Rosetta all nodded as they, too, wiped away tears.

"You'd have done the same for any of us, if you'd realized those quilts just needed a *gut* cleaning," Christine remarked gently.

"*Jah*, when Truman explained who'd made those lovely pieces, we knew you'd want them back," Mattie put in. "We still have two more—"

"And we'll have them finished in a few days," Ruby said with a gentle smile. "Beulah and I were tickled to see that your quilts were still intact, so we brought them out when Truman took us up in the cherry picker."

As she listened to her friends, Irene did some quick calculations. "But—my word, it's been just over a week since the tornado tore into our apartments," she said in a voice hoarse with emotion. "How did you find the time to wash them—and get all that glass out of them—and repair the worn spots?"

"It was a team effort," Frances explained as the other women nodded. "As with everything else, many hands made for light work—"

"And it was a labor of love," Beulah chimed in. "We love our home here and we couldn't ask for better friends and neighbors than we've made at Promise Lodge."

"You can say that again! It's so *gut* to be home," Sylvia blurted out beside Mose.

The two of them had a glow about them, and they were standing closer together than was considered proper for a man and woman who weren't married—although folks could say Mose was supporting the tiny, recuperating woman as she stood on the uneven lawn. "That's why I wanted to share some of the beautiful flowers Mose sent to my hospital room, where we can all enjoy them!"

Irene smiled at the answer to her other little mystery. "What a lovely gift, Sylvia. And we're also happy to see *you* back amongst us!"

As everyone nodded in agreement, Mose cleared his throat loudly. "Sylvia and I also want to announce that we're engaged—"

A loud cheer went up as the crowd applauded enthusiastically.

"—and we'd like to invite you all to the first wedding and dinner at the rebuilt lodge," he continued. His grin made him look unabashedly boyish and head over heels in love. "God's given us the miracle of Sylvia's complete recovery, so we don't want to waste a minute that we could be sharing as husband and wife."

As several men and women in the crowd congratulated Mose and Sylvia, Irene was glad that everyone's attention was focused on the happy couple. Was it her imagination, or did Dale appear a little wistful—a little disappointed— because he wouldn't be making a similar announcement?

Sighing, Irene carefully refolded the quilts into the trunk. Her heart was overflowing with gratitude for what her insightful friends had salvaged from her apartment.

I threw away these quilts, assuming—in my despair— that they were beyond repair. Yet my friends saw something worth saving—something worth the effort, because the quilts have such sentimental, irreplaceable value.

Have I done the same thing to Dale? My friends can't mend that tattered romance, can they?

As Irene closed the trunk, she paused, taken aback by the direction of her thoughts. Dale Kraybill had treated her extremely well, giving her fabric to replace her ruined dresses, and taking her to Sunday dinner at the fanciest restaurant in the region—not to mention insisting that her mistakes in the store on Saturday morning were too minor to get upset about. He was one of the most positive, pleasant men she'd ever known, and he clearly shared the basic values she'd embraced all her life, as well.

Yet, during a few hours when she'd been exhausted and grouchy, she'd written him off.

What if she'd tossed aside the biggest blessing God had given her lately?

Maybe Mose and Sylvia have the right idea. They're moving into the future together, planning for happiness, while I've been hiding myself away, resisting change. I'll be perfectly content in my refurbished apartment, but what if God—and Dale—are hoping to give me so much more?

Chapter 26

After everyone found a place at a table near Rainbow Lake, Bishop Monroe invited them to join him in prayer before the meal.

"God, our Father," he intoned reverently, "we cannot thank You enough for Your protection and Your grace. You've seen to our every need as we each journey on our separate paths, and You've granted us blessings beyond measure as a community. As Promise Lodge completes its second year, You continue to prove that when we work together and help one another, we are *amazing*. And when we honor and serve You, and advance Your kingdom here on earth, we fully realize the benefits of our faith in You."

Dale clasped his hands tightly in his lap, following Monroe's prayer. It felt exactly right, joining this community founded by souls so sincerely devoted to God's word and to serving the Lord by serving each other.

"We thank You especially for the miracle of Sylvia's restored health," Burkholder continued. "And we're grateful to share Irene's birthday on this beautiful evening. Bless this fine food we're about to receive, for we ask it in Jesus' name. Amen."

"Two years!" Mattie crowed as she and her two sisters rose from their chairs. "When we first moved to this property to reclaim an abandoned church camp, we never *dreamed* that so many other folks would come here to share our vision—"

"And who could've predicted that in two years' time, we'd have thirteen houses along our private road—or that we'd witness ten weddings?" Christine said with an exuberant nod. "Of course, we didn't predict the tornado, either— but thanks to help from our friends, we're already moving beyond its destruction and into our future."

"And we'll soon be adding another house or two," Rosetta put in. "Dale has just chosen the plot of land where cabins eight, nine, and ten used to stand. And I suspect Mose and Sylvia will be building a home, as well."

Dale was surprised to be suddenly cast into the limelight, yet the smiles from the folks around him confirmed his sense that he was making the right move.

"And we've gotten mail delivery here, too," Amos recalled with a chuckle. "In the beginning, one of us had to drive into Forest Grove and check our post office box."

"On a more personal note," Rosetta continued as she went to stand behind Irene's chair, "I can recall the very first picnic we had on the shore of Rainbow Lake—and how we invited Truman and his *mamm* to join us . . . and how we all helped Irene along because she was so unsteady on her feet."

"I'd forgotten about that!" Mattie said, flashing Irene a warm smile. "She was having some health issues—acting so much older than her age. Yet now Irene co-owns a pie business and helps at all our wedding meals, as though she's found a whole new purpose here at Promise Lodge. Now that's what I call a happily-ever-after story!"

Dale blinked. He thought back a few years and realized that Rosetta and Mattie were right. He hadn't known the extent of Irene's infirmities—probably because at church, she was either seated in a pew or walking across a level floor. But he could recall a time when he hadn't given Irene Wickey a second thought because she'd seemed so engrossed in her role as a widow. She'd acted a lot older than he, in many ways.

She'll always be older than I am, but so what? Age is more about attitude than aptitude—yet if Irene wants nothing more to do with marriage, I can't change that. Lord knows I've tried to create a happily-ever-after she could share with me . . .

Dale was pulled from his woolgathering when the men around him stood up to go through the food line. As he loaded his plate with sliced ham, fried chicken, corn pudding, fried cabbage, and other delectable foods, he wondered if he could find a way to sit by Irene during the meal. As the guest of honor, however, she and the other Wickeys, as well as Mose and Sylvia, had been the first to serve themselves, so they were well along into eating their meal.

"Tell me about this new house, Dale," the man behind him remarked. "I thought you were snug as a bug in a rug in your apartment above the store."

Dale turned to smile at Preacher Amos, who—along with Bishop Monroe and Preacher Marlin—were sitting together because their wives were serving as hostesses.

"Oh, I am—because you fellows and Lester did such a fine job of building my store and apartment," he replied. "I'm just looking ahead to a time when I might not stay on as the storekeeper."

Amos's bushy brows shot up as the four of them headed back to their table. "I hope this doesn't mean you're having health issues—"

"Oh, nothing like that!" Dale quickly remarked.

"And I certainly hope you don't intend to close up your store anytime soon," Bishop Monroe put in. "We've gotten used to the convenience of shopping with you rather than driving all the way into Forest Grove. And we couldn't ask for any better service than you give us, Dale."

The men's remarks made him feel good. And hadn't he anticipated such questions when folks found out he was building a house?

Be grateful that they don't assume I'll share this home with Irene. I'd have a lot more explaining to do if they'd jumped to that conclusion.

Dale smiled as he tucked into his plateful of food. "I appreciate your concern and your compliments," he said with a chuckle. "But I don't intend to keep working until I keel over at the cash register from old age."

His three companions laughed as they, too, began to eat.

"I understand that remark," Monroe said, nodding. "One of these days, working with Clydesdales that weigh a ton and stand eighteen hands high will be more physical work than I can handle day in and day out."

"I'm looking forward to the time when I turn my barrel factory over to Harley, too," Preacher Marlin said. "I plan to stay busy, but life's too short to be constantly committed to filling orders."

"And there'll come a time when I'll have to quit crawling around on rooftops with a hammer in my hand," Amos put in. "Mattie will see to that."

Dale nodded, glad to hear that these men understood his position. "I'm not ready for the rocking chair, but I'm thinking ahead to my retirement. When I sell the store, I'll be giving up my apartment, too."

Was it his imagination, or did the three church leaders exchange a knowing glance?

"You, um, wouldn't happen to have a certain *woman* in your plans, would you?" Amos asked in a low voice.

"Monroe and Marlin and I can tell you all about how a new wife changes *everything* at our stage of the game."

"For the better!" the bishop clarified with a wide smile.

"It's an adventure in adjustment," Marlin admitted, chuckling. "But I wouldn't trade my life with Frances for anything. In your case, Dale, you won't have to deal with adult children who don't like the idea of another woman replacing their mother."

Dale felt hot around his collar as he picked up a fried chicken leg. With these three men surrounding him, he couldn't gracefully dismiss this topic of conversation, so it was better to go with the flow.

"That certain woman you're referring to seems to be set on returning to her apartment in the lodge," he admitted ruefully. "Irene's a peach, and we've been spending more time together lately, but she's got it in her head that she'll never remarry. Just when I think she's ready to take the leap, she backs away again."

"Cold feet," Preacher Amos put in. "Usually that's a guy thing, because widows often do the pursuing."

"*Jah*, not long ago poor Lester had *two* old biddies chasing after him," Marlin recalled, shaking his head. "He's another man who can tell you that when the *right* woman comes along, she makes all the difference between heartache and happiness."

Bishop Monroe seemed intent on eating, yet Dale sensed he was formulating his response. Burkholder wasn't the type to speak without thinking first—which was one of the many reasons Dale respected him.

"Did you ever meet Irene's husband?" he finally asked. "Sometimes women either want another man just like the one they started out with—or they're determined to find one who'll treat them a whole lot better. That's why Mattie married Amos."

"Or they decide they've got more freedom and independence if they don't have to submit to another man's whims and inclinations at all," Amos remarked with a chuckle. "As we all know, Promise Lodge has its share of women who speak their minds and pursue the lives they want. With or without a man."

"So true," Burkholder agreed heartily. He held Dale's gaze for a long moment. "And maybe that's something for you, as a bachelor, to think about, too. We preachers all insist that God intends for men and women to live together as part of His plan, but if you and Irene can't see eye to eye on the fundamental issues of marriage, it's better to remain single."

"But you'll figure it out," Marlin said quickly. "You didn't become a successful storekeeper and all-around great guy by being clueless."

Once again Dale thanked them for their concern and comments. He had indeed known Ernest Wickey, who'd attended the Mennonite Fellowship in Cloverdale. Ernest had been a rather stoic, standoffish fellow—well suited to hauling loads around northern Missouri in his eighteen-wheeler. The best Dale could recall, he'd died in his sleep six or seven years ago.

Irene hadn't talked much about her life with Ernest—and maybe she had her reasons for keeping her memories to herself. Asking her—or Truman—about the former head of the Wickey family didn't seem like a conversational path Dale wanted to explore, either.

As he finished his meal, however, Dale wondered about a point none of the clergymen had brought up: what if Irene hesitated to marry him because he'd remained single for so long? Was she concerned about his willingness to commit to her, after more than fifty years of living life exactly the way he'd chosen—without any family commitments?

Maybe she wants a husband who already knows how to live with a wife—a man who understands a woman's needs and moods and habits. There's nothing I can do about that.

After a moment, Dale laughed out loud. Did such a man exist? From what he'd heard other men saying all his life, nobody male could fully understand anyone female. That's why folks talked about the *battle of the sexes*.

When he realized his three companions were gazing at him, wondering what was so funny, Dale shrugged.

"It'll all work out," he hedged. "And no matter what happens with Irene, I'll have a comfortable, well-built home—and I'm thanking you fellows in advance for your help with it."

Chapter 27

On Sunday morning, Mose sat taller as the preachers and Bishop Monroe walked down the grassy aisle between the men and the women. Their entrance signaled the beginning of the worship service, because during the lengthy first hymn, they'd decided upon the day's Scripture and who would preach the two sermons. As the church leaders removed their hats, Mose sang the refrain louder, with a sense of finality.

Once again, the congregation was gathered in the Burkholders' side yard, where there was ample space for so many lawn chairs. As the sun rose higher in the clear blue sky, Mose closed his eyes to drink in the sense of reverence that came from holding church outdoors. Most folks probably preferred the lodge's large meeting room, where it was easier to hear the preachers. He, however, cherished the wonder and freedom of worshipping outside. It was so peaceful to see the bishop's Clydesdales grazing in the adjacent pasture—and from where he sat, Mose could also see Queenie keeping watch over Harley Kurtz's flock of sheep.

"If you haven't met them since they arrived on Friday," Bishop Monroe said as he looked at the men and then at the women, "let me introduce Vera and Eddie Brubaker, who've come from the Bloomingdale district for an

extended visit with their aunt and uncle, Minerva and
Harley Kurtz."

When Mose sat up straighter, he spotted a pretty young
woman seated between Phoebe Troyer and Deborah
Schwartz. Her cheeks were flushed as she waved shyly and
pushed up her glasses.

"Vera will assist Minerva, who will soon be on bed rest
to ensure a full-term, healthy baby this fall," the bishop continued. "And Eddie, who has his own painting and staining
business, has arrived just in time to help us restore the
lodge! Let's give these kids a warm welcome today."

Turning in his lawn chair, Mose flashed Vera's brother a
thumbs-up. Eddie seemed young to be in business for himself, but his confident smile suggested that he was looking
forward to the hard work that awaited him in the lodge—
and no one could fault him for such a positive attitude.

"As we behold the wonder of this late-springtime morning, we're ever mindful of God's glory and presence,"
Bishop Monroe said as he looked out over the crowd. "Even
so, we're also thankful that—according to Preacher Amos
and our other carpenters—we'll probably hold our next
church service in the lodge, Lord willing."

The men around Mose nodded, as did the women seated
across the way. He could make out Sylvia's petite form
behind Preacher Eli's wife, Alma Peterscheim. Just the sight
of his fiancée made him thrum all over. It was so good to be
a man in love!

"With that thought in mind," the bishop continued, "if
any of you would rather return to the tradition of worshipping in our homes, this would be a *gut* time to tell me or
one of the other preachers. Christine has reminded me the
founders of our community held church in the lodge because the cabins were the only individual dwellings here at

the time. It's another reminder of how far we've come, with God's help."

As the women nodded, Sylvia peered between Alma's and Irene's heads to flash Mose a smile. What a joy, to be engaged to a happy, healthy woman! Now that Mose knew she'd be around for a while, he had several important issues to consider.

Should I have Amos draw up plans for a house? How are Sylvia and I going to pay her hospital bills? Now that she's promised to spend the rest of her life with me, what will she do with her farm in Pennsylvania?

Mose blinked. Folks were kneeling for the first silent prayer, which meant Preacher Eli's sermon had blown past him while he'd been lost in thoughts of Sylvia. On his knees, he prayed for a more devout frame of mind, as well as for guidance. At thirty-five, he was getting a later start than most men—and Sylvia had already outlived a husband. They'd be off to a lopsided start unless God gave Mose some help.

When everyone was seated again, Preacher Marlin rose to read the morning's Scripture. As he opened the big King James Bible, folks waited attentively. Because Preacher Amos and Preacher Eli had already been living here when the Kurtz family arrived, the congregation was fortunate that Preacher Marlin had agreed to be their deacon—and that he occasionally preached, as well.

"This morning's words of wisdom come to us from the New Testament book of Matthew, the seventh chapter, verses seven and eight," he said in a voice that carried over the crowd. "Hear the word of the Lord! 'Ask, and it shall be given you; seek, and ye shall find; knock, and it shall be opened unto you: For every one that asketh receiveth; and he that seeketh findeth; and to him that knocketh it shall be opened.'"

Folks were nodding, following the familiar passage as Preacher Marlin read the words with authority. Mose considered it a very timely reading, because he had indeed asked God to heal Sylvia, and he'd received the most perfect, positive response that anyone could have hoped for. He had knocked on the door with faith, and it had opened onto the new path the Lord was leading him to.

The preacher closed the Bible with a ponderous *whump* and sat down on the bench between Bishop Monroe and Preacher Eli as Preacher Amos rose to begin the morning's main sermon.

"Ask and you shall receive. Knock, and the door will be opened." The church leader rephrased the verses confidently as he looked around the crowd. "The words and the concepts are as familiar as the backs of our hands, yet maybe it's time to reexamine them. Does this passage really promise that every time we ask for something, we'll get it? And what about those times we *don't* ask for something— like that tornado, for instance—but it hits us anyway? All right now, fess up—which one of you asked for that devastating storm?" he teased.

Folks chuckled, allowing Amos Troyer to lead them along the morning's spiritual path in his laid-back but rock-solid testimonial style. As a kid, Mose had always been happy when Preacher Amos spoke to their Coldstream congregation, because the compactly built carpenter didn't mince words, nor did he meander along seemingly endless, pointless rabbit trails, as some preachers did. It was another reason Mose was glad he and Marlene had sold their farm in Coldstream and moved to Promise Lodge.

"And let's not forget the flip side of the coin here," Amos continued earnestly. "Sometimes we beg and plead for what we want so badly, and we don't receive it. And then, years down the road, we look back and realize that God, in His infinite wisdom, has given us what we truly need rather than what we'd probably be sorry about in the long run."

Mose nodded, reflecting on the preacher's point. How many times had he asked God to free him from his stammering and his fear of dark places? As he thought about it, however, he realized that his perceived disabilities hadn't held him back: he'd finished high school and had gone on to earn his veterinary assistant's degree. And he'd landed his job working with Bishop Monroe's Clydesdales and treating other animals around the Promise Lodge community. And of course, he'd now met the woman God had intended for him. Not bad trade-offs for stuttering among strangers and burning a night-light.

"I used to believe I could go it alone, that starting this new community would fulfill me—especially after Mattie and I finally married," Preacher Amos continued. "But it wasn't until I asked my children's forgiveness that I received the blessing of their presence in my life again when Allen, Barbara, and Bernice came here to live."

Folks nodded again, smiling at the adult Troyer kids and their spouses—and at the twin toddler daughters Barbara and Bernice held on their laps.

As he continued for several more minutes, Preacher Amos brought up examples of the blessings other members of the congregation had received. When Mose glanced at the women across the lawn, it occurred to him that Irene was in the congregation this morning, but Rosetta and Truman were not—which meant they were attending the Mennonite service in Cloverdale.

Hmmm. What does that mean? It's not unusual for the Wickeys to join us for church, but they're usually all together at one place or the other.

"In closing, I'd like to leave you with this thought," Preacher Amos said, turning once again toward the men and then toward the women. "When Jesus preached that we should ask and seek and knock, He was telling us to *believe*—to have faith that God would hear our prayers and respond with His best answers."

Folks in the congregation began shifting in their chairs, anticipating the end of the service. After nearly two and half hours, everyone was ready for the final prayer, the benediction, and the closing hymn—and of course, the common meal.

"So ask the Lord for what you deeply desire, my friends," Amos encouraged. "But be careful what you ask for. *Be careful what you ask for.*"

During a few moments of contemplative silence, his friends' facial expressions told Mose they'd been expecting a few more words of explanation—but the preacher was returning to his spot on the bench. It was Irene's face that registered wide-eyed realization, as though a proverbial light bulb had come on in her mind. Preacher Amos had apparently said something that resonated deeply within her—or his closing remark had served as a warning.

As Mose knelt in the grass for the final prayer, he asked God to guide him and Sylvia as they planned their future—and he asked the Lord to be with Irene and Dale, too, because he sensed his two friends' relationship had been seesawing through some erratic ups and downs lately.

Had he asked for the right things?

Mose smiled to himself. Time would tell.

Chapter 28

Early Wednesday evening, when the carpenters had quit working for the day, Irene slowly crossed the lawn and climbed the steps to the lodge's wide front porch. So many men had been coming and going from the building over the past few days, she had no qualms about stepping inside the structure that had been her home for more than a year. The front part of the building and most of the dining room off to her right had remained intact during the storm. Now that she was the only person inside the lodge she'd come to love so much, she soothed her soul by gazing at its rustic antler chandelier, the stone fireplace, and the glossy double staircase.

It's like coming home to an old friend. I can practically hear folks talking as they enjoy a wedding meal Ruby and Beulah have prepared. I can see the dear faces of those who often join us lodge ladies for supper.

One of those faces belonged to Dale, of course, but Irene chose not to linger on that thought. Her steps echoed as she walked quickly through the dining room—nearly empty, because many of its tables had been used for picnics—and paused at the doorway.

Without the stoves, refrigerators, and sinks, the kitchen

loomed large and had no personality—although the freshly
plastered white ceiling was a welcome improvement.
Workmen were in the process of installing new cabinets, so
the air was redolent with the scents of wood and paint.
Rosetta had mentioned that the new appliances would be
arriving within the next week, and that Allen Troyer had
been rewiring this part of the lodge to accommodate them.

At the back of the kitchen, the old wall phone had been
returned to its usual place, near the narrow back staircase
residents often used to reach their upstairs apartments. Although these sturdy new stairs led right up to her apartment,
Irene decided to take the main staircase instead.

Back in the lobby, Irene noted that the original walls and
ceilings looked faded now. She wondered if Rosetta would
have the entire interior repainted after the workmen completed the kitchen—an update none of them had even
thought about until the tornado ripped their souls open and
tipped their world at a tilt.

Irene held her breath as she started up the grand staircase. She reminded herself that the carpenters and Eddie
Brubaker still had a lot of finishing work to do. Even so, as
she stood in the remodeled hallway that led to her apartment, her nerves were a-jangle. She wanted to see her
home, yet she felt anxious about what she might find.

Stalling, she wandered down the hall to peer into the
apartments in the opposite back corner, where Ruby and
Beulah lived. Their rooms hadn't been hit nearly as hard
by the storm, but for safety's sake the men had torn away
all the interior walls and replaced them. The drywall hadn't
yet been painted, but the plank floors had been stained. A
new toilet, shower stall, and bathroom sink waited near the
back wall of each apartment.

Walking slowly along the upper hallway, which Phoebe
and her three friends had recently painted sunshine yellow,

Irene entered Sylvia's center apartment. The new, unfinished walls of the main room were a far cry from the shades of raspberry Maria Zehr had requested when she'd lived here, and the bedroom looked a lot tamer without the blue walls and ceiling where clouds had been painted. Irene wondered if Sylvia would even bother moving back to her apartment, considering that she and Mose planned to be married as soon as the construction work was all finished.

It'll feel strangely empty with me living in the front corner and the Kuhns on the other end—and nobody else. With Marlene in her new home and Sylvia about to tie the knot, it'll just be us old unattached biddies clucking around up here.

Before she lost her nerve, Irene opened the unpainted door to her apartment and stepped inside. She'd told the carpenters to rebuild the rooms and features the way they'd been originally—yet everything she saw looked eerily foreign. New windows glimmered in the late-afternoon sun. The walls were sanded and ready to paint. The wide-plank oak floors glimmered with maple stain, which matched the rest of the lodge's woodwork. Amos and the other carpenters had given her everything she'd asked for—

Ask and you shall receive. But be careful what you ask for.

As the preacher's words echoed in her head, Irene's breath left her in a rush. She suddenly couldn't stand to be in the empty apartment, so she hurried out into the hallway, shutting the door behind her. She wasn't sure why she'd become so emotional, but all she could do was hug herself and curl forward to cry.

Why am I so upset? Rosetta and I have already decided on the furniture I'll bring from the house. I'll have my hope chest and the quilts my friends have so lovingly restored for me, and—

"Irene, are you all right, dear?"

She clutched herself and froze. Dale must've entered the lodge while she was in her apartment. He was the last person who should see her in such a state, because he would insist on holding the conversation she'd been avoiding. But his footsteps told her he was quickly coming up the stairs to check on her.

Dale slowed his pace as he neared the top of the stairs. Irene had surely heard his question, yet she hadn't turned to acknowledge his presence. Maybe he'd been wrong to enter the lodge without loudly announcing himself.

And maybe he'd been a fool to follow Irene inside when he'd seen her entering a short while ago. If she felt trapped— if she believed he was shadowing her—she might not respond well to the questions he felt compelled to ask. He'd come here with their best interests at heart, but there was no guarantee Irene would see it that way.

"I'm sorry I caught you off guard, Irene," Dale said softly. "If you want me to leave, I will. I can see you're upset—and it's no wonder. Nothing up here looks the way you remember it. Nothing feels like home."

With a loud sniffle, Irene nodded. When at last she turned to face him, he sensed she didn't want him to see her this way. Her face was pale, and her eyelids were red as she inhaled deeply to settle her emotions. Maybe it was his imagination, but for a few moments she seemed to gauge his reaction to her tears, as though she feared his response to them.

"You—you hit the nail on the head, Dale," Irene murmured cautiously. "This isn't home. Not anymore, and maybe not ever again."

He remained a couple of stairs below her, allowing her some space. It was encouraging that he'd said something right this time. He knew Irene had been avoiding him—probably because of something he'd said or done unawares. That was what made relationships so tricky. How was he supposed to know what he'd done wrong?

Dale cleared his throat, praying for guidance. "It's like that old poem by Edgar A. Guest, about how it takes a heap of living before a house becomes your home," he offered. "Everything about your apartment has been replaced—you don't have the mellowed old woodwork or the familiar creak of the floorboards, let alone the furniture and personal belongings you lost in the storm, Irene. You have every reason to feel disoriented, as though you don't belong there—yet."

Irene blinked, nodding. "I—I don't know what I was expecting when I walked in there just now," she said in a halting voice. "But I had to leave in a hurry. That doesn't seem like a very *gut* sign, does it?"

He smiled gently. "I suspect the rooms will look better when they're finished, and after you've moved your furniture in, dear. Truman's told me you've got another family bedroom set and some comfy chairs to bring over. A few nice rugs and some curtains will make it feel cozy again."

"But—but what if I don't like it?" she blurted miserably. "I don't want to live up at the house anymore, either, so what happens if—if *no* place feels like home?"

Dale's heart went out to her as he cautiously ascended the last two steps. He wasn't accustomed to seeing Irene looking so helpless, so overwhelmed. And once again he wondered if he'd been the cause of some of her angst.

"The only other time I've seen you this anxious was

right after the storm. You were at your house sewing a new dress out of old, unmatched remnants of fabric—"

As he'd hoped, Irene chuckled, wiping her eyes. "*Jah*, and I threw that unfinished rag away, too, thanks to you bringing me those three pieces of spring polyester," she recalled aloud. "I felt so desperate—"

"And as I recall, you were exhausted and unwilling to surrender to your need for a nap," he put in gently. "If I remember correctly, *this* helped you."

Dale slowly opened his arms, silently pleading with her. He wanted to help Irene feel better, yes, but he also wanted to know where they stood. If she kept her distance, that would be an answer he couldn't ignore.

For a few tense moments, Irene studied him. She had that deer-in-the-headlights look, as though she might bolt down the hallway. A little sob escaped her, however, and she stepped into his embrace.

Holding her tenderly, Dale closed his eyes and savored the feel of Irene in his arms. She was a solid woman with curves in all the right places, and she fit against him as though they were two pieces of a jigsaw puzzle. His emotions and bothersome thoughts whirled faster, but he kept his mouth shut. If he said the wrong thing, she'd break away—probably for the last time.

"I've missed you," he whispered.

Irene clung to him, resting her head against his neck and shoulder. She swallowed repeatedly, as though unspoken words were clogging her throat.

"I hope you know your pies and fried pies were gone within an hour of when you restocked your display this afternoon," Dale continued softly. "I'm sorry I got cornered by those two English gals looking at the rag rugs, because

I always like chatting with you while we stack your pie boxes on the shelves."

With a sigh, she nodded.

He dared to hold her a bit closer, gently swaying with her. It was a good sign that she was allowing him to comfort her and listening to what he said.

"Irene, I really enjoyed our dinner at the Skyline Inn," Dale murmured. "Ever since our afternoon together, however— our first real date—I feel as though you've—"

"Preacher Amos gave quite a sermon this past Sunday," she put in abruptly. "And when he finished by saying 'ask and you shall receive but be careful what you ask for' it . . . it hit me like a bullet, right between the eyes."

Dale held his breath. Where was Irene going with this idea?

After a moment she eased away from him, stepping back to put some space between them. Her eyes were still red, but she'd mustered the courage to study him at close range. Dale held her gaze for dear life. He hoped *he* had the courage to accept whatever she said next.

"I suspect I've been asking the wrong questions, and maybe asking for the wrong things," Irene murmured. "I've assumed that moving back to my apartment would return me to my comfort zone. And—and I admit that when I over-heard you and Rosetta agreeing on a plot of land where you want to build a house, I jumped to the stupid conclusion that you wanted *me* to live there with you."

"I would move heaven and earth to convince you to share that home with me," Dale whispered. Every fiber of his being trembled, exposed and vulnerable, yet he had to go on. "But that would be forcing the issue—and whenever I do that, you back away. I'm sorry this has been such a painful process for you—"

"I've made it harder than it's supposed to be!" Irene

blurted. "A sweet, wonderful man has declared that he loves me, and he treats me with such patience and kindness—*love* is patient and kind, just like the Bible says!"

She took hold of his shoulders, gripping him with surprising strength. "I've been such an idiot, not to see you for who you really are, Dale. Because when I'm with you, I—I can love myself for who I am, because *you* love me for who I am."

Irene sighed, frowning. "Oh, I'm not making any sense—"

"You're making perfect sense, dear," Dale whispered. His heart was hammering as fear shot through his veins, but it was now or never.

"Will you marry me, Irene? We can still lead our individual lives and conduct our own businesses—we don't have to be joined at the hip, just because other couples live that way," he said earnestly. "But if we're together, we can be so much happier at whatever we do, don't you think?"

Her eyes widened. She got so quiet, he wondered if he'd botched it. Again.

Irene's laughter bubbled up from deep inside her, like a stream singing as it burbled over stones. Her joy filled the upstairs hallway.

"*Jah*, that's it—you always say what I mean, Dale! You know what I want better than I do—so *jah. Jah,* I'll marry you," she added in a whisper that sounded ecstatic yet reverent.

"Ask and you shall receive?" he murmured happily. "I—I guess it really does work, when you ask the right question at the right time."

"I guess it does," Irene said, moving into his embrace. "Suddenly I feel so relieved."

"Oh, *relieved* doesn't half cover it," Dale admitted with a nervous laugh. He exhaled so he could begin breathing normally again after such a dicey, life-altering conversation.

"I don't know about you, but I could dig into a solid supper about now—"

Irene's stomach growled loudly. "There you go, saying exactly what I'm thinking again."

Dale's laughter echoed in the upstairs hallway. "I have a pot roast with potatoes and carrots in my slow cooker. It'll taste so much better if you share it with me."

"In your apartment above the store?" Irene lowered her eyes demurely. "Is this your way of luring me into your lair, Dale? Would it be proper for me to—"

"I think we've reached an age where *we* decide what's proper, *jah*?" he challenged. "And what happens in my apartment stays in my apartment."

Irene laughed, playfully pretending to slap his face. "You say that to all the girls, ain't so?"

Catching her wrist, Dale smiled mischievously. "Not anymore."

Chapter 29

Sylvia smiled as she spoke into the receiver on Thursday morning, seated inside the Troyers' white phone shanty. It was such a relief—such a blessing—that Abe Stoll, her neighbor in Lititz, Pennsylvania was purchasing her home and farm for his newlywed son.

"The price we've arrived at sounds right in line with what the real estate agent told me other properties in the area are selling for," she said. "I'm happy to let you do what you want with the furnishings, Abe, because I don't need them. And if you don't want to ship that old trunkful of clothes to me, donate them to the thrift store. I've sewn up a bunch of new dresses—"

"You sound like a new woman," Abe put in with a chuckle. "I'm so happy to hear about your recovery, Sylvia—not to mention your engagement. Sounds like Promise Lodge and our *gut* Lord have provided you exactly what you were needing."

"*Jah*, that's the way I feel about it, too."

After chatting about Abe's family and what had been happening in their church community, Sylvia hung up. She sat for a few moments, savoring a sense of great satisfaction at the way the loose ends of her life in Pennsylvania had been so neatly tied up. She was especially thankful that she didn't need to rush back there to tend all the details pertaining to the sale. Mose had suggested that they could venture back to her previous community after they'd gotten married, whenever the real estate agent informed her all the documents had been finalized and were ready to sign.

As Sylvia stepped outside into the morning sunlight, she felt especially blessed. She was pain-free. She had a totally new life ahead of her, with a handsome younger husband and new friends who'd looked after her ever since she'd arrived alone, seeking a peaceful place to pass away. Who could've anticipated all the blessings that had come into her life?

The sound of air hammers told her the carpenters were busy working inside the lodge, with the new windows open. Any day now, Preacher Amos would announce when all the rooms and the new kitchen would be ready so she and Mose could set their wedding date.

"Sylvia! Lots of mail for you today!"

She turned, shielding her eyes from the sun as Mattie stood by the mailbox waving several colorful envelopes.

"Who would be sending me anything?" Sylvia asked as she walked toward her friend. "The only folks who even know I'm here are my neighbors in Pennsylvania. And it's not nearly time for birthday cards, because I was born in October."

When Mattie shrugged, her smile suggested she might know what was going on. "I have no idea, dear," she claimed. "But it's always fun to get mail, ain't so?"

As Sylvia thumbed through the envelopes, she became even more puzzled. "Look at these return addresses: Harmony, Minnesota. Jamesport, Missouri. And Arthur, Illinois— and that's just for starters. I don't know a soul in those places, Mattie, and I don't recognize any of these senders' names!"

Mattie hugged her quickly as they started toward the house. "I guess you'll just have to open them," she remarked lightly.

Terribly curious by now, Sylvia popped the seal of the top envelope with her thumb. The last thing she expected was to see a pretty card with a bouquet on the front, which said *Comforting Thoughts as You Recover*. And as she opened it, a five-dollar bill fluttered out!

"What on earth—?" Sylvia skipped the verse inside and read the neat handwriting instead. "'We're delighted to read of your recovery, Sylvia, and we hope this small gift helps with your hospital bills.'"

She stopped to pick up the money and then hurried to catch up with Mattie at the doorway. "Why would anyone in Minnesota know—or *care*—that I've been in the hospital?"

They passed through the Troyers' front room and into the kitchen, which was filled with the aromas of sugar and yeast from the cinnamon rolls rising on the countertop. Too flabbergasted to wait for Mattie's answer, Sylvia dropped the stack of cards on the table and began ripping into them, one after another. By the time she'd finished, she'd read ten cards, seven of which contained cash.

"Mattie, what's going on here?"

Her friend slipped the cinnamon rolls into the oven. "Haven't you ever read the *Showers* column in *The Budget*, which requests cards and/or money for folks who need encouragement?"

Sylvia frowned. "Well, *jah*, but what's that got to do with *me*?"

Mattie went into the front room and returned with the Plain newspaper, which Amos had been reading in his recliner the previous evening. "You haven't seen this week's edition, I take it. Have a look, dear. I suspect your showers of blessings are just getting started."

Checking for the page number on *The Budget*'s front cover, Sylvia turned to the column Mattie had mentioned. She only had to glance at four entries before she came to it.

"'We are delighted that our Sylvia Keim's brain tumor has miraculously disappeared—but her hospital bills have not,'" she read in a rush. "'Let's have a card shower to help a very special lady in her time of need.' But Mattie, I *don't* need this money! I've just sold my farm, and I'll soon be marrying—"

"It's the Plain way to help other folks, ain't so?" Mattie reminded her. "If you want more information, you should check with Gloria, our Promise Lodge scribe. She's the one who writes our weekly letter to *The Budget*, you know."

Sylvia blinked. Indeed, the blurb that included her address, in care of Amos Troyer, also listed Gloria Helmuth's name at the end.

"We haven't seen much of Gloria lately," Sylvia remarked. "I guess she hasn't had a lot of duties as the lodge manager since the storm forced all the tenants to find other rooms. I figured that as a newlywed, she might be setting up her household—"

"Try the Helmuth Nursery," Mattie hinted.

Nodding, Sylvia gathered her cards and took off. As she strode along the road and then cut across the front yard of the lodge, she was once again aware of how much faster she could move these days—how much energy she'd regained since her release from the hospital. Soon she was walking behind the bulk store and past the huge double house where redheaded Sam and Simon Helmuth lived with their wives, Barbara and Bernice, and their little daughters, Carol and Coreen. Her pulse was pounding from exertion and nervous energy as she entered the nursery's main shop.

As she allowed her eyes to adjust to the building's dimness, she spotted the young woman she sought behind the checkout counter, putting pencil to paper. Gloria was Frances Lehman Kurtz's daughter, and Sylvia recalled hearing that her father, Floyd, had been the original bishop of Promise Lodge before he'd passed away after a nasty fall and a stroke. Just this spring, Gloria had married Cyrus Helmuth and moved into one of the new houses built on the other side of the bulk store.

Playfully slapping the bell on the countertop, Sylvia chuckled when Gloria jumped and let out a gasp.

"Got a question for you, Scribe," Sylvia said.

Gloria's big brown eyes sparkled as though she had an inkling of what Sylvia would ask. "And how are you on this fine day, Sylvia?" she asked, straightening her papers. "Congratulations on your engagement to—"

"*You* called for this card shower for me, *jah*?"

The young woman's expression sobered, as though she feared a reprimand. "I did," she admitted, "because—what with you being widowed and a long way from the town where you spent most of your life, I figured—"

"Well, I don't *need* this cash!" Sylvia blurted out, tossing the cards to the countertop. She softened then, smiling. "But it was very kind of you to request a card shower in *The Budget*, Gloria. Already I've received more than forty dollars, from people I don't even know."

"I've heard of folks collecting *thousands*, so I thought— well, after Mamm got the bills for Dat's medical treatments, I realized how expensive it is to even set foot in a hospital." Gloria gazed at her cautiously. "I—I didn't intend to upset you, Sylvia."

Sylvia let out her breath. "I'm not really upset. I just wasn't expecting—well, nobody's ever done such a thoughtful thing on my behalf, Gloria, and I wanted to thank you," she added. "You didn't know I'd be selling my farm, so I'll have that money, and—"

"You and Mose will surely build a house," Gloria put in demurely. "It's true enough that the men here are generous about donating their time and expertise, but lumber and flooring and appliances don't come cheap.

"Your money's your business, though," she added quickly. "I'm sure you'll use whatever you receive in your cards for a *gut* cause. You're a real inspiration, Sylvia. You could've just rolled into a ball and died after you got here, but you stuck it out—and all of us are really glad you did. We'd much rather be digging a foundation for a new home than another space in our little cemetery."

Sylvia's mouth dropped open. She'd heard rumors that back in the day, Gloria had been a flighty, boy-crazy young woman who'd sometimes behaved as though she didn't have a rational thought in her head. That had obviously changed.

"Well, I won't keep you, dear," she murmured. As customers' voices came into the shop, Sylvia restacked her cards. "I look forward to getting better acquainted with you, Gloria. *Denki* for your work as our scribe—and for your delightful kindness, too."

Nodding to the folks who were approaching the checkout counter, Sylvia stepped back out into the morning sunshine. The nursery was alive with growing things, and from where she stood, she could see hanging baskets, potted perennials, and other blooming plants in a stunning array of colors—not to mention the tiny hummingbirds that hovered near the flowers. The air smelled damp and fresh because Gloria's new husband, Cyrus, had been watering with his sprayer hose.

It felt so good to be alive on this sunny June day, surrounded by flowers and friends Sylvia would've missed if she'd remained in Lititz.

This is all Your doing, Lord, and I'm ever so grateful.

Chapter 30

Late the following Wednesday morning, as Irene stood in the center of her apartment's front room, she felt a surge of hope. The girls and young women who'd gathered for a painting frolic—including Fannie Kurtz, Lily Peter-scheim, Laura Helmuth, and Phoebe Troyer—had moved their buckets of paint and ladders into the center apartment about an hour ago, after finishing her rooms first. Although Rosetta and Truman had insisted that she was welcome to stay with them, Irene now felt confident that time in her own apartment would give her a chance to prepare for her life in a new house with Dale.

She opened the windows wider to allow more fresh air to circulate, dispelling the aroma of the pale blue paint she'd requested. It refreshed her to hear youthful laughter coming down the hallway, and to see the fine job the four painters had done. They worked fast and well together, and they planned to complete Sylvia's apartment by early after-noon before tackling the two apartments that belonged to Ruby and Beulah later in the day.

After a burst of air-driven hammering below her, in the kitchen, Irene heard familiar voices calling up from the lobby.

"Are you ready for us, Irene?"

"We've pulled the trailer up to the porch—"

"And the men in the kitchen will carry your furniture up whenever you give the word."

When Irene stepped out into the hall, she waved at the three sisters who were gazing up the main stairway. Mattie, Christine, and Rosetta never seemed to tire of pitching in, no matter what project needed to be tackled next. Rosetta hadn't said a word about visiting Minerva Kurtz, and it had taken all of Irene's patience not to pry the information from her.

"No time like the present," she replied as she started down the stairs. "I think we can put the rugs in place before we interrupt whatever the men are working on, don't you?"

"Not a problem!"

"Where there's a woman, there's a way!"

"And where there are *four* women—watch out!"

Laughing, Irene followed her friends and daughter-in-law outside to the porch. Why wasn't she surprised that they had already taken the three new rolled-up rugs out of the trailer?

"This big blue one goes back in the bedroom," she said, pointing to it. "And I'd like the two oval rag rugs in the front room, please."

"Up we go," Rosetta said as she wrapped her arms around the front end of the blue roll. Mattie took her spot in the center, and Christine brought up the rear.

Irene quickly took Rosetta's place, giving her daughter-in-law a purposeful look. "You can get the door, dear," she insisted. "This is *my* new apartment, so I should be doing more of the heavy lifting."

If Mattie and Christine had seen through her little story, they didn't let on. A few minutes later, the four of them had unrolled the bedroom rug and walked on it to flatten the four corners. The rag rug didn't take as much effort, because it was made of coiled braids that had been hand-sewn, so it was looser.

"Look at these pretty colors," Mattie remarked as she studied the oval on the hardwood floor in the front room. "Where'd you come across this rug, Irene? Did someone you know make it?"

"Some of the ladies at our church in Cloverdale collect discarded clothing and curtains," Irene explained. Now that the rug was on her glossy new floor, she liked it even more than when she'd picked it out. "They get together every week and work on rugs, and they either give them to agencies who help struggling families—or they sell them and donate the proceeds to those agencies."

"Would they make me a couple if I gave them the fabric and paid them?" Christine chimed in. "These really brighten a room!"

"*Jah*, I'd supply the materials and buy a couple of rugs from them, too," Mattie said.

Irene nodded as the four of them went back down the stairs. "That's what I did for this bigger rug we'll carry up next. I had some large fabric scraps, and I bought some new colors I wanted, and I'm really tickled with the way the ladies put them together."

When they'd carried the last rug upstairs and placed it on the front room floor where Irene planned to put her couch, her friends once again admired the blend of prints, solids, and colors that made the oval rug so beautiful.

After the four of them went into the kitchen to speak with Amos, Marlin, Eli, Truman, and Monroe, the bedroom set and the furniture for Irene's front room was put into place very quickly. Once again it amazed Irene that her friends were so willing to stop what they were doing to help her.

"How's the kitchen coming along?" she asked as they all went downstairs. "It sounds like you fellows are making a lot of progress."

"We are," Preacher Amos agreed. "Before you ladies came for us, we were saying that after our paint-party girls finish in here—probably in the next day or so—and Allen installs the new appliances, we can turn the Kuhns loose in their new domain."

"Hopefully by Saturday," Bishop Monroe added. "We might not be completely done with the finishing work in the rooms behind the meeting room by then, but we're planning to hold church here this Sunday. I need to tell Mose and Sylvia about our decision so they can set their wedding date."

Irene nodded, gazing around the large kitchen. With the new cabinets installed in their previous positions, the room didn't look as bleak and foreign as it had last week when she'd gotten so upset. "That's an amazing testimony to the positive power of teamwork," she remarked.

"*Jah*, when you consider that the tornado struck us on May eighteenth, and we'll be worshipping, cooking—and have our residents resettled—by June seventeenth," Preacher Marlin put in, "we have a *lot* to be grateful for."

"Folks here are incredibly generous with their time and talent," Preacher Eli said with a nod. "Not to put down the church district in Coldstream, because the crew from there was a godsend, but our new buildings wouldn't have come together nearly as fast if we were still living there."

"It's the difference in leadership, as well as the general attitude," Mattie put in. "We're so blessed to have you as our bishop, Monroe—and we're all willing to work together here because we've all been *family* from the time we arrived."

"*Jah*, the Promise Lodge district doesn't just belong to the four of us who first bought the property," Christine said, slipping her arms around her sisters. "Every one of our residents has jumped in feet-first and become totally involved—completely invested—in its progress and prosperity."

"There's no place like Promise Lodge," Preacher Amos agreed. "No place like home."

After a few more minutes of discussion, Irene thanked everyone for their help and returned to her apartment, while Truman headed outside. Her few major pieces of furniture were in place, so she unpacked her clothes and put sheets and a coverlet on the bed. On a whim, Irene took one of her quilts from the trunk Truman had refurbished and folded it over the foot of the bed.

From the doorway, she sighed with satisfaction. The bedroom—the entire apartment—would be simple and functional, because she would only live here until the local men could build the house they'd been designing for Dale.

There's no place like Promise Lodge. No place like home.

As Amos's words came back to her, Irene had to agree with them. Who could've guessed how her life was going to change two years ago when she'd first noticed her new Amish neighbors moving in? And who could've predicted that her longtime friend Dale Kraybill would become her second husband?

A quiet knock on the door made her turn. As Rosetta entered the front room, her lips twitched with a smile that made Irene hold her breath. "And how are *you*?" she blurted out when her daughter-in-law reached for her hands.

Rosetta's cheeks turned a pretty shade of pink. "It, um,

took me a while to work up my courage, but when Minerva did a test and examined me yesterday, she—you were *right*, Irene!"

As they embraced, Irene thanked God that Truman and his wife were to be blessed with a child. Rosetta had expressed concern about starting a family at her age, but they would have faith—and the prayers and support of the entire Promise Lodge family—that this mother and her child would remain healthy throughout the birthing process.

Irene wiped her eyes, gazing at Rosetta. "What else did Minerva say? Does everything look all right? When are you due? So many things to think about—"

"And we'll handle one thing at a time, one day at a time," Rosetta said softly. "We're looking at early December. And because I'm thirty-nine, Minerva recommends that I find an obstetrician at the women's clinic in Forest Grove so we can monitor my progress."

"I'm glad to hear that," Irene said with a nod. "And how's Truman?"

Rosetta laughed. "Truman's so happy he's about to pop his buttons, but we've agreed to wait another month or so— and to see a doctor—before we announce this to anyone— *please*? It's early, and I want to be farther along—less likely to miscarry—before we get everyone excited about this baby. This *baby*!"

Irene hugged her precious daughter-in-law again and let out a sigh. "Keeping this news to myself will be about the hardest thing I've ever done, but I—"

"You have excitement of your own to keep you occupied for a while," Rosetta teased, grabbing Irene's hand. "Let's take a walk down the hall, shall we? What's that I hear going on outside?"

As they left the apartment, the rumble of heavy equipment prompted Irene to walk quickly to the other end of the building. Now that the lodge was enclosed with a new back wall, she couldn't imagine what further dozing work Truman would be doing out on the grounds. Earlier in the week he'd removed four concrete slabs where cabins had once sat, leaving the six slabs closest to the lodge, where Rosetta intended to build new ones.

As they slipped into the empty room next to Ruby's apartment, Irene and Rosetta waved at the four young women who were painting Beulah's rooms. Her business partner, Phoebe—who was helping them on her day off from baking Promise Lodge pies—lifted her roller in response. When Irene peered through the window, she sucked in her breath.

Truman was excavating where the last two cabins had sat—digging the foundation for the new house she would share with Dale!

Her decision to remarry suddenly felt more real, and more immediate. Depending upon whether the men built the new cabins or the Kraybill home first, she might be moving out of her apartment sooner rather than later. She suddenly had hundreds of things to do, because she had a wedding to plan! And a grandbaby on the way!

That evening after he'd closed the store, Dale stood near the gaping hole in the ground between the lodge and the homes Cyrus and Jonathan Helmuth had recently built. His body felt like one big grin, and he could hardly stand still: for the first time in his life, he was going to own a home that wasn't connected to his business.

And he was going to share it with a *wife*.

He'd known these things ever since he'd bought the land, of course, but now the physical evidence was before him, marked off by wooden stakes with red rag strips drifting on the breeze. Dale was walking the perimeter of his foundation for the second time when a movement caught his eye.

Irene and Sylvia were coming down the front steps of the lodge, waving when he looked up at them. Dale had hoped to share his thoughts with his fiancée when he was alone with her, but he wasn't surprised that another apartment dweller—who had also recently gotten engaged—was coming with Irene to talk about the excavation site.

"Isn't this *exciting*?" Irene called out as the two women approached.

Dale gazed at her, aware that he was shifting from one foot to the other like a nervous kid caught up in his first serious romance. Irene's face was lit with anticipation and joy, rather than the despair he'd witnessed before she'd moved back into her apartment—and wasn't that wonderful?

He couldn't help himself. He grabbed her hands and pulled her into an exuberant hug, even though Sylvia was beside them. Irene didn't seem embarrassed by his show of affection, either. She beamed at him, lightly kissing his cheek.

"When I looked out the window earlier today and saw what Truman was doing," she said in a rush, "it woke me up to the fact that we have a wedding to plan before we move into this home! And we haven't even talked about a date yet."

Sylvia laughed along with them. "Bishop Monroe told Mose and me this morning that the lodge kitchen should be fully functional by Saturday, and we'll have church in the meeting room this Sunday," she remarked. "When we told the Kuhns we'd like to have our wedding on Thursday, the twenty-eighth, they squawked like a couple of startled chickens. They were afraid they'd need more time to master the new stoves and ovens."

"But that's your date? June twenty-eighth?" Dale asked.

Sylvia nodded. "We figure that'll be time enough for my friends from Pennsylvania to make their plans," she said. "And most of Mose's family lives down the highway in Coldstream. So we're on!"

"Congratulations," Dale said, still grasping Irene's hand. "I think we'd be better off to set our date for when the house is finished—don't you, Irene?"

"*Jah*, considering you can't bunk in my apartment after we marry," she replied with a chuckle. "And I see no reason to move *again* to live in your apartment while we wait for the house to be ready. Do we know when our place might be finished?"

"Nope. But Preacher Amos hinted that they'd build it before they start work on the new cabins."

"So we have a little breathing room," Irene said, sounding relieved. "I'm all for letting Sylvia and Mose be the first to get married in the rebuilt lodge."

Dale nodded. He saw no reason to make it a race. As Sylvia stepped close to the edge of the hole where their new basement would soon be poured, some questions occurred to him.

"Where do you and Mose plan to live, Sylvia?"

She flashed him a girlish smile. "I'll be moving into the loft above the Clydesdale stables until my farm sale has closed and I'm squared away with my medical expenses," she replied. "Then we'll figure out where to put a house, and what will go in it."

"Which leads me to my next thought," Dale put in. "After hearing from the four younger Helmuths about a store in Willow Ridge where they saw some fine Amish furniture and household goods, I'd like to drive over there—and I'd like you to select whatever strikes you, Irene. My furniture is serviceable, but I don't have nearly enough to fill a house—and I want to start our life together with mostly new pieces—don't you, dear?"

Her eyes widened. "Oh my, I have no idea what to choose, or—well, it's been *years* since I shopped for sofas or dining room sets, or—"

"So it's high time you did that, *jah*?" Dale asked gently. He looked over at Sylvia. "Would you and Mose like to go along? The kids were saying it's a full two hours by buggy, so you can spend more time shopping and less time clip-clopping if you come with us."

Sylvia's face lit up. "That would be fun! But—but the stores in Willow Ridge are surely closed on Sunday, so who'll mind your store while you're away, Dale?"

He smiled at her astute question. "Marlene can handle it—especially if we go early on a Monday or a Tuesday, which are my lighter traffic days," he replied. "She's been asking how she can repay me for the time she took off to stay at the hospital with Mose."

"*Jah*, and she did that for *me*, bless her heart," Sylvia murmured. She held his gaze for a moment, pondering something. "You can think about this, Dale, but if you need another helper in your store—and you think there's work a pipsqueak like me can do—I'd be happy to give it a shot. I feel so much better now, without my headaches and medications."

Dale's mouth dropped open. "I *will* think about it."

"This is going to be such an adventure!" Sylvia said, clapping her hands like a happy child. "I'll go tell Mose about our jaunt to Willow Ridge right now! You and Irene set your time and we'll be in the back seat whenever you say—making sure you two *behave* yourselves, you know!"

Chapter 31

Just after nine o'clock on Monday morning, Irene opened the door to the Simple Gifts shop in Willow Ridge, her nerves a-jangle with anticipation. During the ride from Promise Lodge, between snatches of conversation with Mose and Sylvia, she'd thought about the furnishings she and Dale would need if they were to start out with mostly new pieces, as he'd suggested. She suspected the final bill might give her a heart attack.

"I think we're the first ones here," she whispered as she looked around. The building had once been a large barn, and above the large main floor they could see a loft area. Everywhere she gazed, the merchandise was colorful and tastefully arranged. "Oh my, look at these beautiful dining room tables and bedroom sets. They surely must cost a fortune—"

"And I'm going to insist that you don't look at a single price tag today, Irene," Dale interrupted gently. "We've talked about this before. We can afford whatever you want—"

"*Jah*, this is no time to make do with scratched tabletops and quilts draped over your old sofas," Sylvia put in as she, too, gazed around in awe. "This is our second chance at creating a home, Irene. Think of how many women never receive such a wonderful gift."

"That's the spirit," Mose agreed before winking at Irene. "And both of you ladies have latched on to bachelors who've not had anything major to spend our hard-earned money on. Show us what we've been missing!"

Dale laughed out loud. "That's the ticket! I can see why Gloria, Laura, and their new husbands are so excited about this place. Look at those quilts up in the loft—and on these shelves, I see five different patterns of hand-thrown pottery dishes."

"And there's *guy* stuff in the back corner. Saddles and ornamental metal gates and such," Mose said as he looked in that direction. "I'm going to check that out first, but call me whenever you want me to look at something, honey-girl. I trust your judgment—and believe me, the furniture at my place is all 'early American attic.' Someday soon we'll have a whole house to furnish, after all. Go hog wild."

Irene's eyes widened. When had she ever heard an Amish man encouraging his woman to spend whatever she wanted on furniture—let alone *two* fellows who were offering their fiancées blank checks? Her heart hammered faster as she decided what to look at first.

"*Gut* morning, folks! Welcome to Simple Gifts!" a slender redheaded woman called out from an office behind the checkout counter. She wore a calf-length tie-dye dress in bright purples, greens, and white. "I'm Nora Hooley, and I'm happy to answer any questions you might have. Everything you see here has been handcrafted by Amish and Mennonite folks around central Missouri."

"And everything I see here is beautiful," Irene murmured.

Dale nodded as he ran an appreciative finger over the top of a glossy oak dining table. "I like the idea of supporting

Plain families," he said, smiling at Nora. "We drove in from Promise, several miles north of here. Would you deliver our purchases, or would we need to return with a large truck?"

Nora quickly waved him off. "I confess that I overheard you folks talking about furnishing two new homes—and congratulations on all the happiness that surely must mean for the four of you!" she replied. "I'm sure we can arrange for delivery—"

The redhead paused, as though considering her next words. "You're from Promise, you say? You wouldn't happen to be from the community that recently caught a fellow named Cornelius Riehl pretending to be a bishop, would you?"

"That would be us!" Irene said with a laugh. "My three companions moved in too recently to recall all that hullaballoo—"

"But it was the four young folks who came here looking for evidence against him who told us about shopping at your place," Dale said eagerly.

"And they were delightful, too—Gloria and Cyrus, and Laura and Jonathan!" Nora's smile lit up her entire freckled face. "I'm so glad you cornered Cornelius before he could take your church district to the cleaners, I'll deliver whatever you folks order at no cost. I'm grateful you've come all this way to shop with me."

Nodding, Irene looked more carefully at the oak table Dale had admired. Once again, he'd known what she would like before she'd even said anything. "What a handsome china hutch this set has," she remarked as she carefully opened its glass doors. "I have some lovely china that belonged to my grandmother, and if I got it out of the lower kitchen cabinets, the kids would have a lot more room for their gadgets."

"Let's keep these pieces in mind as we continue shopping," Dale said. "Oak has always been my favorite—for floors and furnishings alike."

"Our wood furniture's made right here in Willow Ridge," Nora said. "So if you want pieces you don't see, or you'd like a set in a different style or species of wood, the Brennemans will be happy to build whatever you want."

"I want to see these blue dishes," Sylvia said as she held up a fat, curvy pitcher. "When I moved here from my farm in Pennsylvania, I left everything in the house—which I've now sold. So I'm starting from scratch."

"The woman who makes these dishes lives a couple of towns away," Nora remarked as she began to take blue plates and bowls from the display case. "Folks love Amanda's work so much, I have trouble keeping it in stock. This cobalt blue is one of her most popular colors—and it coordinates with the pretty striped set you see."

"So I could mix and match!" Sylvia's eyes lit up as she picked up a mug with stripes of cobalt, scarlet, and mustard yellow. "Isn't this the most cheerful thing you've ever seen, Irene? Think of how *happy* you'd feel, sipping your morning coffee from this! Nora, I'd like eight place settings of each set, and I'll choose some serving pieces, too."

From there, the shopping began in earnest. Organized as he was, Dale began jotting their wish list in his pocket notebook, nodding as Irene suggested coordinating items she liked. After they'd browsed for a while, they agreed to purchase the oak table, the hutch, and ten chairs, along with a stunning walnut bedroom set. While the two men were examining an unusual rocking chair made of birch, Irene secretly picked up the Brennemans' printed price list.

When she did the mental math for the pieces they'd selected, her breath escaped in a rush. As Irene felt the blood draining from her head, she sat on one of the sturdy chairs she and Dale had just purchased.

Sylvia came over, frowning. "You look as pale as milk, Irene. You're not coming down with something—"

"I'm about to pass out from sticker shock," Irene whispered, making sure Dale and Mose were still out of earshot. "We've just chosen dining room furniture that cost more than the entire house Ernest built when I married him— nearly twice as much, in fact."

Squeezing her shoulder, Sylvia nodded. "Quality furniture doesn't come cheap—but I don't figure to buy any more of it in my lifetime," she pointed out. "And it was *years* ago when we married our first husbands, Irene. The cost of furniture—and houses—has gone up, you know. Chances are you'd be just as appalled by the price tags in a store full of mass-produced, poorly made pieces."

Before Dale spotted her distress, Irene rose from the chair and strolled with Sylvia to a display of handmade pot holders and other kitchen linens. It seemed like a safer, less-expensive aisle to visit.

"I appreciate your sense of perspective, Sylvia," Irene murmured. "This is such a lovely store, I'll keep looking while we're here, but I'm not choosing anything else today. I need to show a little control!"

Sylvia chuckled, tucking her hand through Irene's elbow. "Not a bad idea, actually," she agreed. "That way, we'll have an excuse to come back another time, ain't so?"

The petite woman paused, as though hoping to express her next idea just right.

"When Mose and I decided on June twenty-eighth for our wedding, he immediately asked Marlene and Lester to be side sitters," she said pensively.

"Makes sense, considering how close he and his sister have always been," Irene remarked.

"I don't have siblings or cousins, so I—I was wondering if you and Dale would also stand up with us," Sylvia continued nervously. "I know you're busy making your own wedding plans, so if you'd like some help sewing your dress—"

"I won't make a habit of speaking for Dale, but in this case I'll just say *yes*, Sylvia!" Irene blurted. "What an honor. I haven't been in a wedding party since I was a young woman—"

"Far as I can see, Irene, you're *still* a young woman," Sylvia insisted with a big smile. "It's your attitude that counts, not your age. Shall we let the men know what we've just decided?"

Chapter 32

As Mose stood up to join Sylvia in front of Bishop Monroe, ready to take his wedding vows, his heart overflowed with love—but the rest of him wanted to melt down until he could seep between the floorboards. In a meeting room filled with people from Coldstream, Lititz, and Promise Lodge, he feared that he'd embarrass himself—and Sylvia—so badly that no one would stay in their seats as he struggled to speak. He'd worried about his impediment all week, and during the church service and Preacher Amos's wedding sermon, praying that God would deliver him from his stumbling tongue. But such a miracle probably wasn't going to happen.

What if he stammered so badly that the bishop couldn't understand what he was saying, so his words didn't count? What if even God couldn't understand him?

Or what if I follow Sylvia's suggestion—the way she coached me—and that doesn't count as a valid vow, either? Lord, you've got to help me! Quick!

Marlene gently grasped his elbow, reminding him that she would always love him and never forsake him. Her gentle, brown-eyed gaze settled Mose as nothing else could.

Beautiful, sweet Sylvia, in her dress of deep teal, gazed up at him with so much love and strength as she slipped her tiny hand into his, it almost made him cry.

But at this most sacred, nerve-wracking time in his life, her confidence in him wasn't enough. Mose swallowed repeatedly. His throat was so parched he didn't think he could speak at all.

"Friends and family, beloved folk from far and near," Bishop Monroe began in his resonant voice, "we gather here to witness a holy moment. Mose Fisher and Sylvia Keim are about to declare before God and all of us that they'll commit the rest of their lives to one another. If anyone here knows of a reason they should not become man and wife, say so now."

Silence resounded in the meeting room. Sweat trickled down Mose's spine.

What'll I do, Lord? Shall I take Sylvia's suggestion, or do this the conventional way?

"So be it," the bishop said. "Let's proceed with our sacramental, joyous business."

Mose's heart hammered so loudly he was afraid he wouldn't be able to distinguish one phrase from the next. But he felt confidence and faith radiating from Sylvia, this woman who'd agreed to become his wife. And bless her, she gazed at Mose again with her hazel eyes, entreating him to follow her lead as they took their vows—to reflect the love and devotion she expressed so beautifully. So clearly.

Bishop Monroe's calm green eyes held his gaze, assuring Mose that all would be well—and it would be over in mere moments if he could just hold steady.

"Sing to me, Mose," Sylvia murmured.

Mose doubted anyone but he and the bishop had heard

her. Monroe's nod, barely perceptible, told Mose that Sylvia had spoken with the bishop about this matter—and that he was willing to do whatever would help.

Mose inhaled deeply and nodded. The longer he stalled, the more folks would wonder what was wrong.

"Repeat after me, Mose," Bishop Monroe began gently.

Mose closed his eyes and slipped into the tune of "Jesus Loves Me."

By stretching the bishop's initial words a bit, Mose made them fit the familiar tune. So far, so good—as long as he didn't overthink the process. He opened his eyes to find the woman of his dreams gazing at him with heart-stopping, utterly wonderful love as she silently encouraged him to continue.

So—just as he'd practiced it with clever, patient Sylvia the day before—Mose made it through the wedding vows. He kept his voice low, in a singsong that didn't follow the beloved old tune, but his fearful brain still counted it as singing. As he spoke the final words, Mose thanked God as well as Teacher Carolyn, who'd taught him to overcome his faulty speech pattern by putting his words to music.

Bishop Monroe blessed them—and despite the way Old Order weddings traditionally discouraged a show of affection at the ceremony's end, Mose swept Sylvia up into his arms to hold her as their mouths met. A few folks sucked in their breath, surprised at such a maneuver, but to Mose, it had always seemed the most natural, practical way for a bull moose of a man to kiss his fawn of a woman.

Sylvia didn't seem to mind. She hugged him around the neck, pouring her love into a kiss that made the congregation wait for several long, lovely moments. When she finally eased her lips away, she tweaked Mose's nose.

"You got through it—and you were just perfect!" she whispered.

"Thanks to *you*," Mose murmured back. "I love you so much, Sylvia."

As folks began sidling between the pew benches into the aisles, she kissed him again. "This is only the beginning, dear man," she assured him with shining eyes. "The best is yet to come."

As Dale finished his pumpkin pie that afternoon, he couldn't recall ever feeling so stuffed. Mose and Sylvia had asked the Kuhns to cook a traditional turkey dinner with all the trimmings, to celebrate how thankful they were for all the blessings God had bestowed upon them in the past few months. Beside him at the raised *eck* table in the corner of the lodge's crowded dining room, Irene laid her fork down about halfway through her slice of apple pie.

"Can't do it," she murmured. "I'm afraid I'll pop open— and wouldn't *that* be a spectacle to ruin this fine day?"

Dale grasped her hand beneath the table. "I might not eat another bite between now and our big day," he said. "We need to congratulate Beulah and Ruby—"

"Do I hear someone taking our names in vain?" Ruby teased as she approached the kitchen door with an empty steam table pan.

"Absolutely not!" Irene replied. "For all your worries about learning to use the new ovens and stoves, you cooked up the finest meal *ever*, ladies."

"*Jah*, amen to that!" Mose chimed in from the center of the table. "What a feast!"

"I sure hope we have leftovers!" Sylvia chimed in. "Nothing beats a turkey sandwich with cranberry sauce, on a homemade dinner roll!"

"Who says you'll get leftovers?" Beulah teased as she and her sister came to stand in front of the wedding party's table. "I thought you were moving to Mose's loft, Mrs. Fisher, instead of staying here in the lodge to eat with us."

Irene laughed. "Stick with me, Sylvia. I'm living here for a while yet, so *I* can see that you get those leftovers—if there are any. People seem to be going through a *lot* of food."

"Happens every time we have a wedding," Ruby remarked happily.

"And we're only three weeks away from *your* big day, Irene!" Mattie exclaimed as she joined the little group, along with her two sisters.

"*Jah*, on July nineteenth we'll celebrate Promise Lodge's twelfth wedding," Christine chimed in brightly. "Your house is nearly finished, and you and Dale look like the happiest lovebirds on the planet today—well, right after Mose and Sylvia, that is."

"Here's to happiness!" Dale said, jubilantly raising his water glass. "That's something Promise Lodge seems to excel at."

"Because we *plan* for happiness! Right, sisters?" Rosetta chimed in.

Mattie's expression waxed nostalgic as she gazed at the three couples seated on the dais. As she slipped an arm around her two sisters and hugged them, she looked almost ready to cry.

"Who knew how much strength and energy we had hidden away inside us when we bought this place?" she asked softly. "And who knew how much love would bloom and grow because we took those first steps toward a better life?"

Dale's throat tightened with emotion. The three women before him were the very symbols of the can-do attitude that had inspired every person who'd come to Promise Lodge

for a fresh start. When he thought about the love that had
bloomed and grown so unexpectedly at this stage of his
own life, he gave thanks to God for leading him to a new
beginning—and for the stalwart sisters who'd ensured his
success along with everyone else's.

He raised his glass again, sincerely grateful. "And here's
to you three ladies," Dale stated firmly. "We couldn't have
come so far without *you*."

From the
Promise Lodge Kitchen

Beulah, Ruby, Irene, and the other Promise Lodge ladies have once again prepared some amazing food in this story—because in times of celebration or times of crisis, food remains a tie that binds us together. As always, the recipes here call for simple, basic ingredients most of us have on hand because feeding our families and friends doesn't have to be complicated! I've made each of these dishes (several times, because they're favorites!), and I've included them because they are *so* tasty! Like most Amish cooks, I sometimes start with convenience foods rather than doing everything totally from scratch because I want you to enjoy trying them for yourselves!

These recipes are also posted on my website, www.CharlotteHubbard.com. If you don't find a recipe you want, please email me via my website to request it— or to let me know how you liked it!

—*Charlotte*

Seven Layer Bars

I've come to enjoy this versatile recipe so much that I don't need to look at it anymore! These bars not only taste amazing, but they require little measuring, and you make them right in the pan! Rather than measure the coconut, chips, and peanuts, I usually sprinkle on enough to nearly cover the previous layer. For variety, you can also switch out the flavors of chips you use.

- 1 sleeve graham crackers (8 or 9 crackers)
- 1 stick butter
- 1 cup (or more) coconut
- 1 cup (or more) chocolate chips
- 1 cup (or more) butterscotch chips
- 1 cup (or more) dry roasted peanuts
- 1 cup miniature M&M's
- 1 can sweetened condensed milk

Crush the graham crackers in the unopened sleeve by first breaking them with your fingers and then gently crushing them with a rolling pin. Meanwhile, spray a 9"x13" pan, cut the butter into chunks in the pan, and put the pan in the oven while it preheats to 350°.

When the butter is melted, remove pan from oven and place on a heat-safe surface. Sprinkle the crushed graham crackers over the butter, forming the "crust" on the bottom. Then sprinkle on the coconut, the chocolate and butterscotch chips, the peanuts, and the M&M's in layers and press down slightly. Slowly pour the sweetened condensed milk over the entire top of the pan, using a metal spatula to help spread it around. Bake for about 20 minutes or until the edges and most of the top is bubbling. Cool in the pan. Makes 3–4 dozen, depending on how you cut them. These freeze well.

Baked Banana-Oatmeal Cups

These moist, chewy "muffins" contain nearly the amount of rolled oats in a bowl of oatmeal—but they're portable! This is also a great way to use up very ripe bananas, and because they freeze well, they make great snacks and easy breakfast treats any time you want them.

    3 cups old-fashioned oats
    1½ cups milk
    2 ripe bananas, mashed (about ¾ cup)
    ⅓ cup packed brown sugar
    2 eggs, lightly beaten
    1 tsp. baking powder
    1 tsp. vanilla
    ½ cup chopped pecans or walnuts

Preheat oven to 350° and spray a 12-cup muffin tin with cooking spray. In a large bowl, combine all the ingredients until blended. Place about ⅓ cup of the batter in each muffin cup until all batter is used. Bake 20–25 minutes, until a toothpick comes out clean from the center. Cool in the pan for 10 minutes and then carefully turn the muffins out onto a wire rack.

<u>Kitchen Tip</u>: Frozen muffins may be wrapped in foil and warmed in a low oven for about 15 minutes or covered and microwaved for about 40 seconds.

Cheesy Muffin Tin Omelets

Here's a different "format" for your morning eggs—and these cheesy little gems are easy to take out of the freezer, reheat in the microwave, and enjoy in a matter of moments! The added veggies are a colorful plus! Makes 12.

2 T. olive oil
½ medium onion, chopped
1 cup frozen chopped spinach
1 medium red bell pepper, diced
8 large eggs
½ cup grated Parmesan cheese
½ cup milk
½ tsp. each of salt and paprika
½ cup shredded cheese (your choice; I like Cheddar)

Preheat oven to 325° and liberally coat a 12-cup muffin tin with cooking spray. Heat the oil in a large nonstick skillet. Add the onion, stir to coat, and about a minute later add in the spinach. Cook for a few minutes and then add in the red bell pepper. When vegetables are soft, remove from heat and cool a few minutes. Squeeze them in paper towels or a sieve to remove excess water.

In a large bowl, whisk the eggs, Parmesan, milk, and seasonings until well combined. Stir in the vegetables. Divide this mixture into the prepared muffin tins and top each omelet with shredded cheese. Bake until firm, about 20–25 minutes. Let them stand in the tin about 5 minutes before removing. Serve warm or store in a sealed container in the fridge or freezer.

Chunky Cream Cheese and Fruit Coffee Cake

This recipe is so good I'm giving you the doubled version that makes a 9"x13" pan, because once you've made this versatile breakfast treat, you'll want every bit of it! Feel free to substitute other fruit, or to use two fruits—my favorite combination is fresh peaches with frozen blueberries!

½ cup butter, softened
1⅓ cups sugar
2 eggs
2½ cups flour, divided
1 tsp. baking powder
Dash of salt
2 tsp. cinnamon
1 cup milk or flavored yogurt
3 cups fresh or frozen fruit
8 oz. brick of cream cheese, cut into small pieces

Topping:
½ cup flour
6 T. brown sugar
4 T. butter

Spray a 9"x13" baking pan and preheat oven to 350°. For the batter, cream the butter and sugar in a large mixing bowl, then beat in the eggs. Combine 2 cups of the flour, baking powder, salt, and cinnamon, then add it to the creamed mixture alternately with the milk/yogurt. Stir the remaining ½ cup flour in with the fruit. Stir the fruit and chunks of cream cheese into the mixture—it'll be thick and lumpy.

Make the topping by combining the flour and brown sugar. Cut in the butter to make a crumbly mixture, then sprinkle it over the batter. Bake for around 35 minutes, or until a pick inserted near the center comes out clean.

Pineapple Macaroni Salad

The pineapple juice and cider vinegar add real zing to this unusual pasta salad. Add diced ham and/or shredded cheese (increase the dressing) to make this an entrée.

½ pound elbow or small shell macaroni, cooked
 and cooled
1 tsp. cooking oil
½ cup pineapple tidbits
½ cup diced red bell pepper
½ cup grated carrot
½ cup finely chopped celery
¼ cup mayonnaise
⅓ cup pineapple juice
1 T. cider vinegar
1 tsp. sugar
2 tsp. dried minced onion
Salt and pepper to taste

Cook the macaroni according to package directions, adding the oil to the water to keep it from sticking. Drain and cool. In a large bowl, combine the macaroni, pineapple, and vegetables.

To make the dressing, stir together all the remaining ingredients, and then stir the dressing into the salad. Chill for several hours. Serves 6–8.

Cream Cheese Sugar Cookies

Every time I serve these easy cookies, someone remarks about how wonderful they are! I like to frost them with tinted buttercream (recipe is on my website) and dip them in sprinkles to add a little flash, but you can decorate them as you prefer. They freeze well.

3 cups flour
1 tsp. baking powder
¼ tsp. baking soda
½ tsp. salt
2 sticks unsalted butter, softened
2 oz. (¼ cup) cream cheese, softened
1¼ cups sugar (plus extra, for rolling)
1 tsp. vanilla
½ tsp. rum flavor or extract
¼ tsp. almond extract
1 large egg

Preheat oven to 350°. Line baking sheets with parchment paper. In a medium bowl, whisk together the flour, baking powder, baking soda, and salt. Set aside.

In a mixer bowl, cream the butter, cream cheese, and sugar until well blended. Add the flavorings and the egg, and blend well. Scrape down the bowl and add the flour mixture on low speed until the dough forms a soft ball.

Place additional sugar in a shallow bowl. Pinch off tablespoon-size clumps of dough, drop them into the sugar, and roll them into balls. Place 2" apart on the papered baking sheets and bake about 8 minutes, rotating pans front to back halfway through to ensure even baking. Cookies will remain pale and soft—don't overbake! Cool on pan for a few minutes and transfer to wire racks to cool. Makes about 4 dozen.

Fried Cabbage

So easy, yet so good! Even if you think you're not a fan of cooked cabbage, the bacon and onion in this recipe will change your mind!

    5 slices bacon, cut into small pieces
    1 small onion, chopped
    1 small green cabbage, cored and chopped (about
       5 cups)
    ⅓ cup chicken broth
    Salt and pepper, to taste

In a large skillet over medium heat, cook the bacon until crisp. Remove bacon from the pan with a slotted spoon and set aside, allowing the grease to remain. Add the chopped onion and cook until translucent, about 5 minutes. Add the cabbage and cook for about 10 minutes, stirring occasionally. Add the broth and seasonings and continue cooking until the cabbage is as tender as you like it. Stir in the bacon pieces and serve.

Awesome Corn Casserole

No cornbread mix to come between you and the fabulous taste of this corn concoction! Makes enough for a crowd and stirs up in a heartbeat.

    2 cans creamed corn (15 oz. each)
    1 can corn kernels (15 oz.)
    ¼ cup sugar
    4 large eggs
    6 T. butter, melted
    6 T. flour
    1 T. baking powder
    ¼ cup packaged, cooked bacon bits
    ½ cup diced red bell pepper
    Salt, pepper, and parsley to taste

Preheat oven to 350° and spray a 2-quart casserole or 9"x13" pan. In a separate large bowl, combine the 3 cans of corn, sugar, and eggs and stir until blended. Add in the melted butter, then stir in the flour, baking powder, and remaining ingredients. Pour into the prepared casserole and bake uncovered about an hour, until top is golden brown and the center no longer jiggles.

*Please read on for a preview
of the next Promise Lodge novel,
coming soon!*

Miracles at Promise Lodge
CHARLOTTE HUBBARD

**A season of new life has blessed the Amish of Missouri's
Promise Lodge, as mothers-to-be anticipate the arrival
of their little miracles—and the flourishing community
witnesses one young man's remarkable change of heart.**

Longtime residents of Promise Lodge welcome a wave of
newcomers that includes a pretty potter who's come to help
an expectant couple, and a hard-working dairy expert ready
to manage the herds on the expanding Burkholder farm.
Then there's Isaac Chupp, the handsome, charming son
of a notoriously unyielding bishop from nearby
Coldstream. Isaac has recklessly rebelled against his *dat*,
and his bad boy reputation precedes him. Now he seeks a
fresh start, applying for work at Dale Kraybill's bulk store.

Proving himself reliable while Dale takes off for his
wedding trip is Isaac's bold first step.
But more miraculous awakenings may come as he settles
into the warm new light of the faithful community.
And while Promise Lodge celebrates an abundance of
newborns as summer turns to fall, Isaac discovers
a kindred soul who has her own share of challenges.
In helping her, he just may find his true purpose in loving
selflessly, building up, and giving back . . .

Chapter 1

As Isaac Chupp entered the country store at Promise
Lodge, he was immediately aware of how bright and
clean and new it was—and that all the aisles ran perpendi-
cular to the checkout counter. Compared to Coldstream's
tired old market, it was a step into the twenty-first century:
the glass-front refrigerator units and overhead lights were
electric, and their radiance was reflected in large mirrors
that covered the upper walls. The owner, Dale Kraybill, was
Mennonite—

*And he's extremely savvy. From the computerized cash
register, he can see everyone who's shopping in his store.*

In the mirrors, Isaac noted that several shoppers, Plain
and English alike, were pushing carts along the well-
stocked aisles. He stepped away from the front door, taking
time to browse while the storekeeper was helping a young
woman set up a display of the most colorful pottery dishes
he'd ever seen. He wanted to know something about the inventory and the store's organization before he introduced
himself to Kraybill, who'd recently run an ad for help. The
store's owner had spoken at length with Isaac over the
phone yesterday before inviting him to come for an in-
person interview.

Today, July fifth, could be his personal declaration of independence if he got the job. He'd be stepping into a whole new world, leaving his narrow-minded *dat* behind—

"Vera, I predict your pottery will fly off the shelves!" Kraybill said to the young woman. "I'm glad you've decided to sell your pieces here."

Isaac's eyes widened. If his father, Bishop Obadiah of Coldstream's Old Order community, were here, he'd be ordering the girl to pack up her colorful wares and confess before the congregation on Sunday because she was *sinful*—too artistically inclined. The way his *dat* saw it, God would never accept her because she'd broken free of the conservative mold and mindset to which Amish folks were expected to conform.

Vera modestly turned away from Kraybill's compliment with flushed cheeks. When she smiled at Isaac, the nerdy, endearing way she pushed up her glasses made his heart turn a flip-flop.

"*Denki*, Dale, you're very kind," she said in a low, melodious voice. "You've given me quite an opportunity to display my work."

Opportunity? Have I got an opportunity for you, Miss Vera!

Isaac sucked in a breath, hoping she couldn't hear the hammering of his heart.

I have to get this job! I have to convince this beautiful, unique girl that I'm the man she wants to marry!

Where had the idea of marriage come from? At nineteen, he'd never given a thought to a permanent relationship with any of the girls he'd dated, yet just one look—and the sound of Vera's voice and her thick glasses—had sent him off the deep end.

While Dale and Vera finished the pottery display, Isaac forced himself to focus. He could *not* come across as a lovesick puppy who would constantly moon over Vera. He reminded himself of the years of experience he'd acquired while clerking for his father's auction company—not to mention his expertise at setting up the sale barn's computer and recordkeeping system. He rehearsed all the positive-sounding reasons he was ready to come to work for Kraybill at Promise Lodge, three hours away from his family in Coldstream.

After smoothing his shirt beneath his suspenders and putting on his best smile, Isaac stepped forward with his hand extended. "Mr. Kraybill? Is this a *gut* time to talk?" he asked enthusiastically. "I'm Isaac Chupp, and we spoke over the phone—"

"Isaac! Happy to meet you, young man," the steely-haired storekeeper said as they pumped hands. "And I admire a potential employee who shows up early to get the lay of the land, so to speak. Let's step back to my office. This young woman coming to run the cash register is Marlene Lehman—"

Isaac held Marlene's wide-eyed gaze, challenging her with his confident smile.

Yeah, it's me—looking for a new life, same as you were when you sold your farm in Coldstream without telling anyone.

He'd known Marlene all his life because she and her brother had recently moved here to escape his father's narrowmindedness, as had many of the residents of Promise Lodge.

"—and you'll be answering to her while I'm away for a few days, after Irene Wickey and I get married," Kraybill continued jovially. "As I told you over the phone, I'm looking for—"

"Is that Isaac Chupp up ahead?" a woman behind them asked loudly.

"Lo and behold, it *is* Isaac," another woman replied. "After our last run-in, I didn't figure he'd ever come back."

Isaac hadn't spotted the women in the large mirrors, but he recognized their voices immediately. He reminded himself that he'd been *invited* to interview—that he had every right to be in Dale Kraybill's store—yet his confidence sagged like a balloon with a slow leak. Isaac had no choice but to turn and face two of the three sisters who'd transformed an abandoned church camp into the thriving community of Promise Lodge.

Rosetta Wickey and Christine Burkholder stood beside another familiar young woman from his past, Deborah Peterscheim Schwartz. She held his gaze unflinchingly as she bounced a toddler on her hip.

Never one to beat around the bush, Rosetta crossed her arms. "What brings you to Promise Lodge, Isaac? Did I overhear Dale calling you a potential employee?"

"I hope you've left your beer—and your matches—at home," Christine chimed in. "I've just built a new dairy barn and I don't want to look out some evening and see it engulfed in flames."

From the corner of his eye, Isaac caught Vera's startled expression as she pushed her shopping cart one aisle farther away. He couldn't miss the way Kraybill's face had tightened, either, as he turned toward the three shoppers.

"What are you ladies saying?" he asked carefully. "I'm guessing you knew Isaac when you lived in Coldstream—"

"*Jah*, back when he used to smoke and drink with his English friends in our barns before they burned to the ground," Christine put in sternly.

"And let's not forget that Christine's husband died in that barn fire, trying to save the livestock," Rosetta said as she slung her arm around Deborah's shoulders. "And Isaac shoved Deborah into a ditch out in the country and left her, because she'd called the sheriff when she spotted him in my family's burning barn."

"Isaac's behavior was the main reason my family left Coldstream a couple years ago," Deborah remarked quietly. She swayed from side to side with her child, a far cry from the frightened, vulnerable teenager who'd suffered Bishop Obadiah's vengeance after she'd reported Isaac's wrongdoing.

"And since we've come here, we've heard stories about money gone missing from his father's auction receipts, and we've caught him red-handed at forging his *mamm*'s handwriting in a letter," Rosetta added as she gazed purposefully at the storekeeper. "Be sure you're satisfied with Isaac's response to these issues, Dale. We hope you'll hold him accountable—and we hope you won't be sorry if you hire him."

Isaac's confidence bottomed out. His throat was so dry it clicked when he swallowed. But he had to defend himself. If Kraybill—and Vera—believed only what his accusers had said, he'd be going back to Coldstream with his tail between his legs. And he *refused* to do that.

"I came here hoping for a second chance—a fresh start with some of that forgiveness you Promise Lodge folks are known for," he stated in the firmest voice he could muster. "You and your families left Coldstream and moved on. I want to do that, too."

After a few moments of uncomfortable silence, Kraybill gestured for Isaac to follow him through the swinging double doors into the warehouse. They entered a small office with ledgers on the bookshelf and a computer on a side table. The storekeeper nodded toward the straight-back chair and then seated himself behind the modest desk. He looked at Isaac with calm blue-gray eyes that saw everything and gave away nothing of what he was thinking.

"Isaac, have you ever stolen anything from a store like this?"

Isaac's body tensed. Was that a trick question? Or was it a *test*?

He knew better than to drop Kraybill's steady gaze. The longer the silence stretched between them, however, the more the man behind the desk would figure out about him—in addition to what the Bender sisters and Deborah had revealed moments ago.

"Yeah, I have," Isaac admitted softly. "When I was a kid, I took odds and ends from the market in Coldstream—not because I really wanted the stuff, but because I wanted to get away with it. The old guy who owned the place back then was clueless."

"I imagine the store has changed since Raymond Overholt and his new bride, Lizzie, took it over earlier this year. I was sorry to see those kids go—but I'm sure the Overholt family's delighted that they're living in Coldstream."

As he spoke, Dale Kraybill's gaze didn't waver. His voice remained as cool and smooth as a shaded lake.

But still waters run deep. He knows more than he's saying—and he's going to hold it over me.

In a rare moment of anxiety, Isaac looked around the office, grasping for straws to inspire a conversation that would somehow save his bacon. "Look, about what Rosetta and Christine and Deborah were saying out there—"

"Your reputation has preceded you, Isaac. More than half the families here came from Coldstream, after all, and they've known you all your life," Kraybill put in as he leaned forward over his desk.

Isaac braced himself. Although the storekeeper's voice and gaze remained pleasant and unthreatening, he was about to dismiss Isaac without further ado—and Isaac understood why. After all, his older brothers had informed him last week that he wouldn't be clerking any more auctions. Sticky fingers, they'd called it. And even though Raymond Overholt was younger than he, and hopelessly in love with his ditzy bride, Lizzie, Raymond wouldn't even *talk* to Isaac about working in Coldstream's bulk store after enduring so many years of the teasing and . . . well, *bullying*, Raymond's *mamm* had reported to Bishop Obadiah.

"After I spoke with you on the phone yesterday, I chatted with Amos and Mattie Troyer," Kraybill continued matter-of-factly. "And I asked Marlene how she'd feel about you working here—especially while I was away."

Isaac swallowed hard. Preacher Amos and Mattie—even when she'd been married to her first husband, Marvin Schwartz—had always been on his case, watching him as though they'd suspected he was up to something. Which had usually been true.

And Marlene was gawking at me in disbelief just now, wondering why Kraybill would even consider me for this interview.

"Wh-what'd they say?" Isaac saw no reason to prolong this mental anguish, now that his former neighbors had all expressed their negative sentiments about him. He'd been doomed before he'd even arrived. He sighed, realizing that his instant, smoldering attraction to pretty Vera was also destined to go nowhere.

"They all echoed Rosetta, Christine, and Deborah," the storekeeper replied. He was still leaning on his elbows, observing Isaac so calmly, yet so intently, that Isaac started to sweat. Why didn't this guy just send him packing and get it over with?

"But I figured you knew what you'd be in for when you applied for this job, Isaac," Kraybill continued. "You anticipated being under everyone's constant scrutiny, yet you took a chance and answered my ad—because you surely realized I'd know about your past before you came today."

Truth be told, Isaac had been so focused on getting out of Coldstream, he hadn't really considered the reactions of his former neighbors—and on that count, he'd fallen short. He'd also underestimated the man sitting across the desk from him.

"To me, that means you've got *moxie*—if you're truly looking for a fresh start."

Isaac's eyes widened. In his experience, the people who'd reprimanded him and told him to move on hadn't put any sort of positive spin on his situation. The word *moxie* had never figured into their conversations about his multitude of misdeeds. Isaac waited for Kraybill to speak next— waited for the proverbial other shoe to fall—because the man had an unnerving knack for using silence to manipulate Isaac's responses.

The storekeeper rocked back in his wooden chair. "Were Rosetta, Christine, and Deborah correct, Isaac? Did you burn down the two families' barns and leave Deborah in a ditch to walk home in torn clothing, after she called nine-one-one to report you?"

Isaac sighed. "*Jah*, but the fires weren't intentional. My English friends and I were drunk, and the lanterns must've gotten kicked over—"

"But you did nothing to make up for the damage you caused?"

Isaac glanced down at his lap. "No. I—"

"And your father, the bishop, didn't make reparations to those families, either? And he didn't hold you accountable?"

"Don't ask me to explain my *dat*'s behavior!" Isaac blurted out bitterly. "I have no idea why he didn't punish me or—"

"And the way I understand it, Deborah bore the brunt of her father, Preacher Eli's, judgment as well as the other church leaders' disapproval because she reported the fire?"

"They didn't like it that she got the cops involved. We Amish prefer to handle such matters themselves."

"As I understand it, you have not yet joined the Amish church," Kraybill pointed out, "but being in *rumspringa* does *not* excuse you from acting like a decent human being and apologizing to those you've hurt."

Gripping the sides of his chair seat, Isaac knew better than to smart off—or to storm out of the room, the way he'd done when his father had lectured him. How had the store-keeper known that Dat had used *rumspringa* to gloss over his youngest son's errant behavior—even though no one in Coldstream had accepted that excuse any more than Kraybill did? Isaac couldn't explain it, but the steely-haired storekeeper demanded a different level of respect than his father, who had tried—and failed—to exact Isaac's absolute obedience.

"If you're sincerely interested in a fresh start—and if you're going to work in my store," Kraybill added purpose-fully, "you'll have to *earn* the forgiveness you want from Rosetta, Christine, and Deborah. And you'll have to *ask* them for it, Isaac. You can't expect them to wipe your slate clean just because you say you're making a fresh start. That *moxie* I mentioned earlier means nothing if you can't prove you've become a different, more responsible person."

The small office rang with silence. After being lulled by the storekeeper's quiet conversation at the beginning of the interview, Isaac now felt nailed to his chair by Kraybill's rapid-fire questions and sermonette.

He was in a tight spot. Mamm's words still stung, and there was no way around them: *If your brothers no longer want you clerking for them, you'll have to find your own*

*way, Isaac. I won't have you hanging around the house,
underfoot and useless.*

The thought of facing Deborah, Rosetta, and Christine—
begging them like a whipped dog to forgive the damage
he'd done to their barns, their families, and Deborah's
reputation—made him queasy.

But he couldn't go home.

He could fake his way onto an unsuspecting boss's pay-
roll under another identity, in another town where they didn't
know him. But remembering his cover story, and constantly
looking over his shoulder to see if anyone had caught on,
would be exhausting. It would also mean a life on the run,
and that wasn't what he wanted.

Especially now that he'd seen Vera. He didn't know her
last name or anything else about her, except that she created
outrageously colorful pottery, but Isaac *wanted* to know her.
He wanted to believe Vera could save him from himself.

*I'm asking for a miracle. What's the chance of that hap-
pening for me, when I'm not sure I even believe in God?*

With a sigh, Isaac met Dale Kraybill's gaze again. Wasn't
it a minor miracle that the storekeeper, knowing what he
knew, hadn't already shown him to the door? Isaac widened
his eyes slightly, putting on an earnest expression as he
assumed his most sincere tone of voice.

"So . . . if I ask those ladies for their forgiveness, and
they accept my apologies, will you hire me?"